Nonpareil Books

FICTION

Reuben Bercovitch
Hasen
160 pages, $8.95

Frederick Busch
The Mutual Friend
224 pages, $9.95

José Donoso
The Obscene Bird of Night
448 pages, $12.95

Stanley Elkin
The Franchiser
360 pages, $10.95

Searches & Seizures
320 pages, $10.95

Marian Engel
Bear
144 pages, $9.95

Paula Fox
Desperate Characters
176 pages, $9.95

William H. Gass
In the Heart of the Heart of the Country
340 pages, $10.95

Paul Horgan
A Distant Trumpet
628 pages, $16.95

William Maxwell
The Chateau
416 pages, $10.95

The Folded Leaf
288 pages, $11.95

The Old Man at the Railroad Crossing
192 pages, $10.95

Over by the River
256 pages, $10.95

Time Will Darken It
320 pages, $11.95

They Came Like Swallows
192 pages, $9.95

So Long, See You Tomorrow
174 pages, $9.95

Wright Morris
Collected Stories 1948-1986
274 pages, $10.95

Plains Song: For Female Voices
232 pages, $10.95

Howard Frank Mosher
Disappearances
272 pages, $10.95

Robert Musil
Five Women
224 pages, $10.95

Liam O'Flaherty
Famine
480 pages, $12.95

Mary Robison
Amateur's Guide to the Night
144 pages, $9.95

Days
192 pages, $9.95

Oh!
224 pages, $9.95

Peter Rushforth
Kindergarten
208 pages, $10.95

Maurice Shadbolt
Season of the Jew
384 pages, $12.95

Nonpareil Books returns to print books acknowledged as classics. All *Nonpareils* are printed on acid-free paper and produced to the highest standards. They are permanent softcover books designed for use and made to last. For a complete list, please write to David R. Godine, Publisher.

NONPAREIL BOOKS

David R. Godine, Publisher
300 Massachusetts Avenue
Boston, Massachusetts 02115

TIME WILL DARKEN IT

Other Books by William Maxwell

The Folded Leaf (Godine, 1981)

So Long, See You Tomorrow

The Chateau

Ancestors

They Came Like Swallows

TIME WILL DARKEN IT

★

A Novel by
William Maxwell

NONPAREIL BOOKS
David R. Godine · Publisher
BOSTON

This is a NONPAREIL BOOK *published in 1983 by*
David R. Godine, Publisher, Inc.
Horticultural Hall
300 Massachusetts Avenue
Boston, Massachusetts 02115

First published by Harper & Row, Publishers, Inc.

Library of Congress Cataloging in Publication Data

Maxwell, William, 1908–
Time will darken it.

(A Nonpareil book ; 28)
Reprint. Originally published: London:
Faber and Faber, 1948.
I. Title. II. Series.
PS3525.A9464T55 1983 813'.54 82-81311
ISBN 0-87923-448-2

This book has been printed on acid-free paper.
The paper will not yellow with age, the binding will not deteriorate, and the pages will not fall out.

Fifth printing, January 1992

Printed in the United States of America

For

MY WIFE

The order observed in painting a landscape—once the canvas has been prepared—is as follows: First, one draws it, dividing it into three or four distances or planes. In the foremost, where one places the figure or saint, one draws the largest trees and rocks, proportionate to the scale of the figure. In the second, smaller trees and houses are drawn; in the third yet smaller, and in the fourth, where the mountain ridges meet the sky, one ends with the greatest diminution of all.

The drawing is followed by the blocking out or laying in of colours, which some painters are in the habit of doing in black and white, although I deem it better to execute it directly in colour in order that the smalt may result brighter. If you temper the necessary quantity of pigment—or even more—with linseed or walnut oil and add enough white, you shall produce a bright tint. It must not be dark; on the contrary, it must be rather on the light side because time will darken it. . . .

Once the sky, which is the upper half of the canvas, is done, you proceed to paint the ground, beginning with the mountains bordering on the sky. They will be painted with the lightest smalt-and-white tints, which will be somewhat darker than the horizon, because the ground is always darker than the sky, especially if the sun is on that side. These mountains will have their lights and darks, because it is the custom to put in the lower part—after finishing—some towns and small trees. . . .

As you get nearer the foreground, the trees and houses shall be painted larger, and if desired they may rise above the horizon. . . . In this part it is customary to use a practical method in putting in the details, mingling a few dry leaves among the green ones. . . . And it is very praiseworthy to make the grass on the ground look natural, for this section is nearest the observer.

—FRANCISCO PACHECO (1564–1654)

The quotation from Francisco Pacheco, translated by Marco Treves, is reprinted from Artists on Art *by permission of Pantheon Books Inc.*

Part One

⸻ ★ ⸻

AN EVENING PARTY (1912)

I

In order to pay off an old debt that someone else had contracted, Austin King had said yes when he knew that he ought to have said no, and now at five o'clock of a July afternoon he saw the grinning face of trouble everywhere he turned. The house was full of strangers from Mississippi; within an hour the friends and neighbours he had invited to an evening party would begin ringing the doorbell; and his wife (whom he loved) was not speaking to him.

As yet this quarrel was confined to the bedroom and he wanted if possible to keep it from spreading through the house. On his way upstairs he fixed the picture of Maxine Elliott so that it was straight with the world. As he closed the bedroom door from the inside, his eyes turned to the mahogany four-poster bed where his wife lay, face down, in a Japanese kimono. Her brown hair was spread out on the pillow like a sea plant, and one arm, with a heavy gold bracelet hanging from the delicate inert wrist, extended past the edge of the bed into space.

Austin loosened his tie and took off his coat and trousers and hung them on a hanger in the closet. When he had put on his bathrobe he stood waiting for some slight movement, some indication that the hand which had so often searched blindly for his hand was ready to make peace. There was no price that he was not willing to pay, no bargain too hard if only for the rest of this day all differences could be put aside, all wounds (old and new) disregarded and left to heal themselves. After a moment he sat down on the edge of the bed. Receiving no encouragement, he waited and then put out his hand. His fingers closed around his wife's elbow. The elbow was jerked away and drawn under her body where he couldn't get at it. The childishness of this gesture made him smile, but it also meant that one avenue of reconciliation was closed.

"I'm sorry I did what I did," he said. "I should have talked to you first, before I wrote and told them to come. And if I had it to do over again——" There was no answer and he knew from past experience that there would be none. "I thought you'd understand and they wouldn't," he said.

His eyes rested uneasily on the design of the appliquéd quilt, the round lavender morning glories and the heart-shaped green leaves. The quilt was a present from his mother, who would have been shocked to see anyone lying on it.

Annoyed at himself for thinking about the quilt at a time like this, he crossed the room to the dressing-table, picked up his wife's hairbrush, and closing the bedroom door behind him, went into the room across the hall to look after his little daughter, who was too young to dress without help. Between them they decided which shoes and stockings, which dress she was to wear, and put them on her. Then, sitting in a rocker that was too low for him, Austin held her chin with one hand and managed the hairbrush inexpertly with the other.

The excitement of guests staying in the house made Abbey King talkative. "Is it true," she asked, "is it true that gypsies steal little children?"

Though more delicate and with a difference in spacing, her features were a reproduction of her father's—the high forehead particularly, and the eyebrows and grey-blue eyes. Her hair was light brown, like her mother's, and straight. When it was being brushed, it fluffed out and made crackling sounds but Ab knew, at four years old, that her hair was too fine and too thin to be admired. Both of these drawbacks had been pointed out, not to the little girl but unfortunately in her presence. Mixed in with this sadness about her hair was the pleasure she had from standing between her father's knees.

"Do they, Daddy?"

"Sometimes," Austin King said, frowning intently.

"Do they steal tricycles?"

"I don't think so. They wouldn't have any use for tricycles."

"What happens to the children they steal?"

"Their fathers and mothers go to the police and the police find the gypsies and put them in jail," Austin said.

"What happens if they can't find the gypsies? What if they go so far away that nobody can find them and put them in jail?"

"Then their mothers grieve over them."

"Would Mama grieve over me?"

"Certainly. Stand still, Abbey. Stop jerking your head away. I'm not hurting you."

"You are too," Ab said, because it did hurt a little and because she liked to argue with people—with her father, with Rachel the cook, and most of all with her mother. She liked to wear her mother's temper thin. There was a limit that both of them recognized, a danger line past which Ab couldn't go and safely retreat from a spanking. Occasionally she stepped over it and then, after her mother's anger and her own tears, peace descended on the household. But with her father there was no such line. She could not drive him to the limit of his patience.

"What happens to the children?" she asked again.

"The children? Oh they grow up and become gypsies."

"Then what happens?"

"They go from place to place in their wagons."

Ab's next remark, a question really, though it took the form of a statement, was prepared for by an extended silence, during which Austin turned her around so he could tie her blue sash.

"Rachel says sometimes—*she* says if children are bad and if nobody can do anything with them or make them mind, then their mothers and fathers sell them to the gypsies."

"Surely not," Austin said.

"That's what Rachel says."

"Well nobody's going to sell you to the gypsies so stop worrying about it," Austin said, and got up from the rocker. His hands, as they gave a final twist to Ab's hair-ribbon, seemed meant for some work of exactness like mending watches or making trout flies. Actually, Austin King was a lawyer.

"Now then," he said approvingly, "you're all ready for company even if your father and mother are not. See if you can stay that way for the next half-hour till people begin to arrive."

He stood still and listened. Overhead, footsteps crossed and recrossed the ceiling. In the big, bare, third-floor bedroom (where the heat must be stifling, Austin thought) young Randolph Potter was also making himself presentable for the party. He had come North with his father and mother and sister, hoping to escape the heat, and like a faithful hound running after a carriage with its tongue hanging out the heat had followed them.

Until today Austin King had never set eyes on these foster relatives. When the name Potter crossed his mind at all, it was associated with two faded tintypes in the family album, on the page facing the stiff wedding-day portrait of his Grandfather and Grandmother King. Judge King, Austin's father, often used to speak of the man who took him in after his own father died, gave him a home as long as he needed one, and treated him exactly as he treated his own five sons. Both parties to this act of kindness—the homeless, frightened, boy and the gaunt Mennonite preacher—were now six feet underground, and the obligation could just as well have ended there, except that on the tenth of June the postman had delivered to the law office of Holby and King a letter addressed to Judge King, and therefore all the more binding on the person who broke open the sealed envelope. The letter was signed *Yrs. affy. Reuben S. Potter*, and it was full of allusions to boyhood matters that Austin didn't understand or know about, but he knew what his father would have written in reply to the final paragraph in which Mr. Potter, anxious to pick up the threads that had broken under the weights of time and distance, suggested bringing his family to Illinois for a visit.

Austin's whole long boyhood had been full of visiting aunts and uncles and cousins who came and stayed sometimes for a month or more. Lawyers, judges, politicians, railroad men, business acquaintances, anybody that Judge King liked or was interested in or felt sorry for, he brought home from his office for a meal, for overnight, and never thought of letting his wife know beforehand. The dining-room table could be stretched out until it accommodated any number, and there was always plenty of food. Austin's mother was active and capable, and while Judge King was alive, able to manage any burden that he placed upon her. Having company meant putting clean sheets on the bed in this or that spare room and making up the couch in the billiard room so that some young cousin, or sometimes Austin, could sleep on it, and then settling down to a nice long visit.

Such continuous open hospitality was dying out; it was a thing of the past. Martha King didn't entertain easily and casually the way Austin's mother had, and also, two days before the letter came, Dr. Seymour had told her that she was pregnant again. Faced with a choice between an inherited obligation and the consideration he owed his wife, Austin had sat down at his desk and tried to frame a letter that would explain, politely and regretfully and without giving offence, why it was not convenient to have the Potters at this time. He began and crumpled up one draft after another, until finally, trusting that Martha out of love for him would understand and approve, he dipped his pen in the ink bottle and with a heavy sigh committed them both.

Martha King not only didn't understand, she put an altogether different colouring upon his intentions; but instead of telling him how she felt, she waited, and when the Potters had arrived and it was too late for him to do anything about it, she made a scene behind the closed bedroom door, showered him with accusations (some just, some unjust), said that he didn't love her or he couldn't possibly have done such a thing when she was in no condition to have a house full of company, and then withdrew her support, leaving him to manage as best he could. To add to Austin's difficulties, she was ill in a way that she hadn't been before Ab was born; she was subject to morning sickness, making him feel that he had been unfair not only towards her but also towards the Potters, who should have been told, he now realized. They should at least have been given a chance not to come.

The footsteps stopped.

"Will there be any children for me to play with?" Ab asked.

Austin said, "No, this is a grown-up party and you mustn't interrupt people when they are talking, do you hear? Just be quiet and watch, and afterwards everybody will say, 'What a nice little girl.' "

He gave his daughter a pat on the behind and then, stepping over a doll's bed and a house of alphabet blocks, left her and went back into the bedroom across the hall.

2

Elm Street, the street the Kings lived on, had been finished for almost a generation when the Potters arrived for their visit. The shade had encroached gradually upon the areas of sunlight, and the outermost branches of the trees—maples and elms, cottonwoods, lindens and box elders—had managed to meet in places over the brick pavement. The houses reflected no set style or period of architecture, but only a pleasure in circular bay windows, wide porches, carpenter's lace, and fresh white paint. Elm Street led nowhere in particular and there was never much traffic on it. The most exciting vehicle that passed on a summer day was the ice-cream wagon, painted white, its slow progress announced by a silvery *ka-ling, ka-ling, ka-ling* that brought children running to the kerb. The ice-cream wagon was the high point of the monumental July or August afternoon, and much of its importance came from the fact that it was undependable. The children often waited for it in vain, their only consolation the chips that fell from the iceman's pick. There were also gypsy wagons, but they were infrequent, not to be expected more than once or twice a summer. When they did come, the smaller children, clutching their playthings, withdrew to their own front porches where, in safety, they stood and stared until the caravan of five or six covered wagons had passed by.

For a street only three unbroken blocks long—Elm Street below the intersection was another world entirely—there were an unusual number of children and it was they who gave the street its active character and its air of Roman imperishability. In feature and voice and attitude they were small copies of the women who shook dustcloths out of upstairs windows and banged mops on porch railings, of the men who came home from work in the late afternoon and stood in their shirt-sleeves dampening the lawns and flower beds with a garden hose. But for a time, for as long as they were children, they were almost as free as the sparrows.

With two alleys and any number of barns, pigeon houses, chicken coops, woodsheds, and sloping cellar doors (all offering excellent hiding and sliding places to choose from, all in the public domain), the children seldom left the street to play.

In the daytime boys and girls played apart, but evening brought them all together in a common dislike of the dark and of their mother's voice calling them home. They played games, some of which were older than Columbus' voyages. They caught lightning bugs and put them in a bottle. They frightened themselves with ghost stories. They hid from and hunted one another, in and out of the shrubbery. For the grown people relaxing on their porches after the heat of the day, the cry of *Ready or not you shall be caught* was no more alarming than the fireflies or the creak of the porch swing.

Elm Street is now in its old age and nothing of all this is left. There are cars instead of carriages, no gypsy wagon has been seen in this part of the country for many years. The ice-cream wagon stopped being undependable and simply failed to come. The iceman goes about his business unimpeded by children.

If you happen to be curious about the Indians of Venezuela, you can supply yourself with credentials from the Ministry of Education and letters from various oil companies to their representatives in field camps. With your personal belongings and scientific instruments, including excavating tools for, say, a crew of twelve men—with several hundred sugar bags for specimens, emergency food rations, mosquito netting, and other items essential for carrying on such archæological work —you can start digging and with luck unearth pottery and skeletons that have lain in the ground since somewhere around A.D. 1000. The very poverty of evidence will lead you to brilliant and far-reaching hypotheses.

To arrive at some idea of the culture of a certain street in a Middle Western small town shortly before the First World War, is a much more delicate undertaking. For one thing, there are no ruins to guide you. Though the houses are not kept up as well as they once were, they are still standing. Of certain barns and outbuildings that are gone (and with them trellises and trumpet vines) you will find no trace whatever. In every yard a dozen landmarks (here a lilac bush, there a sweet syringa) are missing. There is no telling what became of the hanging fern baskets with American flags in them or of all those red geraniums. The people who live on Elm Street now belong to a different civilization. They can tell you nothing. You will not need mosquito netting or emergency rations, and the only specimens you will find, possibly the only thing that will prove helpful to you, will be a glass marble or a locust shell split up the back and empty.

3

"If you want me to ask them to leave, I will," Austin said, turning to the four-poster bed. "I'll go right now and explain to them that it was all a mistake, and that we just aren't in a position to have company at this time."

To do this meant that he and the Potters would have to face each other in an embarrassment so hideous that he didn't dare think about it. Nevertheless, if that was what she wanted, if he had put a greater burden on her than she could manage, then he was ready, at whatever cost to himself, to set her free.

"Seriously," he said.

The offer was not accepted.

He turned away and opened the bottom drawer of the highboy, searching for summer underwear. "I'm going to take a bath and shave," he said. "It's almost five-thirty. Somebody has to be downstairs to let people in." He went off down the hall.

Now is the time to be quiet, to stand patiently in this upstairs bedroom and wait for some change in the position of the woman on the bed. So far as a marriage is concerned, nothing that happens downstairs in the living-room or the dining-room or the kitchen is ever as important as what goes on behind the closed bedroom door. It is the point at which curious friends and anxious or interfering relatives have to turn away.

The big double bed, like the quilt, is an heirloom and possibly a hundred years old. At the top of each heavy square post there is a dangerous spike, intended to hold the huge canopy that is now in the Kings' barn, gathering dust. The highboy, also of antique mahogany, contains a secret drawer in which (since Martha King had no secrets and Austin hid his elsewhere) are kept a velvet pincushion in the shape of a strawberry and odds and ends of ribbon. Originally dark, the woodwork in this room has been painted white. The windows extend to the floor and are open to the slight stirring of air that blesses this side of the house, carrying with it the scent of petunias from the window-box. The ceiling of the bedroom is eleven feet high, indicating the house's age and some previous history—quarrels between husband and wife, perhaps, in this very room.

After twenty minutes he came back and went over to the dressing-table. With his head bent forward so that the mirror would accommodate his reflection, he parted his damp hair solemnly on the left side and combed it flat against his skull. In sleep, in repose, in all unguarded moments, his face had a suggestion of sadness about it.

"Was it something that happened this afternoon?" he asked, standing beside the bed. "Did I do something or say something in front of them that hurt your feelings?"

With her voice half-smothered in the pillow Martha King said, "You didn't do anything or say anything and my feelings are not hurt. Now will you please go away?"

He leaned across her, trying to see her face.

"And please don't touch me!"

Austin had a sudden angry impulse to turn her over and slap her, but it was so faint and so immediately disowned that he himself was hardly aware of it. "Listen to me," he said. "You've got to get up now and come downstairs. I don't know what they'll think if you——"

"I don't care what they think. I'm not going downstairs."

"You've got to. We have company in the house and you've asked all those people."

"You go down if you want to. It's your company."

"But what'll I tell them?"

"Whatever you feel like telling them. Tell them you're married to an impossible woman who doesn't care what she does or how much humiliation she brings upon you."

"That isn't true," he said, in a tone of voice that carried only partial conviction—the intention to believe what he had just said, rather than belief itself.

"Yes it is, it's all true and you know it! Tell them I'm lazy and extravagant and a bad housekeeper and that I don't take proper care of my child!"

Austin's eyes wandered to the clock on the dressing-table.

"Couldn't we postpone this—this discussion until later? I know I said something that hurt your feelings but I didn't mean to. Really I didn't. I don't know what it was, even." Again the voice was not wholly convinced of what it said. "Tonight after the party, we'll have it all out, everything. And in the meantime——"

"In the meantime I wish I were dead," Martha King said, and rolled over on her back. Her face was flushed and creased from the pillow, and so given over to feeling that one part of him looked at it with curiosity and detachment. Beautiful (and dear to him) though her ordinary face was, in colouring and feature, in the extreme whiteness and softness of the skin and in the bone structure that lay under this whiteness and softness, and the bluish tint of the part of her eyes surrounding the brown iris, it was a beauty that was all known to him. He saw something now that he might not ever see again, an effort on the part of flesh to make a new face, stranger and more vulnerable than the other. And more beautiful. Tears formed in the right eye and spilled over, and then both eyes were blinded by them. The detachment gave way and he gathered her in his arms.

"I don't see why you aren't happy with me," she said mournfully. "I try so hard to do everything the way you want me to do it."

He wiped the tears away with his hand gently, but there were more. "I *am* happy," he said. "I'm very happy."

"You can't be. Not as long as you're married to a woman who gives you no peace."

"But I am, I tell you. Why do I have to keep saying that I'm happy? If you'd only stop worrying about it and take things for granted, we'd never have these—— Was it Nora Potter? Was it something about Nora?"

Martha shook her head.

"Sweetheart, Nora is like a cousin. She doesn't mean anything more to me than that. You don't have any cousins or you'd understand."

"I saw you when you helped her out of the carriage. You were smiling at her, and I knew you liked her better than you do me. I knew it would happen, before ever they came, and I don't know why I let it upset me. I just couldn't bear it." Now that she had at last accused him, she took his handkerchief and sat up and blew her nose.

"I don't know what you're talking about," he said with a guilty smile, though he had never in his life been more innocent. "Nothing happened. I don't remember smiling at her, or if I did—look, they invited themselves. I didn't ask them to come, and if I'd known they would give you a moment's unhappiness I'd never have allowed them to set foot in this house. You know that, don't you? Now that they're here, we might as well make the best of it. They won't stay long, probably, and we'll never have to have them again. We'll just go on living the way we have been, the three of us, and be happy."

So deeply did he mean and believe in this promise that the barricade of suspicion, the whole elaborate structure of jealousy and doubt that his wife had erected to keep him from reaching her, gave way before his eyes. The flesh gave up trying to make a new face and was content with the old one. Lightly, with the tips of her fingers, she stroked the fabric of his shirt. He took her in his arms again and rocked her.

Neither of them heard the steps on the front porch or the doorbell ringing in the pantry. With no sense of the passing of time, no anxiety because the guests had begun to arrive and there was no one downstairs to introduce the people from Mississippi, they held each other and lost themselves in the opening, unmasking tenderness that always comes after a satisfactory quarrel. At last, feeling utterly secure and able to cope with anything, Austin got up from the bed and finished dressing.

"I'll go right down," he said, "and tell them you were having trouble in the kitchen. Nobody will think anything about it."

"Do I look as if I had been crying?" she asked.

"Hardly at all. Put a cold cloth on your eyes."

At the door he took her in his arms once more and felt her cling to him. If he had held her a moment longer he would have given her all the reassurance she needed for some time to come, but he remembered the people downstairs, and let go. It was not his failure entirely. Women are never ready to let go of love at the point where men are satisfied and able to turn to something else. It is a fault of timing that affects the whole human race. There is no telling how much harm it has caused.

4

Rachel, the Kings' coloured cook, heard the doorbell but Martha King had told her that she would be downstairs to let people in, and so, instead of hurrying through the front part of the house to answer it, she stood still and listened. Rachel never hurried, in any case, but set her course and let wind, wave, and tide take her where she had to go. Her daughter Thelma, who was twelve years old and had been got in to help, said, "They're beginning to come."

"All of them with big appetites," Rachel said, and opened the oven door and basted the ham.

On the front porch, old Mrs. Beach and her two daughters waited. At this hour of the day Elm Street was deserted, its inhabitants drawn to the supper table like nails to a magnet.

"Do you think we should call out?" Alice Beach asked, after what began to seem rather a long time.

"If they're downstairs they'll come," Mrs. Beach said. "And if they're upstairs they wouldn't hear us. Are we early?"

Lucy Beach glanced at the little gold watch that was attached to her shirtwaist by a fleur-de-lis pin, and said, "It's five minutes after."

"Perhaps we ought to go home," Alice Beach said, "and come back later." Though she was in her early forties, she looked to her mother to settle the matter.

"When I was a young married woman," Mrs. Beach said, "and asked people for a certain hour, I was always ready to receive them. I hope when you girls marry that you'll remember to do the same. Not to receive your guests when they arrive is a mark of rudeness." She turned majestically and started for the steps.

Reluctantly her daughters followed. They had looked forward to this evening and there was reason to fear that, once they got home, even though it was only next door, their mother would refuse to stir out of the house.

"Are you coming to the party?" a small voice asked, and the three women, startled, turned around and saw Ab peering at them through the screen door.

"We are if there's going to *be* a party," Mrs. Beach said.

"Oh yes," Ab said.

"Well then, you'd better ask us in."

They trailed into the house, left their crocheted bags and their white kid gloves on the hall table, and seated themselves in an alcove of the long living-room, which by its extreme order and high polish and glittering candlesticks and bouquets of white phlox seemed to support Ab's statement. The little girl sat in a big wing chair facing Mrs. Beach.

"How are your dolls?" Alice Beach asked.

"They're fine, all but Gwendolyn," Ab said, after considering whether or not this interest was genuine, and deciding that it was.

"What's the matter with Gwendolyn? She looked remarkably well the last time I saw her."

"Oh, she broke," Ab said vaguely.

"You must have played too roughly with her," Mrs. Beach said. "I still have every doll that was ever given to me."

"Could I see them some time?" Ab asked.

"They're in the attic," Mrs. Beach said with discouraging finality.

A considerable stretch of silence followed. The guests looked around expectantly and then at each other. Ab, with no basis of social comparison, found nothing strange either in the silence or in the expectancy. All the windows were open and also the French doors leading out onto the side porch, but even so, it was very warm in the living-room. Above the upright piano, in a heavy gilt frame, was an oil painting of the castle of St. Angelo. The clock in the clock tower was real, and its thin tick gradually dominated the silence and filled the room with tension.

Lucy cleared her throat and said, "How do you like your new relatives, Ab?"

"Fine," Ab said, "but I don't think my mother does."

Glances were exchanged again.

"And where *is* your mother?" Mrs. Beach asked.

"Upstairs," Ab said. "My father dressed me. He told me to stay clean till people arrived."

"Well you didn't quite make it," Mrs. Beach said. "You've got a smudge on your nose, from the screen door."

"Come here and let me give you a spit bath," Alice said. Ab got down from the chair obediently and came and stood before her, while she moistened one corner of a small lace-bordered handkerchief with her tongue and removed the smudge. "There," she said. "Now you're as good as new."

"Fix her sash while you're at it," Mrs. Beach said. "Anybody can see that it was tied by a man. . . . I'm sure there's some mistake."

"Perhaps it's the wrong day," Lucy said.

"Oh no," Ab said. "It's the right day."

No longer confident of her appearance she withdrew to the front window as soon as Alice released her, and began to finger the curtains.

The clock in the castle of St. Angelo said twenty minutes past six as Mrs. Beach rose and motioned to her daughters to do likewise. Fortunately there was a step on the stairs. It was not the quick step of Martha King but careful and deliberate — the step of a person farther along in years and well aware of the danger of falling. The woman who entered the room a moment later was so small, so slight, her dress so elaborately embroidered and beaded, her hair so intricately held in place by pins and rhinestone-studded combs that she seemed, though alive, to be hardly flesh and blood but more like a middle-aged fairy.

"Well isn't this nice!" she exclaimed.

"I'm Mrs. Beach," the old woman said. "This is my daughter Lucy——"

"Happy to make your acquaintance."

"—and my daughter Alice."

"I'm Mrs. Potter. Do sit down, all of you. This reminds me of home." Mrs. Potter saw that the wing chair was vacant and settled herself in it. "Nobody is ever on time in Mississippi, but I thought Northerners were more prompt. Austin and Martha will be down directly. Won't you try this chair, Mrs. Beach? I'm sure you'd find it more—— What about you, Miss Lucy?"

Though the old lady and her daughters sat stiffly on the edge of their chairs as if they might get up at any moment, they assured Mrs. Potter that they were comfortable.

"I expect you think this is hot," she said, fanning herself with a painted sandalwood fan, "but I give you my word it's nothing to the weather we've been having down home. People are always saying that Southerners are lazy and they are, but there's a reason. I don't know whether you've ever been laid up with heat prostration but—— Do you live close by?"

"Right next door," Alice Beach said.

"Then it must have been your house I heard that delightful music coming from, while I was getting dressed. Just delightful. Do you play and sing, Mrs. Beach?"

"No," the old lady said solemnly, "but both my daughters are accomplished musicians. My daughter Lucy took lessons of Geraldine Farrar's singing teacher for a short while. Alice didn't have that privilege but we've been told there is a blood blend in their voices which is quite unusual."

"My husband is very fond of music," Mrs. Potter said. "His older brother was a drummer boy in the War Between the States, and we've always hoped that our children would turn out to be musical but neither one of them can sing a note. I hope you'll favour us with a concert while we're here," she added, turning from Mrs. Beach to her daughers. "Both of you."

"We're rather out of practice," Alice Beach said.

"They'll be glad to sing for you," Mrs. Beach said. "They both have very fine voices. My daughter Lucy could have had a career on the concert stage in Europe but I wouldn't allow her to. I didn't want her to be subjected to unpleasant experiences."

"I've never been able to keep either of my children from doing anything they set their minds on," Mrs. Potter said amiably. "I wish you'd tell me how you manage it."

Mrs. Beach did not feel that this remark called for an answer. Her daughters sat with their hands clasped nervously in their laps, and the clock threatened once more to take possession of the room. Before Mrs. Potter could start off on a new track there was a mixed trampling on the stairs and she called out, "Come in and meet these charming folks." And then, "This is my husband, Mrs. Beach . . . and my son Randolph . . . my daughter Nora. . . . Was that the doorbell? . . . Randolph, go see who's at the door."

Secure in the knowledge that this was going to be a party after all, that they had come on the right day and at the right time, even if there was nobody to receive them, Mrs. Beach and her daughters sat back in their chairs.

Ab slipped unnoticed out of the room and wandered out to the kitchen, where there were wonderful smells and an activity that she was familiar with and could understand. Though Rachel cried out at the sight of her, "Now you scat! We got no time for young ones," Ab was not in the least intimidated. She went straight for the kitchen stool, placed it in front of the cupboard, climbed on it and, balancing carefully, helped herself to a cracker.

5

The fear that always haunted Martha King before a party—that people would sit racking their brains for something to say—once more proved groundless. She came downstairs and found the living-room full of her guests, all talking easily to one another. As she slipped into the empty place on the sofa, Mrs. Potter turned and smiled at her. The smile said *Here is your party, my dear. I've started it off right for you. Now I'll sit back and be a guest.* After that it was possible for Martha to look around quite calmly and see who was there. Austin was watching her and ready to come to her rescue, but she didn't need rescuing. She moved the pillow to one side, and then, deciding that Nora Potter was dressed in an unbecoming shade of old rose, Martha King sat back, as passive as the room itself.

"It's a feeling like . . . well, it's not possible for me to put it into words," Nora Potter said to Lucy Beach. "It's something you have to see in someone's face or hear in their voice." Her hair was a curious cinnamon colour, parted in the middle and with bangs covering a forehead that went up and up. Her eyes were a blue-violet and seemed even larger and more vivid than they were because the rest of her face had no colour in it. Her wide smile revealed two upper front teeth separated by a little gap that gave her a childlike appearance, as if she were seven or eight years old and just committing herself to the gangly stage. Though not at all beautiful, the Southern girl's face had a charming, touching quality that the women in the room failed to notice (or if they did, to care about); the men all saw it immediately. The blue-violet eyes were searching gravely for something that was not to be found in this living-room or this town or perhaps anywhere, but that nevertheless might exist somewhere, if you had the courage and the patience and the time to go on looking for it. The same sincerity, the same impossibly high-minded principles, the refusal to compromise in a middle-aged or even a married woman would not have appealed to them. These qualities had to be combined with the sweetness of inexperience. Glancing at Nora the men were reminded of certain idealistic plans they had once had for themselves, plans that for practical reasons had had to be put aside. *You must be careful*, they longed to say to her. *You are young and inexperienced. You may think you know how to take care of yourself but life is hard and there are pitfalls. However, you don't have to be afraid with me. I can be trusted....*

The little coloured girl broke up the conversation in the living-room by opening the french doors and saying "Dinner is served." Every face was turned towards her. The idea that had been, off and on for the last half hour, in all their minds—food—was now a shining fact. Martha King rose and led the way into the dining-room. The other women followed, according to age: Mrs. Beach, Mrs. Danforth, Mrs. Potter, Lucy and Alice Beach, young Mrs. Ellis, who had recently come to town as a bride, Nora Potter, and Mary Caroline Link. Mary Caroline had been asked so that young Randolph Potter would have someone of his own age to talk to.

In the centre of the dining-room table there were two tall lighted white candles. Presiding at the head was Rachel's ham on a big blue platter. At the foot of the table was a platter of fried chicken. Between these two major centres of interest were any number of minor ones—the baked macaroni, the stuffed potatoes, the tomato aspic, the devilled eggs, the watercress, the hot rolls covered with a napkin, the jellies and the preserves, the stack of dinner plates, the rows of gleaming silver, the napkins that matched the big damask cloth. Like a tropical flower, the dinner party had opened its petals and revealed the purpose and prodigality of nature.

"Well, Martha," Mrs. Beach said, without bothering to hide her astonishment, "I must say this looks very nice. I won't have any of the ham. I can see it's delicious by the way it cuts, but ham always gives me heartburn." She glanced at the plate Martha King was fixing for her and was reassured; the chicken was white meat. "And a stuffed potato and a roll, thank you . . . no, that's plenty. I'm an old woman and I don't need as much to keep me going as you young people. Pshaw! you've given me too much of everything, my dear . . . Alice . . . Lucy

Domestic floral window of
trellised trumpet vines,
detail, date unknown.

Twelve Tiffany Bookmarks
Dover Publications

. . . come help yourselves. This is a buffet supper and you're not supposed to hang back in the doorway."

"Aunt Ione, let me give you a better piece of chicken," Martha said to Mrs. Potter. "You've got the part that goes over the fence last."

"It's the piece I like," Mrs. Potter protested. "I never get it at home because it's Mr. Potter's favourite. I wouldn't dare take it if we weren't visiting."

"Well, here's the wishbone to go with it."

"If this keeps up I'll go home stuffed out like a toad," Mrs. Potter said, helping herself to celery and then a ripe olive and crabapple jelly. "You must give me your receipt for pocketbook rolls. Mine never turn out like this."

"I don't suppose there's any way to get the men to continue their conversation in here," Martha said. "Alice, you haven't anything on your plate at all. Here, let me help you. . . . Now then, don't forget the roll. . . . There's no onion in the salad, Mrs. Danforth. I remembered that you don't eat it. . . . Mrs. Ellis, what will you have? A wishbone? The wing?"

"When I was a girl," Mrs. Beach said, "young women of good family were taught to cook as a matter of course, even though there often wasn't any need for them to, after they were married. Unless you know how food should be prepared, you can't tell someone else how to do it." (And even if you tell your daughters how to act at a party, there is nothing you can do about the look of sadness that returns after every effort at animation.) "I used to entertain a great deal when we lived in St. Paul. Mr. Beach was in the wholesale grocery business there, and he loved to invite people to our home. I often spent days getting ready beforehand. Now the young women just slap something together and call it a dinner party."

"Cousin Martha," Mrs. Potter said slyly, "if you just slapped this together——"

"Martha is an exception," Mrs. Beach said, and passed on down the table.

The men appeared to be in no hurry to get into the dining-room. While they stood in a little group outside discussing the price of hogs, Austin King went to the hall closet and got out the card-tables for Thelma. When these were set up, one in the study and three in the living-room, he stood with his back to the fireplace enjoying a moment of pride in the house and in his wife. He had watched her come down the stairs in a white dress with a large silk rose at her waist, looking as lovely (the dress was his favourite and she had worn it to please him) as any woman ever looked. The roomful of people had stopped talking for a few seconds, and then unable to remember what they had been about to say, they went on talking about something else.

In the dining-room Nora Potter said, "I don't know what will happen to me if I ever get married. I can't cook and I hate sewing. Brother says if I never learn to keep house, somebody will always have to do it for me. But just the same, I do envy and admire you, Cousin Martha."

"You haven't any salad," Martha King said. "Here . . . let me help you to it."

Immediately afterwards Nora plunged back into the conversation with Lucy Beach, a conversation that had nothing to do with housekeeping. "Do you think people are happiest," Martha heard her say as they moved out of the dining-room, "when they don't even know that they're happy?"

At that moment the men, who had merely been biding their time, closed around the table and with no pretence of a poor or finicky appetite, helped themselves to everything within reach.

Old Mr. Ellis, returning to the living-room with his plate in his hand, provided a moment of suspense for everybody. He was frail and uncertain in his movements but no one dared to take the plate from him, and the catastrophe they were all expecting did not occur. Avoiding the table where Mrs. Beach had established herself, he sat down between Nora Potter and Alice Beach.

"I've been meaning to call on you," the old man said as he tucked one corner of his napkin into his shirt collar. "And I will, one of these days." He turned to Nora. "You'd never think it, but this young lady I used to dandle on my knee."

"You used to give me peppermint candy," Alice told him.

"I was always partial to you," the old man said.

"How do you like it up North?" Alice asked. Nora had already been asked this question four times, but she answered with enthusiasm.

"You could've come at a better time of year," Mr. Ellis said. "It's too hot in July and August. Spring or fall is best."

"I'd like to come some time in winter," Nora said. "I've only seen snow once in my whole life."

"We get plenty of it," old Mr. Ellis said, "but nothing like what we used to get when I was a boy. I don't know what's happened, but the weather isn't the same."

"Mr. Ellis is full of wonderful stories about the old times," Alice said, turning to Nora. And then turning back, "Tell Miss Potter about The Sudden Change."

"Oh you don't want to hear me tell that story again," the old man said, smiling at her. "You've heard me tell it a hundred times."

"Miss Potter hasn't heard it. And besides, I always enjoy your stories."

"I've forgotten most of them," Mr. Ellis said. Ten years before, he had been an imposing representative of the world sensitive little boys are afraid of—the loud, ample, bald-headed, cigar-smoking, cigar-smelling men. And then suddenly, before anyone realized what was happening, Mr. Ellis' hair had turned white and with it his bushy eyebrows and the long black hairs growing out of his nose and ears. He was now a little old man with a tired mind and the violent emotions of second childhood. He discovered the plate in front of him and made a futile effort to cut his fried chicken.

"Can't I do that for you?" Alice asked.

"I can manage it," the old man said. "I'm still able to feed myself." Then he put down his knife and fork and began: "The Sudden Change occurred on the afternoon of December 20, 1836. It was one of the most remarkable phenomena ever recorded. There were several inches of snow on the ground that day and it had been raining long enough to turn the snow to slush. In the middle of the afternoon it suddenly stopped raining and a dark cloud appeared out of the north-west, travelling very rapidly and accompanied by a roaring sound that . . ."

With her plate in her hand, Martha King stood looking around the living-room. The only vacant place was next to Nora Potter, who glanced up as Martha approached and said, "Mr. Ellis is telling us the most wonderful story. It's a privilege to hear him."

"You're very sweet, my dear," the old man said, taking advantage of his great age to pat her hand.

"Please go on," Martha said. "I came to this table especially to hear you."

"There were two brothers in Douglas County overtaken by this same cold wave I was speaking about," Mr. Ellis continued. "They were out cutting down a bee-tree and they froze to death before they could reach their cabin. Their bodies were found about ten days afterwards. But the most remarkable case of suffering happened to a man named Hildreth. My father knew him well and heard the story from his own lips. He left home in the company of a young man named Frame, both intending to go to Chicago on horseback. They had entered a large prairie and were out of sight of human habitation when the cold came over them in all its fury. Fifteen minutes from that time their overcoats were like sheet iron. The water and slush was turned to solid ice. Their horses drifted with the wind or across it until night closed in. Finally they dismounted, and Hildreth killed Frame's horse, and then they took out the entrails and crawled into the cavity and lay there, as near as Mr. Hildreth could judge, until about midnight. By this time the animal heat was out of the carcass, so they crawled out, and somehow the one that had the knife dropped it. . . ."

A few minutes before, while Martha King was serving her guests, she had been ravenously hungry. Now that she could eat and had a plate piled high with food in front of her, she discovered that she had no appetite. She raised her fork halfway to her mouth and then put it down.

"I wish Pa could hear this," Nora said, turning around in her chair. "He'd be very interested."

But Mr. Potter had discovered that the woman who sat next to him was interested in singing. He was now telling her about all the great singers—Nordica and Melba and Alma Gluck and John McCormack—who had sung at the French Opera in New Orleans, and about the time he happened to be standing on the platform of the railway station in Birmingham when Paderewski's private car passed through. Mr. Potter had heard none of these artists and his own taste in music did not rise above Sousa's marches, but he managed nevertheless, out of scraps and hearsay, to make Lucy Beach's face bloom suddenly, and to place her beyond all doubt in the company from which Geraldine Farrar's teacher, after a few lessons, had dismissed her.

". . . Hildreth returned to the river bank," Mr. Ellis said. "And when he found that the ice was strong enough to bear his weight, he crawled across. The man came out and watched him trying to get over the fence and didn't lift a finger to help him. Finally he tumbled over the fence anyway, and crawled into the house and lay down before the fire. He begged for assistance and when the man relented and would have done something for him, his wife prevented it." Mr. Ellis began searching for his napkin, which had fallen to the floor. Alice restored it to him. He tucked it into his collar again and then said impressively, "The man's name was Benjamin Russ. His wife's name is not known, and nobody cares to remember it. They both had to leave the country afterwards, there was so much indignation among the neighbours. Mr. Hildreth always expressed the opinion that they imagined he had a large sum of money on him, and that they could secure it in case of his death. Such hardheartedness was very rare among the early settlers, who were noted like you Southerners"—the old man made a little bow to Nora—"for their hospitality."

"Grampaw, you've told that story at every gathering you've been to in the last twenty years," Bud Ellis said loudly, from the table in the alcove. "Why don't you keep still for a while and let somebody else talk?"

"All right, all right," the old man said. "I know I'm a tiresome old fool, but just remember that people can't help it if they live too long. You may live too long yourself."

The embarrassment that followed this remark was general. The visitors from Mississippi began talking hurriedly. The Illinois guests were silent and looked down at their plates. No amount of coaxing could make Mr. Ellis finish his story. He sat sulking and feeling sorry for himself until Thelma came to take the plates away and bring the ice cream.

6

After the card-tables had been cleared and put away in the closet under the stairs, Randolph Potter sat down beside Mary Caroline Link and began to tell her about his favourite riding horse, a jumper named Daisy, that had recently gone lame. The young Southerner was so strikingly handsome that he drew the attention of the others in the room to the couple on the sofa. Mary Caroline's pink linen dress was charming, but she herself was plain, with a receding chin and heavy black eyebrows. She had no easy compliments like the girls Randolph was used to, and her shyness forced him to keep thinking up new subjects for conversation.

Across the room, Nora Potter let her eyes come to rest on her brother.

"A penny for your thoughts," Bud Ellis said.

"I was thinking," Nora said, "of the words 'homely' and 'beautiful'—of the terrible importance people attach to whether somebody's nose is too long or their eyes too close together. How it must puzzle the angels!"

"You're way over my head," Bud Ellis said, and got up and joined his grandfather and Mr. Potter at the far end of the living-room.

The sun had gone down but the heat remained on into the long July twilight. The curtains hung limp and still. In the dining-room Thelma moved about, putting away silver and china. The word "nigger", which was so often on the lips of the Southerners, she did not appear to notice, and the Potters were unaware of any lack of tact on their part, even when Austin King got up quietly and closed the dining-room doors.

Martha King had settled down for the evening beside Dr. Danforth, who was old enough to be her father and whose fondness for her was uncritical and of long standing. Though his infirmity—he was hard of hearing—sometimes made him difficult to talk to, she was utterly at ease and herself with him, knowing as she did that if she were to lean forward and say to him: *I think I've killed somebody*, the expression on his face might change from pleasure to concern, but the concern would be for her, and he would probably say: *You did? Well, my dear, I'm sure you had some very good reason for doing it. Can you manage by yourself or do you need my help?*

After a while, Mrs. Potter called across the room to her. "Martha, change places with me. You've had that delightful man to yourself long enough!"

This move having been accomplished, Mrs. Potter sat fanning

herself and smiling around at the company for a moment or two. Then, turning to Dr. Danforth, she said, "Warm, isn't it?"

"I didn't catch that?" Dr. Danforth said, and cupped his hand behind his ear.

"I say it's very *warm*!"

"Ninety-six in the shade on the east side of the courthouse at two o'clock this afternoon," Dr. Danforth said.

"If I'd known it was going to be like this up North," Mrs. Potter said, fanning him as well as herself, "I'd never have had the courage to pack up and come. And in that case, I'd have missed knowing you, Mr. Danverse."

"Danforth . . . Dr. Danforth. I'm a veterinary."

"Well you must just excuse me. I've met so many charming people here this evening, and as I get older I have trouble remembering names. My girlhood friend, Clara Huber, from Greenville, Mississippi, has a daughter who married a man named Danforth. I wonder if you could be any kin?"

"My people come from Vermont," Dr. Danforth said.

"Now isn't that unusual," Mrs. Potter said. "You hardly ever meet anyone who comes from Vermont. Not down home, anyway. But I was going to say, if you're a horse-doctor, you must like horses, so why don't you come down and visit us? We've got a whole stable full of horses you could ride. I tell Mr. Potter he's fonder of horseflesh than he is of his wife. Just joking, you know . . . I say *just joking*. . . . Yes. But seriously, Mr. Danforth, you ought to come down to Mississippi. You've never seen cotton growing, have you? Well, you'll find it interesting. A field of cotton is a beautiful sight if you can just look at it and not have to worry about the practical side. The menfolks will show you around the plantation. The old slave quarters and the live oaks with moss hanging from them. You don't have anything like that up North, do you? And the family burial ground. Just drop us a penny post card and let us know when you're arriving. We're simple country folks. We don't put on any dog. But Mr. Potter loves company and so do I, and we'll show you a good time, you and your very charming wife."

Mrs. Potter had already asked several other people to come and stay at the plantation and each invitation had started, in the person who received it, a chain of subdued excitement and planning that would take months to exhaust itself. She stopped fanning and called across the room to her son. "Randolph, what is the name of the man Clara Huber's eldest daughter married? Danforth? Danverse?"

"Tweed," Randolph said, barely turning his head. "Charlie Tweed." Mary Caroline was telling him about the high school debating contest that had as its subject: *Resolved that Napoleon was defeated, not by the Russians or the English or the Austrians, but by Destiny*. Her side had been given the affirmative.

"Charlie Tweed," Mrs. Potter said to Dr. Danforth. "So he's probably no relation to you. He's a cotton broker and lives outside of Columbus, Georgia."

The conversation of the Southerners was sprinkled with place names that in an Illinois living-room, in 1912, were still romantic—Memphis and Nashville and Natchez and Gulfport and New Orleans—and that conveyed to the people of Draperville a sense of strange vegetation and of an easier, more picturesque life than they themselves were accustomed to. Mr. and Mrs. Potter depended, for the most part, on half a dozen topics: the Delta Country, the plantation, cotton, kinship, their own emphatic likes and dislikes, and the behaviour of various eccentric persons back home. These topics formed a complicated series of tracks and switches, like a railroad yard. Sometimes their separate conversations merged, so that Mr. and Mrs. Potter would be telling the same story simultaneously in different parts of the room. But the next moment they would go steaming off in opposite directions, calling on their son or daughter for confirmation of details, for names and dates momentarily forgotten. They thought out loud, recklessly, and sometimes heard their own remarks with surprise and wonder. They were in the North and among strangers, a situation that was unnatural to them, and that could only be corrected by making lifetime friends of every person they talked to. It didn't occur to them that they might bore anyone, and no one was bored by them or less than delighted with their soft Mississippi accent.

Mr. and Mrs. Potter talked about themselves and the people they knew because they had as yet nothing else to talk about, but as they began to feel better acquainted, the direction of their concern sometimes veered, sometimes reversed itself, and the full heat of their charm and interest was applied flatteringly to the listener, while they extracted his likes and dislikes, his hopes, plans, and history. The person taken hold of in this way had the feeling that they would never let go, that he and everything about him would always engage the attention and sympathy of these Southerners. The fact that the Southerners did let go a moment later, and let go completely, was not important. The contact, though brief, had been satisfying.

Randolph Potter left Mary Caroline and went out to the kitchen on some errand which he did not explain, and Mrs. Danforth came and sat down beside her. It was all Mary Caroline could do not to put out her hand and prevent Randolph's place from being taken. Mrs. Danforth was a very homely woman with a disconcerting habit of twisting her head and looking at the person she was talking to with a parrot-like expression that seemed half-inquiring and half-mocking. Mary Caroline answered Mrs. Danforth's questions about her mother, who had not been well lately, but her eyes kept straying. Mrs. Danforth saw the direction they took, and then, in her survey of the room, that her husband had said something to Mrs. Potter which made her tap his arm coquettishly with her fan. Pleased that he was enjoying himself, Mrs. Danforth turned back to Mary Caroline and said, "What a pretty dress, my dear. Did you make it yourself?"

In a kind of dream, Abbey King had been passed from one lap to another. Worn out by the excitement, the perfume and cigar smoke, and the effort of trying to follow so many conversations, none of which made the least concession to inexperience, she fingered the silk rose at her mother's waist.

"When I was nine," young Mrs. Ellis said to Martha King, "we moved from the part of town where we knew everybody, and I thought I wouldn't ever again have any friends. I used to sit in my swing in the back yard of the new house and watch the two little girls who lived next door. I envied their curls and their clothes and everything about them. And then one day I caught them using my swing. They were swinging each other and eating liquorice, and they gave me some. . . . But it took a long time, it took years for me to realize that wherever I went, there would always be someone who——"

"You'll find people very friendly here," Martha said, stroking Ab's hair.

In the evening air outside, the throbbing sound of the locusts rose and ebbed. Austin King left the circle of men and came across the room. What he had to say was for his wife's ear alone. She nodded twice, and he sat down at the piano and played a series of chords which produced a brief and respectful silence. "We're going to play a game called Mystic Music," he said. Mrs. Potter had never heard of this game and, instead of listening to the rules as Austin explained them, she kept going off into descriptions of parlour games that they played in Mississippi. The men were reluctant to leave their closed circle and the subject of Teddy Roosevelt, who out of egotism had split the Republican Party.

Though it was taken so seriously that night in the Kings' living-room, the split in the Republican Party was as nothing compared to the split between the men and the women. Before dinner and again immediately afterwards, the men gathered at one end of the room near the ebony pier glass and the women at the opposite end, around the empty fireplace.

What originally brought the split about, it would be hard to say. Perhaps the women, with their tedious recipes and their preoccupation with the diseases of children drove the men away. Or perhaps the men, knowing how nervous the women became when their husbands' voices were raised in political argument, withdrew of their own accord in order to carry on, unhampered, the defence of their favourite misconceptions. Both men and women may have decided sadly that after marriage there was no common ground for social intercourse. At all events, the separation had taken place a long time before. In Draperville only the young, ready (like Randolph and Mary Caroline) for courtship, or the old, bent (like Mrs. Potter and Dr. Danforth) on preserving the traditions of gallantry, were willing to talk to one another. They met as ambassadors and kept open the lines of communication between the sexes.

Austin King continued his efforts at the piano until eventually one person at a time relinquished his right to speak and the room was ready for the new game. Young Mrs. Ellis was chosen to be the first victim, and left the room. Austin began to improvise. He played the same mysterious little tune over and over, the end being woven each time into the beginning, until the company arrived at the stunt that Mrs. Ellis must do. She was called back from the study and the music became louder. She changed the direction of her steps and the music diminished. Now louder, now softer, it led her around the living-room on invisible wires until at last, hesitantly, she transferred a vase of white phlox from the table to the mantelpiece and the music stopped altogether.

The next victim, Randolph Potter, had to stand before Mary Caroline Link, bow from the waist, and ask her to dance with him. Under the spell of the music, Alice Beach (whose sister had sung for Geraldine Farrar's teacher, though she herself, being the younger one, had had no such opportunity) took a copy of *Janice Meredith* out of the bookcase in the study, returned to the living-room, sat down in the wing chair, and commenced to read aloud.

Since Austin couldn't see into the study, this required assistance, and so did the next stunt, when Dr. Danforth went all the way upstairs. The piano was moved so that Austin could see into the front hall, and confederates were stationed on the landing and at the head of the stairs. By prearranged signals they conveyed to the pianist whether Dr. Danforth was getting warmer or colder. A false move on his part produced an abrupt fortissimo chord, which was sometimes succeeded by others even louder, because of Dr. Danforth's infirmity. At last he came down the stairs wearing a white coat of Martha King's and a black hat with ostrich feathers on it. This feat was regarded by the Mississippi relatives as a triumph of the human mind.

After Dr. Danforth, it was Ab's turn. She had not expected to have any. But little girls can be seen and not heard and still be the centre of attention. Now, with all eyes upon her, she was obliged to leave the room. She sat with her legs tucked under her in a wicker chair in the study, and listened to the low murmur in the next room. It threatened to become intelligible but didn't quite, and finally they called to her.

As Ab came into the living-room she saw and started towards her mother. The music stopped her in her tracks. She blushed. She would have liked to escape but the music held her fast. She moved tentatively towards the fireplace. The music grew softer. There were three people confronting her—Mrs. Potter, Dr. Danforth, and Miss Lucy Beach. Ab knew she was supposed to do something to one of them, but which one? And what was it that she was supposed to do? She advanced towards Dr. Danforth. Once when she had an earache, he blew smoke in her ear and the pain went away. The music grew louder, obliterating him.

Through the music her father was saying something to her which she couldn't understand, but which was nevertheless insistent and left her no choice except the right one. She stepped back and would have walked in the opposite direction but the *DEE dum dum dum* grew loud and frightening. Lucy Beach sat there smiling at her, but some instinct—what the music was saying seemed clearer to the child now, though it was not yet plain—made her move instead towards her great-aunt from Mississippi. The music grew soft and caressing. The music suggested love to the little girl. She saw an invitation in her great-aunt's eyes and, forgetting that this was part of a game, leaned towards her and kissed her on the cheek. To Ab's surprise, the music stopped and the room was full of the sound of clapping.

"You sweet child!" Mrs. Potter exclaimed, and drew Ab into her arms. While Ab was enjoying her moment of triumph, she heard her mother's voice announcing that it was way past time for little girls to be in bed. A moment later she was led off, having gone around the circle of the company and said good night to everyone.

The sense of triumph was still with her on the stairs, and it lasted even after she had been tucked in bed. She was pleased with her first excursion into society, and she realized drowsily that the grown people were, beyond all doubt or question, pleased with her. The sudden impulse which had seemed to arise from inside her, the impulse towards love, was, as it turned out, exactly what they had meant for her to feel all along.

7

The sounds of an evening party breaking up are nearly always the same and nearly always beautiful. For over an hour the only excitement on Elm Street had been provided by the insects striking at the arc light. Now it was suddenly replaced by human voices, by the voice of Mrs. Beach saying, "Feel that breeze. . . . Good night Martha . . . Austin, good night. Such a nice party. . . . No, you mustn't come with us, Mr. Potter. We left a light burning and we're not afraid."

The light could not protect Mrs. Beach and her daughters from death by violence, or old age, or from the terrible hold they had on one another, but at least it would enable them to enter their own house without being afraid of the dark, and it is the dark most people fear, anyway—not being murdered or robbed.

Good night . . . good night.

Mrs. Danforth had left no light on, but then her husband was with her.

Good night, Martha . . . good night, my boy.

Good night, Austin . . . good night, Martha . . . good night, Mrs. Potter. . . . Here, Grampaw, take hold of my arm.

I don't need any help. I can see perfectly . . . good night, Miss Potter . . . good night.

Old Mr. Ellis had been listened to, and at his time of life he asked for nothing more. All the Draperville people had been so complimented, so smiled at and enjoyed that they felt a kind of lightness, as if a weight had been lifted from their backs. They tried to convey this in their parting words.

Good night, Mrs. King. I don't know when I've had such a lovely time.

You must come again, Mrs. Ellis.

Good night, Mr. King.

Though Mary Caroline lived next door to the Ellises, everyone expected Randolph Potter to take her home and she found him now (so firmly and relentlessly does the world push young people at one another) by her side.

No, you don't have to take me home, Randolph, really. It's only a step. . . . Well, all right then, if you insist.

If it had been twenty miles, the distance from the Kings' front porch to the Links' front walk would have been too short for Mary Caroline. The summer night was barely large enough to enclose a wandering sanity, a heart that must—somewhere on the way home—sigh or break. Such a pressure around her heart the girl had never felt before. Randolph did not touch her or even take hold of her elbow as they crossed the street, but his voice was music, the night insects were violins.

Faced with a sea of empty chairs, Austin and Martha and the Potters sat down to appreciate the quiet, recover their ordinary selves, and exchange impressions of the evening.

"Your friends are just charming," Mrs. Potter said. "I can't get over how nice they were to us."

"There was salt in the ice cream," Martha said.

"It tasted like nectar and ambrosia to me," Mrs. Potter said. "Austin, towards the end of the evening, I couldn't help thinking of your father. You look like him, you know. And he would have been so proud of you."

The expression on Austin King's face did not change, but he was pleased, nevertheless. Mrs. Potter had found the only compliment that could touch him, that he would allow himself to accept.

"I always like a mixed party," Mr. Potter said. "You get all kinds of people together, young and old, and they're bound to have a good time."

Nora smothered a yawn. It had been a long evening, and now she wanted to go to sleep and never wake up again. She kept her head from falling forward.

"Rich and poor," Mr. Potter said.

"There was nobody here who was very rich *or* very poor," Austin said.

"Well, people like the Danforths and the old lady with the two daughters—Mrs. Beach. They're people of culture and refinement. They've travelled all over Europe, she told me. You can see they've always lived well. And poor old Mr. Ellis. We had a little conversation after dinner. I always feel sorry when a man gets that old and has to worry about money."

"The Ellises don't have to worry about money," Martha said, tucking a loose hairpin into place.

"Old Mr. Ellis likes to give the impression that he's hard up," Austin said, "but actually he owns four hundred acres of the best farmland around here."

"You don't say!"

"It's Mrs. Beach who has a difficult time," Martha said. "They used to be well off—not rich exactly but comfortable—and then Mr. Beach died and left them barely enough to get along. But of course you'd never know from talking to her. She's terribly proud."

"Always has been," Austin said, nodding.

"Nora, go to bed," Mrs. Potter said. "You're so sleepy you can hardly keep your eyes open. Cousin Martha will excuse you."

"I'll wait up till Randolph comes."

"What time do you have breakfast?" Mrs. Potter asked, turning to Martha.

"Don't worry about breakfast," Austin said. "Sleep till noon if you feel like it."

The two men withdrew to the study for a nightcap, leaving the women to straighten the rugs and put back the chairs, to discover that Mrs. Danforth had forgotten her palm-leaf fan and Alice Beach a small, lace-bordered handkerchief with a smudge in one corner. Randolph's step on the front porch broke up the exchange of confidences in the living-room and the matter-of-fact conversation about farming in the study. Amid a second round of good nights, the Potters went upstairs to bed.

"You go on up," Martha said to Austin. "I want to see if Rachel has put everything away."

"I'll wait," he said, yawning.

The kitchen was all in order, the remains of the ham in the covered roasting pan on the table in the larder, the sink white and gleaming, the icebox crammed with leftovers.

Martha started back, turning out lights as she went. Finding no one in the study or the living-room she called to him.

"Out here," he answered.

He was on the porch, looking up at the sky. She came and leaned her head against his shoulder. Without speaking, they went down the steps and out into the yard where the grass, wet with dew, ruined Martha King's bronze evening slippers. The moon was high in the sky, so bright that they could see the shapes of the flower beds and here and there, dimly, the colour of a flower. When they came to the sundial, they stopped. The mingled odour of stock and flowering tobacco Austin had smelled before, but he had never realized until now how like the natural perfume of a woman's hair it was. A foot away from him, Martha stood as still as a statue.

Tonight after the party we'll have it all out, he had told her, hours before. Everything, he had said. But if it was that she was waiting for, she wouldn't be standing there with her face raised to the sky. She'd be looking either at or away from him. The small flicker of resentment that had persisted all through the evening—she needn't have put him through so much when there were guests in the house and people coming—he laid aside.

"You must be dead tired," he said.

There was no answer from the moonlit statue. Every rustle, every movement in nature had withdrawn, leaving them in the secret centre of the summer night. *There will be other summer nights*, the sundial said, *nights almost like this, but this night won't ever come again. Take it while you have it.*

"We'd better go in," he said after a moment or two. "To-morrow we both have to be up early."

Taking her arm, he led her gently back through the garden to the lighted house.

Part Two

★

A LONG HOT DAY

I

After three unbroken blocks, Elm Street dipped downhill in a way that was dangerous to children trying out new bicycles, and at the intersection with Dewey Avenue the pavement ended. From here on, Elm Street made no pretence of living up to the dignified architectural standards of the period. Instead, it was lined on both sides with one-story houses that under the steady pressure of a first and second mortgage were beginning to settle, to soften, to crack open.

If there had ever been any graceful trees below the intersection, they were gone by 1912. The cottonwoods and box elders had been planted by the wind—the same wind that later broke off limbs and lopped the tops out of them. There were no flower beds, no fern baskets, no potted palms, no brick driveways. The grass fought a losing battle with dandelions, ragweed, thistles. Chimney fires and evictions were not uncommon.

In this down-at-the-heel neighbourhood a few white families and most of the Negroes of Draperville lived on terms of social intimacy to which there were limits; but no taboo prevented the women from calling to each other (*How's your husband's back, Mrs. Woolman? Is it still giving him trouble? . . . I saw your Rudolf heading for the gravel pits with some older boys and told him to come home, but I don't think he heard me. . . .*) or the children from playing together in swarms.

In winter the residents of lower Elm Street kept themselves warm with stoves or took to their beds when the woodpile gave out. Their windows were nailed shut the year around, and the stale air they breathed they were accustomed and resigned to, just as they were accustomed and resigned to roofs that leaked, ceilings that cracked and fell, floors that were uneven, and the scratching of rats at night inside the walls. In their lifetime few of them had known anything better, though as a matter of fact there was one—there was a coloured boy who finished high school and went off to St. Louis to study medicine, much to the amusement of the white families who brought their washing to his mother once a week in big wicker baskets.

Something like a great pane of glass, opaque from one side, transparent from the other, divided the two halves of Elm Street. Beulah Osborn, the Ellises' hired girl, Snowball McHenry, who worked in Dr. Danforth's livery stable, and the Reverend Mr. Porterfield, who looked after Mrs. Beach's furnace from October until April and her flower garden from April until October, knew a great deal about what went on in the comfortable houses on the hill. But when they or any of their friends and neighbours passed under the arc light at the intersection, the comfortable part of Elm Street lost all contact with them.

In one of these shabby houses, in what was actually a railroad caboose covered with black roofing paper and divided into two rooms by a flimsy partition, Rachel, the Kings' cook, lived sometimes with one man and sometimes with another, and raised her five children. The two small windows on either side of the front door had once looked out on a moving landscape, on Iowa and Texas and Louisiana and West Virginia. Because every house in Draperville had to have a porch, Rachel's also had one—a platform four by four, with an ornamental balustrade that unknown hands had deposited in a tree nearby, one Halloween. In the front yard under the shade of a box elder was a rain-rotted carriage seat with the horsehair stuffing coming out of it, and a funeral basket set on two round stones. There were a number of other things in Rachel's yard that were not easily explained—a bassinet, a rusty coach lantern, a coffeepot, a slab of marble that might have been a table-top or a tombstone. The effect of all this was strangely formal, a fancy-dress nightmare made out of odds and ends, suggesting (if you didn't look too closely) an eighteenth-century garden house.

The morning after Martha King's party, Rachel opened her eyes and saw the commode with a pitcher and bowl, and a full slopjar standing on the floor beside it. A magazine cover was tacked on the wall above the washstand. The child in this picture had rolled off the printing press a little white girl, but someone had since painted the hands and face a chocolate brown, and now it was a little coloured girl who hugged the grey kitten to her breast.

Rachel hung for a moment between sleep and waking, and then, realizing that the other half of the bed was empty, said "You, Thelma—what you doing?"

Thelma appeared in the doorway to the kitchen. She was in her underwear and in her left hand was the piece of wrapping-paper Rachel had used to bring home some leftovers from the party—a little chicken and ham that would never be missed. As a piece of sculpture, Thelma was astonishingly beautiful. The receding slope of her forehead, the relation of the cheek-bones to the slanting, dreamy eyes, the carving of the thin arms and legs, the rounded shoulders, the hollow chest were the work of a tormented artist who had said, in this one fully accomplished effort, all that there is to say about childhood; said (unfortunately, from the point of view of a work of art) a little more, spoiling the generality of his design by something personal.

"You want to see what I been drawing?" Thelma asked.

Rachel brushed the picture aside. "What time that clock say?"

"Twenty minutes to seven."

"Whoo-ee, I got to get up out of this bed right now. Go wake up your brothers."

As Rachel bent over the china washbowl, she heard the

couch in the kitchen being shaken, and then groans and protests.

"Time to get up, Alfred," Thelma said.

"Time to knock your head off if you don't leave me alone," Alfred said.

"Hush up, all of you!" Rachel commanded.

Thelma came back in the front room and sat on the bed. Rachel glanced at her daughter suspiciously and, as she was drying her face and hands, said, "There seems to be something weighing on your mind."

Thelma pulled a feather through the ticking of the pillow and said, "I don't want to go to Mrs. King's no more."

"So that what's bothering you."

"I don't so much like it there. The Southern people they—"

"I guess I'm mistaken," Rachel said. "It don't look as if you was my child after all. Mrs. King give you them nice crayons and when she needs a helping hand, you aren't a bit willing."

"Yes I am," Thelma said quickly. "I'm your child."

"Get away from me," Rachel said, and found herself, at ten minutes of seven when the coffee ought to be in the pot and on the stove, with a broken heart to mend. She took Thelma on her lap and said, "I don't know what to do with you. I just don't. Let me see that picture you drawed." She felt around in the bedclothes and uncovered the piece of brown wrapping-paper. "Alfred . . . Eugene. . . . Get up out of that bed before I come pull you out. Your Pappy come home one of these days and I tell him a few things."

The two little boys asleep on the narrow cot at the foot of Rachel's bed stirred and untwined their bare legs without waking.

Rachel held the picture out at arm's length and considered it critically. The artist had taken certain liberties with perspective and altered a few facts, but there nevertheless, for all time, was the Kings' living-room, the ebony pier glass, the upright piano, and the bouquets of white phlox, just as they had appeared to the innocent eye, the eye that sees things as they are and not the use they are put to. The café-au-lait ladies distributed about the room on sofas and chairs wore long lace dresses, diamond necklaces, too many rings on their fingers, too many jewelled pendants and rhinestone ornaments in their hair. The men were more aristocratic. They might have been dark-skinned dukes and earls. No one was fat or ugly, no one was old.

"Yes," Rachel said nodding. "You're too tender for this world. I got to harden you up some way or you won't survive."

2

The breakfast table was set for seven, and four of the places had not been disturbed. No sound came from the upper regions of the house. When Austin and Martha spoke to each other or to Ab, their voices sounded subdued, as if they were either listening or afraid of being overheard. Except for this, and the empty places, there was no indication of company in the house. One might almost have thought that the Mississippi people had packed their bags and stolen away in the night.

Austin passed his cup down the table to be refilled. With the fumes from the coffeepot, Martha felt a wave of returning nausea, and bent her face away. "Be careful and don't spill it," she said, handing the cup to Ab.

"That's very good coffee," Austin said.

The telephone rang a minute or two later. He looked at his wife questioningly. She nodded, and he got up and went into the study to answer it. Young Mrs. Ellis wanted to say what a nice time they had had and how much they had enjoyed the Potters. Austin barely had time to return and sit down before the telephone rang again. The second call was from Mrs. Danforth, to say the same thing. "Well I'll tell Martha," she heard him say. "Oh no, she's fine."

At eight-thirty he folded his napkin and slipped it through a silver ring that had his first name engraved on it and was a relic of his childhood. "I'll be home a little after twelve," he said as he pushed his chair back from the table. Although he said nothing about the Potters, it was clear from the look in his eyes and from his doubtful expression as he bent down to kiss his wife that he wanted to ask her to be gracious, to be friendly whether she felt like it or not, to do nothing that would make the Potters feel unwanted.

As he was starting out the front door, Martha heard him say, "Hello, where have *you* been?"

A moment later, Nora Potter came through the study and into the dining-room. She was wearing a green dress with black velvet bows and two black velvet ribbons braided into her cinnamon-coloured hair. The dress was becoming, but strange for this time of the day. It made Nora look like a tintype in a family album—some fourth or fifth cousin who is shown, a few pages later, with her rather vain-looking husband, and then again as an old lady, formidable and all in black, with her elbow resting on an Ionic pillar.

"I woke up around six o'clock," Nora said as she began to eat her cantaloupe, "and couldn't get back to sleep so I got up and put on my clothes and went out walking. Wasn't that enterprising of me?"

"Very," Martha said.

"Did I waken you?"

Martha shook her head. "We thought you were still asleep," she said, reaching for the china serving bell.

"I tried to slip out of the house as quietly as I could. What a nice sound that bell makes. Our bell at home makes such a racket. It came down through the Detrava side of the family so Mama insists on using it."

"This one came down through Mr. Gossett's gift shop," Martha said. "Did you enjoy your walk?"

"There was dew on the grass and after the heat yesterday everything seemed so fresh and clear cut. Maybe because I'm in a strange place, seeing everything for the first time. Or maybe it's because I'm happy. All my life I've wanted to come North." She put down her spoon and with her raised eyebrows conveyed the seriousness and the intensity of this desire. "Ever since I was a little girl."

The horrible odour of frying eggs penetrated through two swinging doors and filled the dining-room.

"Well now that you're here, you must make the most of it," Martha said.

"I mean to," Nora said earnestly. "At home it doesn't cool off at night and you wake up exhausted. Here everybody and his dog were out sweeping and watering their window-boxes and I don't know what all. You'd think they were getting ready for a celebration."

Martha leaned over and wiped a dribble of egg from Ab's chin. "You make me wish I'd been out with you," she said. "There was nothing so interesting going on here."

"And red geraniums. Everybody has red geraniums and I'm so tired of magnolias. What would they have done if I'd walked right past them into their houses and had a look around?"

"It all depends on whose house you walked into. The Murphys would have let you go upstairs and downstairs and anywhere you wanted to. Old Mrs. Tannehill would probably have called the police."

"Would she really?"

"Yes, I think she would," Martha said. "But Austin would have come and bailed you out."

"It's a game I'm always playing with myself," Nora said. "That I'm invisible and can go wherever I want to go and watch people when they don't know anybody is watching them." She finished her cantaloupe and pushed it aside. "There was so much going on this morning I almost came back here to get Brother. You know how—not always but sometimes—you feel If I only had someone with me?"

"I know," Martha said.

"And then," Nora said, "sometimes when you do have someone with you and you think they're going to enjoy things the way you do, it turns out not to be the right person." Her eyes came to rest on the silver napkin ring. "You and Cousin Austin seem so suited to each other. I woke up thinking about you."

"And I woke up thinking about you," Martha said.

"Did you really?" Nora's eyes opened wide with amazement. "Wasn't that a coincidence! And yet if we were to try and tell somebody, they probably wouldn't believe that such a thing could happen. I'm always having strange things happen to me. I don't know what it is."

The pantry door swung open and Rachel appeared with a platter of bacon and eggs. "Morning, Miss Nora," she said glumly.

"Good morning, Rachel. How are you this morning—at least *I* think they're strange. But what I was about to say is I'm so glad you and Cousin Austin found each other."

"Do you take cream and sugar in your coffee?" Martha asked.

"Neither," Nora said. "I just take it black." Her expression changed and became uncertain. In Mississippi a genuine liking conveyed with candour usually brought a similar protestation in return. Also, there was something about Martha King's manner—so encouraging one minute and the next so blank, as if she had no idea what Nora was talking about—that made some of Nora's pleasure in the summer morning dwindle away. At the risk of seeming foolish she added, "And so glad I've found you both," and was partly reassured by the wan smile from across the breakfast table. "I often wonder why people marry the people they do marry, and what they find to say to each other, day in and day out. There's so much that must be difficult——"

"You're excused, pet," Martha said to Ab.

"I haven't finished my milk," Ab said.

"Never mind. You don't have to finish your milk this morning. Go in the study and play with your dolls."

"Do you mind my talking in such a steady stream?" Nora asked, as Ab left the room. "We all talk more than we should, except Randolph. It's a family failing. The thing is, you don't have to listen. Not if you don't feel like it."

"Oh but I *am* listening," Martha said. "And with great interest."

"If people don't talk," Nora said, "it's so hard to know what's on their minds. Tell me, Cousin Martha, do you ever hear voices?"

The telephone began ringing, and Martha went into the study to answer it.

"Yes," Nora heard her say. "Well, I'm glad. I hoped everybody was having a good time. . . . Yes, I'll tell them. They aren't up yet. Only Nora . . ."

At the sound of her own name, Nora felt the cold damp wind of dislike blowing through the dining-room, and wondered what she had said or done to deserve it.

"Oh no!" Martha exclaimed, over the telephone. "What a pity! Perhaps it was the fried chicken . . . yes . . . yes, of course. . . . Well, you tell her I'm terribly sorry. . . . I can look it up, but I think I remember it . . . a teaspoonful of baking powder and then you beat it throughly until it's stiff. . . . That's right . . . yes . . . yes, Alice . . . yes, I will. And thank you for calling."

"I'm so sorry about all these interruptions," she said, when she came back into the dining-room. "That was Alice Beach calling to say what a nice time they had last night and how much they liked you all."

"I hope you told her how much we liked them," Nora said.

"What was it you were saying?" Martha asked. "Here, let me fill your cup."

Oh, it's no use, Nora thought. I ought never have tried to make friends with her. She doesn't want to be friends with anybody.

"I hear these voices," she began, as she passed her cup across the table, "saying 'Nora, where are you?' and I say, sometimes right out loud: 'On the side porch' or 'Upstairs'—depending on where I am at the time. They aren't real voices——"

Martha tilted the coffeepot and it gave out a last thin trickle.

"*Now* where are you going?" Nora asked anxiously.

"To make a fresh pot of coffee."

"Can't I do it?"

"I'd better go do it myself," Martha said. "Rachel's in a bad mood this morning. She might bite your head off. . . . They're not real?" she asked, with her hand on the swinging door.

"Cousin Martha, that bed!" a voice said. Mrs. Potter swept into the dining-room, wearing a lace cap to hide her curl papers and an old brocade dressing-gown that Nora had begged her to leave at home. "Good morning, daughter."

"Nora and I have been having such an interesting conversation," Martha King said.

"I hope she hasn't been talking about Life, at the breakfast table."

"Oh no," Martha said. "Nora and I have been talking about voices."

"I can't always follow her, before my eyes are open. Nothing but toast and coffee for me," Mrs. Potter added as she sat down. "Mr. Potter likes his two eggs and a little fried ham, if you have any, but I just have toast and coffee. My dear, it was like sleeping on a cloud."

3

The law office of Holby and King, on the north side of the courthouse square, was reached by a flight of rickety stairs in which deep grooves had been worn by the feet of people coming to inquire into their rights under the Law, or to be treated by Dr. Hieronymous, the osteopath whose office was across the hall.

In the outer room of the law firm, surrounded by tier upon tier of fat calf-bound books on jurisprudence and equity, Miss Ewing guarded the gate through which people were usually but not always allowed to pass. She was a thin, energetic, nervous woman with a raw complexion, pale blue eyes, and pince-nez that reflected no mercy upon mankind. Around her cuffs she wore sheets of legal foolscap held in place by paper clips, and her hair was a grey bird's nest full of little combs, bone hairpins, puffs, and rats. The age of anyone born and raised in Draperville was either common knowledge or easily arrived at by mental calculation—Miss Ewing was fifty-one. But how she did her hair up the same way every morning of her life was a secret known to no other living person.

Miss Ewing was friendly with clients, rude to insurance salesmen and peddlers, and self-important generally; but she did the work of two secretaries and an errand boy, was never ill, and gave up all claim to a life of her own in the sincere and fairly accurate belief that without her the firm of Holby and King would not have been able to function. She alone understood the filing and book-keeping systems, and she had dozens of telephone numbers and addresses in her head, including some that belonged to people who were now retired from business and in certain cases dead.

This morning she was sitting at her L. C. Smith double-keyboard typewriter thrashing out five copies of an abstract that Austin King had left on her desk, and waiting for a farmer named John Scroggins to come out of Mr. Holby's office so she could go in and take his dictation. There were a number of matters that Mr. Holby ought to have been attending to, but instead he was addressing the farmer as if they were both in a crowded courtroom. "We had more enjoyment in the days of bare rough floors and mud chimneys than the people of today, who tread upon velvet and recline upon cushioned seats, clothed in purple and fine linen . . ."

The farmer was clothed in an old dark blue suit, and he had come to consult Mr. Holby about the mortgage on his farm. It was coming due shortly and the bank was threatening to foreclose.

"Life then," Mr. Holby said, "was more real. Humankind possessed more goodness. Virtue had a higher level, and manhood was set at a higher key . . ."

Miss Ewing went on typing.

Austin King's door was closed. Although he was the junior partner in the firm, his office was the larger of the two, and looked out over the square and the stately courthouse elms. It had been Judge King's office. Partly out of respect for his father's memory and partly so that his father's friends could come here and smoke a cigar and perhaps feel his loss less keenly, Austin had kept the office the way it was during Judge King's lifetime. But the big slant-topped desk, the green and red carpet, the stuffed prairie dog and the framed photograph of the old Buttercup Hunting and Fishing Club were not enough. Something was gone from the room and these memorials only made the old men sad. When they came at all, it was generally on business.

Judge King was the nearest the town of Draperville had come to producing a great man. During the last years of his life, honours had been heaped upon him. He was twice judge of the circuit court and several times a director of the country fair association. In 1880 he was a delegate to the Republican National Convention at Chicago, and four years later he was one of the presidential electors for the State of Illinois. In 1896 he was asked to run for governor and declined (the offer had strings attached to it). And shortly after the conclusion of his most celebrated case, *The Citizens of Dunthorpe County v. James Long*, he was publicly presented with the gold watch which Austin now carried.

Judge King's largeness of mind, his legal talent, and his wisdom in political affairs were balanced and made human by his fund of stories, his love of good living, and the pleasure he took in people of all kinds, especially women. He preferred them to be young and pretty, but whatever they were like, he rose to meet them as if they were, entirely in themselves, an object of pleasure and an occasion for ceremony. He made them little complimentary speeches and with his own eyes dancing, looked deeply into theirs, to see what was there. They were always charming to him. Refusing to recognize what everyone knew to be a melancholy fact, he went on notes for friends and made a number of loans of which his executors could find no written record. But in a place where gossip and scandal flourished, Judge King left a good name.

It was never his intention that Austin should become a lawyer. He died in 1901 before Austin knew what profession he wanted to follow. His father's memory, tenaciously preserved in the minds of the people who loved him, the sense of personal loss, and perhaps most of all the realization that he had never really known his father made Austin choose law as a career.

After seven years of practising in his father's office, he still did not feel that it was his own. But when he arrived in the morning, there was usually someone waiting to see him. He was not consulted about political appointments or asked to serve on honorary committees, but men who wanted to be sure that, in the event of their death, their families would not be taken advantage of had Austin King draw up their wills and appointed him sole executor. He could spot a trick clause in a contract far more quickly than his father ever could. He had read more widely and was better at preparing briefs. On the other hand, there were things that Judge King had learned as a lean and hungry young man in the offices of Whitman, James, and Whitlaw in Cincinnati that no law school has ever learned how to teach. Judge King had been a brilliant trial lawyer of the old school. Austin settled cases, whenever he could, out of court; settled them ably and without fanfare. This was not wholly the difference between father and son. The times were changing.

During the period between 1850 and 1900, when Draperville was still a pioneering community, the ownership of land was continually and expensively disputed. The Government extinguished the Indian title to the prairie, and the land was subject to settlement either before or after it was surveyed. The settler had no paper title—merely the right to possession, which he got by moving onto the land and raising a crop. The amount of the crop was not legally specified. A rail fence of four lengths was often seen on the prairie, with the enclosed ground spaded over and sown with wheat. This gave the settler the right to hold his land against all others until he had purchased it from the Government (or until, through some unfortunate clerical mistake, someone else had) and it also left a chaos of overlapping claims. Laws were passed but they were full of loopholes, and consequently for the next two generations able lawyers were held in the highest respect. In the eyes of simple and uneducated men, the Law assumed the status, dignity, and mystical content of a religion. The local lawyers, even though they were the heirs of Moses, sometimes charged very high fees. A farmer accused of having improper relations with his daughter would have to hand over his farm to the Honourable Stephen A. Finch before that eminent swayer of juries would take his case. But the older lawyers also took on a great many cases where there was no possibility of remuneration, merely so they could argue in court. They were dramatic figures and people attended their trials as they would a play, for the emotional excitement, the spectacle, the glimpses of truth behind the barn-burning, the murderous assault, the boundary dispute, or the question of right of way.

By 1912, the older generation, the great legal actors with their overblown rhetoric, their long white hair and leonine heads, their tricks in cross-examination, their departures from good taste, had one after another died or lapsed into the frailty of old men. There was also, throughout the country, an abrupt change in the legal profession. The older Illinois lawyers were trained on and continued to read assiduously certain books. Their bible was Chitty's *Pleadings*, which Abraham Lincoln carried in his saddlebags when he went on circuit in the forties and fifties; they also read Blackstone's *Commentaries*, Kent's *Commentaries*, and Starkie on *Evidence*. The broad abstract principles set forth in these books were applied to any single stolen will or perjured testimony, and on these principles, the issue was decided. With the establishment of the Harvard Law School case system, the attention of lawyers generally was directed away from statements of principle and towards the facts in the particular case. They preferred more and more to argue before a judge, to let the court decide on the basis of legal precedent, to keep the case away from a jury, and to close the doors of the theatre on the audience who hoped to hear about the murder of Agamemnon and see Medea's chariot drawn by dragons. The result was that the Law lost much of its moral and philosophic dignity, and required a different talent of those who practised it. The younger men regarded themselves as businessmen, and Miss Ewing (never quite respectful, never openly disrespectful) considered them one and all as schoolboys slip-slopping around in the shoes of giants.

Through the old-fashioned oratory in Mr. Holby's office she heard the measured tread which meant that Austin King was walking the floor. So far as Miss Ewing could see, it was the only trait that he had inherited from his father. More times than she could remember she had heard Judge King pacing the length and breadth of his inner office. At such times he did not suffer himself to be interrupted. The governor of the State had been kept waiting for forty-five minutes until the pacing stopped.

When she had finished typing the abstract, she arranged all five copies neatly in a pile, got up from her desk, and took them into Austin's office. He stopped pacing and looked at her, but the expression in his eyes was remote, and she was not at all sure that he knew she was in the room.

"Mrs. Jouette called," she said. "I made an appointment for her to see you at ten o'clock on Tuesday."

The thread of his thought broken, he nodded and (judging by the shade of annoyance in his voice) sufficiently aware of her presence, said, "Thank you, Miss Ewing."

If he doesn't want to be interrupted, she said to herself as she sat down at her desk in the outer office, all he has to do is say so.

She knew perfectly well that he would never tell her not to come in when the door was closed, and so long as he didn't tell her, some perverse impulse drove her to break in upon him with details that could just as well wait. At times, when Miss Ewing was overtired, she considered the possibility of getting a position elsewhere, though she knew that there was no office in Draperville where she would receive as much consideration or be paid anything like her present salary.

The outer door opened and Herb Rogers came in. Miss Ewing did not waste on him the smile that was reserved for clients.

"I'm selling tickets for a benefit at the opera house," he said hesitantly.

"Mr. Holby has someone in his office," Miss Ewing said, "but if you'd like to see Mr. King——"

"I don't want to bother him if he's busy. I can come back later."

"It's all right," Miss Ewing said cheerfully. "You can go in."

4

Sit down, won't you? the rubber cousin said. *You're rocking the boat.*

I never try to make my children mind, the elephant cousin said.

I wish you'd tell me how you manage, the rubber cousin said.

Oh I don't know, the elephant cousin said. *I give them presents from the ten cent store. They manage the rest.*

I give Humphrey lots of presents, said the mother.

That's news to me, said Humphrey.

Well I don't know whether it is or not, said the mother.

Sit down, Edward, before I slap you, said the rubber cousin.

My name isn't Edward, Humphrey said.

"From now on, it is," Ab said.

Well my advice, said the father, *would be to go out in the kitchen and see what there is to eat. Wash your hands, everybody.*

The telephone began to ring and Ab made no move to answer it. She didn't even seem aware of the ringing on the other side of the room, but the doll party on the window seat was suspended when Martha King came into the study and took the receiver off the hook.

"Yes? . . . Oh yes, Bud . . . no, we haven't. . . ."

Ab always enjoyed listening to her mother on the telephone. Where grown-up conversations were concerned, the half was usually more interesting than the whole.

"Yes . . ." her mother said several times into the telephone.

"Well I'm afraid it's going to be very warm, but just let me ask them. . . ." Martha King put the receiver on the telephone stand and left the study. Ab turned back to her dolls.

Hot cocoa, said Humphrey, whose name was now Edward.

And crackers with white icing on them, the father said.

That's a good idea, the elephant cousin said. *Whose idea was it?*

That was my idea, said the mother.

Martha King came back and said, "Bud? . . . We'd like to very much . . . yes. . . . All right, I will . . . good-bye."

With a brief, absent-minded glance at the dolls lined up in a row on the window-sill, she went through the living-room and out onto the porch. The doll party came to a sudden end.

". . . and the terrible part of it was," Mrs. Potter was saying as Ab opened the screen door, "they seemed so happy!"

She had taken possession, for the rest of the visit, of a wicker armchair that just suited her. The chair commanded a view of the sidewalk and the street, and the right armrest was designed to hold magazines or a knitting bag. Mrs. Potter kept her silk bag with the round raffia base in her lap. The bag contained crocheting and it went everywhere Mrs. Potter went. Mr. Potter kept the swing in motion with his foot. Nora was out in the side yard reading a book, with her head bowed to the white page.

"So Rebecca came home with a six-months-old baby," Mrs. Potter said, "and she's been home ever since. . . . Daughter, you oughtn't to be out there on the damp ground. Cousin Martha will give you a blanket to sit on."

"It isn't damp," Nora called back, "and I don't want a blanket to sit on."

"Nora is a great reader," Mrs. Potter observed. "She takes after her Great-Aunt Selina, who used to cook with a book in her hand. When Nora was fourteen she started in and read right straight through the historical novels of Harrison Ainsworth. I tried one of them once. It was about the Tower of

London and very interesting. I always meant to go on and read the rest of it. Aunt Selina married a man named . . ." The crochet needle jabbed in and out, emphasizing this point or that in Mrs. Potter's family history. When Mr. Potter showed increasing signs of restlessness, she glanced up and said, "You haven't seen the barn."

"You don't have to worry about me," Mr. Potter said. "I can always look after myself."

But he didn't. He sat in the swing, with one leg crossed over the other and his arms folded expectantly, and did nothing whatever to amuse himself. He was waiting for the telephone to ring, for people to arrive, for last night's party to begin all over again.

"Aren't there any dogs in this town?" he asked suddenly.

"At home Mr. Potter always has at least three hunting dogs trailing after him," Mrs. Potter said. "Every chair in the house has dog hairs on it, and we have to barricade the beds to keep Blackie off of them. She comes and goes like a princess. . . ."

"Blackie's a good dog but she's getting old," Mr. Potter said mournfully. "She can't see any more. Five years ago I wouldn't have taken a hundred dollars for her."

He got up from the swing and announced that he was going to have a look around. He meant the barn; enough time had elapsed so that the idea was his now and not his wife's. As he disappeared around the corner of the house, she said, "Mr. Potter is not himself this morning. You'll just have to excuse him. He misses the horses. His whole life revolves around horses and dogs. Raising cotton is just a sideline. But it's good for him to get away some place where he has to fall back on people for companionship. . . . Now, my dear, I want to hear all about you. Are your mother and father living? I thought maybe we'd have the pleasure of meeting them last night."

"My mother died before I was old enough to remember her," Martha said. "She died of consumption, and my father died shortly afterwards. I was raised by an uncle and aunt."

Mrs. Potter had reached a crucial turn in her crocheting and didn't answer for a minute or two. Then she drew a length of thread through her fingers and said, "Was she your mother's sister?"

"My father's," Martha said. "My mother didn't have any sisters or brothers. She was an actress. I have a picture of her upstairs, in *The Taming of the Shrew*. I can just barely remember my father. From what I've heard of him, I don't think he was much like the rest of the family. They're all very religious."

In her voice there was a note of tension, of fright, as if she were a schoolgirl undergoing an examination for which she was not at all prepared. Mrs. Potter heard it, and without seeming to change the subject, began to talk about the house on Elm Street. Apparently it is not easy for women to make friends. Except for certain critical periods of their lives, they seem almost not to need them. But for Mrs. Potter, too, the visit stretched out interminably. It had not been her idea to come North this summer and she didn't know, actually, why they were here. She only knew that part of the month of July and part of the month of August had to be crossed somehow, and so she set out to cross them. With her crocheting to support her, as it had in every other crisis of married life, she commented on rooms, rugs, curtains, wallpaper, the arrangement of tables and chairs—all this interspersed with descriptions of the plantation house in Mississippi, and how various pieces of furniture had come down through the family. Under the praise of her house (which was praise of her) Martha King began to feel easier, to feel safe. She explained about the alcove in the living-room and the open bookshelves in the study and, after a time, about the people who had raised her and who were now in China working as Christian missionaries.

"My religion has been a great comfort to me," Mrs. Potter began. Ab closed the screen door softly so as not to attract attention to herself, and went back to the library. The dolls were worn out from the party. The elephant and Humphrey Edward lay face down on a cushion and for the time being, they all refused to come to life.

Ab went upstairs to her room and got her celluloid animals —a duck, a green frog, and a goldfish—and started down the hall to the bathroom. When she pushed the door open, Randolph Potter was lying in the tub in water up to his chin. Ab stood holding her celluloid toys, and made no move towards the washstand.

"I've lost the soap," Randolph said. He moved his legs gently so that the black hairs stirred with the current.

"Can't you find it?" Ab asked.

"Not without an extensive search. What have you got there?"

Ab held the toys out to him.

"I have a duck at home," he said, and sat up slowly. "A live duck." The water parted, revealing the bald slope of his knee. "I wish I had him here right now."

"In the bath with you?" Ab cried.

"He swims round and round," Randolph said, nodding. "And when I lose the soap he dives for it."

"Why does he do that?"

"Because he knows I need it."

"Why do you need the soap?"

"For the same reason little girls need to ask questions they already know the answer to." When he drew his hand out of the water, his fingers were closed around a cake of castile soap.

"What is the duck's name?"

"I call him Sam," Randolph said, and glanced at the open door.

Now that they had something to talk about, Ab pulled the toilet cover down and set the celluloid animals on it. Randolph began to soap his arms and chest. Where the soap went, Ab's eyes went also.

"He follows me wherever I go," Randolph said. "And he likes raisins and crackerjack."

"What does he do with the prize?" Ab asked.

"He wears it on a string around his neck. When he gets in the bath with me, I take it off so he won't lose it. And when he swims, he goes like this." Randolph made a movement with his hands which churned the water around the tub clockwise.

"I take a bath with my mother sometimes," Ab said, drawing nearer.

"When Sam gets tired of swimming one way, he turns around and goes the other."

There was a sudden upheaval in the tub and Randolph stood up, dripping, and began to soap his back, his belly, and his thighs. He saw where Ab's stare was directed. Having got what he wanted, he said, "I don't think you ought to be in here with me. . . . You better go now before somebody comes," and watched the child's curiosity slowly turn to fear.

In her desperate hurry to get away from the bathroom, Ab slipped and fell thump-thump-thump, all the way down the treacherous back stairs. Her screaming brought Rachel, who picked her up and moaned over her and rocked her in her arms.

The world (including Draperville) is not a nice place, and the innocent and the young have to take their chances. They cannot be watched over, twenty-four hours a day. At what moment, from what hiding-place, the idea of evil will strike, there is no telling. And when it does, the result is not always disastrous. Children have their own incalculable strength and weakness, and this, for all their seeming helplessness, will determine the pattern of their lives. Even when you suspect why they fall downstairs, you cannot be sure. You have no way of knowing whether their fright is permanent or can be healed by putting butter on the large lump that comes out on their forehead after a fall.

5

The July sun mounting higher and higher in the sky brought both heat and glare with it. By the middle of the morning, animals moved with a noticeable slowness, and the leaves of the trees hung limp and dusty. Women with errands to do downtown kept as much as possible in the shade of awnings. Men meeting on the steps of the courthouse or in front of the bank, stopped to compare thermometer readings, to observe how the new asphalt paving blocks buckled with the heat, and to prophesy a thunderstorm out of the brassy sky before night. Farmers driving into Draperville for their Saturday marketing left their teams on shady side streets or in Dr. Danforth's livery stable. The farmers alone bore the heat patiently and without complaining; no heat, no corn. In stores the overhead fans whirred to little if any purpose. The windows in the two upper floors of office buildings were flung wide open, as if the masonry were gasping with the heat. At eleven o'clock, the big round sprinkling wagon drove twice around the square. The spraying cooled the streets and the air temporarily but by noon, when Austin King left his office, the pavement was dry and dusty again.

He waited under the awning of Giovanni's ice-cream parlour and moviedrome until a street-car came along. It was the open car that went out past the cemeteries to the Chautauqua grounds, and would let him off two blocks further from Elm Street than the other car, but it was cooler and so he took it. As he turned in at his own front walk, Mr. Potter got up from the porch swing. "It's a scorcher, isn't it?" Austin said.

"We're all waiting for you," Mr. Potter said.

"Am I late?"

"The women folks decided to have an early lunch," Mr. Potter said. "Bud Ellis called and invited us to drive out to their farm this afternoon."

"In this heat?"

"Well, he seemed to think today would be a good time. And we're used to heat. Down home——" Mr. Potter hesitated, searching for justification for the ride and apparently expecting Austin to provide it.

For a minute Austin said nothing. Then pleasantly, in his usual tone of voice, "If that's what you all want to do, fine." He held the screen door open for Mr. Potter, and followed him into the house. Randolph was in the study. He had Austin's fishing box open on his knees and was examining the trout flies. Mrs. Potter was in the living-room, playing the piano loudly and firmly. Ab was sitting on the living-room floor, with her collection of Singer sewing machine birds spread out around her.

"Where's Martha?" Austin asked.

"In the kitchen," Mrs. Potter said, still playing.

The whole atmosphere of the house had changed since breakfast. The Potters seemed to have taken hold (after all, he might have been consulted about the drive this afternoon), to have asserted their rights and privileges as guests, and he could feel *his* rights and privileges withdrawing timidly into the cellar, into closets, and beyond the trap door to the attic.

"If you'll excuse me," he said, "I'd better wash up before lunch."

He came down by way of the back stairs, and found Martha in the pantry putting sprigs of mint in a row of tall iced-tea glasses. "You look as pale as a ghost," she said. "Was it hot downtown?"

"No worse than it was here, probably."

"We're just having sandwiches and leftover salad."

"Did everything go all right this morning?" he asked.

"Randolph came down to breakfast at ten-thirty. Ab fell

on the stairs. And they want to go driving."

"So I hear."

"I tried to put it off, but Mr. Potter gets restless just sitting around the house. And Nora has been reading."

"That shouldn't upset anybody," Austin said.

"Maybe it shouldn't but it did. You know that set of books from your father's library—tall green books?"

"The 'Works of Robert Ingersoll'?"

"Well, Nora found them and Aunt Ione discovered what she was reading and made her stop. He's an atheist, isn't he? Aunt Ione has been playing hymns to purify the atmosphere. Nora got mad and went over to the Beaches' house and the girls asked her to stay and eat with them. I wanted to get out of the house for a while myself, to give the Potters more room, but it was time to start lunch."

"I don't think Nora had a very good time at the party last night," Austin said.

"Did she say anything to you?"

"No," Austin said, "it's just a feeling I had. We ought to have invited somebody for her—somebody her own age." He touched a damp curl on the nape of her neck. Martha moved away from him.

"You don't seem too happy yourself at this moment," he said.

"Does everybody have to be happy? Go on in and tell them to sit down. We're all ready."

He looked at her in astonishment. Though he knew he had already said too much, he said one thing more: "I'm sorry you had such a difficult morning." But it was no use. She was already far, far out of his reach. He waited a moment with his hand on the swinging door and then went on into the dining-room.

During lunch Martha King behaved towards her guests exactly as she had before, but she looked past her husband instead of at him—a thing that all three of the Mississippi people were instantly aware of. Out of politeness and not because they had any fear of scenes, they talked—talked constantly, often including Rachel in their conversation as she moved around the table. The gleam and roll of her very white eyeballs conveyed extreme acuteness of perception and sometimes open mockery, both of which the Potters were used to in their own servants.

As soon as Austin had finished his dessert, he put down his napkin and escaped to the barn. The horse, a handsome sorrel, had been harnessed and fed. Austin backed Prince Edward into the shafts of the high English cart that was his special pride, and drove around to the front of the house, where the Ellises' surrey was waiting. He tied the reins to the other hitching-post and then went back inside. Bud Ellis was standing in the front hall with his straw hat in his plump hand. Mrs. Potter had put on a long linen dustcoat and was adjusting her veils in front of the ebony mirror in the living-room. Mr. Potter and Randolph, also in dustcoats, were waiting impatiently.

"Where is Miss Nora?" Bud Ellis asked, shifting his weight from one foot to the other. "Isn't she coming?"

"Nobody knows," Randolph said gloomily.

There was a step on the front porch and Mrs. Potter, turning away from the pier glass, said, "There she is now."

"I'm not going," Nora announced as she walked in. "I'm going to stay home with Cousin Martha."

"There's no need for you to do that," Mrs. Potter said.

"But I don't *want* to go!" Nora exclaimed.

"You don't want to miss the ride," Mrs. Potter said firmly. "And Cousin Martha probably has things that she wants to do this afternoon."

Seeing Nora's face fall, Mrs. Potter thought how selfish her children were, how seldom they did anything for anyone else if it required the least effort or sacrifice. She herself would have liked very much to stay home out of the heat, but here she was, ready to do what everybody else did, and to give every appearance of enjoying it. "We're all waiting for you," she said.

Reduced to the status of a child, Nora put on the linen dustcoat her mother held out to her, and then a series of green veils. The whole company trooped out of the cool house into the blinding hot glare. The English cart, though it was very handsome and painted red, did not have a top to protect them from the sun. Mrs. Potter gathered her long skirts with one hand, put her right foot on the little iron step, and with Mr. Potter's help mounted to the back seat of the cart. After a brief pause, to give Austin a chance to offer him the reins, Mr. Potter got up after her. Screened by the purple clematis on the Links' front porch, Mary Caroline saw Bud Ellis help Nora into the front seat of the surrey, saw Randolph leap into the front seat of the cart beside Austin King.

Actuality, no matter how beautiful or how charming, can never even approximate the heartbreaking vision of the beggar looking in at the feast. To Mary Caroline, Mrs. Potter was not a middle-aged woman from Mississippi but a queen—some legendary queen of France or Denmark; and Randolph was not a person at all, but everything that is kind or fair. For this glimpse of him, as the carriages drove off, she had been waiting since breakfast and would have gone on waiting, patiently, for years.

6

The road to the Ellis farm led out past the fair grounds, the baseball park, and the coal mine into flat open country, where the whole of the horizon was visible, very much as it is in the Delta country. Occasionally, the sweep of land is interrupted there by a line of willows and cypresses, indicating water. Here the interruption was likely to be a hedge fence or a windbreak of pines on the north side of a farmhouse. The clouds that pass over the Delta are larger and in the evening create the gold and rosy colour that they later pass on to the sky. But the Mississippi people, looking around them, saw the heat shimmer that they were accustomed to.

Nora Potter, riding beside Bud Ellis in the front seat of the surrey, found she had misjudged him; he was much nicer than he had seemed the night before, and she could talk to him about the things that were worth talking about. "It's just that sometimes I feel so full of longing," she explained, "all kinds of longing—for happiness, for sympathy, for someone who won't be startled by what I say."

"I've been thinking," he said, "about what you said about faces. It's true what you said, every word of it. People do make too much of a fuss about—men especially—about whether a girl is good looking or not. They ought to look for something deeper. It's a funny thing, but that's what made me call this morning. I wanted to hear what else you had to say."

In the fields on either side of the road the grain had been cut and was now standing in yellow shocks flattened by their own weight and by the weather. The corn was a dark, dusty, summer green.

"We crossed the Ohio River just as it was getting light yesterday morning," Nora said. "I was awake and I kept looking out of the train window. It was like coming into a foreign country. Here the past doesn't hang over you all the way it does over us. You're just yourselves, leading your own lives and not grieving over the War Between the States and Sherman's army. You wake up in the morning and it's that morning you wake up to. At home I wake up in a world that's always remembering something—the way things used to be. And trying to get back. And there isn't any getting back, so of course there isn't really any waking up. Except for the niggers. They're happy and irresponsible. I hear them outside my bedroom window, laughing and quarrelling as if they owned the place and we were just there to take care of them. Sometimes I wish I were a nigger or an Indian or anything that would keep me from having to be myself, Nora Potter, who goes to parties and pays calls, and sits by quietly, with nothing to say, while Mama does all the talking."

"I know what you mean," Bud Ellis said, nodding. "But there are a lot of people who wouldn't."

"I have a great deal to say, but it isn't recipes, and that's all the women at home ever talk about. Cooking and sewing and their children and family matters."

"It's practically all they talk about here."

"If you say something that's an *idea*," Nora said, "they look at you as if you'd just gone out of your mind. They actually get embarrassed and after a minute or two start talking about something else. I haven't anybody at home I can talk to—except Brother, of course. He understands me, in a way, but it isn't a very good way. There's no comfort in it. You can't ever depend on him for anything, and he's so vain. He spends hours looking at himself in the mirror. I can go to him when I've been having trouble with Mama, because he knows how exasperating she is, and how hard I try to get along with her. But when I tell him what I've been thinking, what I really believe, he doesn't listen. Sometimes he looks at me as if he wished I'd quit talking and quit worrying and quit trying so hard. But I have to keep trying. If you don't do that down home, you're done for."

"You're not telling me a thing I don't know about," Bud Ellis said gloomily. "Not a thing, Nora."

"There's so much food, and you eat and eat until you can't breathe, and take longer and longer naps, and plan new clothes and talk about who is related to who, and it's like a dream. All you need to do is use that easy charm all Mississippi people have—Randolph, Mama, and Papa, everybody but me."

"Offhand I'd say you have the most charm of any of them," Bud Ellis said, very seriously.

"You don't mean that. You're only being polite, and you don't need to be with me."

"I wasn't being polite," Bud said. "Cross my heart."

Nora shook her head. "Don't you see——" she began.

Although Austin King knew the road, he kept his eyes on the surrey, maintaining just enough distance between the two carriages so that the dust would have a chance to settle ahead of him. When Bud Ellis stopped, so that Nora, who had never seen a threshing combine, could watch the farmers pitching the bound sheaves into the maw of the red machine and the straw spraying out of the big metal snout, Austin stopped too. The surrey started up, after a minute or two, and he touched Prince Edward lightly with his whip and drove on between more stubbled fields, more fields of tall Illinois corn. He was beginning to get used to the Mississippi voices, and to hear more in them than a soft Southern accent. When Randolph had anything to say it was generally addressed to the back seat. Austin's mind was free to return to town, to the house on Elm Street and the figure of his wife, closing the door of the bedroom where Ab lay in the deep restoring sleep of childhood, taking clean towels out of the linen closet, talking to Rachel, and searching, in all probability, for some new grievance against him. This mirrored image was inaccurate; for a long while that afternoon Martha King sat in the window seat in the library, doing nothing at all. And in one point, Austin's image of his wife reflected more truth about him than about her. But at least it made him forget the heat and the tiresome drive until suddenly the rich Southern voices, raised in argument, brought him back to reality.

"For heaven's sake, stop admiring your hands!"

"What else is there to admire?" Randolph asked.

"You can admire the view," Mrs. Potter said. "Cousin Austin, what are those green warty things?"

"Hedge apples," Austin said.

"Are they good to eat?"

"I've never heard of anybody eating them."

"How interesting," Mrs. Potter said.

"For God's sake, Mother!" Randolph exclaimed. "You've seen hedgerows all your life!"

"Maybe I have," Mrs. Potter said. "I don't always notice every little detail, like you and Nora. I certainly don't remember any such warty things growing on the plantation. . . . Cousin Austin, would it be too much trouble for you to stop the carriage a moment so Randolph can hop down and pick one?"

"I'll do no such thing," Randolph said. "If you'd never seen a hedge apple before, I'd get you one gladly, but the grass is dusty and they don't grow within reach, and the trees have thorns on them. If you want one, you can climb up and get it yourself."

Austin brought the carriage to a stop, handed the reins to Randolph, and jumped out. In the ditch by the side of the road he found a stick and started throwing it.

"Don't anyone ever talk to me again about the manners of a Southern gentleman," Mrs. Potter said.

"You're the one who's always talking about Southern gentlemen," Randolph said. "I don't know that I've ever seen one."

"You've seen your father," Mrs. Potter said.

After several attempts Austin knocked down one of the hedge apples and brought it over to the cart.

"Thank you, Cousin Austin," Mrs. Potter said. And then, as they drove on, "Yes, I do believe I've seen them before. It seems to me that old Mrs. Maltby has a recipe for making jam out of them. Or perhaps it's quince I'm thinking of. In any case, I'm going to take it home and ask her. There ought to be something you can do with them, since there are so many."

In the surrey the conversation had right-about faced, and it was now Bud Ellis who was doing most of the talking.

"When anybody tried that hard, you can't help feeling sorry for them."

"I know," Nora said.

"But feeling sorry isn't enough. It ought to be, but it isn't. Not if you're a person who—well, never mind. I don't know how I got started talking like this, except that you're kind enough to listen to me." He gave a slap with the reins and made the horse go faster. "She's very sweet and affectionate and all that, but I know everything she's going to say before she says it. And the things I say to her half the time she doesn't hear. Or if she does hear, she doesn't understand. She gets it all wrong, just the way when she tries to tell the simplest story every single fact comes out changed. Last night I heard her telling your mother about an old stone quarry that we drove out to, a week or so ago. It's full of water and the kids go swimming in it. I used to swim there a lot when I was growing up, and I heard her saying that the walls were a hundred feet high. Actually, they're only twenty-five or thirty feet high. I know it's a small thing and I ought to be able to overlook it, but I sat there chewing my fingernails, and thinking if she'd only get something right, just once!"

Nora glanced around, to see if the English cart was still following. Once before, in Mississippi, a conversation with a married man had taken just such a turn, and she didn't want this conversation to end up where that one had.

"Even though our paths have led along such distant trails —which I very much regret—I can talk to you and you understand what I'm saying. Mary and I don't speak the same language or see eye to eye about anything. Our pleasures are never the same. When I come home at night I wonder sometimes why I come to that particular house—why not just any house, since there isn't going to be anything for me when I get there."

Nora knew that she ought not to be listening to him. Most of what he said probably wasn't true, and she ought to be heading him off, now while there was still time. But instead she sat and looked at her gloves. She couldn't help feeling sorry for him. He was so idealistic, just the way she was, and it seemed as if everybody in the world, whether they were married or not, was looking for the same thing and never finding it.

Staring straight ahead at the dusty road, Bud Ellis said, "I'm going to tell you something I've never told any living person. I wasn't in love with her when I married her. I thought I was, at first, and then I woke up one morning and knew it was all a mistake."

Now is the time, Nora said to herself, but the flippant remark, the observation that would set them back on the right track again, refused to come.

"By that time the wedding announcements had been sent out and all the arrangements made, and you know how it is. I just couldn't do it. A thing like that, women don't get over very easily. Especially some women. I thought maybe after a month or two I'd fall in love with her, that it would come about of its own accord, but it hasn't and now I know it never will. We just aren't right for each other, and it's a great shame, because she could have made some man very happy. Sometimes I've thought I ought to tell her I don't love her, but when she looks at me in that way—so sort of anxious and waiting to see whether I'm going to like her new dress or something she's bought for the house, I just can't say it. It's all the same to me whatever she wears. But I tell her she looks fine and she believes what I tell her. That's the funny part about it. She's perfectly happy and satisfied. Maybe some day I'll find a woman I really care about, someone I can share my inmost thoughts with and know that they're understood—a woman that just being with means everything in the world. If I do, I'll screw up my courage and make a clean breast of it to Mary. It'll be hard on her to accept, but not as hard as it would be if there is nobody I care about more than I care about her. Meanwhile, we'll just have to go on living together and yet utter strangers. I don't blame her, you understand; it's my fault, the whole business. I shouldn't have been so soft-hearted in the beginning. But there are things I know now that I didn't then. And if a man is going to make his mark in the world, and accomplish his ambitions, he has to have a woman behind him who understands those ambitions and is driving him on. . . . This may be taking a liberty, but there's something I want to ask you, Nora. Do you think you could find room in your heart for one more friend?"

Why, Nora wondered wildly, *why* should it always be a married man who manœuvres his way around the room until he ends up sitting beside me? Is it something I do that I shouldn't, and that makes a serious conversation, a conversation about life, suddenly turn into something else?

People often ask themselves the right questions. Where they fail is in answering the questions they ask themselves, and even there they do not fail by much. A single avenue of reasoning followed to its logical conclusion would bring them straight home to the truth. But they stop just short of it, over and over again. When they have only to reach out and grasp the idea that would explain everything, they decide that the search is hopeless. The search is never hopeless. There is no haystack so large that the needle in it cannot be found. But it takes time, it takes humility and a serious reason for searching.

7

The surrey and then the English cart turned from the road into a narrow lane with deep ruts in it. The lane led through empty wheat-fields to a gate, and beyond it the farmyard, where a buggy stood with the shafts resting on the ground.

Bud Ellis drove around to the side of the house, and Austin followed him. While they were helping the ladies to alight, the old man and his tenant farmer came out of the barn and walked towards the carriages.

"So you came after all," Mr. Ellis called to them. "I wasn't sure whether you would or not."

"You ought to know we wouldn't let an opportunity like this slip by," Mr. Potter said, mopping his face with his handkerchief.

"I wouldn't have blamed you any if you'd changed your mind. It's a long drive in this heat. . . . Meet Mr. Gelbach."

The tenant acknowledged the introduction with a nod and then said, "Be quiet, Shep!" to the dog that was barking at them from ten feet away.

The barking dog and the odour from the pig-pen mingled with the other summer smells were like medicine to the restlessness that had afflicted Mr. Potter's legs all morning. "A fine place you have," he said, glancing around.

"The house needs paint and one thing and another," Mr. Ellis said. "Just now it's not much to look at, but I'll get it all fixed up one of these days. With corn selling at thirty-three cents at the grain elevator, I may end up living here." No one took him seriously and he did not mean that they should. He was knocking on wood in case the ancient gods of agriculture should have noticed his prosperity and consider that it had passed all reasonable bounds.

The tenant farmer unhitched the two horses and led them off to the barn.

"I've got something you ladies would enjoy seeing," old Mr. Ellis said. "My new colt, born two days ago."

The colt and the mare were in a pasture behind the big barn. "Pretty as a picture," Mr. Potter said, leaning on the pasture fence. "Yes, that's worth coming all the way from Mississippi to see." He called a long string of coaxing invitations to the colt but it wouldn't come to him.

They went on to take a look inside the big white barn, smelling of manure, hay, dust, and harness; at the corn cribs empty until fall; at the new windmill; at the sheds filled with rusty farm machinery; at the pigs; at the vegetable garden; and finally at an Indian mound down by the creek. A head, ears, nose, legs, and tail were all easily discernible to the people from Mississippi, and Mr. Potter knew about an Indian mound in Tennessee which was said to resemble the extinct Megatherium.

After the Indian mound, Mr. Ellis turned towards the cornfield, and at this point the women were left behind. They were not expected to take an interest in farming, and besides, their shoes were not suitable for walking over ploughed fields. Austin King and the tenant farmer walked along side by side with nothing to say. Each imagined that the other was mildly contemptuous—the farmer of the city man, the man who worked with his head of the man who worked much longer hours and harder because he had nothing to work with but his calloused hands.

Austin King was in many ways the spiritual son of Mr. Potter's tall, gaunt, bearded father, and would certainly have been a preacher if he had been born fifty years earlier. Mr. Potter had had all the justice and impartiality he could stand in his boyhood. He had more than once been tied to the stake and burned alive in his father's righteous wrath. And so he went on ahead with old Mr. Ellis and his grandson.

No one was ever made to feel morally inferior in Bud Ellis' presence. Money was what Bud Ellis was after, and this cold pursuit has a tendency to elbow its way into the category of the amiable weaknesses, where it does not belong. For the sake of their warmth and protective coloration, the man whose real pursuit is money will also pursue women or drink too much, or make a point of sitting around with his coat off, his tie untied, his feet on a desk, killing or seeming to kill time. And in that way he can safely say that anyone who appears not to be governed by materialistic or animal appetites is a blue-nosed hypocrite.

As they stripped off ears and compared the size of the kernels, Mr. Potter made the opening move in a game that must be played according to certain fixed rules, like chess—a game in which (as no one had more reason to know than Mr. Potter) hurry is often fatal. He admired whatever old Mr. Ellis admired, and listened to his long, rambling, sometimes pointless stories. Mr. Potter also told stories himself, stories in which he himself was invariably the shrewd hero, sly, tactful, humorous, always coming out on top at the end. These stories, taken together, tended to establish Reuben S. Potter as a sound man of business.

Mr. Ellis was himself a sound man of business. His four hundred acres had been acquired at a tax sale. The old man was quick to scent out a game and usually ready to play—on his own terms, of course, which would not in the final showdown be wholly to the advantage of Mr. Potter.

Without his family to restrain him, Mr. Potter's voice grew louder and his bragging more open. "I knew what I was up against. I'd had dealings with Henry Fuqua before. So when he come to me and said he'd heard I had a pair of mules I was fixing to dispose of and how much did I want for them, I said, 'Henry, you got a good mule now. What do you want with two more?' 'Well I do,' he said, 'and furthermore I got my eye on them two white mules.' 'Well,' I said, 'tell you the honest truth, I don't know as I want to sell that pair of mules. They're nicely broken in now and used to each other and I might have trouble finding another pair that would satisfy me. Why don't you go talk to Fred Obermeier? I was out by his place the other day and he's got some nice mules, two or three of them.' 'If I wanted to talk to Fred Obermeier,' he said, 'I'd be talking to him now. I wouldn't be here dickering with you. I'll give you eighty dollars for the two of them.' Well, eighty dollars is a good price down home for a pair of mules, but I figured if they were worth that to Henry, they were worth more to somebody else, because he can't bear to part with a nickel he don't have to, so I said, 'Tell you what I'll do. You can have Jake, if you want him, but Olly belongs to the children. They raised him and he's kind of a pet. You know how it is, Henry,' I said, 'if I was to sell Jake and Olly both, they'd probably feel bad.' 'Make it eighty-five,' he said. 'No, Henry,' I said. 'That's a decent enough offer, but these mules—I don't know as I can see my way clear to selling them. Not at this time, anyway.' So we argued back and forth, and the sum and substance of it was . . ."

Mr. Ellis dropped back beside Austin King and the tenant, a short stocky man of about forty, with light hair, blue eyes, and a dark sunburned neck. "My oats aren't as good this year as last," Mr. Ellis said. "We had a lot of rain in the late spring and planted late. But the corn will even things up—isn't that right, John?"

"It ought to, if this weather holds," the tenant said, his voice low and unemphatic.

"John had his own farm until a few years ago," Mr. Ellis said, turning to Austin. "He's a very good man, a hard worker. They both are. When we're short of help she comes right out in the field and works alongside of him. They've got three nice children and she puts up enough vegetables to last through the winter and keeps the house neat as a pin. I want to get her some linoleum for the kitchen floor when I sell my corn. It always pays to keep the womenfolks happy, you know. Some people are eternally changing tenants but I've had this couple on the place for the last seven years and we get along fine."

When the corn was delivered to the grain elevator, the tenant would claim his share of the profits. Meanwhile, he allowed old Mr. Ellis to take unto himself full credit for ploughing this forty-acre field, for sowing the seed, for disking and harrowing in dry weather. As they walked along under the enormous sky and in the midst of heat so luxuriant and growth so swift that they could almost be seen and heard, the tenant farmer's arms remained always at his side as if he had no power of gesture, and his eyes, not even angry, reflected no pride, no pleasure, no possession of anything that they saw.

8

When the men disappeared into the cornfield, Mrs. Potter didn't have Dr. Danforth to fall back upon. There was Nora, of course, but to fall back upon Nora in time of need was to take up all manner of unsolved problems that Mrs. Potter, who loved peace and harmony, had agreed to let alone. She couldn't make friends with the dog because Randolph had bewitched it, and Randolph himself was never to be counted on. He was only there when she didn't need him. He was kneeling in the dust now, his face hidden by his crossed arms, and the dog was walking round and round, nosing Randolph, trying to get in past his hand, past his elbow. Mrs. Potter retired to the porch, opened her silk bag, and found her spectacles.

When the men came back from the fields, she could stuff her crocheting into the bag again and with the extreme adaptability which marks the lady, be ready to please, to console and comfort, to mother old Mr. Ellis, who was twenty-five years her senior but who would nevertheless need mothering after he had been so long in the hot sun.

"It's cooler out here," Nora called from the shade of a cottonwood tree.

"My knees," Mrs. Potter called back.

Nora offered to drag the rocker out onto the grass, but Mrs. Potter would not allow it. She was happier where she was. Occasionally she raised her eyes from her crocheting and let them wander over as much of the farm as she could see from the porch. She did not insist on the tangles of cane-brakes and somewhere among the enormous cypresses of the primeval forest, the scream of sawmills. She did not expect to see the great rolling sheet of cotton as it came from the gin or to be offered sow-belly and hot biscuits and sorghum molasses. What distressed her was that there should be no old trees around the farmhouse, no lawn, no flower garden. Neatness and order were wasted upon her and so was the fertility of black soil. She wanted something that gratified her sense of family tradition, of home as the centre of the universe. What Mrs. Potter saw was a flayed landscape that a hundred years earlier had been one of the natural wonders of the world—the great western prairie with timber here and there in the distance, following a stream, and the tall prairie grass whipped into waves by the wind, by the cloud shadows passing over it, mile after mile, as if the landscape (once an inland sea) remembered and was trying to reproduce its ancient aspect.

The farmer's three children huddled in a group by the windmill and watched Randolph and the dog for some time before they overcame their shyness and allowed him to charm them with tricks. The laughter and the squealing of the children reached the porch and caused Mrs. Potter to peer down at them over the railing. With a sigh she began another round on her centrepiece. No matter where Randolph was, he had to be loved; he couldn't rest until he had made someone (even if it was only a long-nosed collie) a victim to his charm.

The crocheting grew under Mrs. Potter's fingers until it was the size of a small saucer, and then the farmer's wife came out of the house with a jelly glass in her hand, worked the rusty pump-handle, and brought Mrs. Potter a drink of cold water.

"Now aren't you kind!"

Mrs. Potter could not invite the farmer's wife to visit her in Mississippi but she was ready, even so, to make a friend. She pressed her crocheting flat on her knee and explained the pattern, so like a snowflake under the magnifying glass, and the farmer's wife invited her to come inside out of the heat.

Under the cottonwood tree Nora amused herself by picking blades of sunburnt grass and measuring them, one against another, discarding in each case the shorter one. Drowsy with the heat, her mind drifted helplessly, now coming to rest against the children's voices, now returning to the house in town. What I don't see, she said to herself, is why life should be so simple for some people; why everything that Cousin Martha could possibly want or need should be granted to her, with no strings attached, happiness within reach, where she has only to bend down and gather it, day after day. And other people. . . . These games I play, Nora said to herself, looking out over the cornfields; this mindless measuring and discarding of grassblades; these voices that cry *Nora, where are you?* because no human voice ever asks that in a tone anything like the sound I hear in my mind—I know they aren't real voices, but am I the only one who hears them? Cousin Martha doesn't imagine that she's invisible or want to see what is on the other side of the wall. She doesn't want to watch people when they don't know they're being watched. Motives don't interest her the way they do me. She has things to do, and if I had been allowed to stay home with her this afternoon, I might have found out her secret—what it is that makes it possible for her to be so sure of herself. But since I'm here instead, something ought to happen to me. Things that start ought to be finished, even if it takes twenty or thirty years. We were asked out to this farm and therefore something ought to come of it, for all of us, and for Cousin Austin. Most of all for Cousin Austin, because he didn't want to come. He was tired and he didn't want to drive us out into the country. Nothing but politeness made him do it. He's seen the farm before and he doesn't care about farming or expect anything to come of this drive. It's one thing for me to expect something and not get it, but if people who expect nothing come away empty-handed, then there is really no hope.

No hope, said the heat, the only actor on this wide empty

stage, drawing the last moisture out of the ground into the dry air. *There is no such person as Cousin Austin. The whole business of expecting and receiving is an illusion.*

Frightened by this communication from the landscape, Nora stood up suddenly, brushed her skirt off, and ran towards the porch. Every window in the house had been closed since early morning, and the blinds pulled to the window sills to keep out the sun. The downstairs rooms had an air of scrubbed, solemn poverty. When Nora came into the parlour, Mrs. Potter and the farmer's wife paused and then (since she seemed to have nothing to tell them, no message from the men) turned back to each other and went on talking about their canning, their church work, and their children.

9

Between quarter to two and quarter past three an age of quiet passed over the house on Elm Street, over the richness contained in cupboards, the serenity of objects in empty rooms. The front stairs creaked, but not from any human footstep. The sunlight relinquished its hold on the corner of an oriental rug in the study in order to warm the leg of a chair. A fly settled on the kitchen ceiling. In the living-room a single white wheel-shaped phlox blossom hung for a long time and then dropped to the table without making a sound. On a dusty beam in the basement a spider finished its web and waited. Just when the arrangement of the furniture, the disposition of light and shadow, the polish and sweet odour of summer seemed final and the house itself a preserved invaluable memory, Ab awoke and called out to her mother.

Between three-thirty and quarter to four, the leaves on the trees began to stir. There were dust eddies, dry whirlpools in Elm Street. The locusts grew shriller. One of the little Ritchie girls, walking and skipping on her way to the store for a loaf of bread and two pounds of small yellow onions, passed the Kings' house and saw Martha King in the garden, cutting Shasta daisies. Mrs. Danforth looked out of her kitchen window and saw her at about the same time—saw Ab pulling flowers off the trumpet vine while Martha arranged the daisies in a cut-glass vase on the back steps. So did Rachel's son, Eugene, who came to the back door that afternoon, talked to his mother for a few minutes, and went out the driveway, eating a slice of bread with butter and sugar on it.

When Martha King had finished arranging the flowers, there was nothing more for her to do. She went upstairs to her room and stood looking around and frowning, as though something had brought her here and she could not remember what it was. The closet door, slightly ajar, drew her attention. Half the closet was dedicated to Austin King, his suits, his shoes, his ties, his sober, tobacco-smelling presence. The empty coat-sleeves, the trousers hanging upside down, reminded her of how she had been irritable with him before lunch when he was only trying to do his best by the company from Mississippi and by her. Resolving to do better by him and by them, she let her eyes rove through her own wardrobe, feeling the pleasure of dark purple against flamingo red, stopping at a row of white blouses then going on to folds of velvet or silk. She lifted the white dress she had worn the night before from its hanger, and holding it in front of her, consulted the dressing-table mirror. Then she sat down in the chair by the window and with a pair of sewing scissors she snipped the threads that held the silk rose in place.

When Austin King went away to law school, Martha Hastings was a girl who had only just lengthened her skirts and been permitted to leave off wearing hair-ribbons. Three years later, when he began to practise law in his father's office overlooking the courthouse square, she was a grown woman, quite different from the girl he remembered, with mysterious shadows in her face and beautiful brown eyes that were sometimes sad, sometimes wilful and arrogant. For a long time he merely watched for her, in any group of people where she was likely to be, and wondered about her when he was falling asleep at night, finding now this explanation and now that for the mysterious shadows, investing her with the sweetness and gentleness and pliability of a story-book heroine, walking with her, in his imagination, over moon-dappled grass, their hands sometimes touching, their faces reflecting one another's need. Accident at last brought them together; the Women's Club decided to produce Erminie *with local talent. After a rehearsal at the Draperville Academy, Austin King asked if he could escort Martha Hastings home. He was, and always had been, shy with girls. If she had rewarded him with the slightest encouragement, it is more than likely that he would have seen no more of her. But from the very beginning she fought against him. The never-ending effort to do what was right, upon which Austin King spent so much of his energy, she had already had more than enough of at home. She had been boxed in by Christian unselfishness, by church and Sunday school, by the Epworth League, from the time that she was old enough to be at all aware of her surroundings.*

In an atmosphere laden with Methodism, people smiled at her, the same complacent, oversweet smile that they smiled at everyone else. They had no idea who she was, or what she was like. They weren't taking any chances. They were singing their way to eternal salvation and she didn't want to be saved. She wanted to run risks and there weren't any offered to her. What she missed was excitement, weakness in her knees, the sense of falling and falling and nothing under you to break the fall, nothing but empty space, and who knows what, when you land or if you ever land at all. Wasn't there anyone, she asked herself, standing on the church steps in the brilliant sunshine, or holding a plate of strawberry ice cream at a church social—wasn't there someone who would give her the sense of danger, a man who would look at her and make everything go dim around her? A man that she would see only once and know that she would marry him if he raised his little finger to ask her to; even though she didn't know anything about him, maybe not even his name, or whether he was kind or false, loved her or was making a game of love?

The first time that Austin kissed Martha Hastings good night on the front steps of her uncle's house, her arm rose in an involuntary gesture and then, feeling his uncertainty, she let her arm drop to her side and said, "You didn't have to do that." Boys brought up the way Austin King was brought up are taught, along with table manners, to create a handsome high pedestal and put the woman they admire on it, for purposes of worship. What they are not taught is how to get her off the pedestal, for purposes of love. (Martha King slipped the white dress on over her head. Standing in front of the mirror, turning slowly, she considered the effect without the rose. The face in the mirror became doubtful. Without the flower, the pleated silk sash didn't look right. It might be the way the sash was draped, but on the other hand, sashes were not being worn so much any more. If the dress were plainer. . . . She took it off and very carefully cut the threads that held the sash in place, and then went on cutting and removed the lace inset at the throat. It made the dress look too sweet, she decided, too much like a young girl's first party dress.)

The next day she received a letter asking her to marry him. Her first reaction was pleasure, wholly unexpected, like coming outdoors on a May morning and finding that the Baltimore orioles had arrived. He's so gentle, she thought, and so trusting. Some girls would take advantage of him, and so I'd better marry him and protect him from them. Then, in a spasm of irritation at her own foolishness, she tore the letter into small pieces and dropped it in the wastebasket.

Sitting in the porch swing that night she told him that it was no use, that she didn't love him and never would love him and that sooner or later she would have to ask him to stop seeing her. "When that time comes," he said solemnly, "all you have to do is tell me and I won't bother you any more."

The time didn't come, though she often threatened him with it, always with such pain in her voice, as if it were he who had threatened to send her away and never let her see him any more. This contradiction between what she said and the voice that said it confused and encouraged him. Part of him was ready to agree with her. It was impossible that he would ever possess a beautiful woman. Nevertheless, he kept coming, night after night, drawn by the desire to see her face and hear the sound of her voice, to be near her. Her voice was sometimes young and confiding, sometimes harsh, and occasionally altogether hopeless. Martha Hastings had many different voices, each one so full of shading and meaning that even to think about them was to cause shivers of delight to pass over his body.

Though Austin King was, by Mrs. Beach's standards, an eligible young man, attractive, of good family, well-mannered, ambitious, and kind, his own opinion of himself was not very high; not as high as—taking human nature by and large, all the grossness, selfishness, and loutish cruelty—it might have been. He knew that Martha Hastings did not want to marry him, but he also remembered how her arm had come to rest for a second on his shoulder, and from this physical memory, this sensation which the shoulder could produce at will, he derived hope. He even tried a little experiment. Instead of asking her, as he had been doing each night when he left, if he could see her the next night, he deliberately omitted this question, and when he arrived the following evening—tall, thin, hollow-cheeked, with a bunch of white roses in his hand—she was expecting him. But she did not like the roses. "I don't mind them when they're just buds like this," she said, with a troubled expression on her face. "But I don't like them when they open." After that he brought her other flowers—violets, carnations, lilies of the valley, whatever the florist had that reminded him of her. Instead of kissing her good night, against her will, he watched her carefully, studied her moods, listened for anything in her glance or her voice that would give her away to him.

Since it is the nature of women to want to be loved, too great encouragement ought not to be derived from the fact that if you kiss one of them on a summer night, her arm rises and involuntarily comes to rest on your shoulder. Although so much time and effort have gone into denying it, the truth of the matter is that women are human, susceptible to physical excitement and the moon. This susceptibility is only skin-deep. (Something would have to be done about the ugly seam that held the skirt and waist together, Martha King decided. She tried draping the sash in various ways, and then with a reckless gleam in her eyes, burned her bridges behind her. No dress with one long sleeve and one short has ever yet looked right. If the dress was short sleeved, wouldn't the waist have to be higher? Or was it the embroidered panel that was causing all the difficulty?) *Every woman is a walled town, with ring after ring of armed reservations and hesitations. They can hold off an army for years, and they are not always to be trusted even when they open the gates of their own accord. The citadel has cells, secret places where resistance can survive long after the enemy is, to all appearances, in possession. The conqueror has to take all, the defeated lose everything before the natural balance and pride of either can be regained.*

What distinguished Austin King from the God-fearing, church-going people who attended Wednesday-night prayer meetings, was that he allowed her to be angry and unreasonable and unfair. He also revealed something of himself—not the effort to do right, but a simple falling into it, at times, as if there was no other choice open to him—which touched her heart. Even so she would not marry him.

Nothing is accomplished in the way of courtship that does not first take place in the pursuer's imagination. One evening, as he was crossing the street in front of her house, the words "I, Austin do take thee, Martha" came unbidden into his mind. His life was quite changed and his chances were greatly improved when he reached the other side of the street and stepped up on the grass between the kerbing and the sidewalk. He carried himself more confidently. There was a different look in his eyes. Martha Hastings, watching him cut across the lawn instead of coming up the walk, took fright. The enemy had got through the outer wall.

The gentlest person has depths of cunning, resources of patience and persistence and strategy. Knowing that Martha Hastings was frightened, and wanting in so far as possible to be kind, Austin never again asked her to marry him. Instead he began to talk about the future as though it were now settled. He appeared to be happy and serene when he was with her. She was not taken in by this subterfuge, but on the other hand, there seemed to be no way to combat it. Austin brought to life, one by one, four imaginary children, each with a name and nature of its own. The oldest was a boy, a blond, white-faced dreamer, late to meals, moody, and frequently irritable. Then a girl, a passionate, unpredictable child, never saddened or elated by the same things that affected other children; now needing to be petted and loved, now fearlessly scaling roofs, climbing apple trees. Then a thoroughly conventional boy whose only concern was to be like other people and who disapproved of his family. The third boy was short and stocky and brave, a hero in the small size, all heart and no subtlety, always running to catch up with the others.

The idea of marriage with Austin King, Martha Hastings could reject, but there was no denying that he was the father of these children who were so real to her. For a while in self-defence she spoke of them as his children, and when that failed her, she had to accept not only them but also the house that he conjured up one night in the porch swing—the house surrounded by very old apple trees, with the snow lying a foot deep outside, and the children asleep upstairs, and the two of them talking in low voices by their own fireside.

Realizing, finally, that it was too late to send him away, that his will and his imagination were stronger and more persistent than hers, she did the one thing left for her to do. She packed a suitcase and ran away, leaving no word for him or even an address where he could write to her. Her uncle and aunt, sworn to secrecy, put her on the train one damp November morning, and in a mood of wild and laughing elation she looked out of the train window and saw the town of Draperville slipping away from her.

Between four and four-thirty, the locusts grew still. Martha King finished cutting the threads that held the waist and skirt together and then glanced at the clock. It was later than she thought. They ought to be coming home any time now. She folded the pieces of what had been Austin's favourite dress and put them away in a chest where she kept sewing materials. When she went downstairs she opened the screen door and called "You'd better come in now," to Ab, who was riding her tricycle up and down the walk.

"Just one more time," Ab said.

The sky was clouded over with running clouds. Martha turned and went out to the kitchen. "There's going to be a thunderstorm," she said to Rachel. "It'll cool the air, but I do wish they'd come."

IO

The clock face in the courthouse dome said five o'clock when Austin King drove around the square and down Lafayette Street with Nora on the front seat beside him and Randolph in back, between his mother and father, holding a bloody handkerchief to his forehead. The horse was in a lather. Austin had driven him harder than he would have under ordinary circumstances, on such a hot day, but it had not been fast enough for the Potters, who, by their anxious silence, had urged him to drive faster.

He stayed in the cart in front of Dr. Seymour's office while the Potters went inside. When they came out, ten minutes later, Randolph had a neat bandage over his left eye, and looked handsomer than ever, but the gravity had not left their faces.

The tops of the trees were swaying wildly in the wind and the first drops of rain were splashing on the pavement when the cart turned into Elm Street and drove up before the Kings' house. The Potters got out and hurried into the house, with the hedge apple and several ears of corn. Austin drove the horse and cart around to the barn.

"What on earth happened?" Martha King asked, as the Potters burst in upon her.

"The man warned Randolph about the dog," Mrs. Potter said, "but you can't keep that boy from making friends with an animal."

"Accidents will happen," Mr. Potter said.

"Randolph, go on upstairs and lie down," Mrs. Potter said. "I'll be up in a minute."

"We were about ready to leave," Mr. Potter said, "and I was trying to round everybody up so we wouldn't get caught in the storm when——"

"Randolph began running in circles," Mrs. Potter interrupted her husband, "with the dog after him. They disappeared around the corner of the house, and when Randolph came back there was a gash in his forehead——"

"About two inches long," Mr. Potter said, "down his forehead and through his eyebrow——"

"It was bleeding," Mrs. Potter said.

"The dog wasn't frothing at the mouth?" Martha asked.

Mr. Potter shook his head.

"Randolph isn't used to these Northern dogs," Mrs. Potter said. "He should have been more careful. Apparently the dog got excited and leapt at his face."

"The doctor took eight stitches in it," Mr. Potter said impressively.

"It hurt his feelings," Mrs. Potter said as she turned towards the stairs, "but he'll get over it. Cousin Martha, you should have been with us. We had a very nice drive, in spite of the way it turned out."

Austin unharnessed the horse, led him into the stall, threw a blanket over him, and gave him some oats. Then he stood in the doorway, looking out at the rain. The sky had turned from black to olive green, and the garden was illuminated by a flash of white lightning which was followed by a clap of thunder that made him thrust his neck forward involuntarily and hunch his shoulders, as if the thunderbolt had been intended for him. His face was relaxed and cheerful. The storm had released all the accumulated tension of the long hot day. He didn't mind being marooned in the barn or the fact that the house was full of visitors. Something inside him, he did not know what, had broken loose, had swung free, leaving him utterly calm and at peace with the world.

Mrs. Danforth, looking out of her bedroom window, thought how deceptive appearances are. Austin King, usually so restrained and dignified beyond his years, was running through the rain with long leaping strides like a boy of twelve.

II

The bedroom lights were on because of the unnatural darkness outside, and Austin, all dressed and ready to go downstairs for dinner, was sitting on the edge of the bed. His hair was neatly combed, and his starched collar and Sunday suit imparted a kind of stiffness to his gesture of apology.

"I'm sorry," he said. "It never occurred to me."

"That's what I say," Martha said calmly. "It never occurred to you."

She was seated at her dressing-table in her petticoat and camisole. Her waist was tightly corseted, and her full bust and shoulders had a curving elegance that was of a piece with the carved monogram on the silver brush and comb and hand-mirror on her dressing-table.

"I thought if you wanted to come, you'd say so," Austin said.

"I did say so."

"When?" he asked, in amazement.

"Before lunch," Martha said, still looking in the mirror.

"I don't remember your saying that you wanted to come driving with us. I must not have heard you."

"I said I'd like to get out of the house for a while."

"Is that what you meant?" Austin said. "I wasn't sure at the time. I thought you were just tired and irritable and wished they'd never come."

"If you weren't sure, you might have asked me."

"It was so hot and all, and I'd have given anything to have stayed home myself instead of taking a long drive, so naturally I——"

The rain had started coming in through the screens. Austin got up and closed both windows, and then went back and sat down on the bed. What does she see? he wondered. What on earth does she see when she holds her hand-mirror and looks sidewise into it?

One sometimes notices in public places, in restaurants especially, women dressed elaborately, wearing furs, equipped with diamond rings on their fingers, and their faces so hideous that the observer turns away out of pity. Yet no pity is asked for; nothing but pride looks out of the ugly face.

If Austin King had suddenly said, "You have the most lovely eyes of any woman I have ever seen and wherever I go I am always looking, always comparing other women with you. Of them all, my darling, you are the most beautiful, the most romantic. I love, beyond all reason or measure, the curve and width of your upper eyelids, and your hair that always looks as if you had been out walking and the wind had swept it back from your forehead. I love the things your mouth says to me, and the soft shadow right now at the side of your throat . . ." the chances are that Martha would have listened carefully and perhaps in some inner part of her nature been satisfied for a moment. But only for a moment.

She put the hand-mirror face down on the dressing-table and looked into the large mirror in front of her. She never looked into either mirror a moment longer than necessary. If she had cared to look at her husband, all she needed to do was to shift her glance to meet his, also reflected in the mirror, but she avoided his eyes, apparently without any effort on her part.

The beautiful blind passion of running away is permitted only to children, convicts, and slaves. If you are subject to the truant officer and the Law of Bedtime there will be doorways that will shelter you and freight cars that will take you a long way from home. If you are a safe-cracker and cannot walk in a straight line for more than a hundred yards without coming face to face with a high stone wall, there are ways of tunnelling under the wall, under the five-year sentence, and confederates waiting outside. If you cannot own property but are owned yourself, you may, hiding in the daytime and travelling across country by back roads at night, eventually reach the border. But if any free person tries to run away he will discover sooner or later that he has been running all the while in a circle and that this circle is taking him inexorably back to the person or place he ran away from. The free person who runs away is no better off than a fish with a hook in his mouth, given plenty of line so that he can tire himself out and be reeled in calmly and easily by his own destiny.

"I wouldn't have gone if you had asked me," Martha King said. "There were too many things that had to be done here. It's just that I don't like to have it taken for granted that I never go anywhere."

In a happy panic Martha Hastings left town and went to Indianapolis to stay with Helen Burke, who was teaching school there. They had known each other since they were little girls, and

Helen (whom no man had ever asked to marry) listened patiently night after night while Martha talked about Austin, twisting his words about to suit her own purposes, throwing a sinister light on innocent circumstances, and, on rather flimsy evidence, convicting the man she loved. Helen Burke believed everything that Martha told her, sympathized with and was caught up in the excitement of her friend's dramatic dilemma. "I don't know how you lived through it," she would say, and her eyes would fill with tears over the monstrous cunning and misbehaviour of a boy she had known ever since the first grade and whose name always headed the honour roll. "And I had no one to turn to," Martha would say, "except you." When at the end of ten days, Martha Hastings packed her bag and said good-bye, Helen Burke was too emotionally exhausted to do anything about it. Offering fresh counsel and foreseeing new difficulties, she went with Martha to the station, before school opened in the morning, and had trouble all that day enforcing discipline in the classroom.

The movements of Martha King's arms, her gestures as she pinned her hair in place on top of her head, were dreamy and thoughtful. "The whole thing is of no importance," she said. "I just mentioned it in passing. I don't want to spoil your pleasure in any way. And so long as you are——"

"But it *is* important," Austin protested. "If you think for one minute that I don't enjoy having you with me——"

"I'm useful to you as someone to run the house. I know you appreciate that."

There was an extra loud clap of thunder and Martha winced. She was not afraid of electrical storms but they made her nervous.

Martha Hastings had written to her aunt and uncle that she was coming, but no one but Helen Burke knew that she was on the 11.15 *train. She sat looking out of the dirty window at fields and farmhouses and roads leading in all directions and felt her own hold on life to be very slight, to be slipping away from her like the flat landscape. If she could have stayed on the train for-*

ever she would have, but it was leading her towards a decision that she was not yet prepared to make, and suddenly, as though a familiar voice had spoken, it came to her that she must let chance decide. If Austin was at the station to meet her, she would marry him. It would be the hand of fate, and she would have no choice but to follow where it pointed. If the station platform was deserted, if he didn't know just by his love for her that she was coming back to him, then they were not meant for each other. In a state of peace with the world and with herself she sat and looked out at the red barns and the round silos, at a white horse in a pasture and at cows huddled around a tree for shade. "Draperville!" the conductor shouted. "Draperville!" and the train began to slow down. Through the plumed smoke outside the window she saw a church steeple, the monument works, and then the station. The train would go on to Peoria and for a second, standing in the aisle, she considered wildly the possibility of going on with it. There was no one she knew in Peoria, no friend waiting to give her shelter. As she stepped down from the train he was the first person she saw, his head above the other heads on the station platform. He had seen her and was coming towards her. The face that she presented to him was one he had never seen before, quiet, relaxed, without the slightest trace of indecision or of anxiety.

That night, sitting in the porch swing, she told him that she would marry him. She also asked him not to tell anyone, but this request, in the midst of his happiness, he failed to attach any importance to. The next night, when he went to see her, her serenity was gone. She told him that she didn't want to be engaged yet, that she needed time to think it over. And then, seeing the strange expression that passed over his face, she said, "You haven't told anyone, have you?"

"I've told my mother," he said. "She's going to give you a diamond pin that belonged to Grandmother Curtis. She asked me to bring you to tea tomorrow afternoon."

"Oh, Austin, how could you?"

"And I told Mr. Holby," he said.

"How can I face your mother when I don't know yet whether I want to marry you? I told you not to tell anyone!"

"I'm sorry," Austin said helplessly. "I forgot. If you want me to, I'll tell them we're not engaged. That it was a mistake."

This humiliation she could not bear for him to have.

Sad of heart, he had to go on accepting congratulations. Martha had not actually broken the engagement, she had suspended it, left it open and in doubt. She kept the diamond pin, but did not wear it. He came back night after night, he was gentle with her, he was patient, he was unyielding. During all this time he did not reproach or blame her, even to himself. Martha Hastings was catapulted into a dreamlike series of showers, engagement presents, congratulations, and attentions from Austin's family, and in the natural course of events found herself with Austin's mother addressing a pile of wedding invitations.

"I don't know what else I can say except that I'm very sorry," Austin said. "And since you didn't really want to go anyway, I don't exactly see what harm is done."

"No," Martha said. "What does it matter? It's a small thing that I've married a man who doesn't care for me."

She was rewarded with a look which said quite plainly I am married to a stranger and there is no possibility of ever coming to terms with her. It only lasted for a second and was replaced by a look of such understanding, and such sadness as the result of understanding, that she had to turn her face away. Once more he had found her out, got through the barrier and seen her for what she was, a beautiful woman who could not believe in her own beauty or accept love without casting every conceivable doubt upon it. Now and every other time that they quarrelled, she was merely seeing how far she could go, leading him to the edge of the pit and making him look down, threatening their common happiness in order to convince herself of its reality.

"I'm going downstairs," he said. "Ab's tricycle is out in the rain and it'll get all rusty."

Part Three

A SERIOUS MISTAKE

I

The gash that ran down Randolph Potter's forehead and through his left eyebrow healed rapidly without becoming infected. Because of it he was, for a time, both a hero and a household pet. Nora changed bedrooms with her brother so that he wouldn't have to sleep in the oven-like heat engendered by the sun on the tin roof. During the daytime he lay stretched out on a sofa in the living-room or on the porch swing and held court. Someone was always at his side, anxious to wait upon him, eager to run upstairs for a clean handkerchief or out to the kitchen for a glass of cold water. He saw the evening paper before anyone else did, and he had only to bite his lip or frown or sit up and arrange the pillows at his back, and people stopped talking and inquired if he was in pain.

The Ellises, feeling responsible for the accident, dropped in to see Randolph every day. Sitting between his mother and sister, he took no part in the conversation. In his eyes there was a look of tired contentment. His family and all the people around him had abandoned their ordinary preoccupation with their own affairs and were now concerned about him for a change; not merely about him—about a very small part of him. He was quite satisfied.

Mrs. Beach advised that the collie's head be sent to a laboratory in Chicago for testing. When Martha King failed to convey this suggestion to the Ellises, Mrs. Beach conveyed it herself. The dog was kept under observation for a week, and when neither it nor Randolph developed symptoms of rabies, Dr. Danforth sent the dog back to the farm.

During the week of waiting, Mr. Potter got volume MUN–PAY of the encyclopædia in the study and made Nora read aloud the article on Pasteur. He was particularly moved by the closing words of Pasteur's oration at the founding of the Institute: "Two opposing laws seem to me now in contest. The one, a law of blood and death, opening out each day new modes of destruction, forces nations always to be ready for battle. The other, the law of peace, work, and health, whose only aim is to deliver mankind from the calamities which beset him . . ." When Nora had finished reading, Mr. Potter with tears in his eyes said, "Those are the words of a great man. If it weren't for Pasteur and General Robert E. Lee, the world would be far worse off than it is today. They're the leaders and the rest of us follow along after them and owe what we have to their wisdom and self-sacrifice."

"But that isn't what it means," Nora said.

"That's what I got out of it," Mr. Potter said. "You can interpret it any way you please. I know that if your father were here, Austin, he would agree with me. All this talk about education—what good does it do to teach a nigger to read and write? They're put here on earth for a definite purpose, just like the rest of us, and when you try to change that, you're going against the Lord's intention."

"What Nora is trying to say——" Austin began.

"It's all in the Bible," Mr. Potter interrupted, "right down in black and white: 'A little knowledge is a dangerous thing.' Women and men are different and anybody who says that a woman can do the same things a man can do is talking through his hat. Woman's place is in the home, and if only a lot of crackpots, busybodies, and old maids would stop agitating for equal rights, the vote, and all the rest of it——"

"Nora has just as much right to her opinion," Mrs. Potter said, drawing out her crochet thread, "wrong though it may be——"

"But it isn't a matter of opinion," Nora cried. "It's a matter of words, and they only mean one thing. Scientists, it says, are trying to——"

"They'll ruin the country," Mr. Potter said. "Mark my words. Every radical and every reformer will join hands with the suffragettes, and the first thing you know——"

Nora got up from her chair and left the room. A moment later they heard the screen door slam.

"*Now* what did I say?" Mr. Potter asked, turning helplessly to his wife.

The cigar-smoking, cigar-smelling men, simple, forthright, and forever dangerous—to themselves as well as to other people—swing from prejudice to hanging prejudice in the happy delusion that their feet are on solid ground, and any small table or delicate vase or new idea they come near stands a good chance of being knocked over. Even so (or perhaps because of the very great number of tables and vases and ideas that he had at one time or another upset) Mr. Potter waited for some reassurance from his wife, some gesture of approval.

"I expect she's gone over to the Beaches'," Mrs. Potter said; and then, pursuing the one comparison that never lost its charm for her, "At home Nora always goes to see Miss Washburn when she wants to let off steam. Miss Washburn was one of her teachers at the seminary. She doesn't think I've been all that I should have been to Nora. She told someone that, and I haven't spoken to her since. It's easy for people who—— This fall, she's leaving Mississippi for good. She's going East to teach at some girls' college and she wanted to take Nora with her."

"If I had my way she'd ride out of town on a rail," Mr. Potter said bitterly. "Anyone who tries to come between children and their parents, and especially a dried-up old maid that no man ever looked twice at——"

"Mr. Potter doesn't believe in education for women," Mrs. Potter interrupted him. "And I must say, I don't either. At least, not very much. There are other things they can do, I always say. Some day the right man will come along and Nora will marry and have a home and children of her own and then she'll come to her father and thank him for knowing what was best. But it was a terrible disappointment to her. She's a great reader, you know. Just now, she doesn't know what she wants to make of her life. She's all mixed up, and try as I may, I can't seem to help her."

Randolph touched the edge of his bandage lightly with his finger.

"She just has to work it out for herself," Mrs. Potter said. "Does your wound bother you?"

"I think it's draining," Randolph said.

"Well, stop touching it," Mrs. Potter said. "You've been very brave, but if you don't stop worrying it——"

Having brought the conversation around to where he and not Nora was the centre of attention, Randolph let his bandage alone.

When he grew tired of lying still, he usually got up and went out to the kitchen, and Martha King, coming into the pantry on some errand, would hear derisive laughter that stopped abruptly as she pushed open the swinging door. Rachel had washed and ironed the bloodstained shirt so to Randolph's satisfaction that he wouldn't let Martha King send his shirts to Mrs. Coffey with the family washing. Rachel took them home and did them late at night. He wouldn't allow his mother to heat the water for the hot applications Dr. Seymour had ordered; only Rachel, his favourite, could do this. No matter how late Randolph came down to breakfast, there was a place set for him, at the dining-room table, and usually some mark of favour—fried chicken livers, a lamb kidney or a chop—that hadn't been served to the others. Under his patronage, Rachel's position in the household rose considerably. The Mississippi people plied her with compliments on her cooking and when they got into an argument among themselves, asked her to support and corroborate their opinions. "Isn't that so, Rachel?" they would ask, and

Rachel would answer, "That's right, Mr. Potter. You tell them!" And then, "Miss Nora, that's a true fact what you just said," and retire to the kitchen leaving them both convinced that she was on their side.

The conversations between Randolph and Rachel in the kitchen were not all a matter of sly joking. There were sometimes intimate revelations, things Randolph told her about himself, about the members of his family, that he would not have told any white person. Rachel got so she listened continually for his step, coming through the pantry towards the kitchen, and her manner towards Mrs. Potter was not always wholly respectful. Randolph had become her child, as he had been long ago in the past the child of some other black woman who watched over him in the daytime, put him to bed at night, sang to him, told him stories, and was there always, the eternal audience for anything he had to say.

"The trouble with you," Rachel said to him one day, "is you want everything. And you don't want to do no work for it."

"That's right," Randolph said nodding. "There's a crippled boy at home—Griswold, his name is—had infantile paralysis when he was small and the other boys used to pick on him a lot. I don't think he ever had a friend till I came along and was nice to him. Griswold's very smart. He notices everything, especially people's weak points, and that way, when the time comes, he gets what he wants. The other day . . ."

Most people, when they are describing a friend or telling a story, make the mistake of editing, of leaving things out. Fearing that their audience will grow restless, they rush ahead to the point, get there too soon, have to go back and explain, and in the end, the quality of experience is not conveyed. Randolph was never in a hurry, never in doubt about whether what he had to say would interest Rachel. By the time he had finished, she had a very clear idea in her mind of the crippled boy who knew how to wait for what he wanted, and she also knew one more thing about Randolph Potter.

Turning from the sink, she asked out loud a question that had been in the back of her mind for days: "What you want to go and hurt that dog for?"

"I didn't hurt it," Randolph said, and then when Rachel rolled her eyes sceptically, "I tell you I didn't!"

"You was just petting it and it bit you?"

"Ummm," he said. Their eyes met and he smiled slowly. "I don't really know what happened. I was tired of playing with her and she kept jumping on me and asking for more so I kicked her."

He looked at Rachel to see if she were shocked, but her face revealed nothing whatever. If she had been shocked, it would have been all right. Or if she had been sufficiently under his spell that she had laughed, but all she did was look at him thoughtfully.

"I kicked her in the head," he said. "And if she'd been my dog and bit me like that, I'd have taken a gun and shot her. You don't believe me, do you?"

"I believe you," Rachel said. "I reckon that's what you'd of done, all right."

"That's where you're wrong," Randolph said, and got up from the stool and left her. From that day on, he never came into the kitchen, never looked at Rachel when she was passing platters of food around the table, never spoke to her when they met on the back stairs.

2

Nora Potter tried again and again to make friends with Martha King, and each time the effort spent itself without accomplishing any more than waves accomplish when they wash over rock. Sympathy is almost never to be had by asking. It comes of itself or not at all. And those who are engaged in work of great moment, such as fomenting conspiracy or carrying a child inside them, do not really have it to offer.

Martha would sit and listen to Mrs. Potter (who wanted nothing except to be a decent, pleasant, untroublesome guest) by the hour. But when she found herself alone with Nora, she usually got up after a minute or two and went to look at the loaf of nutbread baking in the oven or to count the sheets that had come back from the wash. Defeated time after time by these tactics and with no idea why they were being used against her, Nora would go across the side yard to the Beaches, who were always delighted when she came. Mrs. Beach put down her volume of aristocratic memoirs, the girls left the piano, and they all settled down on the porch or in the shade of a full-grown mulberry tree in the back yard.

The Beach girls said very little, and the few remarks they made were generally corrected or cut short by their mother, who, like Mrs. Potter, had a long continued story to tell. "The sky this morning reminds me of Florence," she would begin, while with one hand she made sure that her cameo breastpin had not come undone. "The same deep blue. You'd love Florence, Nora. I wish we could all go there together. Perhaps we will, some day. Such a beautiful city . . ." Or, "I'll never forget my first glimpse of Venice. We arrived on a Saturday night and left the railway station in a gondola and found ourselves on the Grand Canal . . ."

No one coming into the Beaches' house could have remained unaware of the fact that Mrs. Beach had travelled. In every room and on every wall there was some testimony to this wonderful advantage which she had had over nearly everyone else in Draperville. A huge photograph of the Colosseum hung in the front hall. The Bridge of Sighs and St. Mark's Square were represented, one in colour, one in black and white, in the living-room. In the dining-room the Beaches ate with the Cumaean Sibyl and Raphael's Holy Family looking on.

The greatest concentration of *objets d'art* was in the parlour where there was a Louis XV glass-and-gilt cabinet full of curios—ornamental scissors from Germany, imitation tanagra figurines, Bohemian glass, Dresden china, miniature silver souvenir albums of Mont St. Michel and the châteaux country, wood-carvings from the Black Forest, a tiny spy-glass that offered a microscopic view of the façade of Cologne Cathedral, and enough other treasures to occupy the eyes and mind of a child for hours. Over the piano a row of familiar heads—Beethoven, Mendelssohn, Schubert, and Schumann—testified to the importance and value of great music, and did what they could to make up for the fact that the piano was not a Steinway.

Nora Potter soon felt so at home at the Beaches' that to knock or pull the front-door chime when she came to see them would have seemed an act of impoliteness. She walked in one morning and wandered through the house until she found Lucy in the kitchen, fixing a tray.

"Mother had a bad night," Lucy said. "We were up with her until past daylight." Nora started to say that she would come back some other time, but Lucy said, "No, don't go. She's awake now and it'll do her good to see you."

Mrs. Beach's room was high-ceilinged and gloomy, with massive golden oak furniture, and on the walls and dressing-table, on the bureau and the nightstand, a hundred mementoes and votive offerings to Mrs. Beach's marriage and motherhood. The old lady herself was lying propped up in bed, and, for someone who had been keeping people up all night, she looked quite well indeed. "Pshaw," she said when she saw Nora. "Just see what they've gone and done to me!"

"If you *will* eat things you know you're not supposed to," Lucy said.

"It wasn't the baked beans. They never hurt anybody, and you can tell Dr. Seymour I said so. There was an onion in the stewed tomatoes. I tasted it."

"I've told you twenty times——" Lucy began.

"Onion never agrees with me," Mrs. Beach said. And then

to Nora, "You were a dear to come and entertain an old woman like this. I wish you were staying with us instead of at the Kings'. I could be dying up here and Martha King wouldn't come near me."

"Mother, you know that isn't true," Lucy said indignantly.

"True enough," Mrs. Beach said. She lifted the napkin that covered her tray and peered under it. "I don't think I'd better eat any toast, especially since you put butter on it. Just a cup of tea is all I want. Did you remember to scald the pot?"

Her daughter nodded impatiently, and Mrs. Beach, still sceptical, put her hand against the side of the Limoges teapot. "All right, dear," she said. "I'll call you if I want anything."

All the things that in her own mother annoyed Nora—her mother's unreasonableness, her arbitrary opinions, her interminable stories about the past—she could be patient with in Mrs. Beach. She dragged a white rattan chair over to the bed and showed such interest in Mrs. Beach's symptoms that the invalid developed an appetite, drank two cups of strong tea, and ate all the buttered toast. Nora took the tray away when Mrs. Beach had finished with it. Then she adjusted the pillows successfully—a thing that neither Lucy nor Alice ever managed to do.

"I can see a change in the girls just since you've been here, Nora," Mrs. Beach said. "You're very good for them, you know. They spend so much time with me when they ought to be going to parties or at least seeing someone nearer their own age. I've tried my best to encourage them to bring their friends here, but they don't seem to want any outside companionship. Or else there isn't anybody that interests them. They've had more than most girls, though I dare say they don't appreciate it. I didn't appreciate the things my father and mother tried to do for me until I was older and had children of my own. But the girls are not like me. They're not like any of my people so far as I can see. Mr. Beach had a sister; possibly Lucy and Alice take after her, though she was a cripple all her life, and could hardly have been expected to . . ."

Nora's friendship with the Beaches was happy because it was with the whole household. She felt herself, for the first time, being plucked at, being forced, whether she wanted to or not, to take sides. Her eyes fell on the faded picture of Mr. Beach—a dapper, middle-aged man who in effigy was no more help than he had been in real life.

"If they would only talk to me," Mrs. Beach said. "I have to worm information out of them. There was a young man who liked Alice for a time. His father owned some land, I believe, out near Kaiserville, and he was a nice enough boy, Mr. Beach thought, but no polish or refinement, of course, and that dreadful red neck all farm boys have. I had a little talk with him one evening and he didn't come back any more. Alice isn't strong, you know. She could never have done the work a woman is expected to do in the country. And besides, the girls had their music. . . . Tomorrow or the next day, when I'm feeling better, remind me to show you the album of pressed flowers that we brought back with us from the Holy Land. . . ."

Nora said nothing while the old lady criticized her daughters, but her silence struck her as disloyal, and if it had been possible, she would have sneaked out of the house without stopping to talk to Lucy and Alice. It wasn't possible. There was only one stairs, and they were waiting for her at the bottom of it. As she stood up, Mrs. Beach said, "Remember me to your dear mother and father, and if Austin should ask about me—I know Martha won't—tell him I spent a bad night but that, thanks to you, I'm feeling much better."

The house next door is never the sanctuary it at first appears to be. If you reach the stage where you are permitted to enter without knocking, you are also expected to come oftener and to penetrate farther and in the end share, along with the permanent inhabitants, the weight of the roof tree.

3

What was missing from Austin King's office overlooking the courthouse square was sociability. With a good cigar in his fist and his feet on Judge King's slant-topped desk, Mr. Potter set about correcting this condition. It was not too difficult, and the only real opposition was supplied by Miss Ewing, who thought all Southerners were lazy and shiftless and should be kept waiting.

Mr. Potter waited once. He waited more than half an hour, and when Miss Ewing finally said, "Mr. King will see you now," he went inside and discovered to his astonishment that Austin was alone and hadn't even been told that Mr. Potter was waiting.

"Now don't you bother, Miss Ewing," he said as he walked into the outer office the next day. "Stay right where you are. I don't want you jumping up and down for me."

"Mr. King has someone in his office," Miss Ewing said.

"Yes?" Mr. Potter said. "I wonder who it could be."

"Alfred Ogilvee," Miss Ewing said indicating with a slight turn of her head the chair Mr. Potter was to take advantage of. "Mr. King will be free in just a few minutes."

"Well, if he's busy, I don't want to interfere," Mr. Potter said. "But I'd better tell him I'm here. Otherwise he'll be wondering about me. I'll go in and get my business over and leave right away. . . . Now you go right ahead, my boy, and don't mind me!" Mr. Potter closed the door of the inner office behind him. "I know you two have something you want to talk over, and I'll just sit here by the window and watch the crowd. . . . I don't know anything about these legal matters, Mr. Ogilvee. I'm just a plain farmer. I run a cotton plantation down in Howard's Landing, Mississippi, and when they start using all those big words, I have to take a back seat. The party of the first part and the party of the second part. It's enough to drive an ordinary man crazy. But Austin here understands it. He can tell you what it all means, in simple language that anybody can follow. I wish I had his education. I wouldn't be a farmer if I did. I'd get me a nice office somewhere and a girl to keep the books and answer the phone, and I'd sit back and watch the money roll in. If we could all write our own wills any time we felt like it and get up in court and address the judge in high-flown language, the lawyers would go hungry. I dare say that time'll never come. You put your money in land and you may have a thousand and one worries, but there's one thing you don't have to worry about. The land won't run off. It's there to stay. I've known men—very smart men they were, too—worked hard all their life and everybody looked up to them, bankers and lawyers and men that had factories working day and night, and every reason, you might say, to feel high and dry—who went to bed worth forty or fifty thousand dollars and woke up without a cent to their name. May I ask what line of work you're in, Mr. Ogilvee? . . ."

Alfred Ogilvee had come to have Austin draw up a deed of sale for a corner lot, but he stayed to visit, to discuss farming and politics and the old days when a horsemill was looked upon as a very important enterprise, and everything movable wasn't placed under lock and key. What happened with Alfred Ogilvee happened with other clients. Recognizing that a change had set in, they not only stayed but came again, a day or two later, and on finding out from Miss Ewing that Mr. Potter and Mr. Holby were in Austin's office, they went on in.

Mr. Potter had no sense of the relentless pressure of time. In keeping Austin from working he was, Mr. Potter assumed, doing him a favour. Once Austin realized that there was no way to dam the flow of Mr. Potter's sociability or cut short his visits, he began to enjoy them. So long as he was kept from working, it didn't matter how many men were sitting around in his office with their hats tipped back, their thumbs hooked to their vests, interrupting their own remarks to aim at the cuspidor, and wondering if there was any reason to suppose that the improvement of the next fifty years would be less than the improvement of the last fifty. Religion, politics, farming and medicine, the school tax, the war between capital and labour, feminism—all had their innings. One way or another, everything was settled, including how to ascertain the age of sheep. For the most part, Austin sat and listened. While the air grew thick with cigar smoke, he had the satisfaction of feeling himself taken in and accepted in a way that he had never been accepted before.

Anxious to be liked, to be looked up to, like the men who had gone to sleep worth forty or fifty thousand dollars, Mr. Potter found ways of ingratiating himself with the merchants of Draperville. Instead of fighting the Civil War over again, he said solemnly, "The South has come to see the error of its ways. What we need down there now are modern farm machinery and modern business methods, factories run the way they are up here. . . ." Any true Southerner, in 1912, would have rejected Mr. Potter's ideas along with the accent that it had taken him many years to acquire. The merchants, with no basis of comparison, saw no reason to find fault with anything Mr. Potter did or said.

As a young man he had left the North to seek his fortune in Mississippi at a time when Northerners were not at all welcome there. In order to set foot inside certain doors, to hold down the job of credit manager to a mill, Mr. Potter had had to be something of an actor. Where he shone was not as Hamlet but as a vaudeville actor, an entertainer. His humorous stories, though they had often been told before, were still wonderful in the way they conveyed (as if Mr. Potter's life depended on it) every nuance of character, every detail of setting, and above all the final rich flower of point. The stories always ended in a burst of laughter, and it was for this that they had been so painstakingly told.

Sometimes, when there was no one else in Austin's office, Mr. Potter actually did sit by the window and watch the crowd, but there were so many activities going on down below in the courthouse square, so many matters of interest that crossed Mr. Potter's mind. Both required comment and the comment usually required an answer. In the end, Austin found himself turning, without too great reluctance, from his littered desk.

4

Though the drive out to Mr. Ellis' farm ended in a disaster, it was nevertheless followed by so many other afternoon and evening drives that it often seemed as if the visit were taking place on wheels. After supper Austin drove the cart around to the front of the house and waited for the screen door to open. There was no use trying to hurry the Potters. They came in their own good time, when Mr. Potter had finished reading the article on the seasons of the antipodes, in the evening paper; when Randolph facing some mirror had considered long enough how he looked with a bandage across the left side of his forehead; when Mrs. Potter had finished telling Martha King about a certain dress that she had not brought with her, high-waisted, of orange velvet and Irish crochet, covered with black marquisette; when Nora had found her gloves. If Austin attempted to hurry the Potters, it only injected a note of crisis into the proceedings. Eventually the screen door burst open and the rich Southern voices arguing happily, saying "What do you need gloves for anyway on a night like this?" or "Cousin Austin, why didn't you tell us you were waiting?" took possession of the stage.

Sitting beside Austin King on the front seat of the cart, Mr. Potter talked on and on, his voice pitched to carry above the unhurried clop-clopping of the horse's hoofs, and the chorale of the locusts. Sometimes Mr. Potter tried Austin's patience by telling him things he already knew.

"You've got a very fine wife," he said. "I don't know how you persuaded her to marry you, but you must have done something because I can see she just worships you. She's a fine girl, pretty as they come, and full of spirit, which I always like in a woman, provided it doesn't go with strong-mindedness. . . ." Or Mr. Potter said, "Now my boy, I'm going to give you some advice, and I want you to take it in the same spirit that it is offered. When I was your age, nobody could tell me anything because I wouldn't listen to them, but I got all that knocked out of me, and I don't know as I would want you or Randolph here to go through what I went through before I got my feet on the ground . . ."

Don't be misled by the advice of old people, the locusts said. *Or the clop-clopping of horses' hoofs. There is no ground under your feet, or any solid place. If you start down, looking for it, you will just keep on going down and down. Nothing is safe any more, but if you must trust yourself to something, try resting on the air. Make a spinning sound like us, and maybe that will support you.* The mindless, kindless voice of nature, audible enough to poets and other crackpots, Mr. Potter did not hear or want to hear.

"If you want to get ahead in the world," he said, "and I'm sure you do—you're ambitious, the same as any other young man—learn to be more like other people. Your father was a very able, clever man, but he was no saint. I could tell you a thing or two about him that isn't generally known, but I don't think any the less of him for being human. If you want people to come to you, you've got to meet them halfway.

Somebody asks you to drop into a corner saloon with them, do it. Don't always be making excuses that you have work to do, or that you have to get home to your wife. The work will keep and so will your wife. I've lived a long time and I know what I'm talking about. . . ."

Try scraping your wings together, said the locusts. *Maybe that will put off the coming of the first hard frost. That's the theory we operate on, and so do the katydids, but if you don't like that theory, find one of your own that you do like and operate on that, and don't trust people who know what they're talking about.*

"We all make mistakes," Mr. Potter said. "It's the only way we learn. But if you can profit by someone else's experience, it saves a lot of time and heartache, believe me."

Except for a nod and an occasional "That's the fair grounds we're passing now," or "That's the jail," Austin sat and held the reins.

If offering advice made Mr. Potter happy, there was no reason why he shouldn't listen to it, even though he often didn't agree with what Mr. Potter said. There were certain matters that Austin would have liked to have someone's advice about: Whether it wouldn't be better if he dissolved the partnership with Mr. Holby and started out on his own. And what to do about his mother, who, now that she was older, leaned on him in a way she had never leaned on his father, and let the money he sent her from time to time slip through her fingers. What to do when Martha (whose happiness was far more important to him than his own) let herself strike out at him, wildly and carelessly, as if it were a matter of complete indifference to her whether the next bitter thing she said would be the remark that neither of them would ever forget. And why what he did for one person took away from what he tried to do for another, so that no matter what he did or whom he tried to please, he still felt somehow in the wrong. These things he couldn't discuss with Mr. Potter.

The evening drives ended before dark. The afternoon drives were longer and required preparation in the way of veils and dustcoats. Sometimes they went in the cart, sometimes with Bud Ellis in his surrey. The men sat in front, and wisps of their conversation—the words "alfalfa" and "timothy," the words "first and second sweepings"—drifted back with the cigar smoke. Ab sat on her mother's lap or if Martha King stayed home, on Mrs. Potter's, which she found quite comfortable after she got used to the projecting corset stays. With its big red wheels, the English cart was enough higher than the general run of rigs and surreys so that, on dirt country roads, they almost never had to eat other people's dust but rode along smiling and superior. The conversation in the back seat came steadily and placidly. There were never any exchanges of private information when the men were present, never that carefully subdued, serious tone, just above a whisper, which was calculated to escape Ab but which invariably acted instead as a warning signal to her wandering attention. When the household secrets, the recipes, the ways of keeping silver from tarnishing, rose loud enough to be overheard in the front seat, Bud Ellis would sometimes wink at Mr. Potter and say, "Blah-blah-blah. . . ." Ab knew (and Bud Ellis didn't) about the unfettered talk of the women on those occasions when no men were present.

In one corner of the porch of the house on Elm Street, there was a clay flower-pot filled with sand which she emptied out on the floor and then put back, a handful at a time, very quietly. Most of the talk that flowed over her head was cheerful and reassuring, but she waited patiently for those moments when the conversation took a darker tone. For example, the conversation between her mother and Aunt Ione, interrupted by the return of Mr. Potter from the barn.

"Nora and I used to be much closer," were the words that caught Ab's attention, "but because of an unfortunate thing that happened—I don't know exactly how to tell you about it or whether I ought to, even, but there was a time when Mr. Potter and I—there were certain things about him that I didn't understand or make allowance for, as I should have. So many doors were closed to us—neither of us was born and raised in the South, you know. And we had a darky nurse who took care of the children, and I sat around all day, ready to receive callers who never came. I couldn't see that Mr. Potter needed me, and it didn't seem that my life was leading anywhere. And then I met someone who cared very deeply for me. . . . It's strange how just talking about it brings all the old feelings back. He kept begging me to run away with him, and I tried not to listen, even though I felt I belonged to him and not to the man I had married, and that it was my one chance for happiness. I know now that we none of us have that right. But anyway, I did finally. I left Mr. Potter and the children and went off with him. We lived in Charleston for a while, and then in Savannah. I thought he was happy. He seemed *quite* happy, but it turned out he wasn't. It was just blindness on my part. He had a very fine mind and I knew I was no match for him in that, but I thought I could make it up to him in other ways. He had to tell me, and even then it was hard for me to realize that he . . . Mr. Potter never reproached me. If he had, it might have been easier. I had no one but Nora to talk to. By that time she was older and there was no way of keeping from her what had happened. I dare say I told her more than I should have. She was always a very serious child. For a while, as I say, we were very close, and then after a year or two she withdrew into herself. She never talks to me any more about what's in her heart, and I try not to burden her with my feelings. . . ."

During this recital, Ab sat as still as a stone. In those moments when life is a play and not merely a backstage rehearsal, children are the true audience. With no lines to speak, they remain politely on their side of the proscenium unless (after the hero has blinded himself with his own hands) the playwright chooses to have one or two of them led onto the stage to be wept over and then frightened with some such blessing as *May heaven be kinder to you than it has been to me.* Although children are not always equipped to understand all that they see and overhear, they know as a rule which character is supposed to represent Good and which Evil, and they appreciate genuine repentance. By all rights, when the play is finished, the actors should turn and bow to them, and ask for their applause.

5

If Ab, tired of eavesdropping, tried to break in upon the conversation of her mother and Mrs. Potter, Martha King would turn her head and convey in a glance that this was not the time to test the invisible line past which Ab could not go without a spanking. Along with a great many other things, spankings had been postponed until the visit of the Mississippi people was over. There was no telling when that would be. They had come a long way (a whole day and a whole night on the train) and Ab had been told that she must not ask them how long they were going to stay.

There were compensations. Mr. Potter brought home thin twisted peppermint sticks in a glass jar, and if coaxed, he would walk the length of the living-room with Ab sitting on his foot. And Cousin Randolph was always at her disposal. He allowed her to crawl all over him, to whisper inaudible secrets in his ear, and one rainy day he even played dolls with her. But every one of these delights was paid for, sooner or later, with confusion. If she told Randolph that gypsies came and set fire to the barn during the night, he not only believed her but made the gypsies set fire to the house as well, and also to the Danforths' house. The fire department arrived and the conflagration became too real, so that Ab was driven back upon the truth, which was that she herself had lighted a match—a thing she was never supposed to do; and the truth Randolph would not believe, in spite of her anxious efforts to convince him of it.

Sometimes when they were alone, he would sit and stare at her with what seemed like intense dislike, though she knew that, since he was her cousin, it couldn't be. Everywhere he went, Ab followed or walked ahead of him like an animal on a leash, and when Martha King tried to put a stop to this on the grounds that Ab was being a nuisance, Randolph insisted that he liked to have Ab with him, that he needed her to protect him from Mary Caroline.

The Links lived four houses down, on the opposite side of the street from the Kings'. Mr. Link owned a small factory where he manufactured inexpensive paper-soled shoes to be worn on one occasion only—by dead people. He believed in frugality and would not let his wife pay out good money for a hired girl when she had two grown daughters to help with the housework. There was a dining-room and kitchen on the ground floor of the house, but the family cooked and ate in the basement.

When Mary Caroline was seven years old she stopped playing with dolls and instead haunted any house on Elm Street where there was a baby. In dozens of ways she conveyed her dependability with the result that, when other girls were playing jackstraws or skipping-rope, she was wheeling a baby-carriage up and down the shady sidewalks, tipping the carriage to produce a toothless smile and a crinkling of tiny eyelids, jiggling the carriage when the baby fretted, or sitting still while a hand as small and miraculous as it is possible to imagine clasped her forefinger. Any baby would do so long as Mary Caroline could guard it from other children who might want to pick it up, and who in their carelessness might forget about the soft spot on the crown of the head; any baby that was helpless, cried, smiled at her, wet its diapers, was sweet sour smelling and silken soft.

All that Mary Caroline would have asked for, if asking would have done any good, was to belong to a large family where babies recur frequently, and not be forced to roam the neighbourhood in search of them. The year between her eleventh and twelfth birthdays moved so slowly that at times it seemed to her she would never get through it. But once it became a physical possibility for her to have a baby of her own, her whole concern was disparagingly for her mirror. She cut out dresses from tissue paper patterns and pieced them together on the floor of her bedroom—an undertaking that often ended in tears. She tried twenty ways of pinning up her hair and in the mirror she was twenty different women—young, old, animated, bored, modest as a nun, evil beyond shame or boldness. She bathed constantly and took great care of her nails.

All this went on in her bedroom, at the end of the upstairs hall. She presented to the world—to her mother and father and sister, her schoolmates, her teachers—the image of a fourteen-year-old girl with sturdy legs, a thick waist, thick eyebrows, a receding chin, an awkward manner, and a tendency to blush. Where there should have been mysterious shadows in her face, to correspond with the mysteries that absorbed all her waking mind, there was only a painful shyness.

In the town of Draperville, the fourteen-year-old girls were the natural prey of older boys. At their moment of budding, the girls left the boys of their own age (still in knee-britches, in love with bicycles) behind. The older boys were waiting in Giovanni's ice-cream parlour, with the dark and the whole outdoors (and sometimes the girl, as well) on their side.

The five boys, all of decent respectable families, who lured a Polish miner's daughter out to the cemetery one May night, would not have dared to do what they did if it had been, say, one of the Atchison girls instead. But they managed, now and then, singly, to seduce some girl whose father was cashier of the bank, or county superintendent of highways, or a hardware merchant or a lawyer or a doctor. The Lathrop boy, so well brought up, so polite always with older people, persuaded Jessie McCormack to go with him out into a cornfield at the edge of town. And afterward, when he urinated on the moonlit weeds, he felt a sensation of burning pain that frightened him and robbed him of all pride in his wonderful new accomplishment. Since there seemed to be no other way to renew this pride except by telling on the girl, he did that—only to one boy, but that was enough. That boy told the others. And in the end, the word *cornfield* was a signal for Jessie McCormack to turn away and find other company.

What was done to the Polish miner's daughter was an act of horror, but at least her body was old for her age. The McCormack girl was prematurely pretty, with blue eyes and straight blonde hair and bangs, and her mother dressed her like the doll in *Tales of Hoffmann* and she had not meant to do anything that the other girls didn't do. A single word can age people, wash away any youth, any attractiveness they were intended to have. At seventeen, no longer a doll and disappointing as a woman, she sat alone in the porch swing on Saturday evenings and watched the couples go by.

The high school boys compared experiences in the locker rooms and washrooms at school (*I don't ever want to have anything to do with her again. I hate a girl that . . .*), but in all their tattling, their wondering and recounting and imagining, they left Mary Caroline untouched. The boy who asked Mary Caroline to the senior play, her last year in high school, wore glasses and went out for the track team (unsuccessfully) and in his social inexperience let her walk on the outside until somebody shouted "Girl for sale!"

And all the while her eyes saw, on every side, the strong arms and straight backs and widening shoulders. Her ears caught the husky music in voices that had only recently deepened. There was, she discovered, a hollow centre in her body which drained all the strength out of her legs whenever she met James Morrissey in the corridor—James Morrissey who had curly blond hair and a cracked laugh and white teeth and cheeks like apple blossoms, and who wrote notes to Frances Longworth and to Virginia Burris but never to Mary Caroline. And then suddenly it was no longer James Morrissey but now Boyd Mangus who affected that highly sensitive nervous centre. Then it was Frankie Cooper. Then Joe Diehl. Like a cloud shadow, love passed over the field, having nothing to do with actual boys but only with something which for a brief time was given to them.

Mary Caroline had always been studious, but when the Potters arrived and she suddenly started acting like her older sister, gossip lumped both girls together permanently. The gossip of Draperville was often irresponsible and unjust. Mary Caroline was not boy crazy; she had received a sign. She who had looked in the mirror so many times with sickness and dislike for herself had seen mirrored in a human eye her need for love. She had seen it only once, at the Kings' evening party for the people from Mississippi, but it had been unmistakable.

Although the world firmly and relentlessly pushes young people together, it does so with an object in view and has very little patience with them once it becomes apparent that the object is not going to be served. *If this one won't love you, then for heaven's sake go find another who will:* so says the world, and the young, unless they are unusually obstinate, obey. Mary Caroline came back, day after day, in the hope of seeing again what she had seen the night of the Kings' party, and always with an excuse in her hands—a dish of home-made fudge, a book of poems for Mrs. Potter (who never read poetry), one of her mother's coffee cakes, or a bouquet of the same flowers that bloomed so abundantly in Martha King's garden. When these offerings had been received and disposed of, Mary Caroline sat in a shy silence, never taking her eyes off Randolph, and sometimes it was necessary for Martha King to ask her to meals.

6

"You'll stay for lunch?" Alice Beach asked at the foot of the stairs.

"I'd love to," Nora said, "but Cousin Martha is expecting me. I told her I'd be right back."

"It's all right," Lucy Beach called from the dining-room. "I just telephoned Martha. It was perfectly all right. She's having a light lunch the same as we are. And this way we can have you all to ourselves for once. Everything is ready. Come and sit down."

From their strange manner, which conveyed a subdued excitement, it was clear that the Beach girls had something on their minds and were debating whether to tell Nora. The secret, like all secrets, came out eventually. Lucy and Alice were thinking of starting a kindergarten. There was a place downtown, it seemed—two rooms over Bailey's Drug Store that were for rent very reasonably.

"I've spoken to Mr. Bailey about them," Lucy said, "and he's waiting to hear from us before he lets anyone else have them. There has to be some equipment—the more the better, naturally, but it all takes money and we haven't got very much. We're going to have some long low tables, and some chairs that are the right size for children, and coloured yarns for them to weave, and scissors and blocks and coloured paper for them to cut out——"

"Tell her about the book," Alice said. "We sent off for——"

"We have a book written by an Italian woman," Lucy said. "Sometime while you're here——"

"It's very difficult reading," Alice said. "There's a lot I can't make head or tail of."

"You haven't tried," Lucy said. "I don't suppose, Nora, with all you have to do, that you'd have time or even be interested——"

"Oh, but I would," Nora said. "I'd be very interested. I am already."

The rest of the lunch party was given over to the kindergarten plans. When Lucy came back from the kitchen with a large dish of sliced peaches and the teapot, she said, "What we want to ask you, Nora, is this: Would you, as a kindness to us, speak to Mother about it? Maybe if you said it was a good idea, she might let us go ahead with it."

"I don't know that I have that much influence over her," Nora said, "or any, as a matter of fact. But of course I'll try. Just tell me what it is that you want me to say to her and I'll——"

Before she could finish, the telephone began to ring, and Lucy jumped up from the table to answer it.

"Yes," they heard her say. "All right, I will."

"Who was it?" Alice asked when Lucy put the receiver back on the hook.

"That was your mother," Lucy said. "She said to tell you that they're waiting for you to go driving with them."

"Oh it's so stupid," Nora said, rising from her place. "I don't in the least want to go driving. Couldn't I stay and talk with you?"

From the upstairs part of the house came the tinkle of a little bedside bell, bought in the open market in Fiesole long ago.

"Couldn't we——" Nora began.

"That's Mama," Lucy said. "I'd better go see what she wants. It was so nice of you to stay and have lunch with us, Nora, and Alice will give you the book."

7

All her stubbornness aroused, Nora sat under the mulberry tree in the Beaches' yard, with the dark blue book that had been ordered from Chicago open on her lap, and in a short while her family (quite as if she didn't exist) came out of the Kings' house with Bud Ellis and got into the Ellises' surrey. When Martha and Ab joined them, the surrey started up briskly and without even a backward glance they drove away. That's what they're like, she thought. And if anything happened to me, they'd just go on being themselves, so why do I worry so about them?

She waited a little longer, until Rachel came out of the kitchen door with a bundle under her arm, and called, "They was looking for you, Miss Nora. They wanted you to go driving with them."

"I know," Nora called back. "I didn't want to go driving."

"Well, you're safe now. You outsmarted them. You got the whole house to yourself," Rachel said and went off down the driveway.

The book failed to hold Nora's attention, under the mulberry tree or in the window seat of Austin King's study. She rejected for a while the temptation to explore the house, entirely empty and for the first time at her disposal, but in the end she put the book aside and wandered from room to room. There was very little that she hadn't seen before, but observing the house the way it was now, unsoftened and unclaimed by the people who lived in it, she saw more clearly. Rejecting, approving, she tried to imagine what it was like to be Martha King.

The house was so still that it gave her the feeling that she was being watched, that the sofas and chairs were keeping an eye on her to see that she didn't touch anything that she shouldn't; that she put back the alabaster model of the Taj Mahal and the little bearded grinning man (made out of ivory, with a pack on his back, a folded fan, and his toes turned inward) exactly the way she found them. The locusts warned her, but from too far away. The clocks all seemed preoccupied with their various and contradictory versions of the correct time. The glimpse that Nora caught of herself in the ebony pier glass was of a person slightly wary, involved in an action that carried with it an element of danger.

A glance into the guest-room, when Nora went upstairs, was enough. This room which might have held some clue on the day they arrived, now offered only an untidiness no different from the untidiness, year in and year out, of a familiar bedroom in the plantation house in Mississippi. Nora hesitated, standing in the upstairs hall, between Ab's room and the room that belonged to Austin and Martha King. The door of this room (the one she wanted most to see when it was unoccupied) was closed. She went into Ab's room, looked around, and came out again, no wiser in the ways of children than she had been before. She listened and heard no sound but the beating of her own heart, which grew louder when she put her hand on the knob of the closed door and turned it.

The bedroom was empty and in perfect order.

Nora stared at the mirror, drained of life and purposeless. She went over to the dressing-table and, careful not to upset the bottles of perfume, she pulled out drawer after drawer: face powder and hair-pins, enamelled ear-rings, a little blue leather box containing Martha King's jewels, tortoiseshell combs, scented handkerchiefs, folded white kid gloves, stockings, ribboned sachets. Here too, Martha King, whom she liked and envied and couldn't ever seem to know, eluded her. The paraphernalia of femininity, softness, sweetness, and illusion might have belonged to any beautiful woman.

Nora passed on to the bureau, pulled open the big drawers and discovered the little secret one, containing a velvet pincushion, odds and ends of ribbon, and a letter addressed to Austin King. Observing how it lay among the ribbons so she could restore it to the exact same position, Nora lifted the letter out of the drawer, examined the handwriting (feminine) and the postmark (Providence, R.I.). With the letter in her hand she went out into the upstairs hall, bent over the banister and listened, ready, if there was the slightest sound, to slip the letter back in the drawer and be in her own third-floor bedroom by the time anyone reached the landing. There was no sound. With her hands trembling, she drew the letter from the envelope and began to read slowly, for the writing offered certain difficulties.

Austin, my dearest, my precious, my most neglected:

You have sent me all the money there is in the world! I know there cannot be more. And I cannot say anything or even thank you at all. I wonder why we are so inadequately equipped with words that will express? Words are the tools of man and could not express what the spirit can feel.

But if you only knew what a load is taken from me, right off my back, as it were, all because you love me. I'm just going to try with might and main (whatever that does mean!) not to feel obligated. That is the worst of me. I am such a poor receptacle. I want to do all the pouring, or so it seems, and do not get the joy out of great or small gifts because I so want to give those that are greater. That is not right, so I intend to enjoy my relief and forget what you gave me. Perhaps I can even go so far as believing that I gave it to you?

The carpenters are here. It has simply poured all day and to see them sitting about unable to shingle was just too much for all of us. But tonight the wind has shifted to the west and we believe we shall have a fine day tomorrow.

And new shingles are on the south side of the house and the west side of the barn. Tomorrow if the day is fair the barn will be all right and in order and that makes me glad. I have worried over the roof for so long that I shall miss it, the worry. There are no planks under the floor of the barn, in front, you know, where it was rotting, and the eaves are to be fixed too, and the barn is to have some paint, much needed. I think I shall freshen up the walls downstairs, in the dining-room. Did I tell you that Jessie gave me Aunt Evelyn's table buffet? I have the most annoying time of it trying to remember what I have written you three children. I cannot for my life tell whether I told you, or Charles, or Maud, or each one of you several times. Well, anyhow, told or untold, she did—Jessie gave me the table. It came yesterday, is sixty inches across and solid mahogany. Enormous. It weighs a ton.

That you weigh one hundred and sixty pounds is a great solace. Do you walk to work each day? Above all, you must get exercise and in fresh air. Last evening your Aunt Dorothy held forth about you and certainly she paid you the highest compliment one human can pay another. I'll not tell you now. But sometime. She is so fine and level. And kind—and generous. But I'll not start on her.

About myself. You see I have been acting sort of uppish ever since last summer's adventures in high finance and I have not responded to all the tests and various treatments according to my usual docility. Now don't get the idea that I am seriously ill. I'm not, but I am also opposed to being ill if it can be avoided. Yesterday I went to see Dr. Stanton again, and that after a week away, and was told to return in two weeks. Meanwhile, I am loaded with pills and potions, and my leg is still lame and blue.

I have not told all this to Maud because I felt certain she would get ideas, think I was worse off than I am and worry about it. Of course I shall say nary a word to her or to anybody about your generosities, but I cannot understand why your sister should feel as she does.

Last Sunday I heard a wonderful sermon by my pet, Dr. Malcolm LeRoy Jones, which ended with a story about Voltaire and Benjamin Franklin. It seems that Franklin took his son, a lad of seventeen, to see Voltaire who was very old. When they entered Voltaire's room Franklin said, "I have brought my son to you and I want you to tell him something he will remember all his life." Voltaire arose and said, "My son, remember two words, GOD & LIBERTY."

Dearest and beloved Austin, take care of yourself. Remember that without health there is no happiness in success. I am very proud of you and no one loves you as I do.

Mother.

8

"Anybody home?" Austin King called, standing in the front hall at five o'clock that afternoon.

The answer came from the study, and it was not his wife's voice but Nora's that he heard. When she appeared, he thought for a moment she was ill, she looked so listless, so dejected, so unlike herself.

"There's something I have to tell you," she said.

"Is that so?"

"Something I have to confess."

"Very well." Austin put his hat away and, as she started for the study, said, "Let's go in here." He sat down, crossed one knee over the other, and waited. He had been particularly careful about Nora all during the visit. He never manœuvred her into the front seat of the cart when they went driving—in fact, he occasionally manœuvred her out of it. And when he came home from the office and found her sitting alone on the porch, instead of following his natural inclination to be friendly, he stood with one hand on the screen door, asked her what kind of a day she had had, and went on into the house. When Nora was set upon by her family for expressing some idea that seemed to him reasonable and just, he sometimes raised his voice in her defence, but what he said ("I agree with Nora. . . ." or "I think this is what Nora is trying to say. . . .") was usually drowned out in the same clamour that did away with Nora's opinions. If this cautious show of friendliness had been enough, and she was able to come to him when she had something on her mind, he was pleased. "Now tell me all about it," he said encouragingly.

In the window seat, facing him, Nora was silent.

"Don't worry," Austin said. "Whatever it is, I promise I won't be angry with you."

"You ought to be angry," Nora said. With her head bent, she examined her hands—the palms and then the backs—with a detachment that reminded him of Martha in front of her mirror.

"I've been through the house," she said at last, and then waited, as if for him to understand from this vague preliminary what it was that she really had to confess, and so spare her the difficulty and pain and humiliation of telling it.

"That's perfectly all right," Austin said. "The house is just as much yours, Nora, while you are staying in it, as it is ours."

"But that's not all," Nora said. "I did something I've never done before, and I don't know what made me do it this time. They went off driving without me, and I found the letter and read it."

"What letter, Nora?" He couldn't think of any correspondence that was in the slightest degree incriminating, but even so, a chill passed through him.

"Upstairs. I don't know what made me do such a thing. All I know is I feel dreadful because of it."

"Upstairs?"

"In the little secret drawer in your bureau. I found the letter from your mother and read it."

"Oh that!" Austin said, and then he nodded.

"It was a very nice letter but I had no right to read it. I felt terrible afterwards. I felt so ashamed."

"You mustn't take it so to heart," Austin said. "There was no reason why you shouldn't have read it if you wanted to." Though it was odd, of course, that she had been going through his bureau.

"But I didn't want to. Something made me. I didn't even want to be alone in the house. I didn't feel right about it. I kept thinking maybe someone would come. And it was so still—the way it is sometimes when there's going to be a storm. And afterwards I wanted to hide so I wouldn't have to face you and Cousin Martha ever again. Because you've been so kind to us all and that's the way we repay kindness."

"There was nothing in the letter that I didn't want you to know. But for your own sake, I'm glad you told me. Because now you won't ever have to think about it again."

"I can't help thinking about it. If you only knew how I——"

"I don't remember ever reading someone else's mail," Austin said, "but I know I wanted to, lots of times, and I did other things—when I was a boy—that I was ashamed of afterwards."

"I've learned my lesson," Nora said. "I won't ever do such a thing again as long as I live."

When people say *I have learned my lesson*, what they usually mean is that the lesson was expensive. This one had cost Nora the conversation she had been looking forward to, the conversation that was to have revealed what Austin King felt about life. Instead of talking to him as one grown person to another, she had to come to him now in a storm of childish repentance and like a child have her transgression forgiven.

"I don't see how you really can forgive me!"

"There's nothing to forgive." Austin was hot and tired and he wanted to escape upstairs and put his face in a basin of cold water. He could not escape because Nora did not allow him to. She sat with her mouth slightly open and her eyes had a sick look in them, as if in a moment of absent-mindedness she had allowed some beautiful and valuable object to slip through her fingers and was now staring at the jagged pieces on the floor.

Outside, a carriage stopped in front of the Kings' house. Mr. Potter got down and handed Ab from her mother's lap to the sidewalk. While the others were telling Bud Ellis how much they had enjoyed his company and the ride (which had been too long), Ab wandered up the sidewalk and into the house.

"Forget about it," Austin said. "So far as I'm concerned, it never happened."

The one person he didn't care to have read this letter was Martha, whose name was nowhere mentioned in it and for whom the letter contained no affectionate messages. Certain parts of the letter he could explain. His brother Charles lived in Detroit and was in the real estate business—a simple, amiable man who loved his wife and children, and threw himself into whatever he happened to be doing with an enthusiasm and pleasure that were never complicated by introspection. "This is wonderful!" he was always saying, no matter whether he was swimming or riding or playing tennis or merely out for a Sunday-afternoon walk. "Gosh, I feel fine!" he would tell people, or "I wouldn't have missed this for anything on earth!"—and mean it. Maud lived in Galesburg, was married to a professor at Knox College, and was a very different story. She had the measuring eye that waits to see how cakes and affection are going to be divided, and was not only jealous but also moody and implacable. If the letter had been from either his brother or his sister, he could have told Nora that he seldom saw or heard from Charles and that, although they liked each other, they had nothing to say when they met; or that his sister had certain terrible difficulties to contend with, inside herself, and he had learned to get along with her by remaining always in a state of armed readiness to avoid trouble. In this way he would have aroused Nora's interest and turned her mind away from the fact that she had had no reason (except curiosity) to read the letter in the first place. Since the letter was from his mother this was impossible. He knew far less about his mother than he knew about Nora. If he had tried to tell Nora about his mother, he would only have ended up telling her about himself, and he did not want any of the Mississippi people, so long as they were guests in his house, to know what he was really like. Otherwise, nowhere, neither in the attic nor in the basement nor behind closet doors would he have been safe from them. And so he said, "If I'd thought, Nora, I'd have told you that any letter you find in this house you can read. I give you my complete permission and approval, do you understand?"

"Do you really mean that?" Nora asked.

He nodded.

"I'm so glad," Nora said. "Not that I'd dream of ever doing such a thing again. But just the idea that you wouldn't mind if I——" She stopped, aware of Ab standing in the doorway watching them.

"If this and that," Austin said, "and a half of this and that, and four make eleven——"

Ab's face lit up at this old joke between them.

"—how much is this and that, and a half of this and that?" Smiling he picked her up and carried her into the front hall, where the tired travellers were divesting themselves of gloves, linen coat, and veils.

To remain free of people you need some disguise, and what better, more impenetrable false face can any man put on than the letters (so various, so contradictory in their assumptions and their appeals) of his family and his friends? It was an inspiration and like any inspiration it worked—far more powerfully than Austin had intended. It put an image between Nora Potter and the sun. From that time on, she was conscious of no other presence in the house but his. And when his grey eyes came to rest on her for a moment, they left her so drained and weak that it was all she could do to stand.

9

"The way I've got it figured out," Mr. Potter said painstakingly (though this story was not going to end in a burst of laughter), "is that now is the time. Land in Mississippi is cheaper than it has any right to be. I'm going to buy the plantation next to mine and cotton-farm the two at a big saving. I reckon on taking three or four people into it with me, to swing the deal, but there'll be money for all."

By "all" Mr. Potter did not mean Miss Ewing, who was listening outside with her head just far enough away from the pane of glass that it would not cast a shadow; or Dr. Hieronymous, the osteopath. He meant Bud Ellis and Judge Fairchild and Alfred Ogilvee and Orin McNab, the undertaker, and Mr. Holby and Dr. Seymour and Louis Orthwein, who owned and published the *Draperville Evening Star*. While Mr. Potter walked the floor and talked and gestured, they sat still and listened and asked questions that had to be answered. In their eyes there was the light of—not ambition, precisely—but of an awareness that life had quickened for them, that they were in the presence of their Big Chance. It was up to them to decide whether they would cling to the caution that had served them well enough, up till now, or throw caution to the winds in the hope that the winds would blow power and influence back to them.

When the door opened and the men filed out, Miss Ewing was seated at her desk and the typewriter was thrashing out so many legal words a minute that no one realized how quiet the outer office had been for the last hour and three-quarters. They said nothing to Miss Ewing about the offer that had just been laid before them, but the sound of their feet on the worn stairs was a dead giveaway. It was not beautiful, like the sound of an evening party breaking up but it had its own excitement and fear of the dark.

Faced with a circle of empty chairs, Austin and Mr. Potter sat down to appreciate the drop in tension.

"When you're dealing with Northern businessmen," Mr. Potter said, "everything has to be worked out so they know where they stand. That's where you come into it, my boy. I want it all down on paper, so it's legal and proper and there can't be any trouble later on. Of course if you want to put some money into the venture, that's another thing. I'm not urging you to. I'd rather not do business with relatives. It sometimes makes for hard feelings. But when a golden opportunity is knocking at your door——"

"What about old Mr. Ellis?" Austin asked.

"Bud wants to put up three thousand dollars," Mr. Potter said. "I don't know whether we can let him have that much stock in the company or not. We'll have to see when the time comes. I haven't spoken to the old gentleman yet. Old people are just naturally conservative, as you may have discovered. Mr. Ellis doesn't know much about any but Illinois land, which is very good, there's no getting around that; but land prices in the North are high. The South has possibilities for development that have never been realized. There has been poor management, poor equipment, poor everything. Mr. Ellis may hold off for a while, until he sees how the others react, but then he'll be glad to be included. I thought I'd let Dr. Danforth in on it, and you, naturally, if you are interested. When your mind is made up, there'll be plenty of time to discuss the details." Mr. Potter dropped his cigar in the cuspidor with a gesture of finality.

"In any case," Austin said, "I'll be very glad to draw up the papers for you."

Mr. Potter reached for his soiled Panama hat. "I'd better be getting along now," he said. "I told the ladies I'd be home by four. Mrs. Potter will be wondering what's become of me. Of course, we expect to pay you for any legal work that you do."

"There won't be any charge," Austin said.

IO

In spite of failing mental powers, which made old Mr. Ellis forget sometimes what he had started to say, he knew a surprising amount about the boll weevil. He also behaved very childishly, lost his temper the second time that Mr. Potter's plan was explained to him, shouted at his grandson, and stalked out of the parlour of the farmhouse. During the party which Mary Ellis gave for the Potters that evening, Mr. Ellis remained upstairs in his room, sulking.

A list of guests, an account of the refreshments, and a description of the Japanese lanterns which made the Ellises' yard look like a fairyland, appeared in the *Star* the following evening but actually it rained during the late afternoon, and the lawn party was held indoors. The children of Elm Street, for reasons of their own which had nothing to do with the Ellises' lawn party, appeared pulling lighted shoeboxes. In Bremen and Hamburg, which the children had never heard of, the same custom prevailed at this period and so it may have been brought to Illinois from one or the other of those German cities. The shoeboxes had star-shaped and moon-shaped windows cut in the sides and covered with coloured tissue paper, and there was a round hole in the top, directly over the candle which supplied illumination. The shoeboxes, each drawn by a string, in a procession, made a soft shuffling sound and threw shafts of coloured light on the sidewalk.

Mrs. Potter, watching the procession from the Ellises' porch, said "You know, I miss the darkies. They're the chief thing I miss up North. Rachel's little girl that Cousin Martha has in every now and then to help serve—I've grown so attached to her. If it were only possible, I'd take her home with me in my purse. . . . When you were a child, Mrs. Danforth, did you wake up expecting that overnight the house you went to sleep in had become a palace with marble floors and footmen to wait on you, and you had to put on a pink satin ball dress to eat breakfast in? I go into the kitchen sometimes to boil the water for a cup of tea and I see Thelma has a piece of asparagus fern and two half-dead daisies in a jelly glass by the kitchen window, and I want to say to her 'Strange as it may seem, I was a little girl once. I remember what it was like.' And I do remember, Mrs. Danforth, and I'm sure you do, too. I had tasks set for me, and all that, but what I liked to do best was to sit with my hands in my lap, thinking about all the wonderful things that were some day going to happen to me. My hair was in two braids down my back and there was a dreadful time when I thought I was going to have big feet, but it was only that they were growing and the rest of me hadn't started yet. . . ."

Involuntarily, Mrs. Danforth tucked her own feet farther under the swing. In the dark, the parrot-like expression was not visible, and people forgot that she was homely and were aware instead of the warmth and gentleness of her voice. There was a good deal of laughing and loud talking in the parlour, which came out to them through the open window. Mrs. Danforth saw that Bud Ellis and Mr. Potter had her husband in a corner and were talking to him earnestly.

"My feet are quite small," Mrs. Potter said, "now that I've caught up to them, but when I started to grow taller, something happened to me. I forgot about being a princess and I stopped being surprised that I was not eating off golden plates. . . ."

To approach Dr. Danforth with a business proposition during a social evening was an error in tactics. Mr. Potter had to raise his voice to carry above the other conversations in the room, and a sure thing shouted has either a dubious or a desperate sound.

"It wasn't as if that little girl died or anything," Mrs. Potter said. "She just stepped aside, and she's still there, waiting. I look at Thelma and I know that so far as she's concerned, the practising that comes from the house next door isn't the Beach girls, it's the court musicians. The garden is full of fountains splashing and rose trees, and the rats that run in the walls at night—you've seen the place where they live, Mrs. Danforth?—are kings' sons coming and going. 'Well, dear child,' I want to say to her, 'that's right. They *are* kings' sons.' "

The children with their lighted shoeboxes were coming back now, on the other side of the street.

"It's all I've arrived at," Mrs. Potter said, "after a long and in some ways difficult life. The rats really are kings' sons, and anyone who says they are rats wouldn't know a king's son if he saw one."

II

During the second and third week in August the centre of Draperville shifted from the courthouse square to a section of wooded land and shallow ravines two miles south of town. Rocking and swaying, the open street-car that all the rest of the year went only as far as the cemeteries now went on to the end of the line. The passengers got off, passed over a narrow footbridge, and presented their season tickets at the gates of the Draperville Chautauqua.

A cinder drive led past the ice-cream tent, the women's building, the administration and post-office building, the dining-hall, and the big cone-roofed auditorium, built on the brow of a hill and open on the sides to all kinds of weather. Every year the sloping floor of the auditorium was sprinkled with fresh tanbark, the bare stage was decorated with American flags and potted palms. The acoustics were excellent.

Spreading out from the auditorium in a series of circles were the cottages, rustic, creosote-stained, painted white or green, or with crazy Victorian Gothic embellishments for children to climb on, and with the names that small, cramped cottages always have—Bide Awee, Hillcrest, and The House That Jack Built. Between the cottages there were brown canvas tents with mosquito netting across the entrance flaps and ropes and stakes for the unwary to trip over after dark.

The cottages were occupied by the same families year after year. They did not come for the simple life—life being, if anything, too simple in town. They came for self-improvement, and because it was a change, with new neighbours and unfamiliar china and kerosene stoves to worry over and a partial escape from the heat. Mornings at the encampment of pleasure were for breakfast, for cot-making, for leisure and social calls. For the women there was the cooking school, for the children the slides and swings of the playground. At two o'clock a bell high up in the rafters backstage summoned everybody to the auditorium for a half-hour of music followed by a lecture. The audience kept the air stirring with palm-leaf fans and silk Japanese fans and folding fans and sections of newspaper. The finer shades of meaning were sometimes wafted away but at all events there was rhetoric, there was eloquence, there was the tariff question, diagrammed by the swallows flying through the iron girders of the cone-shaped roof. When the afternoon programme was over, the baseball game drew some of the audience, the ice-cream tent others. Dinner, and then the bell once more, its harsh sound turned musical as it passed through layer upon layer of lacquered oak leaves.

After the evening concert, the part of the audience that had come out from town for the day crowded the street-cars that were waiting for them outside the entrance gates or got into buggies and drove back to town, choking all the way in a continuous cloud of dust that they themselves helped to create. Because of the dust, the route was marked at intervals by gasoline lamps that spluttered and flared up occasionally, frightening the horses. The campers followed a winding cinder road until they came to their own tents and cottages. By eleven, when the curfew rang, all lights were out and the Chautauqua was as dark and quiet as it was on those nights when the chain hung across the entrance and the north wind and snow had their season.

Austin King came home from his office at noon, hitched the horse, and as soon as lunch was over, drove his guests out to the Chautauqua grounds. Mr. Potter liked best the military band, Randolph the light opera company that gave a performance of *Olivette* (with interpolations from *Robin Hood, The Bohemian Girl,* and *The Chimes of Normandy*), but to Mrs. Potter it was all one and the wonderful same. She did not wait for the bell to ring, but left the others in the dining-hall or on the porch of the Ellises' rustic cottage, and went on ahead with her pillow, her fan, and her bottle of citronella. No string trio was ever too long for her, no lecturer ever dull. She was equally delighted with William Jennings Bryan, the explorer who had been in Patagonia, and the man with a potter's wheel who turned out clay vases and made a larger than life-size head of Marie Antoinette grown old and fretful.

Sunday cast its shadow over the Chautauqua grounds as it did in town, but the religious services were shorter. After Sunday school and church at the auditorium, the atmosphere brightened, and by evening there might be glee singers or the "Anvil Chorus" performed with real anvils. Martha King, feeling unwell, missed the second Sunday in the 1912 season. The picture on the bulletin board outside the administration building showed a group of twenty handsome young men in white uniforms heavy with gold braid. Travelling from Chautauqua to Chautauqua, the White Huzzars may have lost track of the days of the week. Or perhaps they were the instruments of Change, pointing towards the fast automobiles, the golf courses, and the Sunday-night movies of the future. Anyway, their musical selections and their behaviour (especially when they grabbed up their clarinets and trumpets, shoved their chairs in a double line, and indulged in a mock sleigh-ride) were light-hearted and long remembered. The grey-haired members of the audience, guardians of a gentle Calvinistic era and with fixed ideas of what entertainment was appropriate to a day of worship, sat shocked and disapproving. The rest applauded wildly, reminded of something they had almost forgotten or known only in snatches—of how wonderful it is to be young.

When the last encore was over, Austin took Ab from Mrs. Potter's lap and lifted her like a limp sack to his shoulder. Her head collapsed of its own weight and her eyelids remained closed, but she knew they were moving slowly up the aisle of the big auditorium, with people all around them. She was in that delicate state of balance in which the mind grasps one thing at a time. Before they reached the long row of hitching posts, even that limited faculty had left her.

Austin started to hand the sleeping child up to Mrs. Potter in the back seat of the carriage, but Nora said, "Oh, let me hold her!" and Nora's voice was so earnest and so desiring that, over Mrs. Potter's protests, Austin handed the child up to the front seat instead. When the carriage wheels started to turn, Ab stirred and seemed on the point of waking, but then a woman's hand cushioned her head in the hollow between two breasts and held it there, and whatever strangeness had penetrated into Ab's sleep went away again or was absorbed into even stranger matters.

Austin drove back to town the long way round to avoid the dust. The night was cool, and the people in the English cart spoke in murmurs and then not at all. As they passed the cemeteries, Nora said, "I've never held a sleeping child before."

"She's not too heavy for you?" Austin asked.

"Oh no," Nora said. "But it's a very strange feeling."

With the reins lying loose in his hands, he was free to turn and look at his daughter and at the girl beside him. With wisps of soft hair blowing against her cheek, Nora's face looked very young and open and vulnerable.

"Will you promise me something, Nora," Austin King said suddenly.

"What is it?"

"Before you marry, bring the man to see me. I want to look him over."

"What if I never find such a person?"

"You don't have to find him. He'll find you. But it has to be the right kind of a man, or you won't be happy."

"Will you be able to tell, just by looking at him?"

"I think so," Austin said.

"All right," Nora said quietly, "I promise."

As they entered the outskirts of town, Ab felt the change from country dirt road to brick pavement, and wakened sufficiently to hear a voice say, "Cousin Austin, do you believe in immortality?" And then shortly afterward, a great many hands lifted her and carried her up a great many steps, brought her through long hallways, and undressed her. When she woke up, it was morning, and she was in her own bed, with no knowledge of how she got there.

12

The Potters' visit lasted four weeks and three days. During the final week Mr. Potter held a series of business meetings in Austin King's office, and the plan was put down on paper, so that there couldn't be any trouble later on. After sober consideration, Austin King decided that his other obligations (especially the money that he had to send his mother from time to time) made it inadvisable for him to invest in the Mississippi corporation. Dr. Danforth also stayed out of the venture. But in a town the size of Draperville it was not difficult to find six men who were ready and willing to make a fortune.

Mrs. Potter wanted very much to stay on till the end of the Chautauqua season, but Mr. Potter had received a letter from the bank in Howard's Landing and business came before pleasure. The banging sound that Ab heard when she was supposed to be taking her nap turned out to be Mr. Potter and Randolph hauling the two trunks up from the basement.

They went one last time to the Chautauqua grounds and when the afternoon lecture was over, wandered into the museum, a log cabin not unlike the one old Mr. Ellis was born in, except that in the old days log cabins didn't have a water cooler just inside the door and visitors were not handed small printed cards urging them, in the name of the First National Bank, to save for a rainy day.

There were barely enough relics in the museum to go around—a gourd that had been used as a powder flask during the battle of Fort Meigs, a pair of antlers, a baby's dress, a tomahawk, a bed with rope springs, a few letters and deeds. By all rights, the first hoe that shaved the prairie grass and so brought an end to one of the wonders of the world, should have been here; but historically important objects that are useful in their own right are seldom found in museums.

It is hard to say why Nora Potter chose this place to announce to her father and mother that she was not going back to Mississippi with them. Perhaps the regimental flags and the rifle that had originally come from Virginia encouraged her to take a defiant stand. Or possibly it was her mother's annoying interest in a stuffed alligator that was swung on wires from the ceiling. At all events, with no warning or preparation, she turned and said, "I'm not going home." Mr. Potter bent down and signed the register in the full expectation that it would guarantee his immortality. Mrs. Potter gazed up at the alligator. "So lifelike," she murmured, and then "What do you mean you're not going home, Nora?"

"The Beach girls are starting a kindergarten and they want me to work with them. I told them I would."

Mrs. Potter's face took on a sudden angry flush. "It's preposterous!" she exclaimed. "I never heard of such a thing."

The present with its unsolved personal relationships and complex problems seldom intrudes upon the past, but when it does, the objects under glass, the framed handwriting of dead men, the rotting silk and corroded metal all are quickened, for a tiny fraction of time and to an almost imperceptible degree, by life.

"We'd better wait outside," Martha King said to Austin, and pushing Ab ahead of her, she went past the water-cooler out into the sunlight. While the Potters converged (*God and Liberty*, Voltaire said) upon Nora, Austin and Martha and Ab waited uneasily in the cinder drive. Occasionally, the sound of voices, rising higher and higher, came through the open door of the museum. Ab was prevented from hearing what was said inside by her mother and father's resolute and uninteresting conversation about Prince Edward, who was showing signs of lameness from being driven so much. After a time the Potters appeared, with blank faces. Mr. Potter drew Austin aside and said, "Mrs. Potter thinks we'd better not stay for the evening performance." A moment later the whole party started walking in the general direction of the cement entrance gates.

Late that night, after the others had retired to their rooms, Mrs. Potter in her brocade dressing-gown knocked on Nora's door, opened it, and went in. Nora was sitting up in bed reading. Mrs. Potter sat down on the edge of the bed, and picked up Nora's book.

"What's this, if I may ask?"

"Certainly you can ask," Nora said. "It's a book the Beach girls loaned me."

Mrs. Potter read the title of the book aloud, dubiously, "*The Montessori Method* . . . I don't understand. I really don't. How you can talk about leaving your family and your home and everyone dear to you! Why do you want to stay up North among strangers?"

"They're not strangers. They're my friends."

"You have friends at home, if that's all there is to it. Plenty of them. What is it you want, Nora?"

"I want to make my own life," Nora said, raising her knees under the cover and resting her chin on them. "I want to be among people who do things instead of merely existing. I want to see snow. I don't know what I want."

"No, you don't know what you want. Ever since you were a little girl you've been that way. Do you know the first word you ever said? Most babies begin with 'Mama' but the first word you ever uttered was 'No' and you've been saying it—not to other people, just to me—ever since. I've tried to be a good mother to you. As good as I knew how, anyway. I nursed you through scarlet fever and whooping cough, I've fed and clothed you, I've protected you against your father when he was impatient or wanted to make you do things you didn't feel like doing, and all the same you're against me, and have been, since the beginning. Do I get on your nerves—the way I talk, the things I do? What is it?"

Nora shook her head. For a minute neither of them spoke, and then she said slowly, "Mother, listen to me. Now's your chance, do you hear? I know that when I start to talk about what I really think and want and believe, something comes over you, some terrible fit of impatience, so that your knees twitch and you can't even sit still long enough to hear what I have to say. You listen to other people. Anybody but your own daughter you have all the patience in the world with. I've watched you. You know just what to say and what not to say. With everybody but me you're wonderful. I wish I had a mirror. I wish I could show you what you look like right now, your face flushed and set, and that expression of grim endurance. Why do you have to endure your own daughter? I get furious at you but I don't endure you. What is it you want me to be? Do you want me to be domestic, like Cousin Martha, and worry about meals and whether the cook is in a bad temper and whether my husband is looking at some other woman? I haven't any husband to be jealous of, and I haven't any house, either. So I can't very well be domestic, can I? Or worry about the temper of the cook who doesn't exist? Do you want me to be afraid of you the way the Beach girls are afraid of their mother, so that when you're around all the life and hope goes out of me, and everybody thinks what a pity it is that such a charming delightful woman should have a dull daughter? Well, I won't be dull for anybody, not even you. I'm not dull, so why should I pretend to be? Or easy going, or self-controlled or anything else. . . . What you are thinking now I know. I can read it in your face. We've been over this a thousand times, you're saying, so why do we have to go over it again? But we haven't been over it a thousand times. I've never really talked to you the way I'm talking now, never in my whole life. Always before I've spared you, spared your feelings, and this time I'm not going to. I don't see any reason to spare your feelings. You're a grown woman and you had enough courage to leave my father and to come back to him, which I wouldn't have been able to do. I'd have died first. Don't look so horrified. You know what he's up to with Bud Ellis and those other men. You know why he brought us all up North when we were perfectly comfortable at home. You don't live with someone for thirty years without knowing what they're like. Somewhere inside of you, you have accepted him, for better or worse. And you've accepted Randolph. You know why that dog bit him. You know how he gets people and animals to love him and then turns on them suddenly when they're least expecting it. If I were a collie, I'd have bit him a hundred times. I did try to kill him once when we were little. Do you remember? I chased him round and round the summer house with a butcher knife and everybody but Black Hattie was afraid to come near me. You were afraid too, Mother. I saw it in your eyes, but I wouldn't have stabbed you. If you'd only walked right up to me when I was wild with anger and trusted me enough to put your arms around me and hold me—that's all I ever wanted—somebody to hold me until I could get over being angry with Brother—then we wouldn't be sitting here like this, like two strangers who don't know each other very well, or like each other. . . . Why haven't you ever accepted me, Mother? Didn't you want to have a daughter? Or was it that you suddenly started to dislike me, after I—— Oh, it's no use. I don't know why I go on trying. It's like talking to a tree or an iron doorstep. . . . Look, I want to stay up North because I feel, deep down in my heart, that there's something here for me. There's nothing at home and I'm young, Mother. I can't bear to wake up in the morning and know what's going to happen all day long, what we're going to have for lunch, what you and Father and Randolph are going to say before the words are out of your mouth. If a wagon goes by with two niggers in it and a yellow dog, that's enough for you. You run to the window at the first sound of the wheels, and say 'There's Old Jeb and Sally and their yellow dog,' and you're as pleased as if you'd seen a circus parade. But I don't care if it *is* Old Jeb, or if my new dress doesn't fit right across the shoulders, or if Miss Failing's sciatica is worse, or the minister is going to leave. There'll be another minister to take his place. There always has been, and the new one will go right on trying to raise the money to fix the church roof, so what difference does it make? I don't care about the big blue willow salad bowl and platter that should have come to you after Great-Aunt Adeline died, only Cousin Laura Drummond snitched it while the rest of the china was being packed. Let Cousin Laura have her salad bowl and platter. I want excitement. I want to live in the real world, not in Mississippi with my head in a brown paper bag just because you married Father instead of Jim Ferris, who would have given you a big house in Baltimore and a fine carriage and plenty of servants to wait on you. I'm your daughter and you ought to help me. You ought to want to help me get away and lead the kind of life you would have had if things had turned out differently. Who knows? You help me now and maybe I can help you later. Maybe I can make a lot of money teaching kindergarten, and you won't have to be worrying always for fear the whole plantation will collapse on your head some day, and the Detrava sofas be sold at auction. Maybe I'll marry a millionaire. Maybe I'll——"

Like an alarm clock that had finally run down, Nora stopped talking. Her eyes filled with tears. If her mother had argued with her, she could have found new arguments to answer the old ones, but her mother was sitting so quietly on the edge of the bed that it frightened Nora. With her hands in her lap, her mother looked suddenly so like a child, a very good child who is waiting for some grown person's permission to get up and go outdoors and play. The angry flush was gone, and instead of the resisting, restless gestures, only a quiet so intense that the room rang with it, like a hollow sea shell.

"Nora, I need you," she said slowly. "If you leave me now, I don't know how I'll manage. You're more help to me than you know. I can't live in a house where nobody is honest or brave or in any way dependable. I did before you were old enough to understand things, but I can't any more."

13

"I know old man Seligsberg isn't your client," Miss Ewing said, "but since Mr. Holby is out of town and it's rather important, I thought maybe you might want to handle it for him."

"All right," Austin said, without glancing up. "Just put it on my desk and I'll look at it later."

Mr. Holby's procrastination was a problem that had to be handled delicately. If he had been as successful and as universally respected as Judge King, he might have found it easier to make decisions. Office work bored him. What he needed to marshal his energies was the smell of the courtroom, the sound of the judge's gavel, whispered consultations at a moment of crisis, a shaky witness to cross-examine, and an audience that he could sway by reason or emotion, depending on the cards he had up his sleeve.

The mantle of the older lawyers should have fallen on his shoulders, but when the time came for him to receive it, the mantle was threadbare and he found himself cheated out of the honour that they had had. His little overnight trips to Springfield and Chicago and St. Louis extended themselves to three days or sometimes to a week and longer. When he was in the office he spent more time talking to old cronies than he gave to legal work. "Just put it there in that pile I have to look over," he would say, indicating a wire basket full of dusty manilla folders. "I'll take care of it first thing tomorrow morning." Or "Let's wait another month or six weeks and then see where we stand. If we hurry it through——"

Austin King was not entirely free from procrastination himself, and for that reason found it twice as irritating in his partner. Forty minutes passed before he got around to looking at the large document that Miss Ewing had placed on his desk. During that time a fashionably dressed young woman entered the outer office and asked to see Mr. King. "If you'll just take a chair," Miss Ewing said, "Mr. King will see you as soon as he is free." There was nothing she liked better than to keep people waiting, and it often annoyed her that Austin did not use this simple means of building up his prestige. When he called to her, finally, she got up from her desk, smiling, and went into his office.

"Where did you find this deed? It should have been recorded months ago."

"It was in the files," Miss Ewing said.

"Did you know it was there?"

Miss Ewing nodded. "I've spoken to Mr. Holby several times about it, but——"

She and Austin exchanged a brief, understanding look, and then he said, "I'd better get right over to the county clerk's office with it."

"Miss Potter is waiting to see you."

With difficulty Austin turned his mind away from the things he would have to say not only to the county clerk but also to Mr. Seligsberg, and to Mr. Holby when he returned from his trip to Chicago.

"Miss Potter?" he repeated. "Tell her to come in."

When Miss Ewing ushered Nora in, Austin got up from his chair. "Well, this is very nice!"

"The county clerk's office closes at noon today," Miss Ewing said, and withdrew, shutting the door after her.

"I won't stay but a minute," Nora said. "I know you're terribly busy."

Unable to deny it in the face of Miss Ewing's instructions about the county clerk's office, Austin with a wave of his hand offered Nora the chair beside his desk. She remained standing.

"I came to ask you something."

"Something of a legal nature, perhaps?" Austin smiled at her.

"No," Nora said, pulling at her gloves.

The errand that had brought her downtown must be a serious one, Austin decided; otherwise she wouldn't be so uneasy with him. Again his hand made the same gesture without his being altogether aware of it, and Nora shook her head. "There's no need for me to sit down," she said, "and I don't want to take up any more of your time than I have to. It's simply this—I came here to ask why you—why you look at me the way you do."

"Look at you?" Austin repeated.

"Yes. Whenever we're in the same room or anywhere together I see you watching me, and before I go home I want to know why. I want to know what it is that you are trying to convey to me."

Austin flushed. "If I have been making you uncomfortable, Nora," he said, "I'm very sorry. I wasn't aware of what I was doing. Now that you've told me, I——"

"Is that all?" Nora's lips trembled.

"What do you mean 'all'?"

"I mean—oh, why are you so cautious? You can say anything in the world to me, *anything*, do you understand?"

"But I really don't have anything to say to you, Nora."

The clacking of the typewriter in the outer office added to his sense of helplessness. *This is a place of business*, the typewriter said. *Personal matters should be taken care of after office hours, not here.*

Nora turned towards the door, and he said, "Wait!"

"Please let me go," she said with her back to him.

"Not just yet. I want to talk to you. If I had had any idea that you——"

"You must have known that I was in love with you. Everything else about me you understood so perfectly without my having to tell you. I thought you wanted me to be in love with you."

"But I *didn't* know it," Austin said, "and I don't believe that you are in love with me. You don't know anything about me." He looked around for some material evidence in support of this statement. The stuffed prairie dog and the photograph of the old Buttercup Hunting and Fishing Club offered, unfortunately, too much evidence. They proved that nobody knew anything about Austin King, that he had taken very good care that people shouldn't know anything about him.

"I know that you are the kindest, most understanding person I have ever known," Nora said. "And that I love you and you don't love me."

"You're very young, Nora. Any feeling that you have for me now you will soon get over."

"How can I get over it when I can't talk to you? I want to talk to you but I can't say the things I need and want to say. You don't want to hear them."

"Possibly not," Austin said, "but I want to help you."

"Besides, I can't look at you."

Nora went to the window, and stood looking down. The firemen were sitting in their shirtsleeves in front of the fire station. A buggy went by, and then a farm wagon, drawn by two heavy grey horses. A man came out of Gersen's clothing store and stood looking up and down the sidewalk, as undecided as a fly walking on a ceiling.

"I don't have to look at you," Nora said. "I know exactly how you look anyway. I know you are trying to help me. But when you say kind things, gentle things, it makes me want to die." Her voice rose in pitch and Austin was sure that Miss Ewing in the outer office could hear everything. The typewriter clacked one more legal sentence and then was still. Any girl who threw herself at a married man could expect no sympathy from Miss Ewing, and neither could the man.

"What I am feeling now," Nora said, "is, of course, being terribly in love, and I don't know quite what to do. Sometimes I feel this cannot be happening, must not be happening to me."

Austin went over to the window, hoping that if he stood near her, she would lower her voice.

"You will be all right, Nora," he said. "Nothing bad will come of it."

"Tomorrow I am going home and I won't ever see you again. You'll forget that I exist, but I can't bear not knowing where you are every minute of the day or what's happening to you. I may begin to imagine all sorts of things."

Austin saw Dr. Seymour come out of his office, get into his buggy, and drive as far as the iron watering trough on the east side of the square.

"It's more than likely that we will see each other again, sometime. And in any case, just because you are going back home doesn't mean that I will disappear from the face of the earth."

"Doesn't it?" Nora said anxiously. "You mean I can write to you?"

"If writing helps, you can write to me."

"But you won't answer my letters?"

"Perhaps not always. It's hard to know now what will be best later on. But whatever seems best for you, I will do, Nora."

They stood for several minutes more, looking out on the courthouse and the rectangle of asphalt streets. Then, without turning to him, Nora said, "No one has ever felt the way I do when I am with you. They couldn't. I feel as if I had just come through a terrible fever where everything was distorted and weird and frightening. We'll never be any nearer to each other, you and I, than we are this moment. Somehow I don't ever see myself being able to manage the love I have for you, or controlling it so that it isn't apparent to everyone. I can't ever be friends with you—really and truly friends—because no one who knows me could ever see me with you and not know I love you. It's so mixed up, isn't it?"

Very, said the typewriter in the outer office.

"I may write to you, or I may not," Nora said. "But even though I do not write, you will feel me thinking of you. I don't see how you could help it."

She moved away from the window and stood memorizing the contents of his desk—the litter of papers, the stains on the green blotter, the shape of the pen, the position of the old-fashioned inkwell.

"I'm going now," she said. "I'm sorry I stayed so long. You aren't angry with me for coming?"

"No."

"It's hard for me to leave, knowing that we probably won't ever have another chance to talk like this. Standing by the window I began to feel so calm inside. Everything was so wonderful. But I still can't look at you. I look in your eyes and the whole room falls apart. It's a quiet feeling, like being suspended in space, but the trouble is I want to go on looking and looking, and I know I must stop. And it's frightening when you consider that I'm supposed to be a grown woman, not a girl. I was so unkind to Mama last night, and I hate myself for it, and I can't bear being unkind to her. I wish I could die."

With her gloved hand on the doorknob, Nora turned back once more. "I will go on writing to you forever."

"Possibly," Austin said, "but I don't think so."

"You won't disappear, will you? You'll remember you promised not to be angry with me if I——"

"No matter what happens," Austin said, "I won't disappear and I won't be angry with you."

14

The Potters' visit, which had seemed so spacious in the beginning, came to a hurried end. At eight o'clock on the last morning, the railway express wagon came and took away the two trunks and five suitcases. The Potters had only themselves to worry about; only gloves, pocket-books, spectacle cases, last-minute regrets.

At quarter after nine, Austin drove around to the front of the house.

Randolph took one last conscientious look in the pier glass, as if the mirrors here in the North were more to be trusted than the ones he would find when he got home. "Cousin Martha, don't forget," he said. "You're coming down to stay with us next winter."

"Is it time to say good-bye?" Mrs. Potter asked. She picked Ab up, kissed her, said "God bless you!" and set her down. Then she turned to Austin. "I'm going to kiss you, too."

"I'm going to the train with you," Austin said, accepting her embrace.

"So you are!" Mrs. Potter exclaimed. "I completely forgot. Well, I'll kiss you again at the station. Where's Nora?"

"I gave you the address of the bank in Howard's Landing, didn't I?" Mr. Potter said to Austin, and then, turning to Martha, "Good-bye, my dear. You've made us all happy with your wonderful hospitality."

"What's keeping that girl?" Mrs. Potter asked. "I declare,

whenever we want to make a train, she's always late. It's enough to drive you to drink. . . . *Nora?*"

"Coming," a voice called down from upstairs.

"We may as well start on out to the carriage," Mrs. Potter said.

Outside in the bright sunlight all sense of hurry seemed to leave her. At the foot of the steps she put her arm through Martha King's and as the two women went slowly down the walk, Mrs. Potter said, "I don't know what to say or how to thank you. The truth of the matter is that I couldn't feel any closer to you, not even if you were my own child. . . . Write to me, won't you? I want to know everything that you're doing, all about Ab and Rachel and that darling black child of hers who is always drawing when she should be doing the dishes. She gave me one of her pictures to take home. And about the Danforths and Mrs. Beach and the Ellises and all the people we've met. But mostly about you, because you're the one who really matters to me. All those years when I might have had you, instead of those people who didn't understand you. If only I'd had you then, after your mother died . . . but she knows. She's watching us."

Mrs. Potter searched the bosom of her dress for a handkerchief, wiped the tears away, and pulled her veil down over her troubled face. Randolph helped his mother into the back seat of the cart and then got in after her. The screen door opened and Nora came out, dressed exactly as she was when she went upstairs; no hat, no gloves, no pocket-book, no light summer coat.

"*Now* what?" Mrs. Potter cried.

"She's not going," Mr. Potter said.

"Nora, go back into the house and——" Mrs. Potter attempted to rise, but Randolph put a restraining hand on her shoulder.

"Her mind is made up," he said.

"But she can't stay here," Mrs. Potter said, looking around

wildly. "Cousin Austin and Cousin Martha have their own life to lead, and I won't have her imposing on them in this way!"

"Mrs. Beach has offered me a room in their house," Nora said.

"Oh, I don't know what will become of her!" Mrs. Potter exclaimed. "Mr. Potter, do something! Don't just sit there!"

Mr. Potter went halfway up the walk and stood talking to Nora so quietly that the others couldn't hear what he said or what Nora said in reply. He bent down and kissed her, and then came back and climbed into the front seat of the cart. Austin looked at his watch.

"We'd better be starting," Mr. Potter said.

As the carriage drove away, Nora and Martha King both waved, but there was no response from the back seat.

Hiding behind the purple clematis, Mary Caroline had one last glimpse of Randolph. He was saying something to his mother, and suddenly he turned. It could have been an accident; he needn't have been thinking of Mary Caroline as they drove past her house, but with such small signs and tokens all of us keep the breath of life in our chimaeras.

15

For most people, having company for more than three or four days is a serious mistake, the equivalent to sawing a large hole in the roof and leaving all the doors and windows open in the middle of winter. Out of a desire to be helpful or the need to be kind, they let themselves in for prolonged spells of entertaining, forfeit their privacy and their easy understanding, knowing that the result will be an estrangement—however temporary—between husband and wife, and that nothing proportionate to this is to be gained by the giving up of beds, the endless succession of heavy meals, the afternoon drives. Either the human race is incurably hospitable or else people forget from one time to the next, as women forget the pains of labour, how weeks and months are lost that can never be recovered.

The guest also loses—even the so-called easy guest who makes her own bed, helps with the dishes, and doesn't require entertaining. She sees things no outsider should see, overhears whispered conversations about herself from two rooms away, finds old letters in books, and is sooner or later the cause of and witness to scenes that because of her presence do not clear the air. When she has left, she expects to go on being a part of the family she has stayed with so happily and for so long; she expects to be remembered; instead of which, her letters, full of intimate references and family jokes, go unanswered. She sends beautiful presents to the children at a time when she really cannot afford any extravagance, and the presents also go unacknowledged. In the end her feelings are hurt, and she begins to doubt—quite unjustly—the genuineness of the family's attachment to her.

During their stay, the Potters had managed to invest the rooms they slept in with much of their personality. They had moved things, chipped things, left rings in mahogany, left medicine stains, left the impression of their bodies in horsehair mattresses. Living partly out of suitcases and partly out of untidy dresser-drawers, with disorder lying on the floor of their closets, with toilet articles spilling over their rooms, they had achieved a surface of confusion that Martha King had long since given up trying to do anything about. And even after all or nearly all of their possessions had been stuffed into trunks and suitcases and the Potters were on the train, the work of restoration had to be carried on, inch by inch.

With their heads tied up in dustcloths, Martha King and Rachel went to work and, like archæologists chipping plaster from a ninth-century Byzantine mosaic, restored the house on Elm Street. Turn a mattress and who can say what manner of person has been sleeping on it? A bed remade with clean sheets and a fresh counterpane will look as if it had never been slept in. By nightfall, the guest-rooms had regained their idealized, expectant air, and there was a large square package (containing a black velvet bow, a sandalwood fan, a toothbrush, a necktie . . .), all wrapped and ready to mail, on the downstairs hall table.

Without the two extra leaves, the dining-room table was round instead of oval, and brought Austin and Martha and Ab much closer together under the red-and-green glass lampshade.

"Is the steak the way you like it?" Martha inquired from her end of the table.

"Yes," Austin said, from his.

"Not too done?"

"No, it's fine. Just the way I like it."

"I asked Mr. Connor for veal chops and he said he had veal but he wouldn't recommend it, so I got steak instead."

"Mr. Holby is going to Chicago next week," Austin said, after a considerable silence.

"Again?"

"He's going to be gone four or five days. There's a meeting of the State Bar Association."

There was another long silence and then he said, "Old Mrs. Jouette was in the office today. She asked after you."

"That was nice of her," Martha said.

Part Four

THE CRUEL CHANCES OF LIFE BAFFLE BOTH THE SEXES

I

If I live to be a thousand years old, Nora said to herself as she rearranged her ivory toilet articles on the dresser scarf, I'll never get used to these curtains.

Neither will we ever get used to you, the faded black and red and green curtains said. *We may learn to tolerate each other but no more. That bed you slept so badly in, last night, is Mr. Beach's bed. He died in it. This was his room. And even though your comb and brush are on the bureau and your dresses are hanging in the clothes-press, it all belongs to him.*

The black walnut bed was enormous, a bed that was meant for husband and wife, for marriage and childbirth. No single person could possibly feel comfortable in it, or anything but lost to the world. Lying between the high, crenellated headboard and footboard, she had dreamed about Randolph; she was in trouble and he saved her. In real life, of course, he never did save her. He was only harsh and impatient with her for getting into trouble when he, for some reason or other, never did. She could be drowning and as she came up for the last time he would look down at her from the bank and say *I told you it wasn't safe to swim into a waterfall. . . .*

When Nora had made the bed Mr. Beach died in, she looked around timidly for something else to do, some household chore that would justify her being there, and discovered that neither Alice nor Lucy had straightened their rooms that morning. Though there were no cotillion programmes tucked in the dressing-table mirror, no invitations to parties or football games, no letters beginning:

My dear Miss Beach,

So delightfully urged I succeeded in getting an invitation to the Draperville Academy dance next Friday. I write to ask permission to take you and to have the supper dance with you. I will call tomorrow evening and then learn whether or not I may have the pleasure of . . .

both rooms seemed to say that it is not kind to pry into the secrets of young people. Lucy's room was larger, with a window seat and a view of the mulberry tree in the back yard. The prevailing colour was a pink so inappropriate to Lucy's age that Nora decided Mrs. Beach must have chosen it for her. Alice's room, directly across the hall, was in blue and white. The two brass beds were undoubtedly the same ones Alice and Lucy had slept in when they were thirteen or fourteen years old. A stranger to the family, passing down the hall and glancing in at these two doors, would have thought to herself *the girls' rooms*, never suspecting that two mature women came here each night, undressed, took the combs and pins out of their greying hair, and lay down to sleep in the midst of so many frills and ruffles.

Feeling like an intruder, Nora put the two rooms in order and escaped to the downstairs part of the house, where she sat in the parlour and looked at a large souvenir book of photographs of the Columbian Exposition, and waited for Martha King to call.

If the Kings had asked Nora to stay on with them, she would have refused, even though their house was so much more cheerful and comfortable than the Beaches'. But they hadn't asked her. And furthermore, Martha had let two whole days go by without coming across the yard to see whether she was settled and happy in her new surroundings.

The telephone rang several times during the morning, and each time Nora hurried into the dining-room, ready to be pleasant and natural, to keep her hurt feelings from betraying themselves, to make water run uphill. While one part of her said into the mouthpiece of the telephone, "This is Nora

Potter, Miss Purinton. . . . Yes . . . for a while, anyway. . . . Just a moment, I'll see if she can come to the phone. . . ." another part of her cried out: *How can she not call when she knows I'm waiting to hear from her?*

Answers to this question came and crowded around Nora. Cousin Martha had meant to call and then someone had dropped in and was gossiping and keeping her from the telephone; or perhaps she had tried to call and the line was busy. It might be that, out of nervousness (they had never been altogether easy with one another), she had put off calling as long as she could, without being rude; or that the telephone was out of order and she was waiting for a man from the telephone company to come out and fix it. In which case, she could have come over unless she was sick. And if she was sick, wouldn't Austin have called and told them?

It was possible—just barely possible—that Cousin Martha (though she didn't seem that kind of a person) had taken this way of showing Nora that she didn't like her and didn't want her here. Down home, people would never act that way. Whether they liked you or not, they called and pretended that. . . . Or it might be that she was annoyed because . . .

Like the early systems of astronomy, the answers were all based on the assumption that the sun goes around the earth. By lunchtime Nora had considered and exhausted every explanation except the right one—that she was not as important to Martha King as Martha King was to her.

It would be difficult, she decided, living right next door to them and never seeing or speaking to Cousin Martha, but if she didn't call, that must be what she intended Nora to do. She would walk past the Kings' house without looking at it, and if they were on the porch and didn't speak. . . . This image, involving a third person, was too painful and had to be put aside in favour of another. . . . If Nora were, say, with Lucy and Alice and they called *Good evening, Martha*, then Nora would have to pretend that she didn't hear or wasn't aware that anyone was being spoken to. She would have to be ready, when Cousin Martha came over to see Mrs. Beach, to step aside into some room, to be always busy in some remote part of the house. She couldn't take the children to kindergarten, as Lucy wanted her to do, because that meant turning up the Kings' front walk, ringing the doorbell, and standing there in front of the door until Cousin Martha opened it. But everything else she could manage, and maybe even that. If she sent some child and she herself remained on the sidewalk, turned slightly away, looking after the other children. . . . Whatever lay in her power to do, for Austin's sake, she would do. If she couldn't be friends with Cousin Martha, she would do the next best thing. She would keep out of her way. Though it would be difficult and not at all the way it was when her family was here, no one would ever know. People would think it was an accident that she and Cousin Martha were never seen together. And her mother, who was very fond of Cousin Martha, need never find out how badly Nora had been treated.

Having prepared herself again and again all morning for the call that didn't come, Nora had no strength left to fight the idea that recurred to her at quarter to two—that perhaps Martha King was waiting for *her* to call; that it was, in fact, her duty to call, after having been a guest in the Kings' house for over a month. Pride counselled her to wait in the parlour, but Fear said *What if Cousin Martha never calls?* By that time, Nora was too nervous to trust her own voice over the telephone.

"I'm going over to the Kings," she called out to the silent house. "I'll be back in a few minutes," and ran across the yard to get at the little white-throated, whisking animal of uncertainty.

2

After dinner, Martha King took her coffee cup and went into the living-room. Austin followed her and built a fire. The living-room fireplace smoked a little until the flue was warm, and as he stood holding the evening paper across the upper part of the opening, he said, "Did you call Nora or go over to see her today?"

"I meant to," Martha said, "but before I got around to it, she came over here." She was silent for such a long time that he finally looked at her over his shoulder.

"I'm worried about her," Martha said.

"Why?"

"Well, she's up here among strangers, and she's young and impulsive, and with nobody to keep any kind of check on her——"

"The Beaches aren't strangers," Austin objected.

"They aren't like her own family. They don't have any control over her. I wouldn't want anything to happen, for Aunt Ione's sake. I feel that she trusts us to look after Nora as much as we can, even though Nora isn't staying with us."

The flue was now drawing properly and the newspaper no longer needed, but Austin continued to stand facing the brick fireplace, keeping the paper from being sucked up the chimney.

"I have a feeling that Nora is in trouble and that she needs——"

"What kind of trouble?"

"Oh, Austin, you make me so impatient sometimes. You know perfectly well that Nora is in love with you and that that's why she didn't go home when they did."

"Did she say so?"

"Of course not."

"Then how do you——"

"I saw it on her face when she walked in. She wanted to know if I thought she'd done right in staying, and we talked about that and about her family. And then we talked about you."

Austin crumpled the newspaper into a ball and threw it into the fire.

"I offered to introduce her to some young people," Martha said, as he sat down, "but it turned out that she likes being with older people. She finds them more stimulating. Besides, she doesn't think of us—of you and me—as being old."

"We're not as young as we once were. That's no reason to smile at her."

"Very well," Martha said. "I won't smile at her. You have a way, Austin—you've never done it with me but I've seen it happen with other people——"

The creaking of the front stairs made her turn her head for a second. The Kings' house, being old, was subject to unexplained noises, most of which came from the cellar and the pantry, and from the front stairs when there was no one on them. This creaking of the stairs, so like the sound of someone trying not to make a sound, often caused Abbey King's heart to stop beating for several seconds. The footsteps did not, like those in ghost stories, continue down the stairs and stop just outside the library door. There was only one, and then a long agonized waiting for the next step, which never came.

"You have a way," Martha went on, "of being very kind and gentle sometimes, and of seeming to offer more than you really do. If you act that way with Nora——"

"What am I supposed to do? Tell her that she's got no business to be in love with me?"

Martha shook her head. "I didn't say that. But if you tell her—or even allow her to guess that you know, it'll be all over with her. She's got as much as she can manage now to keep from telling you or me or anybody that she thinks will listen sympathetically. The only thing that makes it possible for her to pretend that she isn't in love with you is that she doesn't know how you might take it. You might laugh at her or think she was just being very young and she can't bear that. She has that much pride still. As long as she doesn't know how you feel, she'll go on trying to pull the wool over my eyes and waiting for a sign from you. At least I think she will. If she breaks down and starts to confide in you, you can refuse to listen."

Austin sighed.

"If you can't stop her any other way, you can always turn your back and walk off. I may be wrong but I don't think Nora has ever been in love before. And for that reason——"

"I don't see how she can be interested in a man of my age," Austin said. "But whatever feeling she has for me now, she'll get over, as I told her."

"Do you mean to say she came right out and told you she was in love with you?"

"More or less."

"When?"

"The day before they left," Austin said, and then recounted briefly what had happened between Nora and him in his office. When he had finished, he sat staring at the cortège of nymphs that followed the car of Apollo, over the mantelpiece, and thinking how strange it was that Martha showed no signs of being jealous. So many times before when her jealousy had no grounds whatever, she had been very difficult and unreasonable. Apparently, even though she made scenes and accused him of things he wouldn't have dreamed of doing, she didn't really believe or mean what she said. Otherwise, how could she sit, considering the design of the coffee cup so calmly and dispassionately.

"She seemed very upset because she had to go back to

Mississippi with them, and so I told her that she could write to me—which there won't be any occasion for her to do now. And also that I'd do anything I could to help her."

Martha King picked up her coffee cup, and started for the dining-room. As she reached the doorway she turned and asked, "You're not in love with her, are you?"

He saw that she was looking at him, waiting for his answer with no fear and no anger because she felt it necessary to ask such a question, but in a way that was more serious for both of them, if his answer were yes, than either fear or anger.

"No," he said soberly, "I'm not in love with her."

3

When Nora had finished drying the supper dishes for Lucy, she went upstairs to the room that she shared with Mr. Beach, and, standing in front of the dresser, she brushed and braided her hair. From the room at the end of the hall, she heard an old voice complaining.

In a way that was hardly noticeable to anyone but herself, Mrs. Beach was failing. She had difficulty remembering names. Her handwriting began to take on certain of the shaky characteristics of the handwriting on old envelopes in the attic. Her glasses had to be changed. She had to stop and rest on the stairs. All her life she had been busy pointing out the difference between black and white. Now, as a result of these new symptoms, she had to attend to the various shades of grey. This necessary task was instructive; it forced her to reconsider her marriage and rearrange her girlhood; but she was not grateful for it, any more than the woman who has occupied the prize room of a summer boarding-house until a declining income forces her to move into cramped quarters at the head of the back stairs is grateful for the opportunity to acquaint herself with the kitchen odours and the angry voice of the cook. The complaining was bewildered, as if Mrs. Beach had not yet discovered the proper authorities to complain to, and realized that there was no point in laying her grievance before Alice.

Nora daubed cologne on her neck and throat, and after one last quick look at herself in the mirror, she opened a dresser drawer, took out a soft bundle wrapped in a hand-towel, turned out the light, and went down the hall to the head of the stairs.

Nora settled herself on the plush sofa in the parlour, where Lucy was waiting for her, and unpinned the towel, which contained a ball of grey wool and a pair of knitting needles. With Lucy's help, Nora was learning to cast on. Listening for the sound of footsteps on the front porch, Nora sometimes lost the thread of Lucy's conversation, but then she picked it up again, and nodding said, "I know just what you mean." A mistake in her knitting was more serious. She had to unravel back to the point where her mind had wandered. There was no reason to think that Austin would come tonight, any more than any other night, and if he didn't come, she still had every reason to be happy that she was here. In Mississippi, she could wait a hundred years, for all the good it would do her.

"You're doing your hair a new way," Nora observed.

"I changed the parting," Lucy said.

"It's very becoming the way you have it now. I've tried dozens of ways of doing my hair and this is the only way that doesn't make me look like somebody in a sideshow. Mama has such beautiful hair—or at least it was beautiful before it turned grey. But I don't know why we sit here talking about hair when there are so many more interesting things to talk about. What would you like to have, Lucy, if you could have anything in the world you asked for?"

"If I could have anything in the world? Why I'd like to——"

"Once you've declared your wish, you have to stand by it. You can't change your mind and have something else instead. So before you——" Nora turned her head to listen.

If the Dresden shepherd with his crook and saffron knee-breeches and violets painted on his waistcoat, and the shepherdess with her petrified ribbons, tiny waist, and sweet expression are sometimes separated by the whole width of the mantelpiece, it may be that the shepherdess is an ardent, trusting, young girl, inexperienced in the ways of the world, the shepherd a married man, years older than she, with a china wife and child to think about and scruples that have survived the firing and glazing. Or perhaps the hand that put them there was more interested in ideas of order and balance than in images of philandering.

At quarter to nine Lucy yawned and said, "I rather expected Austin King to drop in." She got up from her chair, picked up the souvenir book of the Columbian Exposition, which Nora had left out on the parlour table, and put it away on the bottom shelf of the glassed-in bookcase where it belonged. "Don't feel you have to go to bed when we do, Nora. We've got into the habit of retiring with the chickens."

"If you don't mind," Nora said, "I think I will wait up a little longer. I'm not a bit sleepy."

Once or twice she got up and went into the dining-room, where she could see the lights in the Kings' house, and at one point she wandered out into the hall and stood looking at the door chime which needed only a human hand to make it reverberate through the quiet house. At ten o'clock the lights went out downstairs in the house next door and the upstairs lights went on, shortly afterward.

When Nora went upstairs, no one said (as they would have if she had been at home): *Is that you, Nora?* From the room at the end of the hall came the sound of Mrs. Beach's breathing, as regular and mournful as a buoy bell. Nora tiptoed past the two open doors that offered absolute silence and turned the light on in her room.

When she was ready for bed, she turned the light off and raised the shade so that, lying in bed, she could still see the thin slice of light upstairs in the house next door. After a time the window was raised a few inches, but the light stayed on. Turning and tossing, lying now on her right side, now on her heart, Nora invited and prevented sleep. The light went out, the clock in the downstairs hall struck twelve, and then one, and finally two. After Nora had given up all hope of ever dropping off, she realized that she had been somewhere, that something had happened to her, that she had been dreaming.

4

As a result of his having drawn up the necessary papers (so that Mr. Potter's plan would all be down on paper, legal and proper, and there couldn't be any trouble later on) Austin found himself involved in an active correspondence with the bank in Howard's Landing, and from this correspondence he learned a number of facts that Mr. Potter had apparently not found time or thought it necessary to go into. The indebtedness on the plantation was larger than Bud Ellis and the other shareholders had been given to understand, and the mortgage (which would have to be satisfied before the Mississippi corporation began to coin money) covered not only the plantation house but the land and the farm implements as well. Mr. Potter's reassurances, by return mail, were convincing enough, if you took each explanation by itself, but they didn't quite dovetail. Austin began to wonder about the elk's tooth charm, the courtly manners, and the stories in which Mr. Potter invariably outsmarted the other fellow.

Mrs. Potter's bread-and-butter letter—full of misspelling and arbitrary punctuation, words written in and crossed out, the margins crammed with messages and affectionate afterthoughts, and bits of information about people that Austin and Martha had never heard of—quieted for a short while his uneasiness about the business transaction that had taken place in his office. They would never forget the wonderful time they had had, she wrote, or their dear friends up North. The pity of it was that they couldn't get on the train and come back whenever they felt like it, which was often. Since her return home, she had been as busy as a cat in a fish store. Cousin Alice Light, who lived in Glen Falls, had come with the children, twins. Little Alice very bright for her age, and the boy into everything the minute his mother's back was turned. And then old Mrs. Maltby died before Mrs. Potter had a chance to ask her for the recipe for making hedge-apple jam, and Mrs. Potter, though no kin to the Maltbys, had taken charge, made all the arrangements for the funeral, buried the dead and entertained the living. After the funeral the relatives came back to the house and fought over the furniture, and the little drop-leaf table that was supposed to go to Mrs. Potter went to one of the daughters-in-law instead.

Mrs. Potter missed the yellow bedroom of the house on Elm Street—as girls she and her sister always had that colour. And Mr. Potter had bought an automobile, a Rambler, and was learning to drive. Randolph had been offered a job in the bank but couldn't decide whether to take it or not. His father wanted him to, but Randolph wasn't sure that he'd like working behind a cage and taking money from all kinds of people. Besides, he would have to live away from home, and naturally he'd rather be with his family. The weather was still warm, like the middle of summer. They had started picking cotton that week. . . .

The letter contained no mention of Nora, not even in the postscript. Reading the letter, one would almost have thought that Mrs. Potter had no daughter, or else that she was afraid. In places where witchcraft is still practised, people are extremely careful about disposing of hairs that they find in combs, and of finger-nail parings. Possibly some such instinctive or superstitious caution kept Mrs. Potter from writing Nora's name.

The postman also left in the mailbox of the house on Elm Street a souvenir of the Mardi Gras, addressed to Miss Abbey King. Across the bottom of the long narrow strip of coloured pictures—horse-drawn floats, boats and thrones, gigantic spider-webs, witches' caverns, cloud-capped palaces, and caves under the sea—Randolph had scrawled *Do you remember me?* which was foolish and unnecessary, since Ab in her nightly prayers remembered everybody.

With these samples of their highly characteristic handwriting, the Potters proved that they had gone home, that they were now safely disposed of in the shadowy untroublesome country of absent friends and relations, but Austin King found himself wondering why Mr. Potter, with his affairs in such an unsettled state, had bought an expensive automobile; why Randolph hadn't jumped at the chance of a job in the bank; why Nora never came to see them. Occasionally he saw her, in the side yard or on the porch of the house next door, and waved to her and Nora waved back. Instead of stopping to talk to her, he went on into the house, carrying with him the image of a startled face, the eyes wide open, the expression doubtful, as if Nora were not certain that he was waving at her.

5

After a long summer of green, the prairie towns have their brief season of colour. The leaves on the trees begin to turn—first a branch, then a tree, then a whole street of trees, like middle-aged people falling in love. The maples turn bright orange or scarlet, the elms a pale poetic yellow, and before the colour has reached its height, the leaves begin to detach themselves, to drift down. Lawns have to be raked, and then raked again. Children play in leaf houses, and leaf fires smouldering in gutters change the odour of the air. The sun finds a way through bare branches to make new patterns of light and shade. The daytime, between nine o'clock in the morning and two in the afternoon, is like summer; but after the evening meal, women sitting in porch rockers send this or that child into the house for a shawl and are themselves driven indoors by the dark a few minutes later. The lawn mowers stand idle, frost stills the katydids and puts an end to the asters, and sadly, a little at a time, people get used to the idea of winter.

During the long September evenings, Austin King found time to collect the family snapshots and paste them in a big black scrapbook. This scrapbook was part of a set, of the great American encyclopædia of sentimental occasions, family gatherings, and stages in the growth of children. The volumes are not arranged alphabetically and it doesn't matter very much which one you open, since each of the million or so volumes is likely to contain, among other things,

a picture of a statue in a park
of children playing in the sand at the seashore
of the horses waiting at the paddock gate
of the float that won first prize
of the new house before the roof was finished
of a winding mountain road
of Sunset Hill, of Mirror Lake
of a nurse wheeling a baby carriage
of a tree leaning far out over the bank of a creek
of the tennis court when there was no one on it.
of two families seated along the steps of a band pavilion
of the dead rattlesnake

of a sign reading Babylon 2 miles
of a row of rocking chairs on a hotel veranda
of the view from the ridge
of girls with young men they did not marry
of a picnic by the side of the road
of a camping wagon
of the cat that did not stay to have its picture taken
of a boy holding his bicycle
of summer cottages on a small inland lake
of the dog that was run over
of the little boy in a pony cart, with a formal flower bed and the stone gates of the asylum in the background
of a man with a string of fish
of the graduation class
of the oak tree in the garden
of the children wading with their clothes pulled up to their thighs
of a parade
of a path shovelled through deep snow
of a man aiming a rifle
of a boy walking on his hands
of a Christmas tree taken when the needles were beginning to fall off
of Starved Rock
of two children in a swing
of the party stepping into a gasoline launch
of the bride and groom with their arms around each other
of the son in uniform, standing beside the back steps, on a day when the light was not right for taking kodak pictures
of the pergola
of a fancy-dress party
of the river bank at flood level

Here and there, among so much that is familiar and obvious, you suddenly come upon a scene that cries out for explanation—four women seated around a picnic cloth and gazing calmly at a young man who is also seated and holding what appears to be a revolver in his right hand; or a picture with the centre torn out of it, leaving an oval-shaped hole surrounded by porch railing, lawn, trees, a fragment of a woman's skirt, and the sky. If there are clues in the form of writing: *Just after smash upon mountain* or *The Hermitage* 1910, they are usually unsatisfactory. You never learn what smash-up on what mountain or where the hermitage is. There is seldom any pretence that the subjects were doing anything but having their pictures taken. The scenes are necessarily static, and in the faces there is that strange absence of tension that exists in all casual photographs taken before the first World War. One's immediate impression, looking through old photograph albums, is likely to be *Why there has been no change, no change since childhood.* And then *But how they give themselves away!* And *Who held the camera?* is a question that recurs again and again; what person voluntarily absented himself from the record in order to preserve for posterity the image he saw through the small glass square on the side of the camera?

Austin King worked over the scrapbook at his desk in the study, with his back to the fireplace. His careful hand moved from the pastepot to the cloth, from the cloth to the box of curling, unmounted snapshots. The logs that had been drying out all summer on the woodpile snapped and shuddered and were consumed quickly by the yellow flames and fell apart. When he looked up, he saw the lighted room and himself reflected in the window-panes against the darkness outside. If Martha had been there, she would have drawn the curtains, but she had taken to going upstairs soon after dinner.

If you are of a certain temperament, patient and methodical, pasting snapshots into an album or any work that is simple and done mostly with the hands is pleasant, but it has one important drawback; it leaves the mind free and open to its own dubious devices. Sometimes, to escape from or clarify his own thoughts, Austin King screwed the lid on the pastepot, got up from his desk, and began to walk back and forth in front of the fireplace. He walked from the door that led to the hall (where he turned) to the door that led to the dining-room (where he turned again). Occasionally, while the minute hand and the hour hand of the Dresden china clock on the mantelpiece moved slowly towards bedtime, the classic drama in the fireplace was interrupted by some irrelevant stage business—a door creaking somewhere in the back part of the house, a ghost on the stairs.

Before Austin King could go up to bed there were a number of things that, night after night, had to be done. He stood the logs on end in the study fireplace so they wouldn't burn away before morning. He tried the lock on the kitchen door. He opened the door in the pantry, went down the unsafe cellar stairs, and banked the furnace fire. Some of these precautions were necessary (Rachel sometimes forgot to lock herself out, and the kitchen door had once or twice blown open in the night); some had a strange ritualistic quality. No one had been in the living-room all day but he looked to make sure that the damper in the living-room fireplace was closed. He glanced out of the dining-room window at the thermometer, which had not changed perceptibly since he looked at it two hours before. He went around turning off certain radiators and turning others on, night after night. These acts were somehow precautions against something—the presence on the stairs, possibly; or the enemy who, when Austin opened the front door before locking it, was never there.

6

In the upstairs hall of the Beaches' house, under a combination gas and electric light fixture, there was a large steel engraving of an old woman selling apples. In a gilt frame that was ornately carved and cracked, it had outlived by many years the sentimental age that inspired such pictures. The old woman had snow-white hair, square steel-rimmed spectacles, and an expression that was a nice blending of natural kindness and the determination to be kind. There were three children in the picture. The well-dressed boy and girl on the old woman's left had a marked family resemblance. A china doll hung dangling from the little girl's right hand and she had already taken a bite out of her apple. The little boy was apparently saving his until a burning question had been decided. Facing the brother and sister a barefoot boy with ragged clothing searched deep in his trousers pocket for a penny. The barefoot boy was the centre and whole point of the picture—his rapt eyes, his expression conveying a mixture of hope and fear. It was evident that he could expect no financial assistance from the well-dressed children. Either there was a penny in that or some other pocket, or else he would get no apple from the old woman with the square spectacles. When Mrs. Beach was a little girl, she had often had trouble getting past this picture, and a voice (now long dead) had to remind her that she had been sent in quest of a gold thimble or a spool of thread.

Nora was gazing at the picture one rainy afternoon when a voice called from the foot of the stairs. From her room at the end of the hall, Mrs. Beach called back, "Is that you, Martha? Come on up."

Unable to move, Nora heard the footsteps mounting and at the last moment, panic set her free and she vanished into her own room. Martha King, having seen the flash of skirts and the door closing, said to herself, Then she *is* trying to avoid me.

"In my room," Mrs. Beach called, and Martha went on down the hall.

Mrs. Beach was seated at her sewing table fitting together the complicated pieces of a pink and white and green quilt.

The big double bed, which dominated the room, was made up and the pillows tucked into a round hollow bolster. The rest of the room was in such disorder as one might expect if the occupant were packing for a long sea voyage, but Mrs. Beach had merely been straightening her bureau drawers. The chairs were piled with odds and ends whose place in the grand scheme of things she had not yet decided upon.

"Just move that pile of shirtwaists," she said, with a wave of her stork-handled scissors. "I'd rather you didn't sit on the bed."

"I can't stay," Martha said.

"You always say that, and it's not polite. If you come intending to leave right away, you might as well not come at all. Have you heard from Mrs. Potter?"

Martha nodded.

"I think it's so strange that she doesn't write to me," Mrs. Beach said, "with Nora staying in our house. If Alice or Lucy were staying with the Potters I'd certainly feel that it was my duty to write and show my appreciation, but I gather that Nora and her mother are not very close. That may be why she doesn't bother to put herself out, where Nora is concerned. Now that I think of it, it seems to me that you might have done more for Nora than you have, these past weeks. Or would you have preferred that she went home with her family?"

In order to carry on an amicable conversation with Mrs. Beach, most people found it necessary to let a great many of her remarks pass unchallenged. Far from being grateful because they had come to see her, she usually found pleasure in pointing out to them how long it had been since their last visit. She also asked questions that were inoffensive in themselves but that steered the conversation inexorably around to matters that were sometimes delicate and sometimes none of Mrs. Beach's business.

"I've had only one letter from her," Martha said. "She

asked to be remembered to you. Austin hears from Mr. Potter."

"I must say she seemed very fond of us all when she was here, but out of sight, out of mind, apparently. This is the wild rose pattern." Mrs. Beach held the quilt out for Martha to admire. "I've made one for Lucy and now I'm making one for Alice. I want them to have something to remember me by when I'm gone."

"It's lovely," Martha said. "But I wish you wouldn't talk of dying on a gloomy day like this."

"After you reach sixty," Mrs. Beach said, "you don't expect to be around forever. I don't know that I even want to be. The world was a much nicer place when I was a girl. Good breeding and good manners counted for something. My mother began her married life with her own carriage and a large staff of servants. In the summer we went to . . ."

Mrs. Beach kept Martha for three-quarters of an hour, talking about the vanished world of her girlhood and about the kindergarten, and then she said, "Please don't think I'm driving you away, my dear, but if I don't have my afternoon rest——"

"If you wanted to lie down," Martha said, rising, "why have you been keeping me here? I tried to leave three times in the last fifteen minutes, and each time you——"

"Don't be so touchy," Mrs. Beach said, and smiled. Her smiles were rare, in any case, and seldom as amused or as genuinely friendly as this one was. "All old people have their failings," she said. "Stop and see the girls on your way out. They'll be hurt if you don't."

The Beach girls were on the glassed-in back porch, painting little wooden chairs. They had spread newspapers over the floor but there was no way they could avoid getting paint on themselves. Lucy had a streak of robin's-egg blue running through her hair where she had touched her head in a gesture of weariness. Their hands and aprons were covered with paint.

"Be careful and don't brush against anything!" she said when Martha appeared in the kitchen doorway.

"They're for the kindergarten? How beautiful!" Martha said. "And what a lot of work!"

"There's no end to it," Lucy said. "If I'd known what we were letting ourselves in for——"

"Mother's upstairs," Alice said.

"I've just been up to see her," Martha said, "but I really came over to talk to you. About Ab, I mean. I haven't decided definitely whether to send her to kindergarten or not. She's so young."

"You mustn't let our friendship influence you," Lucy said.

"Oh I wouldn't," Martha said. "If I don't send her, I know you'll understand. When are you going to start?"

"The first week in October, if everything is ready by that time," Lucy said. "We're having trouble with the tables. Mr. Moseby keeps promising them by a certain date, and then they're never ready. It's so discouraging."

They discussed at some length whether Ab would be happy in kindergarten.

"She doesn't want to be anywhere unless I'm there too," Martha said. "Also, I don't want to be separated from her. I really feel very queer about it, but I suppose it will pass. I can't go on like this, feeling anxious about everything. But if she cries——"

"She won't cry," Lucy said. "At the Montessori School in Rome——"

"Look out for your dress!" Alice cried, too late, as Martha backed against one of the freshly painted chairs.

The blue smudge came out with a little turpentine, and Alice went as far as the front door with Martha King, and then turned towards the stairs. Mrs. Beach was lying on her bed with her eyes closed, but as Alice started to tiptoe from the room, she said, "Well, *is* she or isn't she going to send Ab to kindergarten? I never saw Martha so undecided about anything before."

"She's going to think it over," Alice said.

"This shilly-shallying isn't like her," Mrs. Beach said, opening her eyes. "I think she's going to have another baby."

Mrs. Beach had a talent for divination. With the aid of a soiled pack of fortune-telling cards she sometimes correctly foretold the future, and she could often guess at a glance what was inside a wrapped package or in the back of someone's mind. If this was perhaps nothing but acute observation arriving at the truth by way of shortcuts and back alleys, it never ceased to confound and confuse her daughters, and Mrs. Beach had absolute faith in her own intuitive powers.

"If she were going to have a baby, wouldn't it show?" Alice asked, aware that, while they were talking, Nora had come into the room.

"Not necessarily," Mrs. Beach said. "For Austin's sake, I hope it's a boy. He's so kind and considerate of other people. I wish there were only more like him."

This was not her usual opinion of Austin King, and Alice recognized that her mother was in a special mood—the one where she didn't like to hear anybody criticized.

Out of contrariness, as she knelt down and began picking up scraps of material from the rug, Alice said, "Sometimes I wonder about him. I mean, if he is as nice as he seems. Because if he is that way, why does Martha get so furious with him?"

"I've never seen the slightest trace of irritability in Martha," Mrs. Beach said. "Vague, yes, and unable to make up her mind. But not irritable."

"I've seen her ready to pick up an axe and hit him over the head with it," Alice said.

"You're imagining things," Mrs. Beach said. "May, June, July, August, September——"

"No," Alice said, and realized how still Nora was. Throughout the conversation, she hadn't said a word. And yet Nora had lived in the Kings' house for a month and must have some opinion on the subject of Austin King. He was her foster-cousin, of course, and with some people that would be enough to prevent them from discussing him. But Nora talked about her own mother and father and brother without the least reticence, and if she didn't join in the conversation about Austin, it couldn't be because of any family scruples, but only because she didn't want to say what she thought.

As Alice Beach reached toward a pin, an idea came into her mind that startled and then frightened her. She glanced hurriedly around to see whether her mother or Nora had read her thoughts.

"—October, November, December, January," Mrs. Beach said. "I wouldn't be at all surprised if the baby came in January."

7

It wasn't that Ab didn't want to go to kindergarten. She woke that morning in a warm nest of bedclothes, and when her mother came into the room and said, "Today is the day," Ab felt both proud and singled out. But there was something she didn't understand, that might have been explained to her and wasn't, and disaster is often merely an event that you don't have a chance to get used to before it happens.

"Did you go to kindergarten?" she asked as she stepped into the underwear that her mother held out for her.

"No," Martha said. "There wasn't any kindergarten when I was a little girl."

"Did Daddy go to kindergarten?"

"No."

"Did Rachel?"

"No, Rachel didn't go to kindergarten either. Just you."

Ab submitted to the washrag and soap with less than the usual amount of complaints, and she didn't dally over her breakfast. As soon as she had finished her milk, she asked to be excused and slid down from her high chair. The house was full of clocks, but they were of no earthly use to her. She could go to her mother and say, "What time is it?" and her mother would glance at the china clock on the mantelpiece in the study and say, "Twenty minutes to two," or her father would put down his newspaper and extract his gold watch from his vest pocket, open the case, and announce that it was a quarter after seven; but such statements are never really enlightening. There was no way of telling beforehand when anything was going to happen. So far as Ab could discover, it happened when the grown people decided that the time had come for it to happen.

She played, that morning, within sight and hearing of her mother, who lingered at the breakfast table, her hair piled in a loose knot on top of her head, and the sleeves of her negligee pinned above the elbows. At quarter to nine the doorbell rang. When her mother opened the door, Ab saw Nora Potter with a little boy and two little girls.

"Oh, hello," Martha King said. "I didn't expect you quite so early."

Ab withdrew behind her mother's skirts. Since they had come too early, they would have to sit down in the living-room and wait until her mother was dressed.

Martha went to the long closet under the stairs and a moment later emerged with Ab's blue coat and bonnet in her hand, and even then Ab was unprepared for the shock that followed—the shock of hearing her mother say, "Now be a good girl, won't you?" Her mother must know that she wouldn't think of going to kindergarten without her. It was out of the question.

"I'm not going," Ab announced firmly.

"But we talked about it, and you decided you wanted to go," Martha said.

"I don't want to any more," Ab said, successfully preventing her right arm from being forced into the right sleeve of the coat.

"Abbey, please don't make a scene. You know you're going to kindergarten. It's all decided. Now stand still and let me put your coat on."

"I don't want to put my coat on."

"You must. You can't go through life changing your mind every five minutes and keeping people waiting."

"What will all these little girls and boys think of you?" Nora said.

Ab saw Nora coming nearer and threw herself at her mother's knees, clutching them, clasping her hands around her mother's skirts.

"I'm afraid you'll have to carry her, Nora."

To Ab's unbelieving horror, arms took hold of her and tore her away from her mother (Madame Montessori was far away in Rome) and after that, nothing was real or made the slightest sense; not her mother's tears, not the shamed look on the faces of the other children, nor the detached sound of her own screaming.

The kindergarten rooms were three-quarters of a mile from the house on Elm Street, and Ab was carried, kicking and screaming and fighting for breath to scream again, the whole way. People who passed the strange procession turned and looked back and wondered if they ought to interfere. Nobody did. The frightened screaming ("I want my mother! I want my mother!") sounded like grief—heart-rending, impersonal; grief for the world and all who are obliged to live in it.

8

The porchlight went on, directly overhead, and Dr. Danforth opened the door. "Come in, come in, my boy. How are you? I was just saying to Ella——"

"You aren't busy?" Austin asked, as he stepped over the threshold.

"I didn't get that?"

Austin shouted his question.

"Busy?" Dr. Danforth repeated in the low even voice of the deaf. "What would I be busy about at this time of night? Let me take your hat. Always glad to see you."

The Danforths' house had been built by Mrs. Danforth's father at the height of his material prosperity. Mr. Morris had been a banker and also something of a philanthropist. When his bank failed on "Black Friday", he turned everything he had over to his creditors and eventually got back this house and a fraction of his once considerable means so that his family were not in want. For lack of a better word, people who came to the house for the first time usually said "Oh, what a beautiful house!" by which they meant that it was dark, cavelike, and quiet; that it invited day-dreaming; that it belonged to the past. The rooms were large and opened out of one another, and the varnished cherry woodwork had the gleam of dark red marble. The dark-green walls of the dining-room were stencilled with white peacocks above the dado, and in the music room there were cupids and garlands of pink roses. These long-faded murals had been painted by an itinerant Italian artist whose sick wife, debts, and dirty children had touched old Mrs. Morris' always susceptible heart.

The parlour fireplace was of molasses-brown tile, with mirrors set into the complicated Victorian mantelpiece. On the mantelshelf there was a brass clock with the works visible through panes of thick bevelled glass, and several family photographs. Over the sofa there was a huge oil painting of a storm at sea and a Byronic shipwreck. Mrs. Danforth's chair was beside the heavy carved table where the lamp-light would shine on her needlework. The lamp-shade was of hammered brass, four-sided, with pin-points of light shining through in the design of some long-tailed bird —the phoenix perhaps. Dr. Danforth's chair was beside the sofa. The light that shone on his newspaper came from a mahogany floor lamp with a red silk shade. In front of the other window was a large silvered gazing globe that belonged in a garden but had found its way, pedestal and all, into the Danforths' parlour. Though strange in its context and beautiful in itself, the gazing ball was not pleasant to look into, reflecting all people as ugly and deformed.

The room offered no clue to what the Danforths had been doing when the doorbell rang. There was no open book, no workbasket, no cardtable laid out for solitaire. The big lump of cannel coal in the grate was unlit. Though Dr. and Mrs. Danforth were pleased to see Austin King, there was nothing in their manner to indicate that he had rescued them from an empty evening or from each other.

"How is Martha?"

"Tired out. She went upstairs after supper," Austin said and had to repeat this statement louder for Dr. Danforth's benefit.

"Nothing serious?" Dr. Danforth asked.

"Fall house-cleaning," Austin said.

"She mustn't overdo," Dr. Danforth said gravely. "I have a horse downtown that I'm anxious to have you see. A sorrel, five-gaited and gentle as they come."

"That's all he can talk about," Mrs. Danforth said. "All

through supper he talked about nothing but that horse. I don't wonder people never come to see us."

"We've been meaning to come over," Austin said, "but——"

"You might want to get him for Martha. Prince Edward is too big for a woman to handle. This horse would be just right for her."

"Except that he shies occasionally," Mrs. Danforth said.

"What's that?" Dr. Danforth asked.

"I say Martha doesn't want a horse that shies," Mrs. Danforth said placidly.

"I think I can cure him of that. He wasn't ridden properly in the beginning. You can have him for just what I paid for him."

"I don't know that I can afford to buy another horse just now," Austin said. "But I'd like to see him."

"You come around tomorrow sometime," Dr. Danforth said, nodding.

Austin moved forward until he was sitting on the edge of the sofa. "I brought these over to show you," he said, indicating the sheaf of letters in his lap. "Maybe it's nothing to be worried about, but I'd like your advice."

"Why don't you go in the den where you won't be disturbed?" Mrs. Danforth said. Her husband was looking at Austin and didn't know that she had spoken. She waited until he turned to her again and then repeated the suggestion as if for the first time.

"Come along, my boy," Dr. Danforth said.

"If you don't mind?" Austin said to Mrs. Danforth.

Mrs. Danforth smiled at him and said "Not at all."

Though Dr. Danforth had been a part of this household for twenty years, the den was in no way changed from the room it had been when Mrs. Danforth's father was alive. He found his spectacle case, spread Austin's letters out in front of him on the big roll-topped desk, and began to read.

After a while the swivel chair swung around so that Dr. Danforth's back was to the litter of papers—deeds, documents, the correspondence between Austin and the bank in Howard's Landing, between Austin and Mr. Potter. He rubbed his nose thoughtfully with one finger, started to speak, and then changed his mind. At last he said, "I can't advise you, my boy. You'd better talk to someone who knows something about cotton farming. Fred Meister was down there a few years ago. Why don't you go talk to him?"

"But does it seem all right to you, just on the face of it?" Austin asked.

"No, I can't say that it does. The indebtedness is larger than we were given to understand. I only had that one talk with him about it, and I don't hear all that people say, so maybe——"

"It's considerably larger," Austin interrupted.

"Did he say anything about a second mortgage?"

Austin shook his head. "That only came out after I began writing to the bank. Do you think he's dishonest? He didn't seem like that kind of a man when he was here. He seemed—you knew that Mr. Potter and my father were raised together? In some ways he reminds me——"

"I never saw the Judge go out of his way to make anybody like him, but I know what you mean," Dr. Danforth said. "I wouldn't say that Mr. Potter was dishonest. When I'm trading with a man I'm supposed to get the better of him, and he's supposed to get the better of me."

"But this isn't horse trading."

"I was just giving that as an example." Dr. Danforth turned back to the desk and began to read the letters again, moving his lips silently and occasionally shaking his head.

"Has Judge Fairchild seen this letter?" he asked, finally.

Austin got up and came over to the desk. "No," he said, looking down over Dr. Danforth's shoulder. "That one just came today."

"Show it to him. It could be that there is something funny going on between Mr. Potter and the bank. I'd show him everything."

"Wouldn't it be better to wait?" Austin asked.

"Bring it all out into the open," Dr. Danforth said. "It's going to end up there sooner or later anyway, and you'll be doing yourself and everybody else a favour by hurrying the thing along."

Mrs. Danforth opened a drawer of the parlour table and took out her crocheting. In the carved furniture all around her there was a great variety of natural forms—flowers, grasses, ferns, leaves, acorns, occasionally a butterfly or a grasshopper or some small animal like a lizard or a frog. Before he became a banker, Mrs. Danforth's father had taught woodcarving at Hampton Institute, and after his death, as a kind of legacy, he had left everywhere in the house carved tables, chairs, footstools, firescreens, and chests, his version of the fable of Creation. Mrs. Danforth, being of a more abstract turn of mind, was content with a six-pointed star. Though she had crocheted hundreds of white table mats in the previous eighteen years, and scattered them through a dozen households, she never varied from this one design.

The sound of the men's voices, low and serious, came to her from the open door of the den. After a few minutes she got up and went through the house, turning on lights in the dining-room, the pantry, and the kitchen. When she had unlocked and opened the back door there was a light pattering of animal footsteps and a stiff-legged, shaggy black dog came loping out of the darkness and up onto the porch.

"Well, Hamlet," she asked, "did you decide it was time to come home?"

The dog stretched in front of her, as if he were making an exaggerated bow, followed her into the house and back through the kitchen, the pantry, and the dining-room, to the parlour, where he turned around three times and subsided on the rug at her feet.

When he sighed deeply she peered down at him over her glasses and said, "Nobody knows what it means to be a very old dog, do they?"

He rolled his eyes up at her, thumped his tail, and sighed again, a shipwrecked creature that had, against all hope and expectation, found his way to shore.

9

Dr. Danforth had begun to lose his hearing when he was a very young man. One by one the minute sounds—the clock ticking, the click of a fingernail, the scrape of a cup in its saucer, all buzzing, droning, hammering, sawing, singing, all echoes and reverberations, the whole auditory perspective vanished from his consciousness without his knowing that this had happened. He had to ask people more and more frequently to repeat what they said to him, and was annoyed with them for mumbling. At the same time his own voice was pitched lower and lower so that people had trouble catching what he himself said, though he was under the impression that he spoke distinctly. His naturally kind, calm face was screwed up in a permanent grimace by the effort to understand what was going on around him, until one day he saw a horse stomp and realized that the hush he lived in hadn't in any way been impaired. He went out into the street and stood there, listening. The sounds that he knew must be there, as solid and undeniable as the courthouse itself, failed him. He saw movement, people passing on the sidewalks, carriages in the street, clouds in the sky, but they made no sound. And when old man Barnes came up to him and began to shout in his ear, he turned abruptly and went back into the darkness of the stable, a stranger to himself, and from that day on, a friend to no one.

His deafness had the effect of making the world seem a larger place, the streets wider, the buildings farther apart, the sky vast again, the way it had seemed to be when he was a country boy. It also showed him that every man was a liar, and he himself—the eternal horse trader—was of course the greatest, the most complete liar of them all.

The truth is necessarily partial. Every vision of completeness is a distortion in one way or another, whether it springs from sickness or sanctity. But in the visions of saints there are voices that speak reassuringly of the cloud of Unknowing. Dr. Danforth did not even hear the occasional good that people spoke of him. When they came to the livery stable to hire a carriage, he directed them to Snowball McHenry, the Negro stableboy, and betrayed himself only in the way that his hands petted and stroked and captured the heart of every dumb animal that came near them. In time he learned to use his infirmity to advantage, reading lips when he wanted to understand, and when it served his purpose not to understand, making people repeat, until in the exasperation of continual shouting, they gave the game away.

That's Dr. Danforth, deaf as a post but nobody ever got the better of him in a horse trade. . . . Lives all alone, never goes anywhere or sees anybody. . . . Doc's a fine man. The trouble is, he won't let anybody do anything for him. His father was like that towards the end of his life. . . .

So, charitably, Dr. Danforth was assigned a place; he became a town character, like the Orthwein boy, who was born without a soft palate, and Mrs. Jouette, so given to litigation with the members of her own family.

Dr. Danforth knew everything that went on in Draperville but from a distance, from the greatest distance of all, which is the outside. Ten years passed without its ever occurring to him that he needed a new suit of clothes. He was often seen with a stubble on his chin. He didn't know or care how he looked. On his way home to the boarding-house on Hudson Street, he stepped over little girls who were too engrossed in their sidewalk games to realize that they were in anybody's way; saw them leave their coloured chalk, their jacks and skipropes and rubber balls, and lose themselves in the mirror of some upstairs bedroom, just as he himself was lost in a private hush; saw the inevitable change from adolescents to men and women who told lies about each other, about themselves, and about the true nature of the world they lived in, never for a moment admitting what he and everybody else knew to be a fact—that the apple had gone bad a long time ago, and slugs had eaten the rose, that the hay had mildewed in the barn, and the last hope of fair dealing was lost in third-grade arithmetic.

An incomplete vision may last for generations, but anything complete, like any act of will, is bound to crack in a much shorter time. With Dr. Danforth the change came when he began to understand people, unconsciously, by observation and instinct, as he understood animals. The light in the human eye, the sudden change of colouring under surprise and emotion, the stiffness around the mouth, the movement of the hands were all, he discovered, essentially truthful; as if, in those moments when people were most anxious to deceive, they were also desperately eager to convey to him, to anybody, that they were lying. Lying very plausibly—the eye, the skin, the mouth, the hands said—but lying nevertheless, and with no real desire to be believed. *The motive is money*, said the eye. *Ambition*, confessed the nervous hands. *Fear*, said the mottled skin. *Envy*, said the hungry mouth.

As for his own lies, which had once filled him with horror and pride, he saw that he was not even in a class with

Snowball, who lied like an artist, in several dimensions, for pleasure sometimes, sometimes out of boredom, now maliciously, now sincerely out of a confused sense of fact. Since Dr. Danforth loved Snowball, he had to believe everything that the Negro said—tentatively, provisionally, never trying to pin him down, because one lie exposed always gave rise to another, and Snowball himself was apparently incapable of grasping the idea, let alone the ideal, of truth.

Into this crack, bit by bit, enough of the apocalyptic vision disappeared so that when Ella Morris came into the stable one Decoration Day, to hire a rig, he was ready for her. She was then past thirty; a very homely, very intelligent woman with a queer habit of twisting her head to one side when she talked to people and considering them with detachment, with an unsentimental curiosity. Dr. Danforth, as a young man, had known her father and used to call on Mr. Morris sometimes when he needed advice. Ella wanted a carriage to drive her mother out to the cemetery. She didn't shout at him as people so often did. She didn't even talk slowly, but in a perfectly normal voice asked, "Why don't you ever come and see us?"

He thought at first that he must have misunderstood her, but she seemed to be waiting for an answer, so he said, "I don't go anywhere. People don't like to talk to a deaf person."

"You can understand me, can't you?" she asked, twisting her head and looking at him.

He nodded.

"Mother would be very pleased if you came to see her," Ella Morris said. "She often speaks of you."

For two days he tried to make up his mind what to do. Then he went out and bought a new suit, a new white shirt, and a new tie and hat, and that evening he went to call on the Morrises. The old lady talked to him about her dead husband. When Dr. Danforth said what a fine man he was, she said, "Isn't it strange, nobody misses him. All the people that knew him, and all the people he helped. It's just as if he had never lived. I don't know how people can forget so quickly."

"They don't forget," he said. "It's just that they have so much else on their minds."

Ella sat quietly, listening, following the conversation. But the questioning look, the look of reservation, or perhaps of unkind curiosity was not there. She seemed, in some way, to have made up her mind about him.

They talked about the old days for a while and when he got up to go, the old lady said, "I hope you'll come again," and took his hand and looked deeply into his eyes, trying to see, apparently, whether he really did remember her husband.

When Ella went to the door with him, he was afraid that she was going to comment sarcastically about his new suit, but all she said was, "I hope Mother didn't tire you. She lives a great deal in the past."

He went to see the Morrises again, and then again, and one night they asked him to go to a church supper with them. He was afraid to go, but he went, nevertheless, and because he was with the Morrises, people seemed to treat him differently. They went out of their way to draw him into conversation, and he wasn't shy. He talked to people, with his eyes turning occasionally towards Ella Morris, and on the way home that night a great wave came over him of happiness and hope. Sitting on the front porch, after the old lady had excused herself and gone indoors to escape the night air, Ella asked him to marry her. It was so strange, not being able to hear the words and yet knowing, by his own wildly beating heart, that they had been said. He was frightened at what she had done and he thought, for a second, that the only thing left for him to do was to pick up his new hat and run, but he couldn't even do that, because Ella was still talking, in that inaudible voice, her eyes focused on the porch railing, and her face so beautiful with trouble that he realized he couldn't go; that unless he took her in his arms, something terrible would happen.

"If you're sure," he said; but that was a long time later, and it was all he ever said.

From that night everything was different for him. He wasn't on the outside any more, looking at lighted windows. He was sitting down at the table in the dining-room or beside the parlour lamp. He didn't walk down the street and nod to people on their front porches, on summer evenings. He had a porch to sit on, a place where he was expected.

IO

"I saw you coming out of the bank," Nora said, "but you didn't see me."

"Why didn't you stop me?" Austin asked. He had just come through the revolving door of the post office, and the sun was shining directly in his eyes.

"You were lost in thought," Nora said.

"Was I?" Austin said. Her manner with him was friendly and natural—or almost natural—but since her visit with Martha, Nora hadn't come either to the house or to the office. During the past week he had seen her only once, in the side yard of the house next door. Though he was glad to see her now, if he had had a chance to choose where they met, it would not have been in so public a place as the steps of the post office. He shaded his eyes from the glare and said, "What do you hear from your family?"

"They're fine," Nora said. "Pa had an accident with the new automobile, but it wasn't so very serious. He ran over a culvert and bent the front axle, I think it was, and had to be towed into Howard's Landing. But it's all right now. And

Brother has a new hunting dog, and they've had lots of company." She moved up one step in order to be on a level with him. "Mrs. Beach is complaining because you and Cousin Martha never come to see us."

"We haven't gone anywhere," Austin said. "Martha hasn't felt up to it. You know we're——"

"Yes, I know," Nora said. "I'm very happy for you. I——" She hesitated as a man came up the steps towards them.

"I just sold my corn, Austin," the man said.

"Good time to sell," Austin said, nodding, and waited until Ray Murphy had disappeared into the post office. Then he said, "Are you getting along all right, Nora?"

"Yes," Nora said. "You don't have to worry about me any more. I don't know where I got the courage to speak to you as I did that day, but it must have been from you. Because even now as I look back on it and realize what an unthinkable thing I have done, somehow I'm not ashamed or humiliated. So it must be because of you."

"There's no reason for you to feel ashamed."

"I hope you've forgotten all I said to you, because I have. I've put it out of my mind forever. It was just something that at the time seemed very real but wasn't actually, and I'm very grateful to you for talking to me the way you did, because some men—but you aren't like that, and so there's no use in my going into it. I wasn't in love with you—or if I was, I'm not any more. It's just like you said. I'll always know that I can come to you if I'm ever in trouble, and you'll do everything in your power to help me, and for that reason I'm not entirely sorry. But you mustn't worry any more about me because there's nothing to worry about."

The post-office door opened and Nora went right on talking. "The chief thing I want to say to you is how truly grateful to you I am, and how sorry I am that you should ever have become involved enough to feel that you . . ."

If Ray Murphy was surprised to see them still standing there, his face did not show it. He nodded at Austin and went on down the steps and crossed the street.

"... Sometimes I feel like writing to Cousin Martha," Nora said, "and telling her how kind you were to me, and how you put me on the right track."

"I don't believe I'd do that, if I were you."

"Oh I wouldn't dream of writing to her!" Nora exclaimed. "She might not understand and I wouldn't want to cause you or her a moment's unhappiness. It's just that she has so much—she has you and little Abbey and that beautiful house and all—and I feel like telling her how much she has to be thankful for. But she knows, of course. There's no need to tell her things that she already knows."

"No," Austin agreed. He saw Al Sterns coming across the courthouse lawn and, turning to Nora, said, "Would you like to come up to the office and talk to me there?"

"Don't you see I can't come up to your office and talk to you?" Nora said. "Of course I want to, but what is the good? I'd just rattle on and on. If I could only be still or talk sensibly, but I can't do either. I know I'm an emotional person. I'm aware of all these things. But if you only knew how badly I want you to like me and approve of me!"

"I do like and approve of you," Austin said. Al Sterns waited for a wagon to pass and then started across the street towards the post-office.

"I want desperately to be friends with you, but I don't know how. It's not your fault. You are doing everything possible to make things easy for me, but even thinking about going to your office with you makes me want to run miles away, because I know I'd only make a fool of myself. Sometimes when I haven't seen you for several days I think 'Maybe he isn't like that. Now think. How could you remember exactly what he looks like? Part of it is in your head.' But then I see you coming up the walk and you are just as I remember you, of course. This is my compensation for being all mixed up in general—that I have certain things—faces, mannerisms, and so forth, so impressed on my mind that I can never forget them."

"Austin, how's the world treating you?"

"Can't complain, Al. . . . This is my cousin, Miss Potter."

"Pleased to meet you, Miss Potter," Al Sterns said and put out his hand. "Austin, they tell me you——"

"Or even colour them in imagination," Nora said. "They are just as they are."

"I'll drop in and see you later," Al Sterns said, and went on up the steps.

"*You* are just as you are," Nora said. "I think of you all the time, because I can't help doing that. But I don't think of you in any woe-begone way. Just sometimes when I can't find anything to do to keep me busy or at night when I'm falling asleep, I suddenly wonder where you are and what you're doing. And if we do find ourselves face to face, by some accident, the way we are now, I know I'll always have something to say to you, because I think in terms of you. Whenever I see anything that moves me, makes me smile or feel sad, I always think of you. But no one need ever know. I never talk about you, about how wonderful you are, or drag compliments out of people so I can repeat them to you, or make over Ab, or do any of the things girls do when they're hopelessly in love. I won't run in and out of the house on some flimsy pretext, and on the other hand, if I don't come to see you very often, you mustn't think it's because I don't have any interest in you, because I do."

"I understand," Austin said. He had been expecting Al Sterns to come out again, but he saw now that Al had come out of the side entrance and crossed the street in front of the fire station.

"Last night I dreamed about you, and today I can't remember the dream. All I know is that we were at home and that you were going into town with us, and somehow in the dream we went off and left you. . . ."

It was a long involved dream that Nora recaptured, piece by piece, standing on the post-office steps. Though Austin kept his eyes rigidly on her face, he heard very little of it. In his mind he said *Nora, I have work to do. . . . There's somebody waiting in my office. . . .* over and over, hoping that Nora would grasp what he was thinking, by mental telepathy. *I don't want to listen to your dream. . . .*

". . . we were driving through this section of the country," Nora went on. "I can't remember whether this was part of the same dream or another one. Anyway, there were two other people with us. Actually a couple who are not really friends of our family but the man is one of Pa's business associates, with their twelve-year-old son. I can remember distinctly being at your house, Cousin Austin. I don't remember arriving there, having you greet us and so forth, but suddenly in the dream I was leaning against the window-sill with my chin in my hands——"

The Jouettes' shiny black surrey drove up before the post-office. The coloured boy jumped down from the front seat and took old Mrs. Jouette's letter from her.

"—staring at you," Nora said. "The window was closed, which was queer because it was in summer, and you were outdoors watering the lawn, paying absolutely no attention to us at all."

Old Mrs. Jouette, all in shiny black, like the carriage, turned to the sad-faced young girl beside her and said, "Who is that standing on the steps?"

"Austin King."

"It can't be," Mrs. Jouette exclaimed.

"It is all the same," the girl said listlessly. "I don't know who she is, but they were standing there when we drove by before."

"I had the feeling in my dream," Nora said earnestly, "I had the distinct feeling that you had been cordial and polite to everyone but me. I kept staring at you, trying to make you look at me. . . ."

Seeing the old lady's lorgnette trained upon him, Austin lifted his hat and bowed. The bow was returned, but without any accompanying smile of pleasure, and old Mrs. Jouette turned her attention to the courthouse lawn. Lord Nelson, Austin thought, at Trafalgar, in his admiral's frock coat, with all his medals showing. . . .

". . . And you would not," Nora said. "You absolutely refused to look at me. Yet you knew, of course, that I was staring at you for that express reason. . . ."

II

The voices in the study grew louder and Martha King, sitting in the living-room with young Mrs. Ellis, heard Bud Ellis say, "Of course it's not your fault, Austin. All you did was draw up the papers. But naturally, since he was a relative of yours, we assumed——"

"Let's keep to the facts," Judge Fairchild said. Martha got up and dragged her chair nearer the sofa.

"I'm just stupid, I guess," Mary Ellis said. "But it seems harder than anything I've ever tried to do. I sit down with three cook-books in front of me, and they all tell you to do something different, and never the thing you really want to know. If Bud weren't particular about his food, it wouldn't matter, but his mother was a very fine cook and he tells me things she used to make for him, like peach cobbler and upside-down-cake and salt-rising bread. And when I try the same thing, it never turns out right, for some reason. And I have to worry about things that Father Ellis can chew, and sometimes if he doesn't like what we have, he gets up from the table. Bud says he does it just to make a scene, but naturally it makes me feel bad after I've tried to please him. Bud's mother never used a recipe, he says. I don't see how anybody can cook without a recipe. I don't see how you begin, even."

"Probably she learned from *her* mother," Martha said.

"I never had a chance to do that," Mary Ellis said. "My mother was an invalid and we had a series of housekeepers. I was never even allowed in the kitchen."

"It'll come, with practice," Martha said, trying to follow the conversation in the study. "You get so after a while it's second nature. You don't even have to think about it."

"I don't know," Mary Ellis said despairingly. "I don't think I'll ever get to that point. I like to keep house and I like sewing—I make all my own clothes—but I don't think I'll ever learn to cook. It just isn't in me."

"You mustn't feel that way," Martha said. She was struggling with herself to keep from getting up and going into the next room. Austin needed help. She was sure of it. They were solidly against him, appealing to his sense of honour, which was so easy to do if you were Bud Ellis and didn't have any. But if she appeared in the doorway and said *Stop it. I know what you're doing, Bud Ellis, and I won't allow it,* Austin would never forgive her.

"It isn't that I don't have enough time," Mary Ellis was saying. "Although I'm busy, of course. But not like women who have children to think about. Did you have Ab right away?"

"She was born a little over a year after we were married," Martha said.

"I envy you so," Mary Ellis said. "Bud and I have been married nearly a year now and——"

"Just because you don't have a baby the first year doesn't mean anything," Martha said. "I know women who were married ten or twelve years before their first baby came."

"But I don't want to wait that long," Mary Ellis said. "I want to have my children when I'm young. Every time I see a child I want to touch it and hold it on my lap, and it's making Bud very unhappy."

"That goes without saying," Bud Ellis said in a loud voice. "But four thousand dollars is four thousand dollars. And if we'd known what we do now, we'd never have put money into the venture. I'm not accusing *you* of anything, Austin, but I'd like to know one thing: Why did you stay out of it?"

Martha King waited, hoping against hope for the sound of her husband's fist against Bud Ellis' jaw. There was no such sound.

"I try not to feel that way," Mary Ellis said. "I know it's foolish of me to . . ."

Surely he won't explain, Martha said to herself. Oh don't let him stoop to explain.

"I couldn't afford to take the risk," Austin said, in the next room.

"Then you knew it *was* a risk?" Judge Fairchild said, as if he were leaning down from the bench to question the witness on the stand.

Martha King looked across at the Danforths' house, saw that it was dark, and realized that she wouldn't have called Dr. Danforth even if they had been home. It was Austin's battle, and she would have to sit by quietly and let him lose it.

It is a common delusion of gentle people that the world is also gentle, considerate, and fair. Cruelty and suspicion find them eternally unprepared. The surprise, the sense of shock, paralyses them for too long a time after the unprovoked insult has been given. When they finally react and are able to raise their fists in their own defence, it is already too late. *What did he mean by that?* they say, turning to the person nearest them, who witnessed the scene and who might also have been attacked, although he wasn't. There is never any help or enlightenment from the person standing next to them, and so they go on down some endless corridor, reliving the brutal moment, trying vainly to recall the precise words of what must—and yet needn't have been a mortal insult. Should they go back and fight? Or would they only be making a fool of themselves? And then they remember: This is not the first time. Behind this unpleasant incident there is another equally unpleasant (and another and another), the scars of which have long since healed. The old infection breaks open, races through the blood, producing a weakness in the knees, and hands bound, hopeless and heavy at their sides.

"Have you been to a doctor?" Martha King asked.

"Yes. Dr. Spelman. He just told me to get lots of rest and not to get upset by things." Mary Ellis seemed completely unaware of what was going on in the study. When Bud Ellis said, "I think you might have had the decency to tell us, Austin," her face remained unchanged, hopeless, unhappy.

Martha waited and said, "There's something you can try, if you want to. Grace Armstrong told me about it. It's something her mother discovered. Grace says that she would probably never have come into the world otherwise, and neither would her children. If you want to try it——"

"I'll try anything," Mary Ellis said.

"Well, then," Martha said, "this is what you must do. . . ."

12

The people who lived on Elm Street, friends and neighbours, seldom spoke or thought of the Beach girls as separate personalities. It is true that they had a marked family resemblance and that their remarks and timid mannerisms were often interchangeable, but more important, it was generally recognized that they would never marry, and if they were ever to enter the ark with the other animals, two by two, it would have to be in each other's company.

At the kindergarten the children never for a moment confused them. If a child fell down during a game of tag or drop-the-handkerchief and skinned his knee or struck his elbow, it was Alice Beach that he rushed to. She wiped the children's tears away, approved of their weaving, admired and sometimes correctly interpreted the drawings they brought to show her. When they grew tired of playing, she held them in her lap. If they started quarrelling over an alphabet plate or a necklace of wooden beads, she found something else to distract them temporarily from the emotion of ownership. So long as she was in the room there was a centre of love, of safety.

In a child's world, where there is a mother there must also be a father. There was nothing about Lucy Beach that could be considered masculine and yet she was able, when the children grew over-excited, to calm them. "Now that's enough," she would say. "No more." And it would be enough and there was no more of that particular frenzy. She never spoke harshly to the children or punished them with a quick spanking, but they seemed to have decided by common consent to be afraid of her.

Nora went from house to house in the mornings, collecting the children, who fought for the privilege of walking beside her. And because she was young, because she laughed easily and played London Bridge Is Falling Down and Drop-the-Handkerchief with as much pleasure and excitement as they did, they presented her with samples of their handiwork—crayon drawings and lopsided raffia baskets which she was expected to admire and keep always. When she sat down for a moment on one of the low kindergarten chairs, small arms encircled her neck. The children leaned upon her (all except Ab) and rubbed against her like cats and were in love with her without knowing it, and this in no way interrupted or interfered with their relation to Miss Lucy, the agent of punishment, and Miss Alice, the agent of comfort.

Love and fear are so well taught at home that no educational system need be concerned with these two elementary subjects. The first stage of the Montessori Method is to develop the sense of touch, sight, and hearing. This is done through games, and by guiding the children's attention to the association of objects, names, and ideas. They are taught the difference between hot and cold objects, between objects that are rough and those that are smooth. And by teaching children the words "hot," "cold," "rough," "smooth," you extend their sense of language before any question of reading or writing arises. They get their ideas of form and colour from playing with blocks and cylinders of varying sizes, which are fitted into frames that match them. There are no set lessons, no classes, no prizes or punishments of the usual kind. The only incentive is the pleasure, in a room where all kinds of interesting occupations are being pursued, of succeeding and getting things right. The hothouse plant, forced to bloom early and in time for Christmas or Easter, does not, of course, do very well afterward, but one way to discover the true rhythm of the universe is to try and improve on it.

Though Alice and Lucy Beach had read Mme Montessori's famous book, their own education had been at the hands of their mother. Touch, sight, and hearing were developed not by games but by crises. They were taught the difference between a warm, kind mother and a cold mother and how, by a simple act of disobedience, a failure in sympathy, they could change "kind" to "cold," "smooth" to "rough." As they grew older they became extremely adept at fitting their hopes into a frame that did not match. There were set lessons which, once learned, could not be unlearned. There were prizes, in the shape usually of a trip to Europe. And there were punishments of an unusual kind, which sent them weeping to their rooms and then brought them back to be forgiven by the person who had done something unforgivable to them.

If Mrs. Beach had realized how easy it was to start a kindergarten, how simple to find a dozen mothers who were anxious to have their children out from under foot three hours every weekday morning, she would never have given her consent to the modest establishment over Bailey's Drug Store. It was only one of many ideas that the two girls had hatched up, and the other ideas had always been exhausted in talk. This one they had carried through, to her amazement, and for the time being she could think of no way to put a stop to it.

From nine until eleven-thirty, five mornings a week, the children accepted the kindergarten routine as they would have accepted an act of enchantment. When Lucy played the piano, they marched and sang. They wove hammocks and rugs out of coloured yarns. With scissors and paste and sheets of coloured paper they made houses and stores and churches with pointed steeples. At certain times, memory overtook them as it overtook Ulysses on the shore of Calypso's island, and then they would come to Nora and say, "When are we going home?" or "Will my mother be home when I get there?"

Every day when it came time to deliver the children to their homes, Nora had to stand and see one child after another leave her and run into outstretched, waiting arms. It was something that she never got used to.

13

"Why are you responsible?" Dr. Danforth asked. "All you did was draw up the papers."

"I know," Austin said, "but I invited them here. They were

guests in my house and don't you see, that makes it look as if I——"

Dr. Danforth didn't at first understand, and then he said, "No . . . no, you mustn't do that, my boy. They went into it with their eyes open. Or at least they should have gone into it that way. It was speculation pure and simple. And you have Martha and Ab to worry about, and another child coming. It wouldn't be right at all. The thing will work itself out some way. Just give it a chance."

"I found out one thing," Austin said, examining the tips of his shoes, "while they were here. It seems that there was a time when Mr. Potter was very hard up, and turned to Father for help."

"Is that so?" Dr. Danforth peered at Austin over his glasses. "I never heard about that."

"Father refused him," Austin said, "and I can't figure out why."

"It wasn't Mr. Potter that the Judge was indebted to, if I remember correctly," Dr. Danforth said.

"I know," Austin said.

"It's true that they were raised under the same roof and you might expect, for old times' sake, that the Judge would want to do whatever lay in his power to help some member of his foster family. But you can't judge people's actions unless you know what went on in their minds at the time. Even if the Judge were alive today and you could go to him and ask why he refused to help Mr. Potter, he might not give you any satisfaction. He was a very proud man. It was his only fault, as far as I can make out, and with him it wasn't exactly a fault; he had reason to be proud. He might rather let you think ill of him than defend himself against a charge that he figured you ought to know was false. That's the way he was."

"Perhaps you're right," Austin said. "But I remember hearing him say a number of times how deeply indebted he was to the people who raised him, and how he'd never had an opportunity of paying them back."

"You can't pay people back for the kindness they show to you when you're in trouble," Dr. Danforth said emphatically. "There isn't any way of measuring, in terms of money, what you owe them. You can go on paying them back forever, and still be indebted to them. Sometimes they don't need any help. Or maybe the kind of help they need you can't give them. All you can do is look around for somebody that *is* in need of help and do what you can for them, figuring that it will all be cancelled out some day. I'm sure that's the way the Judge looked at it. He was always helping somebody out of a tight spot, his whole life long. People that are near to you and that you have every reason for trusting—if they do something that doesn't look quite right to you—you have to wait and give them time to explain themselves. And if they don't or can't explain because they've passed on, you still mustn't jump to conclusions, my boy, or you may do them and yourself an injustice. The chances are that the Judge paid off this debt as he paid off every other, but felt obligated, even so, to the end of his life, and that's why you heard him speak as he did. I don't doubt that the story Mr. Potter told you about turning to the Judge for help and being refused is true, every word of it. The Judge could say no. But in every one of these letters there is something held back, and I doubt if he told you the whole story. Maybe that wasn't the first time Mr. Potter turned to the Judge for money. Maybe it was the fourth or fifth time. Maybe the Judge went on his note and had to make it good afterward, the way he did for so many other people that pass as honest men. Or it could even be that he had some reason to distrust Mr. Potter. After all, they knew each other as boys. Maybe the Judge realized that any help he gave would just be frittered away on something foolish like an automobile. Sometimes, with men like Mr. Potter, there is no real way of helping them, even if you try.

The more help anybody gives them, the deeper in they get. You can't tell why he refused him. But I'll tell you one thing —I wouldn't believe any man that spoke ill of Judge King."

"I wasn't speaking ill of him," Austin said soberly. "I just wondered, that's all."

Dr. Danforth looked startled. He took his spectacles off, restored them to their case, and put the case in his vest pocket. "I wasn't talking about you," he said. "I didn't really get to know my own father until just at the end of his life. And even then, there were things I couldn't ask about, or tell him about myself, for fear of upsetting him. I know what he was like as my father, but the rest of him, all that part that had nothing to do with me . . ." With a smile that apologized for the tears in his eyes, Dr. Danforth took out his handkerchief and blew his nose vigorously.

There is nothing so difficult to arrive at as the nature and personality of one's parents. Death, about which so much mystery is made, is perhaps no mystery at all. But the history of one's parents has to be pieced together from fragments, their motives and character guessed at, and the truth about them remains deeply buried, like a boulder that projects one small surface above the level of smooth lawn, and when you come to dig around it, proves to be too large ever to move, though each year's frost forces it up a little higher.

14

"The house seems a little chilly," Mrs. Danforth said when her husband came back from the Kings'. She was sitting in her accustomed chair and her hands were engaged in the creation of the same white six-pointed star.

"I'll see what I can do about it," he said.

The rumble of furnace grates being shaken went through the silent house. A shovel scraped in the coal bin. An iron door clanged shut, and there were heavy footsteps clumping up the basement stairs. Mrs. Danforth looked up as her husband came into the room. He went over to his chair, sat down, rubbed his eyes with his hand, sighed, and said nothing. After a time he said, "Well, I've been over the whole business with him. He listened to everything I had to say, but he's still going ahead with his plans."

"I thought he probably would," Mrs. Danforth said.

"He feels responsible because he drew up the papers and because the arrangements were made in his house. If there's anything in the world that boy doesn't feel responsible for, I don't know what it is. He has to borrow four thousand dollars. The bank won't take the stock as collateral."

"Is that so," Mrs. Danforth said.

"I told him, 'You'll be lucky if you get out of this without having to go into bankruptcy.' "

"What did he say to that?"

"He didn't say anything."

"Austin will never go bankrupt," Mrs. Danforth said calmly.

"The others are willing to ride along without bringing suit, in the hopes of getting their money back some day. It's Bud Ellis who's making the trouble. He threatened to bring suit against Austin."

"Why against Austin?"

"Because if they brought suit against Mr. Potter and won, the chances are they still couldn't collect anything. So far as Austin is concerned, they haven't got a leg to stand on. The case would be thrown out of court."

"Austin must know that."

"Certainly he knows it, and so does Bud Ellis. It isn't right. 'Let them stew in their own juice,' I told him. 'You've paid off your father's debts. That's enough.' . . . He mustn't make a pauper of himself for people who aren't even related to him."

"No," Mrs. Danforth agreed.

"I told him all that and a lot more, but it was so much wasted breath."

"Well, you've had your say," Mrs. Danforth said, searching through the table drawer for a missing crochet hook. "Whatever happens now, it won't be your fault."

15

"How nice you look, Nora," Alice Beach said.

To her surprise, Nora went back into her room and took off her ear-rings. The look of expectancy on her face, as she went down the hall and said good night to Mrs. Beach, could not be taken off. Martha King's long-delayed invitation had included them all, but Mrs. Beach had eaten something that disagreed with her and was in bed, and one of the girls was obliged to stay home and take care of her. Which one should go, and which one should miss this pleasant change from their ordinary routine, had been decided long ago when Lucy took lessons from Geraldine Farrar's singing teacher and Alice stayed below in the little reception hall, listening to the sound of her sister's voice ascending and descending the scale that ended with a chord on the piano.

"Do you have your key?" Mrs. Beach asked, as Lucy got up from the chair beside the bed.

"In my purse," Lucy said. "We'll be home early."

On her face also there was a look of expectancy, but what Lucy Beach expected from this evening was by no means clear. She could not have been hoping that the Kings, after knowing her for many years, would suddenly accept her as their intimate friend, ask her for dinner again and again, and feel somehow incomplete unless she was with them. Nevertheless, the look was there, and it implied something of this kind of order.

"The cat came back," Nora said, as Austin opened the door to them. Having waited so long for an invitation to dinner, she now produced this poor joke in self-defence, to show that the waiting was unimportant, was nothing. The gloved hand that was about to reach out and touch his coat-sleeve, she checked in time, but there was nothing she could do about her own rapturous happiness or the voice that cried *Oh why can't he love me?*

Nervously, knowing that the happiness could not last because he would not let it last, she looked around to see what changes had taken place in the house during the past three months.

"It's nice to see you," Austin said, as he put their coats away in the hall closet.

Though it was so important that Nora look at him, right then, before his expression changed, she could not. Once before he had seemed to want something of her, and then it turned out that he. . . . That was how it all began, the mistake above all other mistakes she must guard against making. But would he have said that he was glad to see her unless he meant to imply something more besides?

"Martha will be down in just a minute," he said, and led them into the living-room.

"Mother and Alice were so sorry they couldn't come," Lucy said.

"I'm sorry, too," Austin said, and then, as Lucy chose an uninviting chair, "Wouldn't you be more comfortable by the fire?"

I know exactly how I feel when I'm with him, Nora said to herself, but I don't know how to stop feeling it.

They sat stiffly, making conversation, until Martha King came down the stairs. She was wearing a silk shawl, but she showed quite plainly that she was carrying a child. Austin talked to Lucy, and Nora was left with Martha King, whose one effort at making conversation with Nora that evening came to nothing. While Martha was talking to her, Nora's glance wavered towards the other couple in the room, and then travelled to the sheet music on the piano. She wondered what it would be like sitting here alone with him in the evening, listening to his playing (so much more delicate than her mother's thumping) and watching his sensitive hands moving over the keyboard. She realized suddenly that Martha had asked her a question and said, "Mama? Oh, she's fine."

"And your father?"

"He's all right. They're all fine and sent their love to you and Cousin Austin," Nora said, and felt as if she had awakened abruptly in the midst of a dream. Though the dream remained in her memory, as sharp and clear as a winter day, she couldn't get back into it. "I notice that Cousin Austin comes home much later than he used to last summer. I'm afraid we interfered with his work."

"He's been very busy with the fall term of court," Martha said.

"Oh," Nora said, and nodded, and then after a pause she said, "I'd like very much to hear him speak in court. Would it embarrass him, having someone there that he knows?"

Martha picked at the fringe of her shawl and Nora thought for a moment that she had not understood. "If you think it would embarrass him, I won't say anything to him about it," she said.

"He won't let me go and hear him," Martha said, "but that's probably just an idea that he's got fixed in his mind. You'll have to ask him and see what he says. He might enjoy having you there."

"You can come if you like," Austin said, turning away from Lucy. "The case I'm trying now is not very interesting, the way a criminal trial would be."

"I wouldn't care about that," Nora said, her face suffused with pleasure. "All I want is to see a case tried."

"Dinner is served," Rachel said.

After they were seated, Nora turned to Austin, prepared to be anything that he wanted her to be, because she loved him so much and because he was so wonderful and she was so happy just being with him. All she needed was some positive indication from him of the role he wanted her to play in his life, and until that came she felt shy with him (it was strange how someone could take up so much of your thoughts and still be as remote as a star) and painfully aware of the fact that she wanted him to love her (knowing that he couldn't) and that it didn't matter, so long as she was here and could love him.

Austin's efforts at commonplace table conversation were not taken up by Nora and he had to fall back on the food. Martha tried to talk to Lucy but there were distractions. Rachel had forgotten to warm the plates, and she passed the mint sauce after they had finished eating their lamb.

Lucy Beach, dining out for the first time in years without her mother and sister, failed to notice the frequent silences. Her hand kept reaching for the cut-glass tumbler. She drank a great deal of water, and smoothed and folded the napkin lying across her lap. When, after an interruption, Martha King took up the conversation at some place other than the place where Lucy had left off, she was neither discouraged nor hurt. Her European table manners returned to her; she ate without transferring her fork from her left hand to her right. She complimented Martha on the lamb, the canned peas, the mashed potatoes. She smiled vivaciously (when there was really nothing to smile at) as if she were a beautiful worldly woman with a black velvet ribbon encircling her throat, her long white gloves drawn back and bunched at her wrists, offering herself first to the distinguished grey-haired man on her right, and then to the gallant and witty young man on her left.

When they had finished the main course and were ready for dessert, Martha rang the little china serving bell beside her place, and nothing happened. As if it were customary for people to ring and have no one answer, they sat and waited. Eventually, Rachel put her head in at the pantry door and said, "The frogleg man."

"At this time of night!" Austin exclaimed. He felt in his change pocket and drew out fifty cents for Rachel. Then turning to Nora, he explained, "Mr. Barrett. We never know when he's coming, and if we don't take them, he won't come back any more. They're bullfrogs, and I suspect that he catches them with a flashlight, which is against the law, but . . ." The frogleg man carried them safely through the rest of the meal, on his eccentric back. When they left the table and returned to the living-room, they discovered the fireplace had been smoking in their absence. Austin opened the windows and while they shivered with the cold and broke into coughing, Nora started telling about a strange odour that had developed in the plantation house at Howard's Landing. "It wasn't like any smell I've ever smelled before. It was dry and dusty, and a little like the smell of vinegar, and nobody could make out where it was coming from, until one day——" Austin left the room and Nora waited until he had come back with a big log in his hands before she went on and finished her story.

The log made the fire burn properly. The smoke went up the chimney instead of out into the room, and in time they were able to close the windows. The Kings and their two guests sat in a circle around the fire, and Austin, finding an appreciative audience, talked shop. Martha sat quietly braiding the fringes of her shawl. Austin's stories about the involved litigations, lawsuit after lawsuit, of the picturesque Jouette family, she had heard before. From time to time she pressed a yawn back into her throat and, exerting all the will-power at her command, kept from glancing at the clock in the castle of St. Angelo. Lucy Beach contributed nothing to the conversation but her animated interest. Looking at her, one would have thought that a great many things were now being made clear to her that had not been clear before.

Actually, she was planning in her mind what she would say to Alice when she got home. *Austin got started talking about the law*, she would say, *and he talked very well. I wish you could have heard him. . . .*

Lucy sat and listened as long as Austin included her in the conversation. When he forgot to do this, she turned to Martha King and began to talk about a problem that had arisen in connection with the kindergarten.

"We have an arrangement with Rachel's son, Eugene, to come and start the fire in the stove so the rooms will be warm when the children get there. A couple of weeks ago I noticed that the chairs had been rearranged and the alphabet plates were on a different shelf of the cupboard from where I'd put them the day before. I didn't know whether to speak to Eugene or not. He's a very nice boy, and I didn't want to hurt his feelings. But soon after that, a piece of green paper was missing, and some of the crayons were broken. Something had to be done, so I went downtown an hour earlier one morning, and guess who the culprit was?"

"I can't guess," Martha said. "Who was it?"

"Thelma."

"What did you say to her?"

"What could I say to her," Lucy said, "except that if she came any more, I'd be forced to tell her mother about it."

This version was heavily censored. What actually happened was that Lucy walked in, the fire was crackling in the stove, and Thelma was sitting at one of the long kindergarten tables with crayons and paper spread around her, at work on a detail of the grand fresco that would some day, like the Boro-Budur, depict every human emotion, a design made up entirely of gestures. Suddenly she looked over her shoulder, her eyes large with fright.

"Have you been coming here every morning, Thelma?"

"Yes, Miss Lucy." Thelma looked down at the small black hands that had at last got her into serious trouble.

"You know that you shouldn't have used the crayons and paper without asking?"

"Yes'm."

"And that I'll have to tell your mother on you?"

"Yes'm."

With a long pole Lucy opened one of the windows at the top and let out some of the hot dry air in the room. When she had put the pole in the corner, she turned and said, "What will your mother do when I tell her?"

"Whip me."

"And do you want her to do that?"

"No, Miss Lucy."

Her eyes downcast, her hands shaking, Thelma put on her coat and started to leave. So contagious is remorse that Lucy said, "You can take this with you if you like," and presented Thelma with her own half-finished drawing of a woman in a garden, with shears and a basket full of flowers—poppies or anemones or possibly some flower that existed only in Thelma's mind. Shortly afterward, the children arrived, as noisy and active as birds, and took possession of the kingdom that was reserved for them.

Some dissatisfaction with her part in this scene or with the circumstances which had obliged her to act as she did kept Lucy from going into the particular details, which could have no interest, she felt, for Martha King. She turned her head so as not to miss what Austin was saying.

". . . so Father called old Mr. Seacord into his office and said, 'George, I want you to go down to the bank in Kaiserville and tell Fred Bremmer to look around and see if he can find that will anywhere. If an offer of two hundred acres of land will help him find it, you can make the offer in my name, and I don't care how you split the land between you.' The will was in Father's office by nine o'clock the next morning."

"How amazing," Nora said, and felt the world moving off on an entirely new orbit from which it would very likely never return to pursue its usual path. She had had a vision during the past half-hour, and the way was now open to her. She would read, she would study, she would pass the bar examination with flying colours. She saw herself defending the innocent (who would otherwise be convicted of crimes they had no knowledge of), astounding old and learned judges with her irrefutable logic, the foremost woman lawyer in the State of Illinois, a partner in the firm of King and Potter.

Lucy looked down at her gold watch and exclaimed, "Why, we must go home! We've stayed much later than we should have. . . . Nora, I hate to talk about going, when everybody is having such a good time, but we really must."

In the front hall, while Austin was helping Nora on with her coat, she said, "It's all so fascinating. I won't be able to sleep for thinking of the things you've told me." And Lucy said to Martha King, "It's so nice of you to ask us. As soon as Mother is over her little upset, you must come and have dinner with us. Then Alice can be in on it, too."

She carried her expectant look with her out into the November night.

16

The night of Martha King's dinner party, a traveller returned —a Negro with no last name. He came on a slow freight from Indianapolis. Riding in the same boxcar with him, since noon, were an old man and a fifteen-year-old boy and neither of them ever wanted to see him again. His eyes were bloodshot, his face and hands were gritty, his hair was matted with cinders. His huge, pink-palmed hands hung down out of the sleeves of a corduroy mackinaw that was too small for him and filthy and torn. He had thrown away his only pair of socks two days before. There was a hole in the sole of his right shoe, his belly was empty, and the police were on the lookout for him in St. Louis and Cincinnati.

The shadow that the Negro met under the arc light at every cross street did not surprise him. He had seen it in too many back alleys where it is better to have no shadow at all, and he was a man who lived by surprising other people. When he came to Rachel's shack he stopped and looked up and down the street. Then he moved quietly up to the window and looked in. He stood there motionless for some time before he turned towards the door.

"Where's your Ma?"

The five frightened faces might just as well have been one. There was no variation in the degree or quality of terror.

"I asked you a question."

"She ain't home, Andy," Everitt said.

"That's mighty strange. I thought she'd be here tonight," he said, and closed the door. "She ain't expecting me?"

There was no answer.

"I don't call that much of a welcome," he said. "Your Pappy come three hundred miles to see you, and they ain't none of you get up off their ass to welcome me home."

"We didn't know you was coming," Eugene said in a whisper. "You didn't send no word."

"So I got to send a notice to my own family before they condescends to receive me. I got to write them a letter say I be home on such and such a day, after I been away three whole years. Well, next time maybe I do that. And maybe I don't. Who's your Ma working for, these days? That same old white woman?"

"No," Eugene said.

"Where she work?"

"She work for the Kings," Everitt said.

"Huh? You don't say. She getting up in the world. Fast. Mighty fine clothes you all got, for niggers. Looks to me like you're well fed too. Mighty sleek. Looks to me like I come to the right place."

"I'll go tell her you're here," Thelma said, glancing towards the door.

"Another country heard from. . . . Eugene, git up off of that couch and let your Pappy lie down. He's come a long way and he's tired. Your Ma fix me a little supper and then I'm going to sleep. I'm going to get in the bed and sleep for a week. Get up, you hear? Before I make you. You think you're grown, maybe, but you ain't grown enough. I show you. I show you right now."

What happened inside the shack was of no concern to the funeral basket, the two round stones, the coach lantern, and the coffeepot. They were merely the setting for a fancy-dress nightmare, not the actors. Evil moves about on two legs and has lines to speak, gestures that frighten because they are never completed. He can be blond, well bred, to all appearances gentle and kind. Or the eyes can be almond-shaped, the eyebrows plucked, the lids drooping. The hair can be kinky or curly or straight. Features and colouring are a matter of make-up to be left to the individual actor, who can, if he likes, with grease paint and eyebrow pencil create the face of a friend. If the actor wears a turban or a loincloth, the dramatic effect will be heightened, providing of course that the audience is not also wearing turbans or loincloths. What is important is that Evil be understood, otherwise the scene will not act. The audience will not be able to decide which character is evil and which is the innocent victim. It is quite simple, actually. The one comes to grief through no fault of his own, knows what is being done to him, and does not lift a hand to defend himself from the blow. If he defends himself, he is not innocent. The other has been offered a choice, and has chosen Evil. If the audience and the actors both remember this, they will have no trouble following or acting out the play, which should begin, in any case, quietly, in a low key, suggesting an atmosphere of peace and security and love. The funeral basket, the two round stones, the rain-rotted carriage seat, the coach lantern, and the coffeepot are very good. And for a backdrop let there be a quiet street on a November night in a small midwestern town. A woman comes down the street towards an arc light at the foot of a hill. Under her arm she has a brown paper parcel containing scraps of leftover food. A coloured woman, with her head down, her shoulders hunched, indicating that it is cold. If there is a wind-machine in the wings, the effect will be more realistic. There should be lights in the houses. The trees have shed their leaves. The woman stops suddenly and conveys to the audience by a look, by the absence of all expression, that a chill has passed over her which has nothing to do with the wind from the wings. She looks back at the arc light. And then she begins to run.

17

There was no reason why the ringing of the doorbell the following night should have made the hairs rise on the back of Austin's neck unless he expected, when he opened the front door, to see the disembodied spirit that lived in the cellar, in the butler's pantry, and on the stairs.

"Oh," he said. "I couldn't imagine who it was. Come in, Nora."

"I saw your light," Nora said. "I won't stay but a minute. I know you're very busy."

"I brought some work home from the office," Austin said, as he closed the door. "How is Mrs. Beach?"

"She's feeling better," Nora said as she followed him into the study. "Cousin Austin, there's something that I want very much to talk to you about."

"Yes?"

"Something of the utmost importance. To me, I mean," she added. She sat down in the chair Martha King used when she was doing her mending, and tucked her legs up under her skirt.

Austin's eyebrows rose, conveying both a question and a slight apprehensiveness.

"I spent the afternoon in the public library," she said, "reading Blackstone's *Commentaries.*"

This piece of information was delivered in such a way as to suggest that Nora expected Austin to be amazed by it. If he was amazed, his face failed to show it. He said, "Is that so?"

"I read the first forty-two pages," Nora said.

"What did you make of it?"

"There were lots of things I didn't understand," Nora said. "The language was new to me, but I found it very interesting. . . . Cousin Austin, do you think I could be a lawyer?"

"That's a hard question to answer."

"I know it is," Nora said, "and I don't expect you to tell me right off. I didn't know whether you'd even listen to the idea. Really I didn't. I thought, I'll tell him and then see what he——"

"Why should you want to be a lawyer, Nora, when there are other fields that are just as rewarding and much more——"

"Because it's the one thing that appeals to me," Nora said. "I know there are other things I *could* do, but I want something where I can do some good. All day I've hardly allowed myself to hope. I was afraid that if I did and then it turned out that there was no chance for me, the disappointment would be too—tell me this much: Do you think, knowing me as you do, that it's impossible?"

"It's not impossible," Austin said, "but on the other hand, it's not easy."

"Oh I know that," Nora said quickly.

"There was a girl in my class at Northwestern, quite a nice girl as I remember. It was generally assumed that a girl in law school wouldn't last more than one semester, and as a matter of fact, this girl did drop out. I never knew why or what became of her, but I do know that there are several women practising law in this State at the moment. They may not have an easy time of it, at first, but then nobody does. It all depends on how serious you are about wanting to do it, and whether you're willing to apply yourself. You'd have to work very hard for a long time. Otherwise there's no use even considering it."

"I'm very serious," Nora said. "Terribly serious. Something inside of me says I can do it. I know I can if you'll only help me. I wouldn't want to embarrass or inconvenience you, but would it be possible for me to come to your office in the afternoons and read there? For a short while, I mean. Just long enough for you to decide whether or not there is any use in my trying."

The case against women in the practice of law has been nobly expressed in an opinion by Chief Justice Ryan (39 Wis. page 352):

This is the first application for admission of a female to the bar of this court. And it is a just matter for congratulation that it is made in favour of a lady whose character raises no personal objections; something perhaps not always to be looked for in the women who forsake the ways of their sex for the ways of ours. . . . So we find no statutory authority for the admission of females to the bar of any court in this State. And, with all the respect and sympathy for this lady which all men owe to all good women, we cannot regret that we do not. We cannot but think the common law wise in excluding women from the profession of the law. The profession enters largely into the well being of society; and, to be honourably filled and safely to society, exacts the devotion of life. The law of nature destines and qualifies the female sex for the bearing and nurture of the children of our race and for the custody of the homes of the world and their maintenance in love and honour. And all life-long callings of women, inconsistent with these radical and sacred duties of their sex, as is the profession of the law, are departures from the order of nature; and when voluntary, treason against it. The cruel chances of life sometimes baffle both sexes, and may leave women free from the peculiar duties of their sex. These may need employment, and should be welcome to any not derogatory of their sex and its proprieties, or inconsistent with the good order of society. But it is public policy to provide for the sex, not for its superfluous members; and not to tempt women from the proper duties of their sex by opening to them duties peculiar to ours. There are many employments in life not unfit for the female character. The profession of law is surely not one of these. . . . Discussions are habitually necessary in courts of justice, which are unfit for female ears. The habitual presence of women at these would tend to relax the public sense of decency and propriety. If, as counsel threatened, these things are to come, we will take no voluntary part in bringing them about.

The habitual presence of women in courts of law was to come, even though Chief Justice Ryan took a voluntary part in preventing Miss Lavinia Goodell from practising before the Supreme Court of the State of Wisconsin.

Nora's interest in the law had taken Austin by surprise and appeared to be rather sudden, but it was also true that she had a very good mind, clear and logical, except where her emotions were involved. The fact that she had ploughed through forty pages of Blackstone was in itself remarkable. Very few women would have got past the first page. With help, and if she applied herself . . .

"Let me think about it, a day or two," he said. "Mr. Holby will be back in town on Tuesday. I'll talk the matter over with him. He may object to your being in the office, in which case——"

"If you only knew what it means to me," Nora said.

As she said good night, her face, under the porchlight, was transformed with radiance and hope.

18

"If you want Nora near you," Martha said as she dealt herself a hand of solitaire.

"But that's not the point," Austin said. "I don't want her near me, I'm merely trying to help her. It will be something of an inconvenience having her in the office, day in and day out. It means giving her a certain amount of my time, if she is going to make any progress——"

"Well, if you have the time, why not?"

"I don't have. I've never been entirely caught up since they were here last summer. And Mr. Holby does less and less. From a purely selfish point of view, there's no use even considering the idea. It's bound to cause a certain amount of talk, and it may lead to friction with Mr. Holby. Since I'm doing three-quarters of his work and he is taking sixty per cent of the profits of the firm, I suppose I shouldn't worry about exerting pressure on him."

"The person I'd worry about is Miss Ewing."

"I'm going to have a talk with him about that, too," Austin said. "The time has come when the percentage should be reversed. I'm going to insist on at least a fifty-fifty basis. . . . Why Miss Ewing?"

"I don't know, but I rather imagine she won't like having another woman in the office, especially under the arrangement you're considering."

"She'll have to like it," Austin said. "In the old days I used to be able to come to you with problems that were bothering me, and we could talk them over. Now, when I try to talk something over with you, you seem to resent it. I always understand things better after I've talked to you, and I often follow your suggestions."

"Not recently," Martha said, glancing over the rows of cards for a black ten that the nine of diamonds could go on.

"Maybe not recently," Austin said, "but that's because you have a kind of blind spot where Nora is concerned, and always have had. There's more at stake here than Nora. Every time a woman manages to break through the barrier of prejudice that keeps them out of the professions——"

"This interest in feminism is fairly recent with you, isn't it?"

"Not as recent as you think."

"Well, in any case, this much I do know," Martha said, scooping the cards into a pile. "If you were a doctor, Nora would be spending her time poring over a medical dictionary, and persuading the nurses to let her into the operating room at the hospital. And if you were a school teacher, she'd care terribly about education."

"You're not being fair to her."

"I'm being quite fair to Nora, and you're wrong in thinking I dislike her," Martha said. "I not only like Nora, I admire and respect her courage. The last three months can't have been easy for her. The person I am unfair to is you, Austin, because you want to be helpful, you want to help everybody, and instead of encouraging you to do that—after all, it's a perfectly natural desire——"

She began shuffling and reshuffling the cards, as if shuffling were all that there was to the game.

19

"Well, my boy," Mr. Holby said, "I'm glad you brought the subject up. It's time we gave it some consideration. I have a tendency to let things ride, as long as they seem to be going well, and it didn't occur to me that you might not be satisfied with the present arrangement."

"I'm not dissatisfied," Austin said, feeling, from Mr. Holby's tone of voice, from the kindness and also a certain sadness in his manner, that Mr. Holby was not going to put up a fight; that his case was won. "It's just that when I came into the firm, it was with the understanding that someday——"

"I know," Mr. Holby said, nodding. "I realize all that, and I've been aware for some time that you were carrying perhaps a little more than your share of the burden. But that's what happens, of course. As a young man I went through the same thing, and charged it off to valuable experience, figuring that it would eventually correct itself, as of course, it did. Part of it has been beyond my control. As you know, Mrs. Holby's health hasn't been any too good this last year. I'm quite worried about her. I wouldn't want anybody but you to know this, but I can talk to you as I would talk to my own son. I've had to think about her more than I would have if she'd been as strong and active as most women of her age. I've had to take her to Hot Springs and other places that we hoped would do her good, which means, of course, spending a good deal of money, but these things come up in family life, and there's really no choice. They have to take precedence, for a time, over everything else. I'm telling you all this so you'll understand that it hasn't been just my own pleasures and desires that I've had to consider."

"Oh, I know that," Austin said quickly.

"As we get older, we tend to lean more on the younger men around us, to depend on their energy and willingness to see that the details are carried out, without which, of course, the maturer wisdom and judgment that come with age and that are concerned with broader matters, would be seriously hampered. I fancy that an outside viewpoint would consider that the two just about cancel each other out. At least they make a very good working team. You've done extremely well for so young a man, and I'm confident that some day your name will mean as much, will command the same respect that your father's did. But it takes time, and you mustn't be impatient. It will all come to you, everything that you hope for and deserve in the way of recognition. I've done what I could to guide you and keep you from making rash mistakes, and I intend to go on giving you the benefit of my experience and knowledge, so that when the time comes that I have to step down and you have to carry on alone or with the help of some younger man, the ideals that the firm of Holby and King has always stood for will be ably represented. I look forward to that day, as I'm sure you do, too. Meanwhile, of course, there are other, more pressing matters to consider. In your eagerness to get ahead, I think you under-estimate one or two angles of the situation. I'm the last man in the world to countenance an injustice. Not even for five minutes. My life has been dedicated to the cause of truth and fair play. People who complain that lawyers are interested only in their fee fail to take into consideration that the Law is the only profession whose aim is to correct the evils of society, defend the innocent, and see to it that the guilty are meted out their due punishment. Without the legal profession the world we live in would be chaos. In Law you have order, you have responsibility, you have decency, you have the only arrangement whereby society can function. It isn't enough to pass laws. They must be interpreted. One cause, one legal claim must be balanced against another. You and I, sitting in this room, cannot—and still be worthy of the name we call ourselves by—see the question of partnership in any but the broadest light. When I've been away from the office, it may have seemed to you that I was frittering away my time in social pleasures, enjoying the company and cultivation of time-honoured associates, reaping my just rewards, probably, but nevertheless—and for the moment—allowing my mind to be diverted from the work that lies waiting for me, this very minute, on my desk. I wouldn't blame you if you had thought that. It would be a very natural mistake for you to make under the circumstances. The truth of the matter is that my mind is never idle. I am continually deliberating and meditating upon some legal problem, so that when the times comes and the decision must be made, I have covered the whole question, every crack and cranny of it, and am ready to act. In a world where people are continually acting on some blind impulse, never stopping to consider what is the wise, what is the right course to pursue, the intellectual faculties are not always given their due, but without them where would we be? What hope would there be for mankind? On the one hand, you'd have barbarism and ruthless aggression, on the other, slavery. Someone must digest, must ponder and weigh the consequences, study the causes, give thought to the ultimate values that must never be lost sight of, and dismiss those considerations that are trivial or misleading, that are mere side issues. Now as things stand, I find myself in agreement with you about the division of profits of this firm—that an equal sharing, even though it tends to set a valuation on certain qualities that cannot in the very nature of things be evaluated, is reasonable and fair. Or if not precisely and mathematically so, then it will so soon become that way that we ought to feel ourselves free to anticipate the future and act according to it, with a certain amount of confidence that we are acting properly. I say 'as things stand.'

"A short time ago you mentioned to me the possibility of taking a young woman into the office—Miss Potter—with the understanding that she would read and prepare herself for the bar examination. It is perhaps a rather radical departure from what is customary, but even so, I have no objection. I believe, as I'm sure you know, that conditions change, that we must abide by the Law of Progress in so far as we can interpret it. I'm sure you have looked into Miss Potter's qualifications thoroughly and would not countenance such a step if she were lacking in the requisite mentality. And I appreciate also that, in view of your association with her family, you would want to offer her any assistance that lies in your power. But I hope you have also considered what it means to the firm. She will require desk space, it will put an added burden on Miss Ewing, who is already overworked. And if Miss Potter is to advance with any speed towards her goal, she will require a great deal of your time and guidance. So much of each, in fact, that it seems to me quite to upset the balancing of values, yours and mine, that we were just now speaking of. If you want to have her here, I am willing to withdraw any objections I might have to it, with the understanding that, for the time at least—I don't mean that the question of division of profits cannot be reopened in the future, you understand—until we see how this new arrangement works out, I feel that it is better to let things ride along the way they have been going. I leave it entirely up to you, my boy. Whatever you decide will be satisfactory with me."

Part Five

THE PROVINCE OF JURISPRUDENCE

I

Of the literary arts, the one most practised in Draperville was history. It was informal, and there was no reason to write it down since nothing was ever forgotten. The child born too soon after the wedding ceremony might learn to walk and to ride a bicycle; he might go to school and graduate into long pants, marry, move to Seattle, and do well for himself in the lumber business; but whenever his or his mother's name was mentioned, it was followed inexorably by some smiling reference to the date of his birth. No one knew what had become of the energetic secretary of the Chamber of Commerce who organized the Love-Thy-Neighbour-As-Thyself parade, but they knew why he left town shortly afterward, and history doesn't have to be complete. It is merely a continuous methodical record of events. These events can be told in chronological order but that isn't necessary any more than it is necessary for the historians to be concerned with cause and effect. Research in Draperville was carried on over the back fence, over the telephone, in kitchens and parlours and upstairs bedrooms, in the back seat of carriages, in wicker porch swings, in the bell tower of the Unitarian Church, where the Willing Workers met on Wednesdays and patiently, with their needles and thread, paid off the mortgage on the parsonage.

The final work of shaping and selection was done by the Friendship Club. The eight regular members of this club were the high practitioners of history. They met in rotation at one another's houses for luncheon and bridge. The food that they served was competitive and unwise, since many of them were struggling to maintain their figures. After the canned lobster or crabmeat, the tunafish baked in shells, the chicken patties, the lavish salads, the New York ice cream (all of which they would regret later), the club members settled down to bridge, with their hats on and their shoes pushed off under the card table, their voices rising higher and higher, their short-range view of human events becoming crueller and more malicious as they doubled and redoubled one another's bids, made grand slams, and quarrelled over the scoring. No reputation was safe with them, and only by being present every time could they hope to preserve their own. The innocent were thrown to the wolves, the kind made fun of, the old stripped of the dignity that belonged to their years. *They say* was the phrase invariably used when a good name was about to be auctioned off at the block. *They say that before Dr. Seymour married her she was running around with . . . They say the old lady made him promise before she died that he'd never . . . They say she has cancer of the breast. . . .*

If you come upon footprints and blood on the snow, all you have to do is turn and follow the pink trail back into the woods. You may have to walk miles, but eventually you will come to the clearing where hoofprints and footprints, moving in a circle, tell of the premeditated murder of a deer. You can follow a brook to the spring that is its source. But there is no tracing *They say* back to the person who said it originally.

They say Ed came home one afternoon when he was not expected and found her and Mr. Trimbull . . . They say old Mr. Green went to him and said either you marry Esther or . . . They say that Harvey had a brother who was in an institution in Fairfield and that he kept it from Irene until their second child was born. . . .

The flayed landscape of the western prairie does little to remind the people who live there of the covenant of works or the covenant of grace. The sky, visible right down to the horizon, has a diminishing effect upon everything in the foreground, and the distance is as featureless and remote as the possibility of punishment for slander. The roads run straight, with death and old age intersecting at right angles, and the harvest is stored in cemeteries.

They say Tom went right over and made her pack up her things and leave. They haven't any of them spoken to Lucile since. . . . They say he drinks like a fish. . . . They say it was all Mr. Tierney's fault. He came home with a mild case of diphtheria and their little girl—such a pretty child—caught it from him.

By December, the historians had gathered together all the relevant facts about Austin King's young cousin from Mississippi, knew that she was madly in love with him, and were not surprised when he took her into his office. The historians called on Mrs. Beach with gifts of wine jelly and beef broth, and when they met Nora on the street with the children, they stopped her and asked questions that appeared to be friendly but that were set and ready to spring, like a steel trap. The historians were kind to Miss Ewing, and they remembered that Martha King (on whose side they were) was very careless about repaying social obligations and when asked to join the Women's Club had declined on the grounds that she didn't have time. This ancient border skirmish, nearly forgotten in the light of more recent improprieties, was resurrected detail by detail with appropriate comments (*If I have time, with three children, and Sam's mother living with us* . . .) as fresh as if it had happened yesterday.

What is the chief end of Man? the historians might well have asked over the bridge tables, but they didn't. When they met as a group, they slipped all pity off under the table with their too-tight shoes, and became destroyers, enemies of society and of their neighbours, bent on finding out what went on behind the blinds that were drawn to the window-sill.

They say . . . they say . . . from quarter to one till five o'clock, when the scores were tallied; the prize brought out, unwrapped, and admired; and Jess Burton, Bertha Rupp, Alma Hinkley, Ruth Troxell, Elsie Hubbard, Genevieve Wilkinson, Irma Seifert, and Leona McLain tucked their hand-painted scorecards into their pocket-books to give to their children, slipped on their torturesome pumps, and went home full of news to tell their husbands at the supper table.

2

"What?" Nora asked, looking up from *Province of Jurisprudence Determined.*

"I said I hope my typewriter doesn't disturb you," Miss Ewing said.

"Oh, no," Nora said. "I wasn't even aware of it. Please, you mustn't worry about me, or I'll feel I oughtn't to be here."

"Some people find it very disturbing until they get accustomed to the sound," Miss Ewing said. "Do you find jurisprudence interesting?"

"What?" Nora asked, looking up once more. "Oh yes. Very."

"I noticed you're wearing a sweater today. It's a good idea if you're going to sit so near the window. With an old building like this, there are always all kinds of draughts, and if there's one thing I can't stand, it's a draught down the back of my neck. The janitor said he'd do something about stuffing the cracks with paper, but of course he hasn't. I'll have to speak to him again about it."

"That's very kind of you," Nora said, "but please don't bother. I'm quite comfortable, really I am. All I need is a good light to read by."

"You find the light all right there?"

"Oh yes."

"These dark winter days, I usually turn the lights on at three-thirty or quarter to four, but if you'd prefer to have it earlier, just say so."

"I will," Nora said, without looking up this time.

"You don't want to strain your pretty eyes, reading that fine print," Miss Ewing said, as the typewriter commenced thrashing.

The telephone rang, clients came and went, with a curious glance for the desk at the window, where a red-haired girl sat reading with her chin resting in her hand. The mailman walked in, on his afternoon rounds, handed the bundle of mail to Miss Ewing, and said, "I see they've finally taken pity on you and given you an assistant."

"Not exactly," Miss Ewing said, as she paid him two cents postage due on a long thin letter. Though she usually took the mail from him and sent him on his way, this afternoon she kept him for five minutes with questions about his mother, who was ailing, of what disease neither the doctor nor the mailman could say. The ancient filing cabinet made a grinding noise every time Miss Ewing pulled out one of the drawers.

At three-thirty Miss Ewing said, "I'm going to take Mr. Holby's dictation. Do you think you can manage all right?"

"Yes, thank you," Nora said.

While Miss Ewing was in Mr. Holby's office, a man came in, looked around hesitantly, coughed, and said, "I beg your pardon, Miss——"

Nora looked up and said. "Oh, excuse me. Did you want to see Mr. King?"

"Well, as a matter of fact," the man said, "I came to see Mr. Holby. On business."

"Just a minute," Nora said. "I'll see if he——"

"You're new around here, aren't you? I'm Will Avery."

"I'll tell him you're here, Mr. Avery," Nora said. She knocked timidly on Mr. Holby's door and Miss Ewing opened it, with her notebook in her hand.

"There's someone who——" Nora began.

"Mr. Holby doesn't like to be interrupted when he's giving

dictation," Miss Ewing said. "Oh, hello, Mr. Avery. Would you like to see Mr. Holby? Just go right in."

As she sat down at her desk Nora said, "He asked to see Mr. Holby, and I didn't know what to do, so I——"

"It's quite all right," Miss Ewing said. "There's bound to be some confusion at first. I just thought I'd better tell you so you'd know, after this, not to interrupt him."

Will Avery left the door open, as he went in, and Nora was able to hear the entire discussion of whether Mr. Holby should slap a sheriff's notice on the family who lived over the billiard parlour and were three months in arrears with their rent. When Will Avery got up to go, Mr. Holby accompanied him as far as the stairs, and then came over to see what Nora was reading.

"An extremely important subject for you to grasp," Mr. Holby said. "It involves the larger concepts of the Law, which all of us must keep straight in our minds, even when we are dealing with the most petty concerns. The human race —suppose we conceive of it in this way—the human race is parcelled out into a number of distinct groups or societies, differing greatly in—shall we say—circumstances, in physical and moral characteristics of all kinds. But you will find that they all resemble each other in that they reveal, on closer examination, certain rules of—if you like—*conduct*, in accordance with which the relations of the members *inter se* are governed. Each society naturally has its own laws, its own system of laws, its own *code* as we say. And all the systems, so far as they are known, constitute the appropriate subject matter of jurisprudence.

"The jurist may deal with it in the following ways: He may first of all examine the main conceptions found in all the systems, or in other words . . ." Mr. Holby raised his voice so that it would carry above the sound of the typewriter. ". . . define the leading terms common to them all. For example, the terms *law*, *right*, *duty*, *property*, *crime*, and so on, and so forth, which, or their equivalents, may . . ." The filing cabinet slammed shut. ". . . may, notwithstanding certain delicate differences of connotation, be regarded as common terms in all systems. That kind of inquiry is known as analytical jurisprudence. It regards the conceptions we've been talking about as fixed or stationary, and aims at expressing them clearly and distinctly and showing their logical relations with each other. What do we really mean by a *right* and by a *duty*——" The harsh overhead light went on. Mr. Holby, startled, turned and looked at the light fixture, and then, turning back to Nora, he said, "Where was I?—oh yes—what is really meant by a *right* and by a *duty*, and what is the underlying connection between a *right* and a *duty* are types of questions proper to this inquiry. Now suppose we shift our point of view. Regarding systems of law in the mass—do you follow me?" Nora nodded. "—we may consider them not as stationary but as changeable and changing. If we do that we may ask what general features are exhibited by the record of the change. This, somewhat crudely put, may serve to indicate the field of historical or comparative jurisprudence. In its ideal condition it would require—Come into the office, my dear, where we won't disturb Miss Ewing."

3

Martha King, her movements heavy and slow, went back and forth between the dining-room and the kitchen, stacking the breakfast dishes. This can't go on, she said to herself. I'm going to have it out with her when she comes. She can either turn up in the morning when she's supposed to, or——

There were footsteps outside, and Rachel pushed the back door open. Her eyes were bloodshot and doleful. She looked around at the confusion in the kitchen without seeing it, and then took her coat and stocking cap off and hung them on a nail beside the door.

"Now don't you worry about me being late, Mrs. King. I'll just do these dishes and get to the upstairs."

Martha's anger had deserted her at the sight of Rachel's face. In a helpless silence she turned and lit the gas under the coffeepot and then said, "Are you sick, Rachel?"

"No'm," Rachel said, "I'm not."

"You'd better have a cup of coffee with me. It may make you feel better."

Sitting across the kitchen table from her, Martha said nothing and let Rachel drink her coffee in peace. Day after day when she looked around her and found nowhere the strength to begin, it was Rachel who gave her a push—by encouragement, by example, by insisting (just as she was being sucked down in a whirlpool of things undone) *Now you leave that to me*. In exchange for four dollars a week, Rachel took the mop out of her hand and sometimes the weight off her heart. When the house seemed large and lonely, all she had to do was to go to the kitchen. Rachel was never disapproving, never surprised by anything that Martha King said or did. Her occasional bad moods had nothing to do with the woman she worked for, any more than Martha King's moods had anything to do with Rachel. But in spite of the freedom which they allowed each other, Rachel could say, *Now don't you feel blue, Mrs. King*, or *You're making things out worse than they are*, and Martha King could not.

"I won't ask you if you're in trouble," she said aloud. "I don't need to ask. I've never pried into your affairs, but you know that you can come to me, don't you, if you need help?"

"I know," Rachel said, but she did not explain why she sat with her shoulders hanging limp and heavy and her feet twisted under the chair, or why she looked old and frightened.

"There's been many a time," Martha said, turning and looking out of the window, "when you've helped me."

"It's not that kind of trouble," Rachel said.

Martha King finished her coffee in silence. Rachel got up and carried the cups and saucers to the sink, and began to dispose of the orange peels and eggshells that Martha had left there in the hurry of getting Austin to his office and Ab ready for kindergarten. Martha pushed her chair back and started for the pantry door.

"Would it be all right," Rachel said, above the sound of the running water, "if I was to keep Thelma here when she's not in school?"

This request ought to have made the whole thing as clear as daylight, and perhaps would have, if it hadn't been for the great pane of glass, which kept one part of Elm Street from knowing what the other part was up to. Even so, the gulf that separated Rachel and Martha King was not a simple matter. It was more than the difference between the front and back door. Rachel's trouble was something that Martha King would never have to cope with. She was protected by the thousand and one provisions in the code of respectability, and had been, from the moment she was born. Her husband took out his anger against her by straightening pictures and turning off lights that had been left burning in empty rooms. He carried a pearl-handled pocket-knife, not a razor, and he used it to sharpen pencils with.

And it was not fear of the razor that made Rachel look old. She had been born and raised in the knowledge of it. It was the way his eyes followed Thelma, the fact that his cuffs and kicks were for the boys, never for her; the thick softness in his voice when he spoke to her; the idea that had formed in that low black skull, as simple and easy as death.

"Why, yes," Martha King said. "Of course it'll be all right. Keep her here as much as you like." And pushing the door open, she went on into the front part of the house.

4

"Here, puss. . . . Here, puss, puss, puss. . . . Here puss. . . ."

Leaning over the railing of her second story porch, Miss Ewing looked up and then down the alley. Though she called and called, the big yellow tomcat did not come. "I can't wait any longer," she said to herself out loud. "I'm late enough as it is," and went back into the kitchen, locked and bolted the back door, and put the saucer of milk in the icebox. This was not the first time that the cat had failed to come when she called, and it could just look after itself until she got home.

Left to her own devices, Miss Ewing would never have taken on the care and responsibility of an animal. This one had adopted her. One autumn night when she got home from work, the cat, half-starved, was sitting on her front steps. She stopped to stroke it and the cat purred at her touch. It sat so quiet, so gentle, and so trustful that she toyed with the idea of keeping it, and then after a moment said, "Go home, pussy!" and went on up the stairs to her flat. Ten minutes later she hurried down and opened the street door. The cat was still there, and bounded up the steps after her as lightly and eagerly as a kitten.

She let the cat out every morning when she left for work and when she got home in the evening it was there waiting for her. She learned (or thought she learned) its habits and the cat learned hers. It was company, it was someone to talk to and worry over, and it was, in spite of its condition when she found it, a very superior creature. After she had fed it a few weeks it filled out and became quite handsome. But then it took to wandering, so that she never knew whether it would be there or not when she was hurrying home. Sometimes it was gone for two or three days. And one morning when she opened the back door, she saw something that caused her to let out a low moan. What she took at first sight to be the pieces of a cat—*though not her cat*—proved to be something else; a section of bloody fur, a piece of raw red flesh, and the hideous dismembered tail of a rat. The cat, having eaten all the rest, had left these three pieces on Miss Ewing's porch in front of her back door, to chill her with horror (or perhaps as a mark of friendship and favour). And after that terrible and instructive sight Miss Ewing could not pet the cat or hold it on her lap or feel towards it as she had before. She continued to feed it, and the cat, accepting the change in her, came and went as it pleased.

Miss Ewing's flat was in a row of identical two-story buildings a block from the railroad. It was dark in the daytime and larger than she needed. It would have been too large for her except that she had crammed into it most of the furniture that had once been scattered through a house on Fourth Street, leaving herself barely enough room to move around in. As an only child, Miss Ewing had inherited everything, including, for about fifteen years, the problem of supporting her parents, both of whom were now dead. In the front room there were two large, oval, tinted photographs under convex glass of her mother as a young woman and of her father before he took to drink.

Ordinarily, it was easy for her to get to the office of Holby and King, dust and arrange the two desks in the inner offices, and be at her typewriter when Austin King walked in. But for over a week now, she had found it harder and harder to get up in the morning. She heard the alarm clock go off and lay in bed unable to move, unable to lift her head from the pillow, exhausted by the effort of producing plays and parts of plays in which the characters changed roles with one another and spoke lines that were intended to make the audience laugh (although the play was a tragedy), and the dead came back to life, and everything took place in a half-real, half-mythical kingdom against a backdrop of pastel sorrow. The cat figured frequently in Miss Ewing's dreams. So did her mother. And so, in one disguise or another, did Nora Potter.

When Miss Ewing went to work for the firm of King and Holby she understood, without having to be told, that the big calf-bound books that lined the walls of the outer and inner offices were not to be taken down and read by her. She could copy deeds and abstracts to her heart's content. She had the run of the filing cabinet. She could take dictation, and she could put in long-distance telephone calls and say (sometimes to Springfield, sometimes to Chicago), "Just a minute please, Mr. Holby calling . . ."

Miss Ewing knew as much about mortgages, wills, transfers, property rights, bills of sale, clearance papers, all the actual everyday functioning of a law office as the average attorney ever needs to know. With a little reading on the side, she might have been admitted to practice, along with Miss Lavinia Goodell, but instead she had chosen to dedicate her energies to the best interests of the firm of King and Holby, and later, the firm of Holby and King. She not only knew all their clients by name, but also where the income of these clients was derived from and among what relatives their property would be divided when the undertaker had made away with the mortal remains. She knew what Austin King thought of Mr. Holby and what Mr. Holby thought of Austin King. She knew who (in all probability) killed Elsie Schlesinger on the night of October 17th, 1894. The only thing Miss Ewing didn't know was how to drive Nora Potter out of the office, how to send her weeping down the stairs.

She interrupted Nora's reading whenever she had a free moment to do this in. She took delight in leaving the door into the hall open so that, although a cold draught blew around her own ankles, it also blew around Nora's. She found a black velvet bow and, holding it between her thumb and forefinger as if it were unclean, deposited it in the wastebasket. She spoke one day with a Southern accent and instead of appreciating the true nature of this pleasantry, Nora smiled at her and said, "Why Miss Ewing, you're beginning to talk like a Southerner just from being around me." Nora offered to stamp and seal envelopes when Miss Ewing's desk was inundated with outgoing correspondence. Nora said, "Can't I do some typing for you, Miss Ewing? I can only use two fingers but that won't matter, will it?" Nora said, "Can't I help you with that old filing?" Nora said, "If you'd like me to, Miss Ewing, I'll . . ." Day after day Nora was kind and thoughtful and cheerful and pleasant and friendly in a way that no one (if you exclude the cat that Miss Ewing could no longer bear to touch) had ever been. And perhaps it was this as much as anything that made Miss Ewing wake up so tired in the morning.

In her hurry to get as much work as possible done and out of the way before one-thirty, she made mistakes. She filed papers away in the wrong folders, she found sentences in her shorthand notebook that she could not decipher, she left a whole clause out of a contract that Austin King had given her to copy. When he pointed this out to her, she flushed, mumbled excuses, and retired to the outer office to copy the whole thing over. This time, she inserted the carbon paper the wrong way so that one of the carbon copies had the same words on the back, inverted, and the other was a clean white page. As it drew nearer and nearer to one-thirty, Miss Ewing's eyes kept turning to the clock. Her hands were clammy and moist, and she had to wipe them continually. She was short with the wrong people and patient with people whose reasons for climbing the stairs were dubious. But when one-thirty came, and Nora walked in, there was an abrupt change. Composed, patronizing, ironical, Miss Ewing looked up from her typewriter and said, "Good afternoon, Miss Potter. What is it to be today—Blackstone or Sir James Maine?"

5

The bed creaked in the room across the hall and then a voice answered, "Yes, Alice, what is it?"

"Are you awake?"

"Well, I'm talking to you. I suppose I'm awake. What is it?"

"I thought I heard something."

"In Mother's room?"

"No, downstairs. It sounded like somebody walking around down there. Did you lock the back door?"

"Yes. Go to sleep."

In the summer night such marauders as are about—the night insects, the rabbit nibbling clover on the lawn, the slug sucking the iris blade—all go about their work of destruction in a single-minded silence. Sleep is disturbed not by noises but by the moonlight on the bedroom floor. But in the late fall and early winter, especially before the snow comes, there is a time of terror when field mice, rats, and squirrels, driven indoors by the cold, make ratching-scratching sounds inside the walls; the stairs creak; some part of the house settles a thousandth of an inch (the effect of a dead man's curse or a witch in the neighbourhood); and people whose dreams are too active wake and hear sounds that (so the pounding in their left side tells them) have been made by a prowler.

"If it *is* somebody," Alice Beach said, "they probably won't come upstairs where we are. They'll probably just take the silver and leave. That's what I'd do if I were a burglar."

"Oh, Alice, you're so silly. There isn't anybody downstairs."

They both held their breath and listened, with their hearts

constricted by fear, the pulse in their foreheads beating against the pillow.

"Sh—sh——"

"Very well," Lucy said. "I'm going downstairs and find out what it is. Otherwise you'll keep me awake all night."

"Oh, Lucy, please! *Please* don't! It isn't safe!"

"Fiddlesticks!"

The light went on in the room across the hall and Alice got up out of bed also, put her dressing-gown on, and followed Lucy to the head of the stairs. The light at the foot of the stairs went on, then the light in the parlour, in the dining-room, the kitchen, the laundry. With every light in every room of the whole downstairs turned on, Lucy Beach opened the door to the basement and stood at the head of the cob-webbed stair, waiting. The cause of their disturbance was not there.

It is never easy to live under the same roof with someone in love. Even when the secret is known to all and can be openly joked about, there is something in the atmosphere that promotes restlessness. If the family is divided into those who know and those who don't know and mustn't under any circumstances find out, then instead of restlessness there is a continual strain, the lamps do not give off their usual amount of light, the drinking water tastes queer, the cream turns sour with no provocation. The conspirators avoid each other's eyes, take exhausting precautions against one another, and read double meanings into remarks that under normal circumstances they would not even hear. The person they are doing their best to protect keeps giving the secret away. Now on one pretext, now on another the cat is continually let out of the bag and it is then up to those who know about this animal to rush immediately and corner it before the fatal damage is done.

"You see?" Lucy said, and closed and locked the cellar door. Turning out lights as they went, they found themselves, at last, in the front hall. Lucy opened the door of the coat closet, where a man could have been hiding among the raincoats and umbrellas. "Now if you're satisfied," she said, "we can go back to bed."

6

"I know you're busy, Mr. King," Miss Ewing said, "but Mr. Holby has someone in his office and I thought—if you could give me a minute, that is. I—if you don't mind, I'll close the door."

Austin had given her a great many minutes without her feeling any need to ask apologetically for them, and her manner now was so hesitant, so deeply troubled that he motioned her to a chair. Miss Ewing sat and twisted her handkerchief and at last said, "I haven't been feeling well lately. The doctor tells me I ought to take a rest."

"The office is very busy just now," Austin said, "but I guess we can manage somehow. We don't want you to get down sick. How much time do you plan to take off? A week? Two weeks?"

"I'm afraid it would have to be longer," Miss Ewing said. "I know this is a hard time for you, and I don't like to do it, Mr. King, but Dr. Seymour thinks I ought to give up my job entirely."

"I'm sorry to hear that," Austin said, neither his voice nor his expression conveying an adequate amount of regret. It takes time to accept a catastrophe, and in the face of the first intimation that the golden age of Miss Ewing had come to an end he was almost cheerful.

"I'm sorry to have to tell you," she said. "I thought maybe I could keep on a while longer anyway, but I haven't been sleeping at all well and——"

"It's not a question of money, is it? Because if it's a question of money, I'd be glad to speak to Mr. Holby about a raise for you. I'm sure it could be arranged."

"No," Miss Ewing said. "It isn't that. You and Mr. Holby have always been generous with me. More than generous. It's just that I'm getting along in years and I don't seem to be able to stand the work I used to. My mind is tired, and it makes me so nervous when things don't go just right—when I make mistakes."

Austin searched his conscience for some mild reprimand, some abrupt or impatient gesture that might have hurt Miss Ewing's feelings.

"I'll never forget how good your father was to me when I first came to work here. I was just a girl and I didn't know anything about law or office work. He used to get impatient and lose his temper and shout at other people, but with me he was always so considerate. He was more like a friend than an employer."

Austin nodded sympathetically. What she said was not strictly true and Miss Ewing must know that it was not true. His father had often lost his temper at Miss Ewing. Her high-handed manner with people that she considered unimportant and her old-maid ways had annoyed Judge King so that he had, a number of times, been on the point of firing her. He couldn't fire her because she was indispensable to the firm, and what they had between them was more like marriage than like friendship. But there is always a kind of truth in those fictions which people create in order to describe something too complicated and too subtle to fit into any conventional pattern.

"He was a wonderful man," Miss Ewing said. "There'll never be anybody like him."

Austin's glance strayed to the papers on his desk, and then returned to Miss Ewing. "When would you want to leave?" he asked.

"As soon as possible."

"I'm afraid there are a good many things that Mr. Holby and I don't know about. We've leaned so heavily upon your experience and knowledge of the firm. If you could stay on a few weeks, say until the new girl is broken in."

"Oh I expect to do that," she said eagerly. "The way things are now, I'm the only one who——"

She stopped talking and looked at him with such a strange pleading in her eyes that, half in fright, he started to get up out of his chair.

"Mr. King, I'm not the person you think I am. You shouldn't have trusted me. I've done things I never thought I'd do. Something so. . ."

What was left of her ordinary self-composure gave way entirely and she began to cry and to tell him that she had done terrible things, so terrible that he'd have to put her in jail for it. From her hysterical confession he could make only one incredible fact—Miss Ewing had stolen money from the firm. How much he couldn't discover, but apparently it had been going on for over a year. First, small sums from the cash box. Then she had forged his and Mr. Holby's signatures and in that way withdrawn considerable sums from the bank, which her knowledge of book-keeping had enabled her to conceal.

"If you had come to me and told me that you needed money," Austin said.

"I didn't need it. I don't know why I took it. At first I just wanted to see if I could, as a kind of game, I guess. And when I found out how easy it was to deceive you and Mr. Holby, I went on doing it. If Judge King had been alive I wouldn't have dared. He'd have guessed somehow, and he'd have done something terrible to me. But you kept coming in, day after day, always the same, always trusting me, and I couldn't stand it any more. I just had to tell you and get it over with before I went crazy. You don't know what it's like,

Mr. King, to have something gnawing at your conscience day and night. No peace of mind, no rest, until finally you think everybody knows and is just waiting to catch you at it. Anything, even going to jail, is better than the worry you go through in your own mind. I hope you never know. But that's what you have to do with someone like me—call the police and have them take me away. . . ."

She broke into a fresh storm of weeping, and Austin got up from his chair and went around the desk and put his hands on her thin shoulders to comfort her.

"Please don't!" she exclaimed, shaking herself free. "I don't deserve kindness, and I can't stand it. I can't stand anything more."

Austin left her weeping in the chair that was reserved for people who came to inquire into their rights under the Law, and went out into the outer office and called a cab. When it came, Miss Ewing put her hat and coat on, and took one last wild hopeless look at her cluttered desk. Austin helped her down the stairs and told the Mathein boy who was driving his father's hack to take her home. Then he went back into his office, closed the door, and called Dr. Seymour.

In his excitement, while he was talking over the telephone, there was a certain hardness—the hardness of triumph. All these years Miss Ewing had rubbed his nose in the fact that he was not the man his father was. And how the mighty were fallen! But he said "She's put in many years of faithful service, and if she's sick—she'd never have behaved this way otherwise—naturally we'll take care of her"; and so preserved that inner image, the icon that no one, kind or unkind, is ever willing to change.

7

"Why my darling!" Martha King exclaimed as she lifted Ab onto her lap. "My precious angel! Nobody can ever take your place, not even for one solitary second!"

Ab's tears were stopped by the quick comfort of softness and her mother's "There, there . . ." When she sat up she was smiling.

"Where will the baby sleep? Will the baby sleep in my room?"

"If you'd like it to," Martha said. With her hand she brushed Ab's bangs back from her high forehead, and then bending down, kissed the soft place where the bones had long since grown together.

When Ab left her to go and play, Martha got up from her chair and went over to the window seat and the pile of mending. Rachel had failed to show up, that morning, and Martha King was weighed down by a premonition. The tangle of socks, the shirt collar that needed turning, remained untouched. For over an hour she sat with her forehead against the window, looking out on the driveway and the house next door, on the kitchen pump and the mulberry tree now stripped of both leaves and fruit.

What she thought of, sitting there all that time, she could not have told later. She saw a leaf dropping, people passing on the sidewalk, the grey overcast Saturday. But all this was out of any time sequence and often part of a long chain of ideas and images that seemed to have no connection with each other and that led nowhere. There is a country where women go when they are pregnant, a country with no king and no parliament. The inhabitants do nothing but wait, and the present does not exist on any calendar; only the future, which may or may not come. Yet something is accomplished there, even so, and that inescapable tax which in the outside world is collected once every lunar cycle, in blood, is forgiven and remains in the hands of the taxpayer.

The castle in which all are confined is surrounded by a moat fed by underground springs. There are no incoming and outgoing heralds, no splendour falls on the castle walls. The windows are narrow slits looking out through stone upon a landscape of the palest colours. The view from the highest turret is always the same, except that sometimes there is no view at all.

The inhabitants of the castle are often seized with cramps and vomiting. They are extravagantly hungry one moment and without appetite the next. Consistency is not required of them. Eccentric wool-gatherers in summer they huddle each one beside an ornamental stove that is always lit and there for her alone. In winter they put their arms through the slits in the stone walls and feel the warm rain. Emotions are drowsy, remembered, and vague. Bitterness, hatred, and fear are watered and tended and turned so that they can grow evenly, and then are forgotten before they have a chance to flower. Intending becomes pretending. The children's voices that are heard occasionally are not the voices of children who will grow up and marry and beget more children, but those of Cain and Abel quarrelling over the possession of a tricycle or a rubber ball.

Now and then someone tries to escape from the country but this is difficult. There is bound to be trouble at the frontier. The roads, although policed, are not safe after dark. People are robbed of the calcium in their bones, and of their life's savings in dreams. The featureless landscape turns out to be littered with dirty things, maggots crawling, disgusting amoeba that move and have hairy appendages, or the bloated body of a dead deer.

A sound outside made Martha King turn in time to see Mr. Porterfield wheeling his bicycle up the brick driveway. As she opened the kitchen door, her eyes travelled to the note in his right hand.

The Reverend Mr. Porterfield was a slight, neatly dressed Negro of uncertain age. His hands and face were grave, his manner (neither obsequious nor race-proud nor quick to see insult where no insult is intended) a model for white people to follow in dealing with black. Every Sunday evening from the platform of the African Methodist Episcopal Church he justified the ways of God to his congregation, and when they were in trouble, they came to him for help.

"I don't know what I'm going to do without her," Martha said, after she had finished reading Rachel's note. "Is she all right?"

"Yes, ma'am."

"She didn't say where she was going or what her plans were?"

"Well, no," he said carefully. "She requested me to deliver the message to you and I said I would. But where she was going, she didn't exactly say."

"I see," Martha said. "Won't you come inside? It's very cold out today."

"Thank you, ma'am, but I have to be getting on downtown."

As he righted his bicycle, Martha said, "Did she take the children with her?"

"Oh, yes," Mr. Porterfield said. "Yes, she took the children."

"Well, if you hear anything from her . . ."

"Be glad to. If I hear anything, I'll certainly inform you of it. . . . Good day, ma'am, and remember me to Mr. King."

He knows and he won't tell me, Martha King thought as she watched him wheel his bicycle down the driveway. She started back into the house and then hesitated. Her eyes took in the icebox and the accumulation of things destined for the barn loft, as if somewhere—behind the mildewed print of the U.S.S. *Maine*, perhaps, or in the box of tarnished evening slippers—was hidden the disturbing reason for Rachel's conduct, why she trusted Mr. Porterfield and not Martha King.

8

"Wait till I get there, Nora," Alice Beach called out from her room, where she was getting dressed.

"We're waiting," Nora called back. "I haven't told them a thing."

Each evening when she came home from the office of Holby and King, she brought life and excitement not only into the Beaches' gloomy house but also into the even gloomier sickroom. The atmosphere of illness had had to give way before it. The invalid's eyes were bright with curiosity, and she had permitted Nora and Lucy, as a mark of special favour, to sit on her bed.

"Austin asked me if I'd come back this evening and help out. They've been searching all afternoon long for somebody's will. Apparently Miss Ewing had her own system of filing and——"

"You are too, telling them," Alice called out.

"No, I'm not," Nora said. "Nobody can figure out what it is. The whole place is turned upside down, Mr. Holby is leaving for Chicago in the morning, and poor Cousin Austin——"

"Now," Alice said coming into the room. From the colour in her cheeks, the eager expression on her face, she might have been expecting a gentleman caller.

"Miss Ewing's mother used to sew for me," Mrs. Beach said, forgetting that she had told Nora this vital fact several times already. "I had her for a week in the spring and a week in the fall. She was honest as the day is long, but slow—terribly slow."

"Well," Nora said, sitting back and with her arms crossed, looking from one interested face to another, "guess what."

"Oh, don't keep us in suspense any longer!" Alice cried.

"I won't," Nora said. "It was all in her imagination. The auditors have gone over the books with a fine-tooth comb, backwards and forwards, and every penny has been accounted for."

"No!" Lucy exclaimed.

"Well, I'm glad, for her mother's sake," Mrs. Beach said.

"There isn't a word of truth in Miss Ewing's story," Nora continued, "and I don't know how many people she's told it to. For instance, she hasn't been near the doctor in two months."

"It's the strangest thing I ever heard of," Alice said.

"Austin can't convince her—he stopped in to see her this afternoon and I went with him. She still insists that she's a thief and ought to be sent to the penitentiary. It's very hard to know what to do with someone in that upset state. When you try to reason with them——"

"Was she in bed?" Lucy asked.

"No," Nora said. "She was up and dressed. She has a cat, a big yellow tomcat and she didn't want me to pick it up, but it came straight to me and sat in my lap as contented as you please, all the time we were there."

"Austin shouldn't have left everything in her hands," Mrs. Beach said. "I'm surprised at him. I thought he was a better businessman than that."

"But if you knew Miss Ewing——" Nora began.

"I had to watch her mother like a hawk," Mrs Beach said. "If I didn't, every stitch had to be ripped out and done over again. Part of the trouble was that she was going blind and didn't know it. Miss Ewing must have wanted to steal the money. Otherwise, it wouldn't be so on her mind. . . . When Lucy was six years old, she took a dollar bill from my pocketbook to buy lemonade," Mrs. Beach went on, as if Lucy no longer had any feeling about this crisis in her moral life. "I knew all about it. The neighbour boy who had the lemonade stand stopped me as I was coming home and gave me the change, but I wanted her to tell me and so I waited . . ."

Lucy flushed, and when the painful story came to an end, Nora tactfully led the conversation around to Miss Ewing again.

"They've arranged for her care in a nursing home in Peoria until she's better. The thing is to get her to go there."

"Who's footing the bill?" Mrs. Beach asked.

"Cousin Austin offered to. Mr. Holby refused to have any part of it. But something has to be done with her. She's threatened to kill herself. Tonight as we left each other, Cousin Austin asked if I'd mind going to see her again tomorrow, alone. He thinks maybe she might listen to me where she wouldn't listen to a man, and of course I told him I'd be glad to. I feel that anything I can do to help her, I ought to do, especially when they've all been so kind to me."

9

The chairs in Dr. Seymour's waiting room were straight-backed and hard, and time passed very slowly there. The dark varnished woodwork, the soiled lace doily on the centre table, the ancient *Saturday Evening Posts*, the brass lamp, and the leering, pink plaster billikin, all went with the atmosphere of antiseptic and worry, which remained intact, in spite of the continual substitution of one worried person for another. The waiting room was full: Austin and Martha King, an old man with his left hand wrapped in a dirty bandage, a woman with a little girl, a red-cheeked man who was the picture of health but who could not have been what he appeared to be or he wouldn't have been here. They sat, sometimes looking at each other, sometimes staring at the two pictures that hung on the wall. One of these pictures was of a doctor in a long frock coat walking down a moonlit road with his medicine bag in one hand and his umbrella in the other. The umbrella was held in such a way that the doctor cast ahead of him the shadow of the stork. In the other picture, the doctor was at the bedside of a sick child, whose anxious father and mother were standing in the shadows.

After a time, an elderly woman being treated for the cataract on her right eye was led out by a woman who might have been her daughter. While she was inside, the elderly woman had been told something that she had not expected to be told; something good or something bad that it would take her a while to get used to. In the meantime, she had to be guided. Someone had to manage her purse for her, and show her the way to the door.

The man with the dirty bandage went inside, and Austin looked at Martha. She surprised him now by a patience that he (who was always so patient) did not have. He fidgeted, he was restless, he turned nervously and looked out of the window. His usual sense that everything would be all right, that he was not threatened by the disasters that overtook other people, had deserted him. These consultations had taken place before and they were always the same, always reassuring. He ought to have been at his office at this moment, but Martha couldn't have managed the street-car, and he didn't want her to come in one of Jim Mathein's dirty old hacks, so he had harnessed Prince Edward and driven her down here himself.

The little girl was suffering from some skin disease. She looked at Martha and then away, looked again, and finally buried her head in her mother's lap. The two women exchanged glances and smiled. Gradually the little girl overcame her shyness to the point where she could come and lean against Martha's knee.

"How old are you?" Martha asked.

"Five," the mother said. "She doesn't talk."

"Oh," Martha said. She leaned forward so that the child could finger her beads. It was all that Austin could do to keep from interfering, but Martha had no concern apparently about the skin disease and whether it might be contagious.

For a while nothing happened in the waiting room—nothing more interesting or dramatic than the sun's coming out from behind a cloud, outlining the window on the linoleum floor and transferring the lace curtains there also, as if they were the kind of decalcomania pictures that schoolboys apply to their hands and forearms with spit. Of the illness that for forty years had passed through the waiting room, there was no trace. People with tuberculosis, people walking around with typhoid fever germs inside them, women with a lump on their breast that turned out to be malignant, men with an enlarged prostate, children who failed to gain weight. People with heart trouble, with elephantiasis, dropsy, boils, carbuncles, broken arms, gangrenous infections, measles, mumps, a deficiency of red corpuscles, a dislocated spine, meningitis, facial paralysis, palsy. Women with wrinkled stockings who would shortly be led away to the asylum, women who could not nurse their children, babies born to linger a short while, like a bud on a sickly plant. The little boy whose legs are in braces, the little girl who has breasts at three and begins to menstruate at four but is otherwise normal. The man whose breath is choked by asthma, whose heartbeat is irregular and tired. The woman with swollen joints. The woman whose husband has infected her with gonorrhœa. All saving their worry and fright for the inner office, all capable of being cured or incurable. The illness of the soul inextricably bound up with the illness of the body. The ones who ought to recover and won't, the ones whose condition is hopeless and yet who live on. Like the pattern of the lace curtain on the linoleum, they came and went, leaving no trace.

The man who had gone into the inner office with a dirty bandage wrapped around his hand came out with a clean one. The office girl said, "The doctor will see you now, Mrs. King," and Martha raising herself out of her chair, walked across the room with the curious, unnatural gait of a woman far gone in pregnancy.

Austin waited until the door closed behind her, and then his eyes dropped to the floor, searching for the outline of the window frame, which was so pale now that it was hardly visible, and soon went out altogether. He sat, crossing and uncrossing his legs. After a time he took out his watch and looked at it. The examination in the inner office was lasting longer than usual. He looked out of the window once more at the English cart and didn't at once realize that the office girl had spoken to him.

"I beg your pardon?" he said, turning away from the window.

"Dr. Seymour would like to speak to you," the office girl said.

10

"I don't know what you must think of me," Mary Caroline Link said. "I've been meaning to come ever since you got here, only there's so much to do. This is my last year in high school. I'm graduating in June. And what with the glee club and the triangular debate and outside reading— Did you ever have to read *The Heart of Midlothian*? It's a terribly sad book—I don't know where the days go. But it isn't right not to have time for your friends."

Her conversational manner suitable to a woman of forty, Mary Caroline sat on the sofa in the Beaches' parlour. She had come on a Sunday afternoon with an offering of Boston brown bread.

"I didn't think anything about it," Nora said.

"I hear you're reading law in Mr. King's office," Mary Caroline said. "I'm sure you must find it interesting."

"Yes," Nora said. Her smile was both vague and lavish with some shining inner pleasure.

"How is your brother?" Mary Caroline asked.

"He's fine," Nora said. "I guess he's fine. He never writes. Nothing in the world would make him write a letter."

When Nora smiled, Mary Caroline noticed that there was something about the shape of her eyes and the curve of her mouth that was like Randolph. Nora was nice looking, she looked like someone it would be exciting to know, but her face didn't, of course, make all other faces look flat and commonplace the way his did. There was only this fleeting similarity of expression. Mary Caroline was surprised that she had never seen it before, when it was quite noticeable.

"Do you like the girl he's engaged to?"

"Engaged?"

"Perhaps I shouldn't have asked about it. He told me in confidence, but I thought of course that you knew."

"No," Nora said kindly. "I'm afraid I don't even know what girl you're talking about."

"There must be some mistake," Mary Caroline said, colouring. "I must have misunderstood him. But he told me ——at least I thought he said he was engaged. It seems to me —I could be mistaken—that he said she was a beautiful girl from New Orleans, whose father was a millionaire."

"Oh, that one," Nora said. "No, he's not engaged to her, and never has been, so far as I know. Did he really tell you that?"

"Yes."

"I don't know what makes him tell such terrible lies," Nora said. "Except that he can't bear things the way they really are. Do you have any brothers?"

Mary Caroline shook her head.

"I've often wished that I had another brother besides Randolph," Nora said. "Because as it is, there's no basis of comparison. I don't know whether the way Randolph acts is usual with boys or not."

Nora could have told Mary Caroline how to get even with Randolph, and have led her to the holly tree from which the arrow would have to be fashioned that slew the darling of the gods. What Randolph could not endure was indifference. All Mary Caroline would have had to do was not to be touched by him, not to care in the least whether he lived or died, and he would have moved heaven and earth to make her care.

"I know lots of boys at school," Mary Caroline said, "and I assure you that Randolph isn't at all like them."

"Probably not," Nora said, patting a pillow into shape. "But sometimes I wish he weren't so vain."

"Is he vain?" Mary Caroline asked, sitting forward in her chair.

"Terribly."

"Well, I've never seen that side of him," Mary Caroline said. "But I suppose it's hard not to be vain if you look like Randolph. I'm glad you told me. I feel I understand him better. And it's nice, don't you think, when people who seem so perfect in every way turn out to have some small fault? It makes you like them all the more."

As a result, apparently, of this remark, the vague and yet shining smile was once more interposed between them.

From where Mary Caroline was sitting, through the parlour

window, she saw a rig drive up and stop in front of the Kings' house. She leaned closer to the lace curtain and then said, "It's Dr. Seymour. Is somebody sick at the Kings'?"

"Mrs. King," Nora said gravely.

"Oh dear," Mary Caroline said. "Nobody told me."

"She has to stay in bed all the time, from now until the baby comes."

"What a *shame*!" Mary Caroline said. "I must go and see her."

Feeling that she had already said more than she should about Randolph to his sister, Mary Caroline began to talk about the glee club cantata. She stayed until it began to get dark outside, and Nora went with her to the door. She had heard very little of what Mary Caroline said during the last half hour, and she had no idea that part of an undying devotion had been transferred from Randolph to her.

"I'll call you in a day or so and perhaps we can do something together," Mary Caroline said.

Watching Mary Caroline go off into the twilight and the rain, Nora said *You must not think I don't appreciate all you have done for me. If I don't speak of it, it's because . . .*

Deeply committed to a conversation with Austin King that never ended, Nora did not forget that he had a wife, but she found no room in her heart for jealousy. Cousin Martha was married to him and that was all. She had no interest in his work, no curiosity about what went on in his mind. For that he turned to Nora, who gave him her complete and rapt attention, no matter where she was or what claims the outside world made on her. *I realize perfectly that there are things which I cannot possibly say to you, which you do not wish to hear*, she said as she shepherded the children past the dangerous inter-urban crossing. *I think I have discovered something important*, she said as she put the pots and pans away in the cupboard. *No, I didn't actually discover it. You directed my thinking and there it was. . . . You may have friends who are nearer and dearer to you,* she said to the image in the mirror while she brushed and braided her hair, *but I doubt if there is anyone who cares more deeply about your happiness than I do. . . . I hear everything you say, everything,* she said, and let the coffee boil over on the stove.

II

"I appreciate your thoughtfulness in coming to tell me," Martha King said. "But you and I know, Miss Ewing, that Mr. King isn't that kind of a man."

This statement, which didn't follow logically what Miss Ewing had just been saying, confused and dismayed her. She was not in the habit of paying social calls on Mrs. King, and the long wait downstairs had given her ample time to consider whether it wouldn't have been better not to come. If she had known that Mrs. King was not well, that she would be received in Mrs. King's bedroom, her courage would have failed her. It was sustained now by the belief that what she was doing was for the best interests of the firm of King and Holby. Leaning forward anxiously, she said, "Of course, there's no one like Mr. King. That's why I was so surprised when he called her into his office and——"

What other strange visions Miss Ewing's eyes had seen lately—the synagogue of Satan, the four beasts full of eyes before and behind and within, hail and fire mingled with blood and all green grass burnt up, the star that is called Wormwood falling from heaven, and the air darkened by reason of the smoke of the pit—their unnatural glitter attested to.

"Naturally I'm sorry to learn that people have been talking about him and Miss Potter," Martha said kindly. "But it's something he is in no way responsible for. People have to gossip and if they can't find something that's true to gossip about, they're likely to make something up. I'm sure you'll do everything in your power to stop it. What a lovely umbrella! Is it new?"

"It was my mother's," Miss Ewing said, her attention shifting helplessly to the carved umbrella handle, in the likeness of a monkey's head with the two paws covering the mouth. Though Martha King was lying in bed, she managed to convey that her guest had stayed as long as politeness would allow. Miss Ewing rose and, further dismayed by the glimpse of herself which she caught in the dressing-table mirror (she certainly had no intention of being a busybody and a meddler), took leave. Outside in the hall, she made a wrong turning and soon afterward found herself face to face with the backstairs. Rather than run the risk of having to stop and explain this social error if she retraced her steps, Miss Ewing went on, arrived in the pantry, and, trembling with agitation, eventually found her way out of the labyrinth.

"I don't think anybody would believe her stories," Martha said when she finished telling Austin about her visitor that evening, "except that she isn't the only person who has been talking. You said it would cause a certain amount of talk and it has. Mrs. Jouette felt obliged to warn me of what people—mostly Mrs. Jouette, I have no doubt—are saying. I also heard it from Mrs. Ellis."

"Why didn't you tell me?" Austin asked.

"Because I didn't want to worry you. I knew you'd take it seriously, even though it's so preposterous, and a week from now they'll be gossiping about somebody else. But Miss Ewing's stories were really quite vicious. She's let her imagination run away with her, and if she's told anyone else what she told me this afternoon——"

"Let them talk," Austin said.

"It can't do us any harm," Martha said slowly, "but what about Nora? If being in your office is going to give her a bad reputation——"

"But how *can* they talk that way about her?"

"They can and they will as long as Nora behaves as she does," Martha said.

"What do you mean?"

"Apparently she tries very hard to pretend that she's simply a friend of the family. But she mentions your name a good deal oftener than there is any need for, and the way she looks at you as you walk through the outer office is enough under the circumstances to convict you both. If she shouted her love from the housetops, people wouldn't be any quicker to believe the worst."

"Oh," Austin said. And then, "I suppose if she gives up her plan of becoming a lawyer, and it's understood that she isn't to come to the office any more, or here, and if she manages to avoid speaking to me when we happen to meet somewhere, then they'd be satisfied?"

"It would help," Martha said.

"They can't hurt Nora," Austin said.

12

"Come in, come in," Austin called cheerfully, and to his surprise, Dave Purdy said, "Hello, Austin, how are you?" and walked into Mr. Holby's office instead.

A few minutes later Miss Stiefel brought Austin some letters to sign. Unable to find a trained law secretary, he had taken a girl out of business college. Her typing was adequate, but not to be compared, of course, with the perfection of Miss

Ewing's spacing and paragraphing. Miss Stiefel was pale, with blue eyes, and hair and eyebrows and eyelashes so blonde that they seemed almost white. Her face, just now, indicated that she knew more than it was expedient to show.

"That *was* Dave Purdy, wasn't it?" Austin asked.

Miss Stiefel nodded.

"Did you tell him I was busy?"

"No," Miss Stiefel said. "He wanted to see Mr. Holby."

"But I handle all his legal business," Austin said. "Mr. Holby doesn't know anything about it."

"Shall I ask him to step in on his way out?"

"Never mind," Austin said. And then, as she was leaving the room, "Will you let me know when Mr. Holby is free?"

Although he had not asked her to, she closed the door into the outer office, absentmindedly, perhaps. But it could also be, Austin realized suddenly, that she was following instructions from Mr. Holby—instructions based on the fact that the junior partner was socially no longer an asset to the firm.

When Miss Stiefel opened the door half an hour later, Austin was sitting at his desk with his head in his hands, and she had to speak to him twice before he heard her.

"Mr. Holby is free now."

Mr. Holby didn't as a rule stand upon his dignity. If he knew that Austin wanted to see him, he came to Austin's office. In a dull flush of anger, with the words of his resignation all framed in his mind, ready to offer if the occasion required it of him, Austin got up and went through the outer office. Mr. Holby went right on reading for a moment and then, glancing up, said, "Did you want to see me, young fellow?" He had not called Austin "young fellow" since the early weeks of their partnership.

Austin sat down. Mr. Holby offered him a cigar but no explanation of Dave Purdy's visit. Austin was sure that Mr. Holby would have preferred to ignore the incident. Mr. Holby didn't like explanations when rhetoric would do just as well. When the occasion demanded—in cross-examination, for instance—he could get to the point with the speed and directness of aim of a rattlesnake.

"Dave Purdy came to see you instead of me," Austin said.

Mr. Holby nodded. "He wanted to change his will. Nothing very complicated. I made a note of the change. Would you like to see it?"

"No," Austin said, "if he came to see you about it, you'd better go ahead and handle it. What I want to know is if there have been any others?"

For almost half a minute Mr. Holby didn't reply, and Austin saw that he was trying to make up his mind whether to take refuge in pompous vagueness or to speak frankly. In the end he took the cigar out of the corner of his mouth and spoke frankly.

"It's the women. They're out to get you."

"Why? How do you know?"

"I don't know," Mr. Holby said. "I only guess it; what usually happens when a man begins having trouble with his wife. They band together and take her side, and if they want to, they can do a good deal of damage in a business way."

"But I'm not having trouble with my wife," Austin said, with a rising sharpness in his voice.

"I didn't say that you were," Mr. Holby said blandly. "These stories start circulating, sometimes with no basis in fact, or at best a very slight one, and the first thing you know——"

"You're sure that's why Dave Purdy came to see you instead of me?"

"Positive."

"Have there been others?"

Mr. Holby inhaled twice in succession on his cigar and then nodded slowly.

"Would you like to dissolve the partnership?" Austin asked.

"It may not be necessary," Mr. Holby said. "It all depends on what happens. I mean between you and Martha."

"But I tell you——"

"I know I can speak frankly to you," Mr. Holby interrupted, "as one man of the world to another. Miss Ewing, I'm sorry to say, has done a good deal of talking. I'm no saint and I don't know anybody who is, but you can't expect to have an affair with another woman right under your wife's nose and not get into trouble. I'm not blaming you for it. Miss Potter is a very attractive young woman and it was probably something that you couldn't either of you help. What's done is done, and there's no use crying over spilt milk. We'll——"

"If you'd just listen to me for a minute!" Austin exclaimed. "Miss Ewing is as mad as a March hare. She——"

"The time has come," Mr. Holby said, "for *you* to listen to *me*. We'll weather the storm, and I don't mind telling you there has been a storm. It isn't only a matter of people coming to me instead of you. Bud Ellis has served notice on me that he is taking his business to Chappell and Warren from now on. Well, let him, I say. It's going to cost him a pretty penny before he's through. Meanwhile, anything you can do to patch things up between Martha and you, I advise you to do. Take some time off. Take a trip with her somewhere. It'll be all right with me."

"I'm afraid I can't afford a trip just now," Austin said. "And Martha is expecting a baby in January, so I doubt if she'd enjoy it."

"Suit yourself," Mr. Holby said, and got up from his desk and went toward the hatrack. Standing in the door, with his overcoat on and his silk muffler neatly arranged, he turned and said, "If Martha would care to talk to me, I'd be very happy to see her at any time," and went out, leaving Austin alone, his long legs stretched out in front of him, his eyes staring, and his anger with no outlet.

13

On the morning of the day before Christmas, Martha King did not come downstairs and the door of her bedroom remained closed. Austin stayed home that day and Ab followed him wherever he went, except that she was not allowed to use the basement stairs, which had no railing, and so, while he was searching for some boards to make a stand for the Christmas tree, she stood at the top and asked questions of the dark and dusty rooms below. With the wreath of holly on the front door, the red candles on the mantelpiece in the living-room and the study, and the tree lying on its side beside the icebox on the back porch, her mind was crawling with questions, the answers to which bred new questions that occasionally had to be repeated because Austin's mind was taken up with matters that had nothing to do with Santa Claus. *Put her to bed and keep her in bed,* Dr. Seymour had said. The slight hæmorrhaging had lasted only that one day, but the fear that it might begin again at any time kept Austin from sleeping, made him irritable and unlike himself. If she's only all right, he said to himself as he came up the stairs with the boards for the stand; if she just gets through this last month without any more trouble, that's all I ask.

With Ab after him, he went to the pantry and began searching through the drawer where the hammer should have been and wasn't. I should have realized, he said to himself, that something was the matter, that it was different this time from the way it was before Ab was born. I should have gone and talked to Dr. Seymour myself. Instead of which, I was so immersed in my own affairs that I—— "Frieda, have you seen the hammer? It should be here in this drawer."

"No, Mr. King," Frieda said from the kitchen. "You were the last person that used it. If it isn't there, I don't know where it could be."

The Kings' new cook was a middle-aged widow who had raised a family of five sons and then, just as she was ready to sit back and be taken care of by them, they had one after another married. She was very religious, with thin tight lips and a streak of grey running through her hair. They ate early on Wednesday evening so she could get to prayer meeting on time, but that wasn't of course the same thing as contributing to the support of foreign missionaries in far-off places like India and China, who would have been grateful (she managed to convey as she cleared the table) for the piece of gristle, the remainder of a slice of bread that Austin or Ab left on their plates.

The hammer turned out to be in the larder, a room that Austin King hadn't been in for over a month.

"How does Santa Claus bring presents to children who live in a house where there isn't any fireplace?" Ab asked at his elbow.

Austin answered this question to the best of his ability and then said, "Now if somebody hasn't made off with the nails."

"With his bag and all the presents?" Ab asked.

"Certainly."

With the boards, the hammer, and nails, Austin went out to the back porch and saw a grey sky and soft rain descending. The ground, which should have been covered with snow, was soggy after a week of rain.

"How does Santa Claus get here in his sleigh if there's no snow?"

"There's plenty of snow at the North Pole," Austin said, sawing at one of the boards he had brought up from the basement. When he had finished making the stand, he nailed it to the bottom of the tree and carried it through the kitchen, the pantry, and the dining-room, leaving a trail of pine needles behind him, and discovered that the tree was too tall to stand upright in the bay window of the living-room.

He decided that, for the sake of the shape of the tree, he would have to rip the stand apart and saw another foot off the trunk. He dragged the tree through the house once more, and out on the back porch.

If she takes good care of herself, Austin said to himself, as he pried the stand apart, and if she gets plenty of rest. And if I see to it that nothing happens that could in any way upset her . . .

But suppose she does take care of herself and something happens to her anyway? said the rain, the same slow steady rain that was falling on the graves in the cemetery. *Suppose you are left in this house? Suppose you have to go on living without her, the way other men have had to do who lost their wives?*

She's just got to be all right, Austin said to himself.

The stand, which had been all right the first time, now gave him trouble. The tree leaned to one side, and so he tried more nails, explaining meanwhile to Ab about Mrs. Santa Claus and her remarkable geese.

"And whenever she plucks one of her geese, it snows."

"Then why doesn't she pluck one of them now so Santa Claus's sleigh will have something to run on?" Ab asked.

"Because nothing is ever that simple."

"Why isn't it that simple?"

The tree, when he stepped away from it, teetered and in a spasm of exasperation he threw down the hammer and cried. "Oh, Abbey, I don't *know*!"

She backed away from him in surprise. He had never before spoken sharply to her and now, just when everything else was so confusing, it turned out that with him, too, there was a line that she must not cross. She looked at him as if, before her eyes, he had suddenly turned into a stranger. He picked her up in his arms and carried her into the house.

"You stay inside with Frieda," he said. "You're getting cold."

He was once more her kind, patient father, but that did not in any way alter what had just happened.

She sat watching him from a remote sofa while he set the tree up in the alcove of the living-room. Her face was long and thin with reproach. When he sat down beside her and lifted her onto his lap, her expression changed gradually. He saw that she had forgiven him and that she had another question which she was afraid to ask. He was tired to death of questions, hers and his own and everybody else's, and he sat holding her and looking at the bare Christmas tree. At last, feeling her so quiet against him, he said, "Well, Abbey, what is it?"

14

At quarter after eleven, on Christmas morning, the Kings' living-room was strewn, from the ebony pier glass to the dining-room doors, with tissue paper. The candles on the Christmas tree had burned low and been put out, for fear of fire. Their red and white and green and blue wax had dripped on the pine needles, the artificial snow, the gold tinsel, and the coloured balls that managed to reflect the whole disorderly, uninhabited room in their curved sides.

The square flat package on the hall table was for Nora. It was wrapped in red tissue paper tied with white ribbon and contained a handkerchief. On the sofa in the living-room, the presents that Austin had received were arranged in a neat pile that contained nothing more interesting or exciting than a belt with a silver monogrammed buckle (he already had a pearl-handled pocketknife) and a game that required the throwing of dice. The person or persons who had sent Ab the box of dominoes, the box of tiddlywinks, and the dancing mechanical minstrel would never be properly thanked, because Martha King was not in the living-room when these presents were opened, and the cards that came with them were now somewhere in the mass of tissue paper.

When the doorbell rang, there were footsteps in the upper hall, and Austin came down the stairs, with Ab following, one step at a time.

"Merry Christmas!" Nora cried, as he opened the front door.

"Merry Christmas," Austin said, and took the pile of Christmas packages that she held out to him so she could close her umbrella.

"When I went to bed last night," Nora said, disposing of her coat and the umbrella in the hall, "I was so sure it was going to snow by morning. How is Cousin Martha?"

"Just the same," Austin said.

Nora did not hear him. She had caught sight of the Christmas tree, and was exclaiming over it.

"This room looks as if a cyclone had struck it," Austin said apologetically.

"We just have a small one," Nora said, "on the dining-room table. At home every year—Oh, Austin, I've left you standing there holding all those packages! I'm so sorry." She took them from him and put them on a table. "Cousin Abbey, this is for you," Nora said, handing Ab the largest and most impressive-looking of the presents she had brought over.

Ab, jaded by the continual opening of packages, ripped the big rosette of red ribbon and the tissue paper off and discovered a Noah's ark. It was large, it was painted in bright colours, and it was undoubtedly the most expensive toy that had found its way into Mr. Gossett's shop in time for Christmas.

Nora glanced around the room and said, "Oh, isn't that a sweet doll's house! I had one when I was little—with real andirons in the fireplace that I just loved."

Ab found the catch that released the hinged roof, and dumped Noah and his wife and the wooden animals matter-of-factly on the floor.

"I'm afraid you've been much too generous," Austin said. "We'll put it away until she's older and can appreciate what a beautiful thing it is."

"No, let her play with it. . . . Cousin Abbey, show me what else Santa Claus brought you." In the midst of this tour of inspection, Nora suddenly turned to the pile of packages once more. "This is for Cousin Martha—it's a quilted bed-jacket. And this is for Cousin Martha, too. I couldn't remember what kind of cologne she likes, so I got her violet. And this is for Cousin Martha from Mama. It's the crocheted centre-piece that she started when she was here. She said to tell Cousin Martha that it was her masterpiece. . . . And this is for you, Cousin Austin."

Austin's present turned out to be a grey woollen scarf that Nora had knitted herself.

"That's very thoughtful of you, Nora."

"If you don't like the colour," she said, "I can make you another. All I have to do is get some wool and——"

"No," Austin said. "This is just right. Thank you very much."

"There's a present here for you," Ab said to Nora.

"Go and get it," Austin said. "It's on the hall table."

As Ab started out of the room, Nora said, "I didn't know what to get for Frieda."

"You didn't have to get her anything," Austin said.

"Well, I wanted to," Nora said happily. "I didn't know what she'd like so I got her a handkerchief. . . . Is this for me?"

"Yes," Ab said.

Austin turned his face away while Nora carefully and painstakingly untied the ribbon. Her exclamations of pleasure, her praise of Martha's taste, he only partly heard.

"Abbey, take these up to your mother," he said, handing her the three packages. "And be careful you don't slip on the stairs."

There was no use waiting until tomorrow to tell Nora what he had to tell her. He might as well get it over with, along with all the other unpleasantness.

With her head framed by the Christmas wreath in the window, Nora sat and listened quietly while he explained to her how grateful he and Mr. Holby were for all the help she had given them after Miss Ewing's breakdown, but how with the added burden and confusion of breaking in a new girl, they couldn't—they neither of them had the time to——

Without any noticeable or sickening jar, the world slid back into its accustomed orbit, the one it had been following for hundreds of thousands of years. Nora looked at her hands, at the holly on the mantelpiece, at the wooden animals that had fallen out of the ark. She said, "I know. . . ." She said, "I understand, Cousin Austin, I know exactly. . . ." And by the time he had finished, she was apparently quite reconciled. She tried to pretend that it wasn't a great disappointment to her, but only something natural and to be expected on Christmas Day. She smiled, she went on talking about other things for a short while, and as she was leaving, she said, "Tell Cousin Martha I love the handkerchief. I always lose mine wherever I go and never have enough."

15

"What I'd really like is to behave naturally toward you," Nora said. "And the knowledge you have that I do love you —and knowing *I* know that nothing can be done about that, but that you are willing to act as though this did not affect your attitude toward me as a person and so forth—I don't know whether I am expressing myself so badly that you may not be able to follow what I am trying to say. I hope you do understand, because it is terribly important to me—all these things help me to act toward you as I know I should. I may appear to be giving a very poor performance of trying to help myself, but I *am* trying."

For a while she sat silent, with her arms embracing her knees, lost in thought. The loudness of the clock testified to the lateness of the hour. Nora stared at the design of the carpet without realizing how the silence prolonged itself. At nine-thirty, when she came for the fourth night running, she had said that she was only going to stay for five minutes. She had been discussing, analysing, explaining herself for over three hours now.

"I can't accept the nice things you say to me," she said. "Accept them gracefully, I mean. And yet the very least little thing that you say to me pleases me so. It makes wonderful things happen inside of me. Do you know how good it makes me feel, how glad, sitting across from you in this room? I know that, being you, you know exactly what I am going through, and you are trying to help me. It seems like something without beginning or end, you and I in this room. Everything is so simple now, I say to myself. He knows how you feel. He knows you love him. He knows, in fact, everything. Go ahead and talk, if you must talk, only don't look at him. . . . Isn't it strange the trouble I have looking at you, Austin? I can't look at you."

If she had looked at him, she would have seen that his eyelids were drooping. The lines that gave his face character and distinction had melted. He was very tired. He had tried, like a man walking a tightrope blindfolded over Niagara Falls, to keep himself and the wheel-barrow in balance, but whereas Nora went away each night looking relieved, easier in her mind, and more hopeful, he himself was so exhausted by her that he could hardly get up the stairs.

"Sometimes I've thought about you and wondered. If you had known me first, would things have been any different? I don't mean necessarily that you would have wanted to marry me, but you'd have liked me, wouldn't you? Because I'm not like other girls, am I? Not just another girl who loves you and is afraid of becoming a nuisance?"

"No," Austin said.

"In spite of my general muddle-headedness," Nora said, "certain aspects of this thing are clear, irrevocably clear. I know that nothing can ever again be as empty as the life I lived before I knew you. When I have moments of despair and think it would be so much easier for me just to give up, I can't. Everything in me fights it at every turn. What do you do? What happens when you are caught between two things? When you can't get where you are headed, but it is impossible to turn back? I know that you have been kind and gentle when you might have been angry and lost all patience with me, and I would not have done anything but accept it from you, because that's how it is. Besides, in letting me come and read in your office, you have opened an entirely new world to me. I'm sorry, naturally, that it had to stop, but that doesn't alter the fact that you have been good and wonderful. How can you help but love a person who has been the sort of person you have been? I have nothing but the most profound admiration for you. . . . Oh, don't you see, if I keep this up, this wild talking, it's because I'm saying over and over 'I love you and you don't love me and how can I go on? What am I going to do?' Sooner or later you will become discouraged with me. You will feel I am not making any real effort to overcome an emotion which can only spoil everything for us. I mean make it impossible for us ever to talk to each other again the way we are doing now. . . . But if, in permitting me to say anything and everything to you, we have only succeeded in having me fall more in love with you, we must be on the wrong track. . . . Oh, it wasn't entirely wrong because if, up to a point, I hadn't been able to talk to you as I did that day in your office and as I have been, these last few nights, I think——"

There was the sound of a step on the stair, which Austin didn't pay any attention to, until it was followed by a second and a third.

"And I am thinking of this very carefully," Nora said. "I think I should have——"

The third step was followed by a fourth and a fifth. Austin's eyelids lifted. His face came back into focus. He turned toward the doorway into the hall. Nora went on talking and broke off only when Martha King came into the room, wearing a long lace negligee over her nightgown, and with her light brown hair down her back. She walked between them, over to the window seat, sat down, and drew the lace skirt together over her knees. For a moment nobody said anything. Nora coloured with embarrassment. "I'm so sorry," she said. "I didn't mean to disturb you."

"It's quite all right," Martha said. "Your voice carries." Then turning to Austin, "What do you want of her? Why do you go on making her suffer?"

Nora felt a flicker of elation which gave way to sorrow, to a sorrow that was very deep, as if the woman sitting in the window were her first friend and final enemy, someone whose coming had been long expected and planned for. "He hasn't made me suffer," she said. "He hasn't done anything. It's all my fault. I'm so sorry. I'm so very sorry this happened. Please forgive me!"

"Nora, I think you'd better go now," Austin said. "It's late. It's after midnight."

From the hall doorway, Nora turned and looked back and saw that they were waiting in a silence from which she was excluded.

"I really didn't mean to do this," she said, fumbling with the latch on the front door. "I couldn't have meant to do this."

16

There are only two kinds of faces—those that show everything openly and tragically, and those that (no matter what happens) remain closed. From the one every old loss cries out each time you meet it. Every fresh doubt calls attention to itself. The beginning of cancer or of complacency are immediately apparent, and so is the approach of death. From the other kind you get nothing, no intimation of strain, of the inner war of the soul—unless, of course, you love the person who looks out at you from behind the blank face. In that case, some day, instead of saying *How well you are looking*, as the last acquaintance before you has done, you may be shocked and ask abruptly *What on earth has happened*?

The same thing is true of houses, for anyone who is interested enough to look at them, at what is there. Rachel's shack cried out that she was gone, taking her children with her. The funeral basket lying on its side ten feet away from the two stones said *Keep away unless you are looking for trouble*. The wicker bassinet, half full of leaves, said *Man is his own architect*. The coach lantern and the coffee-pot had disappeared, the front door stood open.

On the unmade bed, on sheets that were twisted and sooty, Andy lay abandoned, flat on his back, barefoot, with trousers on and a woollen shirt unbuttoned over his chest. The breath that came from his open mouth, with each snore, was frosty. He turned onto his side, and huddled there like a fœtus, his hands locked in agony and in sleep.

A dry leaf had drifted in and was now resting on the edge of the rag carpet before it went even further. On the table were dirty dishes, dried food, cigarette butts, and a small pool of vomit. The patchwork covers were in a heap at the foot of the bed, but the hand that reached slowly out went in a different direction, over the side, down, fumbling until the fingers closed over the neck of a bottle and stayed there. The drawers of the old varnished dresser had at some time or other been pulled open and ransacked, and then left with garments dripping over onto the floor. In the kitchen Thelma's picture of the evening party at the Kings' had come loose and hung from one tack, flapping. All the food and cooking utensils had been knocked down from the shelves. There was a broken cup under a chair, and on top of the stove a mixture of coffee grounds and cornflakes.

The man on the bed sat up slowly, with the bottle in his hands. His eyes opened. Bloodshot and frightened, they looked around the room with no recognition in them, not even when they were focused on the open door. The man raised the bottle to his lips, and drank until the bottle, upended, proved conclusively that it was empty. He flung it across the room and the bottle bounced without breaking. The figure on the bed sank back solemnly, the hands opened and closed twice, as if in surprise (*Pharaoh's army got drowned*) and then the only movement was the frosted breath rising thinner and thinner from the purple mouth.

The Kings' house showed nothing, that day. To Mary Caroline Link, on her way to high school, and to old Mr. Porterfield, riding by on his ancient bicycle, the house looked exactly the same as it always had. The iron fence was enough, in itself, to keep out every threat the world has to offer, all danger of change, but Mrs. Danforth was uneasy. From her parlour window she had seen the setting sun reflected from the windows across the way several thousand times. She could predict almost to the minute when the lights would go on—first in the kitchen, then in the front part of the house. She knew also how the Kings' house looked when it was completely dark. She had looked out on the flower garden in summer when it was a mass of bright colour, in clumps and borders, and when the mounded beds, with snow on them, looked like a small family graveyard in a corner of a country field. The Kings' house—the east side of it—and her own house were like her left and right hand. And when there is something wrong with your hand you know it, whether other people are aware of it or not.

Mrs. Danforth opened the pantry door and listened, convinced that she had heard the telephone, that they were trying to communicate with her from the house next door. Then she went about her housework, made the big double bed in the front room, and with the dust-mop in her hands, worked her way down, frowning at the lint that had collected on the stairs.

17

"Now where are you going?"

"Upstairs," Ab said.

Frieda moved between her and the doorway into the dining-room.

"No, you don't, young lady," she said. "I have my orders and I'm to keep you with me, so just sit down on that stool over there and don't make any trouble, if you know what's good for you."

"I want my mother," Ab said.

"Well, you can't have her."

"I can too have her," Ab said. "And I don't have to mind you."

"Your mother doesn't want you up there. She's sick. You

try anything funny and you'll get what Paddy gave the drum."

"I'll tell my father on you when he comes home," Ab said.

"Go ahead and tell him. See how much good it does you."

"I will tell him."

"You're not to bother your Daddy either. He has other things to worry about. You stay here in the kitchen with me and be a good girl and maybe I'll let you lick the dish."

"I don't want to lick the dish, and I don't like it here. You're a bad woman."

"Sticks and stones may break my bones but words will never hurt me," Frieda said.

"If you don't let me see my Mama, I'll call the police. They'll come and take you away and put you in jail."

The thin mouth stretched to a grim slit, and a dark red flush told Ab that she had once more stepped over the line.

"Very well, young lady, call the police. I've taken all I'm going to off you. March right into the library with me and call the police. You'll see soon enough who they'll take off to jail."

She took hold of Ab's arm roughly, pulled her from the high stool, and forced her, stumbling, through the swinging doors, through the dining-room, and into the study.

"Sit right down there," Frieda said, giving Ab a final push toward the desk. "I'll wait here while you do it."

Ab looked at the black instrument on its hook. In spite of many imaginary conversations into a glass telephone filled with red candy, she had never thought of using the real instrument and she did not know what would happen, what voice would answer if she took the receiver off the hook. It might be Mrs. Ellis or Alice Beach or the man at the grocery store, or it might be the voice of her Sunday school teacher or of the man who came to the back door with froglegs.

"Go ahead," Frieda said. "I'm waiting."

Ab looked at the telephone and then wildly around for help.

18

"If only Alie hadn't come down with the grippe," Lucy said.

"Oh, it's so beautiful!" Nora said, standing at the parlour window with her fur hat on, and peering through the lace curtain at a world that was even more lacelike. The evening before, along about dusk, it had started snowing, and the snow had been coming down all night long. The walk and the front yard were buried several inches deep. Beyond that, Nora could not see because of the snowflakes that filled the air with a massed downward movement. "I want to get out in it," she said. "Twice in the night I got up out of bed and went to the window and stood shivering in my nightgown, trying to see the snow. Now I want to be out in it. I want to feel it on my face."

"I don't think you ought to try it," Lucy said. "Let me call the mothers. It probably would be better to, anyway. If the children get their feet wet, they'll all come down with colds."

On a newspaper beside the front door there were three pairs of overshoes. Nora found hers and sat down to put them on.

"By tomorrow," Lucy said, "it will have stopped snowing and the walks will be cleaned and you won't have such a time getting there."

"Who knows what it will be like tomorrow," Nora said gaily. "Maybe the snow will be six feet deep. Maybe we won't be able to get out of the house. Do the drifts ever come up as high as the second-story window?"

"I think I'd better come with you," Lucy said. "I really think I'd better. It'll be hard enough for you, but you don't know what it's like for children. You'll have to carry them, and you can't all that distance."

"They can walk behind me," Nora said. "I'll make a path for them."

She put her arms into the man's winter coat that Lucy held for her. The coat had belonged to Mr. Beach. It was very heavy, it was much too large for Nora, and it was lined with rabbit-skin.

"Now for the mittens. This is just like 'East Lynne,'" Nora said, and pushed the storm door open. The snow was banked against it, blown there during the night, and the storm door cut a deep quarter-circle into the new level of the porch. "Don't worry about me."

The front steps were rounded over so there was scarcely an inch drop from one to the next. Nora put her foot down cautiously where the walk ought to be, and discovered that the snow was six or seven inches deep. She took a big step and then another and another. At the place where the lawn curved down to meet the sidewalk there were three more steps, which she found under the snow. And then she stopped and looked around. The houses across the street had rounded white roofs with black chimneys sticking out of them. The trees, thickened, whitened, lightened with snow, gave a curious perspective to the street that Nora had seen only in the double post cards that went with the stereoscope in the dentist's office in Howard's Landing, Mississippi. "Oh, no wonder!" she exclaimed.

Love falling on her face, love falling on her hair, love smooth and untracked, filling up every previous impression, space closing in, distance diminished, the shape and outline of every house, every tree, every hitching post transformed, made beautiful, made into the great lace curtain.

With the heavy coat weighing her down, Nora floundered through the snow until she got as far as the Kings' front walk. Someone had shovelled a path from the porch steps to the sidewalk, and the path was already filling in, more than half obliterated. She saw large footprints which must be Austin's, and as she walked where he had walked, put her foot down in the print of his, all sense of cold left her. She rang the doorbell and then, turning around, saw the world as he had seen it, a few minutes before, from his own front steps. If I can have this and no more, Nora said to herself, it's enough. I'll be happy forever. I've had more than I ever expected to have on this earth.

But there was more. The arrangements (by whomever made) were generous. The snow kept on falling.

"She isn't going," a voice said in the intense stillness. "Her mother thinks it's snowing too hard for her to go to kindergarten."

"Thank you, Frieda."

"You're welcome, I'm sure, Miss Potter."

It isn't snowing too hard, Nora thought as she turned and went back into the excitement of high freedom. It isn't snowing hard enough.

Of the eleven children that she was supposed to collect, only four were expecting her, and walking with them was as difficult as Lucy Beach had foreseen. They had to walk backwards part of the time so that they didn't face the wind. There were stretches of sidewalk where no one had walked. There were deep drifts. They were sometimes forced out into the street. The children walked behind Nora, in the path that she schuffed for them, and when they got as far as the high school, the little Lehman boy began to cry. The snow had come over his shoe tops and his feet were cold and wet and he had lost one of his mittens. Nora tried to coax him and succeeded for a little way. Then he sat down in the snow and refused to go any farther, so she picked him up and carried him, as heavy as lead, until they reached the beginning of the business district. Here the sidewalks had been cleaned, and walking was easier.

"When we get to the kindergarten it will be all right," Nora kept saying to them. "The kindergarten will be warm. We'll play games. We'll play that it's Christmas."

At nine-thirty, she unlocked the door of the kindergarten rooms and walked in with the children following after her. Though it was immediately apparent, by their visible breath, that there was no fire in the stove, she went over to it and touched it with her hand. The stove was cold. The boy had not come.

There was a closet off the hallway, and in it Nora found some kindling; not much, but if she was careful it would be enough. There was a bucket of coal by the stove, with a folded newspaper lying on top. The fire smoked, but there was no crackling sound, and very soon it went out.

"It probably has something to do with the draught," Nora explained to the children. She raked the coal and blackened kindling out on the floor. There was no more newspaper, and so she snatched a long coloured-paper chain from the chandelier and stuffed it into the stove. The fire, rebuilt, burned feebly, without giving off any heat. The children stood around, all bundled up and shivering. In the hall closet, while she was rummaging for more paper, Nora found a can of kerosene.

19

Mary Ellis had been asked to the Friendship Club, at Alma Hinkley's house on Grove Street, as a substitute for Genevieve Wilkinson, who was out of town. There were the usual two tables and the scorecards were decorated irrelevantly with a hatchet and a spray of cherries. At five minutes after five, the four women in the living-room had finished their final rubber and were replaying certain hands in retrospect while they added up their scores. The table in the parlour had fallen behind because of Bertha Rupp, whose hesitations were sometimes so prolonged and whose playing was so erratic that for years there had been talk of asking her to resign from the club.

Ruth Troxell opened the bidding with a heart and then said, "It must have been a shock to Martha King, in her condition."

"It was a shock to everybody," Mary Ellis said.

"I pass," Irma Seifert said.

Mary Ellis passed and the bidding reached a standstill while Bertha Rupp considered the thirteen cards that chance had dealt her.

"Two clubs," Bertha Rupp said impulsively and then tried to change her bid to two diamonds, which the other players refused to allow.

"But I meant two diamonds!" she exclaimed.

"It doesn't matter what you meant. Two clubs is what you bid," Ruth Troxell said, and then glancing at the score pad beside her, "Two hearts." She was high at the table.

Irma Seifert and Mary Ellis passed.

"Why did they have a can of kerosene in the kindergarten rooms in the first place?" Irma Seifert said.

"That's what I can't figure out," Mary Ellis said. "Alice says that both she and Lucy knew it was there but they never ——Are you waiting for me? I passed."

"We're waiting for Bertha," Ruth Troxell said.

There was a long silence and then Bertha Rupp said, "Two hearts."

"Ruth has already bid two hearts," Irma Seifert said.

"Two spades then," Bertha Rupp said, clenching her cards.

"You're sure you don't want to go three hearts?" Ruth Troxell asked.

"No, two spades."

"Three hearts," Ruth Troxell said.

"With only the word of four-year-old children to go on," Irma Seifert said, "I don't suppose we'll ever know. Three no trump."

"I pass," Mary Ellis said. "Mrs. Potter is the one I feel sorry for."

"They say she has aged overnight," Ruth Troxell said.

"Austin met them at the train," Mary Ellis said, "and they drove straight to the hospital. Nora was conscious. She knew them."

"Who are they staying with?" Irma Seifert asked. "Your bid, Bertha."

"Oh, they're staying with the Kings, the way they did before," Mary Ellis said.

"I wouldn't have had any of them in my house if I had been Martha," Ruth Troxell said.

"At a time like that," Irma Seifert said, "you don't know what you'd do. Take these nuts away from me, somebody, before I make myself sick."

Part Six

THERE IS A REMEDY OR THERE IS NONE

I

"I wouldn't care how disfigured her face and hands might be," Mrs. Potter said, "if she'd only get well; if I could take her home with me and keep her there, forever and ever."

"From the moment they're able to walk, they start trying to get away from you," Mrs. Potter said. She was lying fully dressed on the bed in the yellow guest-room. One arm was thrown across her face, to hide the effort it required for her to remain in possession of her feelings. "They want to escape from your arms, get down out of your lap and leave the house where they were born. I don't know what it is. Nora never had anything but kindness at home. Her father worships the ground she walks on. So do we all. Love her to pieces. But it isn't enough, apparently. I don't know why this had to happen or what we could have done to prevent it."

"Nothing," Martha said. "You couldn't have prevented it or you would have. And you mustn't blame yourself."

Mrs. Potter had experienced The Sudden Change. While she was still trying to close the useless umbrella of the Past, the cold wave of the Present had come over her, and, miles and miles from home, she wandered sometimes with the wind, sometimes across it.

"She keeps trying to talk to me through all those bandages and it's so terrible. Are you sure Dr. Seymour is a good doctor, Martha?"

"We've always had him," Martha said. In open disregard of Dr. Seymour's orders, she was up and dressed, and sitting in a chair by the front window of the guest-room. But she had her own reasons for what she was doing—reasons that

Dr. Seymour wouldn't understand or approve of, but this wouldn't prevent her from putting herself in his hands when the time came to trust someone with absolute trust. "If you don't feel satisfied and want to call some other doctor in for a consultation, I'm sure it would be all right with him."

"I keep wishing we'd brought Dr. LeMoyne with us," Mrs. Potter said. "He's just a country doctor but he knows a great deal. He brought both my children into the world, and he would have come except that he's so old now. He's eighty-three and he would never have stood the train journey."

There had been a fresh fall of snow during the night. The limbs of the trees were outlined in white against a tropical sky. The tree ferns and palm fronds that went with the blue sky were drawn in white, on the window pane.

"This doctor seems very fond of Nora and anxious to do anything he can to relieve her suffering. The thing I don't understand is that she doesn't want to live. She keeps saying there's no place for her anywhere. I haven't told Mr. Potter. It would only upset him. But there must be some reason, something that is troubling her."

Looking out through the patterns of frost, Martha saw that the Wakeman children were trying to make a snowman. The snow would not roll properly; it was too dry, and instead of becoming larger and larger, the snowball crumbled and fell apart.

"You mustn't think too much about what she says in her delirium."

"I can't help thinking about it," Mrs. Potter said. "And besides, she wasn't delirious when she said that. She was in her right mind. 'I don't have to go on living if I don't want to,' she said. . . . Part of the time she knows me, and then other times when I say something to her, she doesn't hear."

A chunk of snow dislodged by the wind left a branch of the big elm tree and was scattered on the brilliant sunshine.

"If I only knew what it is that's troubling her, I might be able to do something about it. But I've asked her and she won't tell me. Did she ever talk to you and Cousin Austin?"

"She talked to Austin," Martha said.

"It surely wasn't the kindergarten," Mrs. Potter said.

"No," Martha said. "She was very good with the children. They all loved her."

"It must be something else," Mrs. Potter said. "Sometimes I think it was those law books. I told you, didn't I, that she never wrote us that she was reading law in Cousin Austin's office?"

"Yes."

"Was it Cousin Austin's idea?"

"No, it was Nora's," Martha said.

"Well, it was very thoughtful of him to allow her to do it. I should have thanked him before this. He's always so ready to help. Some day he'll get his reward. . . . I've been low in my mind, but I have always wanted to live, and I can't seem to find the right thing to say to comfort her. There's something else she said last night: 'It looks different without the leaves.' Whatever could she have meant by that?"

"I don't know," Martha said. "You're sure she said 'leaves'?"

"Yes. And then she said, 'I ought never to have allowed myself to hope.' I asked her what it was that she hoped, but she didn't hear me. And right after that, the nurse said something about her condition and she flared up and we had difficulty quieting her. I oughtn't to tell you these things, Martha. It isn't good for you when you're expecting a child. Everything ought to be happy around you. I don't know why you didn't tell us last summer—why you let us come and impose on you that way when there was no need."

"Last summer was a long time ago," Martha said. "Your being here now doesn't change anything so far as Austin and I are concerned. I'm just sorry that there's so little we can do."

"Don't say that," Mrs. Potter said, withdrawing her arm. "You and Cousin Austin have meant more to us in these last few days than I can ever begin to tell you."

"I'm going to leave you alone for a little while," Martha said. "You must get some rest before you go back to the hospital. If you want anything, call me."

The comforter who says *I know, I know* (and doesn't know) or *You must be brave* (when all people are brave and it doesn't help them when the blow comes) is nevertheless serving a purpose. Martha King made it possible for Mrs. Potter to talk about her grief, and when the words were out of the way and the bedroom door had closed and the comforter had gone off down the hall, then the dammed-up feeling was free to flow over the whole winter landscape, covering roads, setting houses and barns afloat, and determining at last the level past which the flood waters would not rise.

2

On the door of room 211 in the hospital was a sign that read NO VISITORS. This did not apply to Dr. Seymour and the nurses or to Mrs. Potter, who slept on a cot in Nora's room and went home some time during the day to change her clothes, to be with her husband, and to rest. The sign did apply to Austin King.

While he was at his office, he was safe; he could turn his mind to other things and forget for a while about Nora, though even here the trouble intruded. He would find himself staring at a legal paper he had read over and over, without knowing a single word he had read. When he was at home, his eyes kept turning toward his desk where, in the left-hand cubbyhole, there was a letter from Nora. Though Austin needed to talk to someone about this letter and all that had led up to the writing of it, there was no one willing to listen night after night with eyelids grown heavy and no one came down the stairs and put an end to his investigation of blind alleys and his consideration of what might have happened in the light of what actually had. He was quite clear in his mind about what he had meant to do for Nora, but he had been patient, he had listened to Nora instead of turning his back on her the day she came to see him at his office, and if he hadn't treated her gently, would Nora have stayed up North? So much depended on the answer to this question and there was only one person who could tell him (through bandages) what he needed to know.

The Mississippi people returning brought three small suitcases with them and left behind all desire to please, to charm, to acquire new friends. Though there was a question of how long they would stay, their reason for coming was clear to everyone. Time did not pass the way it had before in a whirl of carriage rides, picnics, and trips to the Chautauqua grounds. Time had slowed down and was threatening to stop entirely.

The friends the Potters had made on their previous visit did not desert them. The callers filled the living-room and overflowed into the study. What had happened was too tragic to be mentioned, and so the callers depended on their mere physical presence to convey how sorry they were, and talked about other things, about the weather, about the new oiled road from Draperville to Gleason, about the new fashions in women's dress, about their own sciatica or rheumatism or the great number of people who were down with the grippe, in an effort to divert the Potters from their only purpose in coming to Draperville. Lucy Beach threw herself into Mrs. Potter's arms and wept, but then the Beach girls had always been queer, and if they hadn't taken it into their heads to start a kindergarten, the whole thing might have been avoided. When Lucy had been led from the room, the conversation was resumed where it had left off, the full social strength was mustered to cover this lapse from decorum.

Mr. Potter acted like a man who had been stunned. He was neither restless nor interested in anything that went on around him. He sat most of the time in the big chair in the study, unable to take part in any conversation or to check the involuntary tears that at certain moments filled his eyes and slid down his leathery cheeks. Rather than disturb him, Austin and Martha King found themselves turning to Randolph when there were messages of sympathy that had to be acknowledged, decisions to be made.

Of the many things that would not fall into any proper place during this second visit, one of the strangest was the change in Randolph Potter. He was able to pass the mirror in the hall, the ebony pier glass in the living-room, without so much as a glance at his reflection. His handsomeness forgotten, he had become overnight the prop of the family. Mrs. Potter leaned on him as if from years of habit. When Ab offered herself to him, Randolph lifted her onto his lap but instead of playing games or teasing her, he went on talking quietly to the callers or to Austin and Martha, and after a few minutes she got down and went off to play. Mary Caroline Link called and Randolph talked to her in a way that was pleasant and friendly, but that aroused no expectations. It was almost as if he were her older brother, home from college and trying to fit once more, or at least appear to fit, into the family circle he had now outgrown. He asked about Rachel the first night, when a strange white woman moved around the dining-room table with platters of food. When Martha King explained that Rachel had disappeared shortly before Christmas, taking her children with her, Randolph nodded absently as if he had known all along that was what Rachel would eventually do.

He was not grotesquely cheerful the way his mother sometimes was, nor openly grief-stricken, like Mr. Potter. It was almost as if Randolph, who always walked by himself and never made common cause with his family, were now justifying the wisdom of his past selfishness by assuming full responsibility for his family and for the confusion and distress which they brought with them, sooner or later, wherever they went. Randolph was kind, he was thoughtful, anxious not to make trouble for Martha King and solicitous about her health, and sensible about the problems which Austin and Martha brought to him. More wonderful than anything else, he carried for eight whole days, all alone, the burden of conversation in a house where nobody felt like talking. His mild jokes and stories said or seemed to say: *You understand that it is not lack of feeling that makes me able to tell about the time Pa paid a call on the new minister. I know my sister is lying in the hospital badly burned and that there is nothing any of us can do about it. But if you listen carefully, you will perceive that the jokes I make, the stories I tell, are not the ones I would use if we were all lighthearted and Mama were not waiting for us to leave the dining-room table so she can go back to the hospital. But somebody has to carry the load, otherwise you would sit and stare at your food, and Pa would begin to cry again, and it only makes things worse.*

One day when he and Austin were alone in the study, Austin brought up the subject that no one was willing to talk to him about. "For a while," he began, "we didn't see as much of Nora as we ought to have. living right next door."

"You and Cousin Martha weren't in any way responsible for what happened," Randolph said.

"I know, but I blame myself for——"

"You mustn't. Sister shouldn't have stayed up here on her own. Mama tried to prevent her. We all did. But she had this idea about being a kindergarten teacher, and wouldn't listen to reason. I know you both love her and that's enough, as I keep telling Mama. She thinks if she'd only allowed herself to realize that Nora was a grown woman, and not kept harping at her—but you know Mama is just as set in her ways as Nora is. After a little, when things are straightened out, I hope you'll come and stay with us. You'd like it very much down South, Cousin Austin. I'll take you around and show you the country. Take you coonhunting, if you like."

3

"I just don't know," Mrs. Potter said.

Austin's question had taken her by surprise. The hack was waiting in front of the house and Mrs. Potter, with her hat and coat on, was waiting at the foot of the stairs for Mr. Potter to come down and drive off to the hospital with her. She glanced around for a place to sit down. The only chair near her was an antique of carved walnut that had been put in the front hall purposely because in the hall there was less likelihood of anyone's being tempted to sit on it. The chair creaked ominously but it sustained Mrs. Potter's weight, which was not much, in any case.

"The doctor said——"

"I realize that she isn't allowed to have visitors for a while yet," Austin said, "but now that she's out of danger, I thought maybe it would be all right for me to see her."

His hesitancy and embarrassment in asking for this favour made it clear that he had some serious reason for wanting to be admitted to the hospital room where Nora was, some reason that wouldn't or couldn't wait any longer.

"You couldn't give me the message?" Mrs. Potter asked.

Austin shook his head.

"You want to see her alone?"

"Yes," Austin said, colouring. "I wouldn't want to do anything contrary to Dr. Seymour's orders, but if it's all right with you, and you don't mind asking him——"

"Oh, it's perfectly all right with us," Mrs. Potter said doubtfully. "And I'm sure that if Nora weren't in pain, she'd be delighted to see you. She's always admired you so. But if it's something that would upset her——"

"I'd be very careful," Austin said.

"I know you would," Mrs. Potter said.

From the troubled expression on her face, she might have been sitting in front of some closet door that she had walked past a hundred times in the last week without once noticing that it was there. The beating of her own heart told her now that the closet contained something of interest to her. But was it something that needed to be discovered? Wouldn't it be better and wiser to keep on walking past the closet door as she had been doing? She raised her eyes and met Austin's questioningly.

Then it's here—Nora's secret—where I never thought to look for it? Is this why she doesn't want to go on living?

That's right.

Mrs. Potter parted the fur on her black sealskin muff with her fingers while she deliberated. At last she said, "I don't know why you shouldn't see her, if you want to. You're our own kin, practically. I know you won't stay too long or do anything to wear her out. I'll speak to the doctor about it. If he says it's all right for you to see her . . . Whatever can be keeping Mr. Potter? He knows we have to be at the hospital by four and it's now——"

"I'd be deeply grateful if you would," Austin said.

4

"I didn't mean to hurt your feelings, Miss Stiefel," Austin said, in the outer office. "But you do understand, don't you, that legal work has to be done right. Otherwise there's no point in——"

When it came time for Miss Stiefel to take dictation, she sat with her note-book on her knee and a frightened look on her face that nothing could erase. Austin dictated much slower than usual, and spelled out words as he went along, but the letters she brought in to him to be signed were, more often than not, full of mistakes. Worried lest he himself let something slip by that would cause difficulties later on, he had called the head of the business college. She had no one to send him who was any better than Miss Stiefel, or as good, and so he went on struggling with her, the struggling being interrupted occasionally by tears and apologies.

"I realize that the work is still new to you," he said, "and it takes a while to get used to the legal phraseology, but after this when you aren't sure about something——" Miss Stiefel's eyes were on the doorway and she was not listening to what he said. Austin turned around and saw Randolph Potter. "Be with you in a minute," he said. "After this, come to me with it and don't try to guess what it should be, because nine chances out of ten it won't be right, and it only makes more work for both of us. Mr. Griffon is coming in at four. Do you think you can have that lease ready by then?"

Miss Stiefel nodded, her pale face suffused with slowly rising colour.

"You'd better make two carbons, while you're at it," Austin

said. "We'll keep one here in the files. . . . Did you walk down?" he said, turning to Randolph.

"I came on the streetcar," Randolph said.

"Any news from the hospital?"

"Mama asked me to tell you that she's spoken to Dr. Seymour and it's all right. You can see Sister tomorrow afternoon at four o'clock."

Austin said, "Come inside."

"I know you're busy," Randolph said. "I just dropped in for a minute. I've got a cheque here that I wanted to get cashed, and I thought maybe, since they don't know me at the bank——"

"How much money is there in the cash box?" Austin said, turning to Miss Stiefel.

"Not very much," Miss Stiefel said. "Mrs. Holby was in, and Mr. Holby took ten dollars out of it for her, so——"

"Never mind," Austin said. "I'll endorse it and you can take it over to the First National Bank. You know where that is?"

Randolph nodded, took out his leather billfold, and extracted a cheque, folded in two. Without bothering to look at the amount or the bank that the cheque was drawn on, Austin borrowed Miss Stiefel's pen and wrote his name.

"Take this to the third window," he said. "If there's nobody there, ask for Ed Mauer. I'll call him and tell him you're on the way over."

Before Austin could make this telephone call, the client he was expecting came in, and soon afterward the telephone rang. "Excuse me just a minute," he said, and picked up the receiver. A voice that he recognized as Ed Mauer's said, "There's a fellow here says he's a cousin of yours. He's got a cheque——"

"Oh yes," Austin said. "I was just about to call you."

"——for a hundred and seventy-five dollars. I wanted to make sure the endorsement was genuine."

Though Austin was in the habit of dealing with his suspicions so summarily that he was hardly aware that he had them, this one was not to be ignored. It leered at him and said *Well?* The receiver shook in his hand. He thought of the letter from Nora that was in a cubby-hole of his desk at home. He thought of Mrs. Potter's face the day he had met her at the station and she said *Don't keep anything from me, that's all I ask. . . .* He thought of the night in the study, when Bud Ellis said *Naturally, since he was a relative of yours, we thought . . .* Some day, somehow, there would be an end. And meanwhile . . .

"It's all right, Ed. I endorsed it. Much obliged for calling me."

5

That evening it appeared that for once there would be no callers. Randolph left for the hospital with Mr. Potter soon after dinner, and Austin and Martha King settled down in the living-room.

"Do you feel all right? Is the house warm enough?"

"Yes," Martha said.

"I'll be glad when it's over with," Austin said.

"You're not worrying?"

"No, not exactly," Austin said. "It's just that——"

"There's nothing to worry about," Martha said. "I feel fine, and it's going to be a boy."

"You thought Ab was going to be a boy."

Like two people meeting by accident at a large party after years of not seeing each other, their two faces reflected the same slow recognition that nothing had changed, that everything was remembered.

"Do you remember, Austin, the beautiful fires you built for me when we were first married?"

"You don't care for this fire?"

"It's all right. I have no objection to it," Martha said. And then, "Ab can stay at the Danforths, but I don't know what to do about you."

At such meetings, silences have the weight of words chosen carefully, and words convey now single, now double meaning. The conversation moves forward in strides that take miles and miles for granted.

I keep hearing the sound of my own footsteps, Austin tried to tell her, silently. *Everywhere I go.*

"Maybe if you went to the office, at least part of the time——"

"No," Austin said, " I want to be here."

In desperation at the clotted feeling inside him that cried out *Oh I do love you,* he raised his hand as far as his forehead, and slowly took off his mask. No one is ever fooled by false faces except the people who wear them. The doorbell rings on Halloween, and you go to the door and what do you find? A policeman or a Chinaman, four feet high. The face might be convincing enough if you are near-sighted, but how can you fail to recognize and be touched by the thin arms and legs of the little Ludington boy who lives two houses down the street and who, for all his fierceness on this occasion, you know to be a delicate child and a worry to his mother?

The face under Austin King's mask was just the same as the mask, but the eyes betrayed anxiety.

"I know you do," Martha said.

They sat looking into the fire in a silence that was familiar and trusting. Austin wanted to tell her that he was going to see Nora, and he also wanted to explain his reasons for doing this, so that the trust and deepest level of contact between them wouldn't be destroyed. He let five minutes slip by and then said, "Aunt Ione has arranged for me to see Nora, tomorrow afternoon. I wanted to tell you about it first so you'd understand. I would have waited until she was out of the hospital, but——"

"You asked to see her?"

"Yes," Austin said. "I had a letter from Nora, written that night after she left here. You said you didn't care to discuss her or anything to do with her——"

"I still don't," Martha said.

"—so I didn't show it to you. Martha, in the letter she——"

The doorbell chose this moment to ring. Austin looked around the room helplessly and then at Martha, who had turned away and was looking into the fire. He got up and went to the door.

Sitting on Martha King's antique sofa, with his rubbers still on, and one leg crossed over the other, old Mr. Ellis looked very small, like a shrunken boy. He had dressed himself up very carefully, but there was a large spot on his mottled green tie, and his shirt collar was badly frayed. Mary Ellis would never have let him out of the house with it on, but then she and Bud had gone out after dinner. They had gone to call on the Rupps, and as soon as the old man was sure that it was safe, he had shaved—nicking his face in several places—dressed himself, and with a fine satisfaction in disobeying orders, had come calling.

"It's been a strange winter," he said. "I don't ever remember one like it. Everyone is on edge, it seems like. You go in the stores and the clerks act like they don't want to wait on you. People I've known for forty years pass me by on the street. I know I'm an old man and I forget sometimes what it was I was going to say, but I used to feel that I was welcome when I went places, and now I don't any more."

"You're always welcome here," Martha said quietly. "I oughtn't to have to tell you that."

"I know I am," Mr. Ellis said. "I saw your lights and so I thought I'd just drop in for a minute. Bud and Mary don't want me to go anywhere. They're afraid I can't take care of myself, but I'm just as able to take care of myself as I ever was. I was out sprinkling ashes on the walk this morning and you'd have thought——You folks weren't going any place?"

"No," Martha said. "I don't go out much in this weather."

"I don't want to keep you if you've got to go someplace," Mr. Ellis said. "And they're always keeping things from me. Things I have a right to know. Nelson Streuber died and they didn't tell me. I didn't get to the funeral."

"They probably didn't want to upset you," Martha said, avoiding Austin's eyes.

"He was five years younger than I am, and I never expected to outlive him. . . . That nice young girl—what's her name?—from Mississippi?"

"Nora Potter," Martha said.

"I saw her the other day," old Mr. Ellis said. "I saw her on the street with some children and stopped to talk to her. She's always nice to old people. 'You don't belong here,' I said to her. 'You ought to go home. You don't look happy like you did when you come out to the farm that day with your folks,' and she said, 'Mr. Ellis, I'm going soon. I've learned my lesson.' " Old Mr. Ellis nodded solemnly. " 'I've learned my lesson,' she said. I always enjoy hearing Southerners talk. It's softer than the speech you hear ordinarily, and it seems to belong to them."

Austin examined his hands as if they contained the terribly important answer to some riddle like *As soft as silk, as white as milk, As bitter as gall, a thick wall, And a green coat cover me all.*

"Mr. and Mrs. Potter will be sorry that they missed you," Martha said.

"Are they still here?" Mr. Ellis asked in surprise. "Why, I thought they'd gone home long ago. . . . Austin . . . Martha . . . There's something I want to say to you. I'm an old man. You may not see me many times more. I've seen a great many things happen. I've had almost as much experience as it's possible to have in a lifetime, and people ought to value it. Because that's all there is to growing old. You just gradually accumulate a store of experience. But nobody wants it. Nobody cares what I've seen or what I think. Times have changed, they say, but that's where they're wrong. There's nothing new. Only more of the same. Gradually you accumulate a store of experience—but I said that, didn't I? Bud gets so annoyed with me when I repeat myself. In the summer it's all right. I can go out to the farm every day, and I'm not under foot. But now I have to stay pretty close to home, on account of the ice and snow, and I don't want to catch cold and have it turn into pneumonia. An old man like me, I could go off just like that. I wouldn't mind too much. I've outlived my usefulness, but dying isn't something you can do whenever you have a mind to. You have to wait out your time. My father lived to be almost ninety. The last two years he was bedridden, but his mind was clear. And when he died we were all there around the bed and saw him go. . . ."

Mr. Ellis stayed a long while—long enough for Austin to surrender his last hope of restoring the atmosphere of trust that had been broken in upon. What he had to say he would say, but it would not be the same now, and neither would it have the same effect, in all probability.

He helped Mr. Ellis on with his coat and handed him his muffler. In repayment for this courtesy, old Mr. Ellis said with a twinkle in his eyes, "The greatest hardship in the old days was courting the girls. There was only one room in the house and the old folks would sit and watch the proceedings. It was exceedingly hard on a bashful young man like me. But I managed. We all did, somehow or other."

He would have gone off without his hat, if Austin hadn't forced it on him, and he refused to be helped down the icy steps. "I'm all right," he said. "I'll just hang onto the railings." And slowly, a step at a time, as if it were the grave he was descending to, he made it and said one last good night, quite cheerfully for one so old and so tired out by waiting.

Austin shut the door upon the cold, and turned around in time to see Martha start up the stairs.

"Don't go up just yet," he said. "I haven't told you why it's so important that I see Nora right away."

"I understand that it *is* important and that's enough," Martha said.

"You don't understand a damn thing," Austin said. The sound of footsteps on the porch made him turn. Mr. Potter and Randolph had come home from the hospital.

6

The waiting room on the ground floor of the hospital had a tile floor, cream-coloured walls, a mission table, three hard straight chairs and a wooden bench. The one window looked out on the back wing of the hospital—a red brick wall with a double row of windows that were green-shaded, curtained, quiet, and noncommittal. The grey day had been warm. There were bare patches in the snow. The trees had here and there a trace of their white outline, and from the icicles hanging along the gutters, drops of water fell at regular intervals as if from a leaky faucet. The light was failing, the afternoon all but over when Austin put his hat and coat and muffler on a chair and sat down to wait for Dr. Seymour.

Over the bench was a sepia print of Sir Galahad with his young head bent, brooding, and his arm thrown over his charger's neck. There was also a wall vase with artificial flowers in it. The flowers were made of crêpe paper dipped in wax. They did not resemble any actual flowers and there had been no attempt to convey a general truth, such as what a flower is or why there are such things as flowers, but merely to make one more disconcerting object. There were no magazines on the mission table. It was not part of the hospital's intention to offer entertainment or to make the time pass more quickly for visitors who, more often than not, stayed too long and ran the patients' fever up and were a nuisance, all around.

Austin crossed and uncrossed his legs impatiently and waited for Dr. Seymour to appear in the doorway. Nora's letter he had put off answering until it was too late for anything but remorse because he hadn't answered it. He wasn't, as she thought, indifferent to her feelings or to what happened to her, and never had been. He didn't despise her and there was no reason for her to feel that she had forfeited all claim to his approval and friendship. She had done nothing wrong. If anyone was to blame, he was, for not realizing sooner that there was no way he could guide her through an emotional crisis that he himself was the cause of. But to think of her lying there day after day, in pain, not wanting to live because she thought the one person in the whole world that she loved had no use for her, that she was nothing, that there was no place for her anywhere . . . *You're young, Nora. This won't go on forever. And I do love you, in a way. . . . No, that isn't right. It's not love exactly but tenderness and concern. I want you to be happy and to have everything that life has to offer. I don't want you to lose hope or think that you have to compromise. I want you to go on fighting for the things you believe in. The feeling I have for you isn't like the feeling I have for Martha or for anybody else. It's somehow different and unlimited, and whether we see each other or not . . .*

When Dr. Seymour walked in, he brought with him the hurry of an orchestra conductor arriving late with the audience already seated and impatient and the musicians waiting in the pit. He was a clean-shaven man in his sixties, small-boned, brusque, with mild blue eyes that had a certain vanity in them (his treatment of chronic nephrosis had been published recently in the monthly bulletin of the American Medical Association) and very little interest in or patience with people who were walking around on their two legs.

"How's everything at home?" he asked.

"All right," Austin said.

"Nothing happening yet?"

Austin shook his head.

"It will shortly," Dr. Seymour said. "If it doesn't we'll make it happen. Her pains should have started by now. . . . About this visit upstairs—I don't want you to tire her out, do you understand? If it had been anybody else, I wouldn't have let them come, but I know I can depend on you not to stay too long. Terrible thing that was. I don't know why people can't learn not to pour kerosene on a fire. Remember now—five minutes and no more."

7

If everything I do is wrong, Austin said to himself as he paced the length and breadth of his office overlooking the courthouse square, *then I will not do anything. I will not raise my hand.*

The meeting with Nora in Room 211 of the hospital had not come off the way he had hoped it would. Instead of putting her mind at rest, he had had to go searching from room to room, all up and down the corridor, looking for a nurse to come and quiet Nora's hysterical weeping, and then he had to stand, shamefaced and humiliated, while the nurse gave him a piece of her mind.

He would not try to help anybody in trouble ever again. There was no help, and even if there were, he was in no position to offer it. He could only make things worse—unbearable trouble out of what was no greater and no less a calamity than being born. After this he would keep out of it, let them sink or swim.

It was a pity Martha wasn't at the hospital. She ought to have seen that performance. If he told her about it now, she wouldn't believe it. Nobody would, in their right mind, but it was the last show of that kind he would ever put on. He knew now what it was and why he did it. Other men were vain of their appearance or their clothes or because they were attractive to women or because they could drive a four-in-hand, but he had to be better than anybody else; he had to distinguish between right and wrong.

She came to his office that day all dressed up in a long white dress and a big hat with red roses on it, but that was all the good it did her. He was incapable of doing anything that wasn't upright and honest. He couldn't carry on behind his wife's back with some girl who threw herself at him because that wouldn't be Austin King. He didn't laugh at Nora or treat her like a child (which was what she was) or lose his temper or do anything that would have made it easier for her to forget him or him to forget her. He sent her away thinking of him as a sincere, high-minded man who wouldn't allow himself to fall in love with her because he was already married to somebody else. For that she admired him, naturally, because she was young and didn't know any better. But he knew better. And so did Martha. After they were married, he expected Martha to be to him what his mother was to his father—unquestioning, loyal, bound by a common purpose. He waited to hear her say to Ab *Your father says . . .* in the same tone of voice his mother used with him, and Martha never did and never would. He had made her marry him against her will, or if not against her will, then before she was ready. He rushed her into it. Later he said *If she won't work with and beside me, then I will do it for both of us . . .* In his pride he said *I can do everything that is necessary. I can make a marriage all by myself. . . .* Well he hadn't, and the only thing that seemed at all strange was that he had tried so hard, that it was so hard for him to stop trying, even when he no longer cared what happened unless possibly something inside him didn't want to try, didn't want their marriage to work out.

And how did he know that his mother was unquestioning, loyal, and devoted? When the first of the year came around, his father, confronted with a long bill from Burton's, walked the floor night after night worrying about where he'd get the money to pay it and shouting *Why did you need these three spools of cotton thread?* and *What's this five yards of flowered calico?* and then his mother cried and in the end went right on charging things. They were in business together, the business of having a home and raising a family. And if he hadn't been trying so hard not to discover it, he would have seen, by the time he was ready for long pants, that nobody loves, that there is no such thing as love.

Well, he was finished. Let the bills accumulate on the hall table. He was tired of paying bills. Mr. Holby could find a new partner and take over the front office for himself, as he had all along wanted to do. This wasn't really his office anyway but his father's, and he couldn't fill his father's place here and ought never to have tried. He ought never to have tried to do anything. What happened was bound to happen, from the beginning, and all you needed to do was to lie back and let it happen. . . .

The ringing of the telephone broke in upon his thoughts. He stopped and waited a moment, and then realized that it was nearly seven, that Miss Stiefel had gone home, and the outer office was dark. Like a man walking in his sleep, he made his way a step at a time towards the ringing, which was repeated and insistent and like a voice calling his name. With his hand on the receiver he hesitated.

I'm through, he said to himself. *Let accident decide. Let——*

The telephone stopped ringing.

8

"About six o'clock or a little after," Mrs. Potter said. "We were all at the supper table, and I heard her call Austin, so I put down my napkin and went up to see if she wanted anything and——"

"You say the pains have stopped coming?" Dr. Seymour said.

"They stopped soon after I talked to you," Mrs. Potter said.

"How long did she have them?"

"Oh, about an hour," Mrs. Potter said. "I had some trouble getting you at first. I called your office and they told me you were at the hospital and when I called the hospital they said you had just gone, so I waited and called the office again, and that time——"

"I'll go on up and have a look at her," Dr. Seymour said. He took off his coat, his scarf, and his fur-lined gloves and left them in a neat pile on the chair in the hall.

"She's resting quite comfortably," Mrs. Potter said. "I took her up some toast and tea, and she ate that, and she says she feels fine."

"I'd much rather she didn't feel fine at this point," Dr. Seymour said, and started up the stairs.

When he came down ten minutes later, Mrs. Potter said, "Is everything all right?"

"No," Dr. Seymour said, "it isn't. The pains may start again in a little while, but if they don't——Where's Austin? Why didn't *he* call me?"

"Cousin Austin isn't here," Mrs. Potter said.

"Where is he?"

"I don't know," Mrs. Potter said. "When he didn't come home for supper, I supposed that he had made some other plans. But Martha doesn't know where he is either."

"Did you call his office?" Dr. Seymour said.

"I've called three times," Mrs. Potter said.

"Well, keep on trying," Dr. Seymour said. "I don't like what's going on upstairs. I'm going to move her to the hospital, and then if anything happens, we're at least prepared for it."

"She was expecting to have the baby here," Mrs. Potter said.

"I don't care where she was expecting to have it," Dr. Seymour said, "and two hours from now she won't either, I hope. I want you to go up now and get her dressed and ready. Don't hurry her. I don't want her to be frightened. Just get her dressed and bring her downstairs. The telephone is in here, isn't it?"

9

"He *was* here," the waitress in the dining-room of the Draperville Hotel said. "He came in and ordered the steak dinner."

"What time was that?" Randolph asked.

"About seven o'clock or a little after."

"You're sure it was Mr. King and not somebody else?"

"Oh, no," the waitress said. "It was Mr. King all right."

She was tired and her feet hurt. From years of watching

people cut up their food and put it away, a mouthful at a time, she had contracted a hatred of the human race (and of travelling salesmen in particular) that was like a continual low-grade fever. If arsenic had been easily obtainable and its effect impossible to trace, she would have sprinkled the trays with it and carried them into the dining-room with a light heart. But the handsome young man with the Southern accent confused and troubled her. She wanted to say to him, with her hand on his coat-sleeve: *Why do you care?* Instead she said, "He sat over at that table in the corner and he was alone. At least—no, I'm sure there wasn't anybody with him. I noticed that he didn't eat anything after it was brought to him, and I meant to ask if his steak was all right, but I was busy and pretty soon he got up and went out."

"How long ago?"

"Oh, maybe half an hour, maybe a little more. I couldn't say exactly. He left a dollar bill on the tablecloth, and the dinner only came to——"

"If he comes back," Randolph said, "tell him to call home immediately—no, tell him to go straight to the hospital."

"Is anything wrong?" the waitress asked, ready to cut her gown of green an inch above her knees, be his footpage, run barefoot by his side through moss and mire, and tell no man his name. Her question went unanswered.

As Randolph opened the door of the hack that was waiting outside, he said, "Drive around to the south side of the square. He may have come back in the meantime."

There were no lights in the windows that were lettered *Holby and King, Attorneys at Law.*

"I'm going to try once more, even though the place is dark. Keep an eye out for him. He may be walking around the streets somewhere," Randolph said to the cabman. He jumped out of the hack, ran up the stairs, and rattled the doorknob. It was still locked.

"Austin?" he shouted.

There was no answer. Randolph pounded on the locked door, waited and then pounded again. A door opened at his back and Randolph, turning around, saw Dr. Hieronymous, the osteopath. He was a large man with grey hair and a grey face. With his hands he could easily have broken the door down for Randolph but his voice was mild and he said, "Were you looking for somebody?"

"I'm looking for Mr. King," Randolph said.

"He was just here," Dr. Hieronymous said. "At least I heard somebody come up the stairs. I don't know whether it was Mr. King or not."

"About five minutes ago?"

"Why, yes," Dr. Hieronymous said. "I'd say it was about that. Not more then ten minutes anyway."

"And was there anybody just before or just after?"

"No, I don't think there was."

"Then it wasn't Mr. King you heard, it was me," Randolph said, and resumed pounding on the door.

IO

The nurse rang the bell of the elevator repeatedly before the elevator ropes and then the elevator descended past their eyes. It was operated by a lame Negro who had difficulty opening and closing the doors. This elevator and the one in the county courthouse were the only permanent mechanical contrivances for levitation in Draperville.

"We're going to put you in the room at the end of the hall," the nurse said as she stepped out of the elevator. "It'll be quieter."

"I'm not sensitive to noise," Martha King said.

"I was thinking of the other patients," the nurse said cheerfully and then laughed. The laughter was not unkind but merely a way of sweeping up the pieces of a joke that, never much to begin with, had finally come apart in her hands.

The room at the end of the hall had two windows, one looking out on Washington Street and the other on the street in front of the hospital, where Dr. Seymour's horse and rig were waiting, with the reins tied to the hitching post.

This is not at all the way I wanted it to be, Martha said to herself. I thought I'd be at home, in my own bed, with everything around me the way it always is. I thought Austin would . . .

"Do you want a cup of tea?" The floor nurse asked.

"Yes, I do," Martha said. "I had some tea just a little while ago, but I'm terribly hungry."

"You'll have to work fast," the floor nurse said, "or you'll be hungry a long time. How long ago was your first baby born?"

"Four and a half years ago."

"Dr. Seymour is going to deliver you?"

"Yes," Martha said.

"The first thing to do is to get into bed," the nurse said. "Do you have any pains now?"

"No," Martha said. She surrendered her pocketbook and gloves, and allowed the nurse to help her off with her coat.

Standing across the street from Mike Farrell's saloon, Austin heard mournful singing, and then an argument that ended abruptly with the sound of breaking glass and a man being thrust out through the swinging door.

In the alley that ran beside the pool hall, Austin stopped beside a window with the blind drawn three-quarters of the way to the sill, offering a view of several pairs of feet under a table. The window was open about an inch, and the watcher heard the sound of cards being dealt and shuffled and dealt again, and very little difference between the moment of triumph and the moment of disaster.

He stood in the alley looking under the drawn blind for a very long while. On a street beyond the post office, where there was a row of shabby houses, Austin leaned against a tree and saw the third house from the corner visited by a man on guard against watchers—a man who came in stealth and left twenty minutes later, less alive and (judging by his walk, his carriage) less hopeful than when he came. The man who crossed over to the other side of Lafayette Street to keep from being recognized, Austin would not have known anyway, but neither did he know the man with the miner's cap who spoke to him by name.

Here and there he saw a light in some house, a night light left burning for a child or a sick person afraid of the dark. Austin was grateful for any illumination—for the dim light in the lobby of the Draperville Hotel, and for the light in the hackstand next door, and for the light in Dr. Danforth's livery stable, where Snowball McHenry slept on a pile of horse blankets.

The jewellery store had an iron grating across the windows and a heavy padlock on the door, and a light was left burning so that Monk Collins, the policeman on night duty, could see into the back of the store. Shapiro's Clothing Store and Joe Becker's shoe store were dark, and so was the hardware store, the barber shop, the lumber yard, the two banks. The signboards outside of Giovanni's confectionery and moviedrome (where, if you bought an ice-cream soda, you could sit in the back room and watch a moving picture of a man hanging over the edge of a cliff by his fingers) had been taken in off the sidewalk for the night, but there was a light on the first floor of the courthouse, for the night watchman, and the second floor of the telephone building, and there were also the overhead arc lights where Austin King met and parted company with his shadow. The shadow under the arc light disturbed him as no reflection in a mirror ever had. For a moment it was recognizable, and then as he took a step toward the periphery of the circle of light, the shadow stretched out into a hideous distortion hanging between one shape and the next.

The sound of a violin coming through closed shutters kept Austin standing on the sidewalk in front of a shack on Williams Street for twenty minutes, during which time he experienced all the sensations of earthly happiness. The music stopped and Austin walked on.

Standing across the street from the jail he found himself talking to an old man named Hugh Finders, who had been connected with a brutal murder some twenty years before. Where he came from, Austin had no idea. The old man simply materialized out of the night.

"I seen you around, since you were in kneebritches," he said to Austin, "but this is the first time I ever talked to you, I guess. Everybody's so busy these days. I see them ride by in their fine carriages, but they don't have no time to talk to poor old Hugh."

There was a time when people talked to poor old Hugh. For three days, various lawyers kept him on the witness stand, trying to find out about the bloodstains that were discovered on the inside of his hack. The questions they asked, he did not feel called upon to answer, and all that the street light revealed now was an old man with a cancerous skin condition and wisps of dry white hair sticking out from under a filthy cap. "You live on Elm Street, don't you?" he said. "I know. Big white house. The old Stevenson place. You're married and got a little girl, ain't you? Pretty little thing. I seen her with your wife. She don't know me, I expect. I was always interested in you on account of your father. He was a fine man. Nobody ever went to him in trouble that didn't get help. First he'd give them a lecture, and then he'd reach down in his pocket. He used to think I drank too much and I guess maybe he was right, but we can't all sit up there, high and mighty, and pass judgment on our fellow men. Some of us poor devils has to be judged. Otherwise your daddy would of been out of a job. I always meant to pay back the money he loaned me, but I never managed to, and he never pressed me for it. . . . I don't know what you're doing out at this time of night, but you take an old man's advice and go on home. You'd be better off in bed."

With a slight weave in his walk, he started on toward the street light at the end of the block, but to the best of Austin's knowledge he never got there. Somewhere between the jail and the corner Hugh Finders disappeared and his secret vanished with him.

Austin walked through a park where there were band concerts in the summer-time, and then through the deserted courthouse square. The lighted clock face, so like his father's gold watch hanging in the sky, told him that it was late and that he would have to begin the next day without enough rest, but clocks have been known to be wrong. There might be no next day.

He passed the stairs that led up to the office of Holby and King, without taking advantage of the refuge they offered him, without even knowing they were there. Turning right at the corner, he walked one more block, crossed the interurban tracks, and ended up on the brick platform that ran in front of the railway station.

The through train from St. Louis, due in at 2.37 A.M., was late, and Austin waited on the station platform with his back turned against the icy wind. It was late January, and so the wind was due also, bringing another consignment of winter to the ice-blocked lakes of Wisconsin, the snow-covered cornfields of Illinois. There was a potbellied stove in the station, and Austin went inside, thinking to warm his hands, but the heat and the stale odour made him lightheaded, and so he walked out again immediately. He was in a state of shivering excitement that required air.

Facing the station was a block of stores. The corner cigar store and Mike Farrell's saloon were lighted. The rest—Dalton's grocery, the shoe repair shop, the bicycle shop, and the monument works—were dark. Across the tracks the bird house on a pole—with its porches and round windows, doors, gables, and cupola, a fairly accurate statement of the style of architecture most admired around the year Eighteen-eighty and still surviving along College Avenue—was untenanted. The flower bed that in summer spelled Draperville in marigolds and striped petunias had been erased by heavy frosts. This could have been almost any station anywhere along the line. As Austin passed and repassed the station master's lighted cage, in an effort to keep warm, he could hear the telegraph clicker and see the ticket agent with a green eye-shade on his forehead.

The signal lights switched far down the tracks, south of town. The ticket agent came out of the station. His description afterward of what happened that night would in no way have paralleled or corroborated Austin King's. *Number* 317 *was coming a little late*, one of them would have said. The other would have said *Time was cool and flowed softly around me. I didn't like to put my head down in cold that might not be too clean, and it was hard to swim against the current without doing that, so I drifted downstream toward the monument works and then fought my way back. Twice I tried to crawl out onto the platform but it didn't work. Each time I lost my hold. The platform, the station, the empty birdhouse, the stars, and Mike Farrell's saloon fell away from under me and I was swept downstream. The third time I put my head under water and swam straight toward the light. It was easier than I imagined. When I stopped swimming I was well within the wedge made by two parallel steel rails meeting at infinity, and the light was shining right on my face. I tried to stand up but there was no bottom. There was nothing to stand on, and when I came up for air a second I was still inside the wedge. Although I had been swimming much harder than before, I hadn't got anywhere. I was out of breath and I knew I was somewhere I had no business to be.*

You don't have to have water to drown in. All it requires is that your normal vision be narrowed down to a single point and continue long enough on that point until you begin to remember and to achieve a state of being which is identical with the broadest vision of human life. You can drown in a desert, in the mountain air, in an open car at night with the undersides of the leafy branches washing over you, mile after midnight mile. All you need is a single idea, a point of intense pain, a pin-prick of light growing larger and steadier and more persuasive until the mind and the desire to live are both shattered in starry sensation, leading inevitably toward no sensation whatever. . . .

The station master said something that Austin (with the light falling all around him from a great height) did not hear. . . . *He's right, I guess. He must be right. I've known Fred Vercel for years and never knew him to say anything that wasn't so. If he did call to me, as he says—if he warned me, I probably stepped back, in plenty of time, and the rest is some kind of strange hallucination. But I never had any such feeling before. I know he spoke to me, but the way I remember it, I couldn't hear what he said. I couldn't hear anything but the sound of the approaching engine, and even that stopped when I went under. I had never been in a situation I couldn't get out of, and I held my breath and felt myself being rolled over and over, helpless, on the bottom. My mind, in an orderly fashion, reached one conclusion after another and I knew finally that there wasn't going to be any more for me. This was all. Here in this place. Now. And I felt the most terrible sadness because it was not the way I expected to die. It was just foolish. I shouldn't have looked into the light so long. I knew better. And I was not quite ready to die. There were certain things that I still wanted to do. I suppose everybody feels that way when their time comes.*

For a second there was air over me and I opened my eyes. I was still inside the wedge. Using the last strength I had, I called (or thought I called) for help, and saw Fred Vercel's face stiffen as the giant wheels released clouds of steam. I'm describing the way it happened to me, you understand. If Fred says it happened some other way, you'll have to decide for yourselves which of us is right. Maybe he's the one who was having hallucinations. How do I know? This time I couldn't hold my breath. What came in or went out was beyond my control. I let go, knowing where I was, knowing that gravel touched my forehead, that I was being turned over and over, and that I would never escape from this trap alive. I came to the surface again, without struggling, and saw the two lights on the last car of the train getting smaller and smaller.

I should have waited for another train, maybe, but I didn't. I was very tired. I don't ever remember being as tired as I was that night. I'd been letting myself down. A little bit at a time, over a period of several hours I guess, I'd been letting myself down. I'd been watching what other people do, so I could learn to be more like them, and somehow—maybe because I didn't understand what I saw or it could have been that I was just too tired—it didn't seem worth the bother. I don't know how I got home. I just found myself there, looking through the dining-room window at the thermometer to see how cold it was, turning off the lights, going up the stairs to bed.

II

"The waiting room is right down the hall," the nurse said smiling. "Try not to take it too hard."

"I know where it is," Austin said.

This time he wasn't to have the waiting room all to himself. The man sitting on the wooden bench was bald, heavy set, and decently dressed. His face was familiar but there were a hundred faces like it in the town of Draperville—middle-aged and rather tired with no trace of the earlier, more eager, perhaps even handsome boy's face from which it had emerged. Its only distinguishing feature was a mole on the left cheek, and this, anywhere but in the waiting room, and by anyone except a man who had all Time's delight at his disposal, might easily have passed unnoticed.

Austin sat down and let his head back so that the wall would have the burden of supporting it. There was such an air of uneasiness and of being unwanted about the other man that Austin felt as if he were looking at his own state of mind, and shifted his glance away. The artificial flowers and Sir Galahad reminded him that he had been here the day before, and of what had happened afterward. He tried not to look at them, either. He was conscious of a strange sensation in his mouth, as if his teeth were watering. The rims of his eyelids felt hard and dry.

"You're Austin King, aren't you?" the man asked. "I'm George Diehl. I work in the lumber yard."

"I remember you now," Austin said, nodding.

"Your first kid?"

"Second."

"You've been through this before, then?"

"Not here," Austin said. "The other child was born at home." Because of this man eyeing him as if possibly they ought to become better acquainted, he would have no privacy. His worry and exhaustion would both be exposed to the public gaze.

"Misery loves company. Have a cigar?"

"No, thanks," Austin said. Having recognized George Diehl, Austin set out to ignore him. There is a misery that loves company and another kind that would rather be alone.

In the confusion of dressing and breakfast and getting a suitcase packed for Ab and delivering her at the Danforths' front door, Austin had left his gold watch under his pillow. He got up and went out into the hall. What had seemed like half an hour had actually been two and a half minutes. This error in calculation was destined to repeat itself at varying intervals all through the day.

12

With her nose pressed to the window pane and her forlorn back reflected in Mrs. Danforth's silver gazing globe, Abbey King looked out on the same perspective that she was accustomed to seeing from the window in the front hall and the front living-room window at home. The only difference was that she could see one more house to the left and one less house to the right. No one came in or went out of or walked by the houses. The ground was bare, the trees and shrubbery appeared to have given up forever the idea and intention of producing green leaves. With shreds of brown attached to it, a lateral shoot of the pink rambler trained to grow up the trellis on the east side of the Danforths' house was bowing and trembling in the wind, a few inches from Ab's face. If there is no such place as Purgatory, there is at least Elm Street on a grey day in January.

"Would you like to put on your things and go outside and play?" Mrs. Danforth asked.

"I don't care," Ab said.

"We'll bundle up warmly, and if you get cold, tell me and we'll come in."

Entrusting her mittened hand to Mrs. Danforth's gloved one, Ab made a tour of the yard, and Mrs. Danforth lifted her up so that Ab could look in the window of the playhouse, made of two piano boxes. The key to the playhouse was lost and no one had been in it for many years. Ab saw a school desk, a blackboard, and some dusty paper dolls, and was satisfied that the playhouse, like the flower garden, was finished for a while. Occasionally, her eyes turned to the house next door. She knew that her mother was not there. Whether anyone else was, and what they were doing, the house did not say, and Ab, in exile, did not ask.

A dray went past the Danforths' house, past the Kings' and stopped in front of the Beaches'. A man got down from the driver's seat, and immediately, as if by some prearranged signal, a pack of children appeared around the corner of the house across the street, crossed over, and gathered on the sidewalk.

"You want to join them?" Mrs. Danforth asked.

Ab stood timidly pushing her hands further into her mittens. She was not allowed to go beyond the confines of her own yard, but then she wasn't at home now and the Danforths' yard had no fence but was open to the street.

"It's all right," Mrs. Danforth said. "I'll stay here and watch you."

The sight of the blue kindergarten chairs and the children's excited comments were enough to break the thread (slight in any case) that bound Ab's right mitten to Mrs. Danforth's left glove. She started slowly off down the sidewalk, broke into a run as she passed her own house, and then slowed down again to a walk. The children, boys and girls of all ages, paid no attention to her and there was no Miss Lucy or Miss Alice to coax Ab into the group. She stood on the outskirts, ignored by the others, who left her standing there and went from the sidewalk down into the street, that most dangerous of all places. Ab looked back. Mrs. Danforth nodded. Taking her life in her hands, Ab pressed through the group until she was able to look into the back end of the dray.

"Look out," a boy in a plaid mackinaw said to her. "You'll get conked on the head if you aren't careful."

This offhand admonition, neither friendly nor unfriendly, was very important. First of all, it recognized her existence, a fact that would otherwise have remained in doubt. Second, it conferred citizenship papers on her. From now on she was free to come and go in a commonwealth where the games were sometimes rough and where the older inhabitants sometimes picked on the younger ones, but nobody ever had to deal with or try to understand emotions and ideas that were thirty years too old for them. Abbey King attached herself to the hero in the plaid mackinaw, followed him from the street to the sidewalk and back again, and with her eyes on his dirty, tough, young face, waited to see what remarkable words, what brave acts, he would spontaneously produce.

Satisfied that Ab no longer needed watching, Mrs. Danforth turned and went back into the house that invited daydreaming, that was dark, cavelike, and full of objects which had demonstrated conclusively how often things survive and people do not.

13

When the dray loaded with kindergarten furniture drew up before the Beaches' house, Alice propped the storm door open wide, with a brick covered with carpet from the house in St. Paul, and then went back inside. As she peered out through the front window, the expression on her face was of relief, almost of happiness. The chairs were scattered over the frozen lawn, and the children sat down on them as if they had been invited to a party. The two movingmen started up the walk, carrying a table between them. Except that they held it by the ends instead of by silver handles at the side, the effect was that of pallbearers carrying a coffin. The box of coloured yarn which they had set on top of the table might so easily have been flowers sent by some close friend of the family. When they reached the steps, Alice opened the door again. The man in front put his end down for a moment, tipped his hat, and said, "Where do you want it, lady?"

He was short and stocky, his face so capable and kind that she was tempted to tell him everything, but the other man was still holding his end of the table, so she said timidly, "In the attic, please." She was prepared, if the two men exchanged a glance, not to notice it, but no such unpleasantness occurred. Tracking soot in after them, they headed for the stairs. "Easy," the man in front said. "Watch the newel post." The man at the back was enormous, loose-limbed, open-mouthed, and entirely at the mercy of the mind that directed his strength. At the turn of the stairs, he managed to leave a cruel scratch that no amount of furniture polish would ever remove from the banister.

Halfway down the upstairs hall, the attic door stood open. On the wall beside it, a glass knob the size of a dollar shone red, an indication that the light was on in the attic. The hall was narrow and the table had to be turned gradually and carefully on end before it would go through the door and up the steep attic stairs. Lucy stood waiting for them by the chimney, with a man's heavy sweater on over her cotton dress. She had cleared a space for the kindergarten equipment from the accumulation and welter of years—suitboxes, trunks, old furniture, lampshades, riding boots, books and magazines stacked in piles, boxes that were not always marked as to their contents and might contain Christmas tree ornaments or Mr. Beach's clothes. The men made five trips in all, and Alice went with them each time in an effort to prevent further damage to the stairs.

Lucy remained in the attic, where the kindergarten equipment looked strangely bright and fresh; too bright and too fresh to be what it really was, the death of all her hopes. Why is it we never give anything away? she wondered. Other people discard and dispose of things and start afresh with only what they need and can use, but everything we ever had is here, ready to speak out against us on the Day of Judgment. . . . She pushed the chairs closer together so that the kindergarten equipment took up less room, and rearranged the coloured paper, the yarns, and the boxes of scissors in a neat pile.

"Are you still up there?" Alice called from below, and, receiving an answer, came up the attic stairs.

"It doesn't look like very much, does it?" she said, staring at the tables and chairs.

"Well, it's paid for," Lucy said. "That's the main thing. Maybe we can sell it some time."

"Or maybe we can use it ourselves," Alice said, "after people have forgotten."

"No," Lucy said. "It's done for. I don't know why we keep it. We'll never have any use for it, and we'll never sell it. It's just going to stay up here, with the trunks and the Baedekers." Her eyes wandered to the suitcases in the corner, with faded cracked labels—Lake Como, Grand Hotel, Nice, *Roma*, *Firenze*, and *Compagnie Générale Transatlantique*.

"Any time we want to start living our lives all over again, everything we need is here—except courage."

"Maybe some day we'll have houses of our own," Alice said, "and then whatever will we do with it all?"

"That's done for, too," Lucy said. "I'm forty-seven and you're forty-three. People may call us the Beach girls but we're no spring chickens, either of us. We've had our chance and missed it, and I'm so tired I don't care any more. All I want to do is rest. I don't know why people don't tell you when you're young that life is tiring. It probably wouldn't have done any good, but then again it might have."

"I don't feel that way," Alice said. She took a kindergarten chair and sat down, facing a bookcase crammed with glass and china. On a level with her eyes there was a milk pitcher which she remembered from her childhood. It was blue and white, and two young women (sisters, perhaps) walked in a garden, each with her hand through a young man's arm. A duenna with a dog at her feet sat watching them, approvingly. And in the background there was a ruined temple, undoubtedly to the shaggy god who, from his place under the handle, kept an eye on both couples. Under the spout there was a motto which Alice Beach knew without having to read it:

For every evil
under the sun
there is a remedy
or there is none,
if there be one
try and find it,
if there be none
never mind it.

She turned her face away from this familiar message and looked out of the attic window at the bare branches of a big maple tree. After a while she said, "Sometimes I have to stop and remember how old I am."

"You've got a few more years to go," Lucy said. "Then you'll be tired, too, like me. You won't care any more what happens to you or what might have happened. Don't look at me like that."

"I can't bear to have you say such things."

"You don't have to listen. And besides, I don't have to say them. I can just think them instead, if that will make it any easier for you."

"It won't."

"Well, then, you'd better go away. I'll even help you."

"Where would I go?"

"Anywhere. I can manage here without you, now. You can go anywhere in the world you please. There never was enough money for two but there's enough for one, and you might as well take it and go abroad. You always liked the Dalmatian Coast. Go back to Ragusa and try there for a while."

"What about Mama?"

"Well, what about her?"

"It might kill her if I left home now."

"Nothing will kill her. She'll outlive both of us. She'll outlive everybody on Elm Street. She's not ever going to die. It's time you realized that. She's going to live forever. And she can't stop you from going because I won't let her. I could have stayed in Europe if I'd really wanted to. I can manage her now and I could have managed her then. Deep down in my heart I didn't want to. I wanted her to manage me. And she has, I'll say that for her. She's never been so sick or so tired and discouraged with Papa and us and herself that she didn't manage things the way we wanted her to manage them. So pack your bag and put on your hat and go, and it'll be all right. Go to Mississippi if you don't want to go abroad. Go stay with the Potters on their plantation. Mrs. Potter asked us to last summer. All you have to do is tell her you'd like to go with them when they go. Maybe you'll find someone down there. Sometimes a widower with children will——"

Lucy turned her head to listen. Both of them heard, faint and far away, the ting-a-ling of a bedside bell.

"I'd better go see what she wants," Alice said.

"Let her wait," Lucy said. "This is more important. And don't look so frightened. Try and think calmly and clearly. Try to see what it is that you really want to do. And whatever it is—I don't care if it's to be a bareback rider in a circus—I'll help you."

These offers which come too late or at the wrong time, in words that are somehow unacceptable, are the saddest, the most haunting part of family life.

"Lucy, please stop!" Alice exclaimed as she started for the stairs. "I don't pick at you. Why can't you let me alone?"

14

"Mama?"

"She isn't here," Mr. Potter said. "You've got a new nurse."

"Where is she?" Nora asked.

"She went back to the house to rest. She didn't get much sleep last night, so I said I'd take over. Is there anything you'd like me to do for you?"

"What's that awful shouting?"

"Some poor soul is having a hard time of it, I guess," Mr. Potter said.

"It seems like it's been going on for hours and hours. I don't see why they don't put her somewhere where nobody can hear her. It's awful to have to listen to. . . . When's Mama coming back?"

"Pretty soon. How do you feel?"

"All right. Only I'm so tired of lying here."

"It won't be much longer. The doctor says you're coming along fine."

"I want to go home," Nora said.

"We'll take you home," Mr. Potter said, "just as soon as you're able to be moved."

"I want to be in my own room. I don't ever want to see this place again."

"Just be patient a little while longer," Mr. Potter said. "It doesn't do to try and rush things."

"But I've been here so long and this bed's so uncomfortable."

"Rome wasn't built in a day."

The screaming was resumed.

"What time is it?" Nora asked.

"Half after two."

"Did Mama say what time she was coming back?"

"She'll be along directly. Now that you're getting better, you mustn't expect her to be at your beck and call all the time. You've put her through considerable strain, and she's worn out. From now on, it's up to us to spare her anything we can. . . . It's a bad thing to grow old, Nora, and know that you've been a fool."

After this abrupt revelation, the first that he had ever made to his daughter, Mr. Potter sat quietly and watched her eyes close and saw her breathing change gradually to the breathing of sleep.

Most maxims are lies, or at any rate misleading. A rolling stone gathers moss. A stitch in time doesn't save nine. The knowledge that you have been a fool hurts just as much, is just as hard to admit to yourself if you are young as when you are old. Every error that people make is repeated over and over again, ad infinitum, ad nauseam, if they know what they are doing and cannot help themselves. The curtain goes up night after night on the same play, and if the audience weeps, it is because the hero always arrives at the abandoned sawmill in the nick of time, the heroine never gives in to the dictates of her heart and marries the man with the black moustache. There is not only a second chance, there are a thousand second chances to speak up, to act bravely for once, to face the fact that must sooner or later be faced. If there is really no more time, it can be faced hurriedly. Otherwise, it can be examined at leisure. The result is in either case the same. Windows that have been nailed shut for years are suddenly pried open, letting air in, letting love in, and hope.

Cause is revealed to be, after all, nothing but effect. And the long, slow, dreadful working out of the consequences of any given mistake is arrested the very moment you accept the idea that for you (and for your most beautiful bride, who with garlands is crowned, whose lightness and brightness doth shine in such splendour) there is an end.

15

Part of the time Martha King was convinced that there was some dreadful mistake, that they were trying to bury her alive. At other times she was quite rational, knew why she was there, answered correctly when Dr. Seymour leaned over the bed and asked, "How many fingers have I?" and was able to distinguish between her own screaming and the chant that came from the next room: *Oh doctor, doctor . . . oh my doctor . . .* sometimes pleading, sometimes a shriek, sometimes a singsong, but in the next room. Not the same as *Oh this is strong! The pain comes in waves! It's all in my back!* (she said that); or, *It's gone, isn't it?* (the nurse); or *Are my eyes swollen? It feels as if I were peeking through them . . . Oh now it's starting, it's starting!*

At three-thirty the nurse stopped referring to her watch, and time was measured by the slow progress of a patch of sunlight on the hospital floor.

"By rights," George Diehl said, "she shouldn't be having this child. She's too old. She's nearly fifty and worn out with bringing up kids, but she wanted one more, and I couldn't refuse her. It's not good, though—a woman of her age. She's been in labour for fifteen hours and the doctor is worried about her heart. They let me in to see her for a couple of minutes, just before you came. We've been married for nearly thirty years, and yet whenever I try to tell her I love her, it sticks in my throat. I know she knows, but I thought she might like to hear me say it, so I did, and she said, 'Who's been getting you all upset?' 'Nobody,' I said. 'It's just the sight of you lying there, looking like a young girl.' Which was not the truth, you understand; she looked all worn out, but it pleased her, even though she didn't want to let on. 'You've been a good wife to me,' I said, and afterwards I felt better, as if I'd got a weight off my chest."

(The sunlight reached the foot of the hospital bed and began to climb.)

"But this waiting is hard on a man," George Diehl said. "I've seen a whole year go by faster than these last two hours."

To experience the emotion of waiting, in its purest form, you must pass through that stage when pacing the floor, or drumming with your fingers, or counting, or any of the mechanical aids gives release, and enter into the stage when the arrival of the minute hand of the clock at twelve is separated from the sound of striking by so long an interval that the whole nervous system cries out in vain for an end of waiting. Pain is movement, the waves of the sea rising, receding; waiting is the shore they break upon, the shore that changes, in time, but never noticeably. The will that waits and endures is not the same will that makes it possible for people to get out of bed in the morning or to choose between this necktie, this silk scarf, and that. It is something you never asked for and that never asked for you. You have it and live. You lose it and give up the ghost.

During the course of that interminable day, Austin's relation to the man with a mole on his left cheek kept changing. When the wall would no longer support the weight of his head, he got up and walked, his nerves on edge, his mind coming up against a high blank fear every six or seven paces. He felt his ribs encased in a delicate pressure that might, if he took too deep a breath, be shattered, and with it the last chance that things would turn out all right. A single nervous gesture, a word addressed to himself out loud and his life, like a round glass paperweight turned upside down, would be filled with revolving white particles of terror. At those moments when his natural patience seemed to have gained the upper hand and he was able to sit down and wait, the man with the mole would get up and walk, and it was impossible for Austin not to share in that walking, not to feel his own forehead contracting in the same furrows as that other forehead, and his eyes clouding over with the same suspicion that everything that could be done upstairs was not being done.

The first time that George Diehl, with his hands clasped behind his back, stopped in front of Austin as if there was something that he felt the need of saying, Austin turned his eyes away. He was sorry immediately. The mouth already open, about to speak, closed and the pacing was resumed. When George Diehl sat down and it was Austin's turn to walk the floor, he hesitated and then said abruptly, "I guess we're in this together. If you want to talk—if it will make it any easier for you to talk, go ahead."

"No, thanks," the man said, refusing this offer of sympathy as Austin had refused his cigar. Though neither offer was repeated, George Diehl did begin to talk eventually, about the lumber business, which was not too good, and then about how there wasn't as much game as there used to be and how the creeks were beginning to be fished out or else ruined because the miners had been using dynamite in them; and Austin found himself with a lighted cigar in his right hand and a gradually unfolding history to contemplate that was quite different from his own, until this moment when the two had merged. The story of George Diehl (including the mistakes he had made—there were several that were serious—and the lucky breaks that had alternated with events not so lucky; the jobs he had lost through no fault of his own, the neglected opportunities, how George Diehl's oldest girl wanted to be a teacher, how his son didn't care about anything so long as he had a little spending money in his pocket and they didn't ask him, when he went out in the evening, where he was going and what time he would be home) was a story full of interest and suspense, of strangeness and incident and even poetry.

Austin tried to limit himself to listening, but certain scenes and situations kept rising to the surface of his mind; words got as far as his lips and had to be pushed back. Finally, the fabric of reserve gave way under the weight of George Diehl's confidences and Austin began to talk.

Martha King's pains recurred at the same unchanging interval. A scrubwoman, in slavery to a bucket of soapy water and grey mop, reached the doorway and looked in.

"What's the matter? Won't the baby come out?"

It was not a question but merely comfort, freely given and gratefully received.

"Have you any children?" Martha King asked, turning her face to the door.

"Nine alive and one dead."

"Was your second as hard as the first?"

"That's right. And with the second one I suffered the same pain."

The scrubwoman went on mopping the corridor. She did not know or ask who the patient in 204 was. There was no lace on the hospital gown, and pain had first disfigured and was now busy disposing of the beautiful woman. Pain did its work so well that old Mr. Porterfield would not have recognized Mrs. King. Neither would the Beach girls nor Mrs. Danforth nor anyone who ever saw her gathering flowers in her garden of a late summer afternoon. First the beauty went, then the smile, then the light in the brown eyes, then the perfume, then the softness, then the fiery temper and finally the deeper patience of love. All that was left was a creature writhing on a bed, trying to come to acceptable terms with agony.

George Diehl listened attentively, and now and then made some observation that indicated he had been turning over in his mind the events that Austin was describing. He had long ago come to the conclusion that there was so little difference in people or in how they met their problems that to criticize or take a high moral stand was more or less a waste of time. When Austin realized that no matter what he told George Diehl (he had already told him everything and nothing), George Diehl would not be surprised or shocked or blame him, a kind of exhilaration set in, which the older man understood but did not share—a state of excitement it was perfectly all right for Austin to feel, because he was younger than George Diehl and had more of his life before him.

The fading outside light was replaced by the glare of electric bulbs, and a black velvet cloth was hung outside the hospital windows.

"The only thing that frightens me is hearing that woman scream," Martha King said.

It was her own screaming that she heard, this time. The next room was as quiet as doom.

Disfigure and dispose of Martha King as, say, Mrs. Beach or old Mr. Ellis knew her and you have a nameless animal creature, but the creature is not the end and certainly not the answer. There is finally the self, biting its hands and shouting *It's awful . . . Oh please . . . It's so awful . . . Oh God I don't like it. . . .*

Out in the corridor there was the sound of dishes rattling, of talking and occasionally laughter. People who work in hospitals have their own sanity to think about and preserve.

At quarter to seven, Austin and George Diehl left the waiting room and walked downtown to a restaurant that Austin had never been in before, and ordered steak sandwiches. Austin couldn't eat his when it came. He pushed the plate away from him, on the verge of being sick. He watched George Diehl's face while he ate, and thought how little of all that had happened to him showed in the very ordinary features, the eyes that were tired but friendly and had no comment to make beyond the fact that, if Austin wasn't going to eat his sandwich, it oughtn't to go begging. Austin passed the plate across the table and George Diehl transferred it to his own plate and went on talking and eating.

In silence, talked out at last, they walked back to the hospital, where, as soon as they opened the door, a nurse came toward them with a message for George Diehl, who seemed quite dazed by news that was good. He did not hear Austin's congratulations or even seem to know who Austin was.

"Well, that's that," he said.

Austin found himself in full possession of the waiting room and, after nearly thirteen hours of George Diehl's company and conversation, little or no interest in being alone. He began to walk the floor and the sixth or seventh step brought him face to face with the barrier that he couldn't get past. He sat down and waited for the paperweight to be turned upside down, the miniature snow to begin falling.

16

When Ab had said her prayers, Mrs. Danforth lifted her into the big bed in the guest-room and drew the covers around her. "I'll leave the light on in the hall," she said, "and if you want anything in the night, call me and I'll hear you."

Ab looked up at her without answering, her eyelids weighted with sleep. Nobody but her mother had ever tucked her in bed before, and though Mrs. Danforth was kind and gentle with her, it wasn't the same. She wanted her mother. The sound of Mrs. Danforth's heels descending the stairs was not the sound her mother made.

The gaslight in the hall threw moving shadows and filled the bedroom with an uneasy light. From where Ab lay she could see a picture on the wall: A man in a white nightshirt, his legs sprawled across the sheets, was dreaming of a steeplechase. Above the man in bed there was a brook, and horsemen in pink coats were jumping their horses over this hazardous obstacle. Ab did not understand the dream picture as such. What she saw, by the flickering gaslight, was that the horses would land on the man in the bed and trample him. With her heart beating faster, she tried to turn over in her own bed so as not to be an unwilling witness to the death of the man in the white nightshirt, but her legs were chained and she couldn't move. Even after her eyelids shut out the ugly sight, she still saw it in her mind, and would have cried out except that no sound came.

17

The mop, swishing in wet wide circles, brought the scrubwoman face to face with a glass window which acted as a frame to a picture that never hangs on the walls of the waiting room of doctors' offices. The operating table was tipped, so that the patient's feet were higher than her head, and the upper half of the body was covered by a sheet. The hands strapped to the side of the operating table looked bluish. The sheet moved up, down, up, down, with hard breathing. Dr. Seymour was cutting into the abdominal area, blotting up blood with a towel as the incision grew larger and larger. The scrubwoman made several wide swipes with the mop and then looked again. This time the incision was completed and the skin, held back by clamps, revealed a lake of blood which the nurses were struggling to dispose of. Dr. Seymour, looking like a butcher, fitted the forceps into the abdomen and pulled. The forceps slipped and he put them in again and pulled with all his strength. Then, dispensing with the forceps, he reached in with his hand, wrist deep in blood and water, and pulled out a baby, dripping, waxlike, and limp.

The scrubwoman who had ten children (of which nine were still living) stayed long enough at the window to make sure that this child was alive, and then moved slowly down the corridor, swirling the mop in wider and wider circles that left cloud patterns and wave patterns on the hexagonal tiled floor.

18

In the middle of the night Abbey King was awakened by knocking, by pounding, by a commotion downstairs at the front door. All sounds, all sensations that in the daytime are weakened or explained away by the mind's comforting interpretation, in the night are magnified. This sound, so loud that her heart almost stopped beating, Ab never doubted for a second was on account of her. They were coming for her. They were going to get her and punish her at last for having been so many times a bad girl. Her only hope—that Mrs. Danforth wouldn't hear the pounding, or if she did hear it, wouldn't answer it—lasted only until she heard footsteps in the hall and saw Mrs. Danforth in a long dressing gown, with her hair in two braids down her back, pass the bedroom door.

Just one more chance, Ab begged, to her mother far away and to God farther away still. The steps went on down the stairs and could not be stopped. Ab heard the chain unfastened, the key turn in the door, and a voice that wasn't a policeman's or a gypsy's but her father's voice said, "It's a boy."

Though there was now no reason for terror, it drained away very slowly.

"How's Martha?" Ab heard Mrs. Danforth say.

"She's all right. The doctor says she's fine."

"Did she have a hard time?"

"Toward the end. But they gave her morphine and she came through the operation without any difficulty. The baby weighs five pounds." There was an excitement and a happiness in her father's voice that Ab had never heard there before. She lay perfectly still waiting for him to ask about her, to start up the stairs, to call out when he reached the landing.

"Let me make you some coffee," Mrs. Danforth said. "It won't take but a minute."

"No," Austin said. "Thank you just the same. It's been a long ordeal and I'm done in. I'd better go on home."

The last thing Ab heard was the sound of Mrs. Danforth's soft slippers on the stairs. Sometime during the remainder of the night, the pink-coated horsemen rode over her on their terrible horses, and she died without dying, and woke with arms around her and heard a voice saying "There, there . . . There, there . . . You've been having a bad dream."

19

"But I've told her repeatedly," Mary Caroline said. "She knows it's my favourite blouse and that I don't want her to wear it. She has lots more clothes than I do, and I don't think it was a bit nice of her."

"You mustn't be selfish with your things," Mrs. Link said.

"I'm not," Mary Caroline said. "But when I showed her

the spot that won't come out, she just said she was sorry and let it go at that."

"The next time I'm down town," Mrs. Link said, "I'll get some material and——"

"I'd rather pick it out myself. If you don't mind," Mary Caroline said.

"No, I don't mind."

Tolerant and serene, loving both her daughters equally, Mrs. Link viewed the neighbourhood as they walked along. There was a hack waiting in front of the Kings', and as Mary Caroline and Mrs. Link passed on the opposite side of the street, the Mathein boy came out with two suitcases which he stowed away on the front seat of the hack.

"Did you remember to go and say good-bye to the Potters?" Mrs. Link asked.

"Yes," Mary Caroline said. "Mrs. Potter asked me to come and visit them."

"Well, that was nice," Mrs. Link said.

The lace curtains in the Mercers' front window were new, and the Webbs' house looked all shut up as if they might be away. For a week now, Mrs. Link had been meaning to sit down with her needle and thread and change the yoke in her navy blue dress, so she could wear it to church on Sunday, and they really ought to stop and see Mrs. Macomber, who was all alone in that big house. . . . Dimly conscious of the fact that Mary Caroline had just asked her a question, Mrs. Link said, "What's that, dear?"

"I said are Mr. and Mrs. Mercer in love?"

"Why? What makes you ask?"

"I just wondered," Mary Caroline said.

If she'd only thought to bring Mrs. Macomber's blue cake plate, she could have killed two birds with one stone. On the other hand, it was hardly polite to return the plate with nothing on it. She would take over a loaf of orange bread after she baked on Tuesday. This time of year it always seemed as if there was nothing to look forward to but ice and snow, but it was February and so the winter was really half over. It didn't get dark till nearly five-thirty, and if Mr. Link was ever going to order the seeds for the vegetable garden, he'd better get ready and do it right away. The Sherman house, too bright a yellow when it was first painted, had faded to a pleasant colour, but it would never look the way it had when it was white. And Doris shouldn't have taken Mary Caroline's blouse without asking.

"Are Mr. and Mrs. Sherman in love?" Mary Caroline asked as they turned in at their own front walk.

The hack was still standing in front of the Kings'. How poor Mr. King had managed all this time, with his wife in the hospital and a house full of company.

"Are Mr. and Mrs. King in love?"

"I don't know, dear," Mrs. Link said. "I suppose they are. How can you tell?"

20

Half an hour before the hack arrived to drive them to the station, the Potters were all downstairs, ready and anxious to leave. Mr. Potter took his watch out and compared it with the clock in the hall. As he put the watch back in his vest pocket, he said, "Cousin Abbey, I think we're making a big mistake not to take you with us. You could have a pony to ride and lots of little piccaninnies to play with."

"Mr. Potter, stop teasing that child," Mrs. Potter said. With her hat and coat on, and her veil pinned over her face, she sat down at the piano. She had just remembered a hymn that she hadn't thought of in years. With several false starts she made her way through the first half, and then time after time produced a wrong chord and had to go back and start over again.

"Do you feel all right?" Randolph asked, bending over the sofa.

"Yes," Nora said, "but I wish Mama would remember the rest of that hymn. It's driving me crazy."

"If you want Mama, you'll have to take her hymns with her," Randolph said, and wandered out into the front hall, where a suitcase was waiting for somebody, some conscientious helpful person, to carry it out to the kerbing.

"Cousin Austin said he'd be here by ten," Mr. Potter said, "and it's five after." And then, in response to the ringing of the front doorbell, "Now I wonder who that could be?"

"He'll be here. Don't go borrowing trouble," Randolph said.

"There's someone at the door," Mrs. Potter called from the piano.

"Do you think we ought to answer it?" Mr. Potter said. "We've said good-bye to everybody I can think of."

"Maybe Cousin Austin forgot his key," Randolph said. He opened the door and a long conversation followed, while the cold swept in along the floor.

"For heaven's sake, shut the door!" Nora exclaimed.

"Is that right?" Randolph said. "Well, I'm sure they didn't mean to. How much is it? . . . I'll tell him. I certainly will . . . yes . . . Well, I don't think that's at all fair to you. . . . I'll tell you what you do. You come back next Saturday, and there'll surely be somebody here then."

He closed the door and, turning to Mr. Potter, said, "The paper boy. He hasn't been paid in weeks."

"How much was it?" Mr. Potter asked.

"Forty cents. They take it out of his earnings instead of waiting till he gets paid. He showed me a book with a lot of little coupons in it, so it must be right. Funny that Cousin Austin hasn't paid him. The boy's name is Dick Sisson, and he's saving his money to buy a new bicycle."

"It's twelve minutes after," Mr. Potter said, eyeing his watch.

Mrs. Potter, having remembered the rest of the hymn, got up from the piano triumphantly and said, "Randolph, come help me with your sister."

Together, they got Nora up off the sofa, put her hat and coat on her, and sat her, like a doll done up in bandages, on the chair in the front hall.

"The hack is here," Randolph said, "and no Cousin Austin. Now what do we do?"

"We can't leave without saying good-bye," Mrs. Potter said. "Cousin Austin would be hurt."

"Well, why isn't he here then?" Randolph asked.

"Oh, I don't know!" Mrs. Potter exclaimed. "I wish you wouldn't ask questions that nobody knows the answer to. . . . It's all right, Nora. If we miss this train, we'll take the next one."

The Potters, accustomed to keeping other people waiting, now sat and waited themselves—waited and waited. At last Mrs. Potter said, "Cousin Abbey, will you tell your father that——"

"It's no use," Mr. Potter said. "The train leaves in seven and a half minutes. We'd just have a wild ride for nothing."

They sat looking at each other. A minute went by, and another, and then the front door burst open. "I'm terribly sorry," Austin said. "I was detained."

"It's all right," Mr. Potter said. "We'll take the evening train. Or the one tomorrow morning."

Nora's eyes filled with tears that were not, Austin saw, for him. She wanted to go home. The tears were merely from childish disappointment. A long time ago, he thought, I used to feel like that sometimes.

"If I can't take that train, I'll die," Nora said.

Mr. Potter shook his head. "It's no use," he repeated.

Without bothering to search through that part of his mind where old unhappy memories were stored (whatever the disappointment was that had been more than he could bear, he had lived through it) Austin picked up the remaining suitcase and opened the front door. "We can try," he said. "The train may be late."

21

When Martha King came back to the house on Elm Street it was as a traveller returning after a long adventurous life to the place where that life had begun, fifty years before. The lights in the windows, the known dimensions of the yard, the half-seen shapes of trees and shrubbery all appeared to her from a perspective of distance too great for her to feel any direct happiness but only wonder at the place for being, after all this while, so intact and so much itself.

The nurse went ahead with the baby, while Martha with Austin supporting her made the trip slowly, pausing at the porch steps. She still hadn't got her strength back and there was a question in her mind whether she ever would. The lamps were lighted, the floors and the furniture shone. A hand that might have been hers had been at work, and nothing varied by a hair's breadth from its right place.

"It looks as if we were about to give a party," she said as Austin was hanging her coat in the hall closet.

"Hadn't you better go straight up to bed?"

"After dinner," Martha said.

When she was settled on the sofa in the living-room with a wool afghan over her knees and pillows at her back, she said, "Austin, would you go upstairs and see if there's anything she needs? . . . And find Ab," she called as Austin started for the stairs.

She lay back on the sofa with her eyes closed. The whole feel of the house was wrong, in spite of the order and polish and preparation for her. The living-room curtains, that she had decided to leave until next summer, would have to go. And the picture of Apollo would have to come down. She had looked at it long enough. She would get a divided mirror for over the mantelpiece. The chair in the hall would have to go to the upholsterer's to be glued and re-covered. There would have to be other changes, not all at once, but gradually one thing after another until the house was . . .

A sudden thunder of feet on the stairs made her sit up and turn towards the hall. Austin came into the living-room with Ab riding on his back. They were both flushed and laughing, which annoyed Martha. Ab was a child, of course, and couldn't be expected to know what her mother had been through. But Austin was another matter.

Ab slid into her arms limply and Martha said, "You oughtn't to come down the stairs like that with her."

"I wouldn't drop her," Austin said.

"You might stumble and fall," Martha said. As she rocked Ab and smoothed her hair, she felt as if something she had been deprived of without realizing it had now been restored to her.

"Rachel's out in the kitchen," Ab said.

"No!" Martha exclaimed. And then, "That's what you were so pleased with yourself about?"

"I wanted to surprise you," Austin said. "I found out where she was and wrote to her."

"Did you fire Frieda?"

"She gave notice the day the Potters went. She said she couldn't stay in the house alone with me. It wasn't proper."

"And you've had nobody to cook for you all this time?"

"I managed," Austin said.

At the sound of someone in the dining-room, Martha called, "Rachel, is that you?"

Rachel appeared in the dining-room door and smiled—a broad, bright, gleaming smile that made Martha feel taken up and held, as she herself was holding Ab.

"If you only knew what it was like without you," she said, "and how I missed you."

"Is that right?" Rachel said. "I give the whole house a good going over."

"I see you did. It's beautiful. Have you been up to see the baby? He's not much to look at. He only weighs five and a half pounds."

"I reckon he'll improve, now that you've got him home," Rachel said. "Dinner is served."

"I can't tell you what it feels like," Martha said as she started to get up from the sofa.

Hours later, lying in bed and watching Austin undress, she said the same thing. What it was like was music, like wave upon wave of rising, ringing happy voices singing *Let us praise the Creator and all that He has made.*

With the light off and Austin in bed beside her, she found herself suddenly wide awake, restless, and wanting to talk. "There's something the matter with Ab."

"I didn't notice it," Austin said.

"She acts as if she had some kind of a grievance against us."

"She'll be all right. Don't worry about it."

After a short while, he withdrew his arm from under her head and turned over on his side. She was still not ready to go to sleep. "There's something else that worries me. When Ab was born I loved her right away, but I don't feel the same about this baby."

"You will."

"When I hold him he cries as if he doesn't want to come to me."

"Show me the baby that doesn't cry."

"Austin, does Nora write to you?"

"No."

"You're telling me the truth? You wouldn't lie to me about it?"

"Why should I lie to you? She hasn't written to me and she won't, and if she did write I wouldn't open the letter."

"There's no reason for you to say that. I wouldn't mind if you did. If you want to write to her, it's all right with me."

"But I don't want to write to her. And I don't want her to write to me. It's all past and done with."

"For you, maybe."

"Oh, darling, forget about it. Go to sleep."

"All the time I was in the hospital I kept thinking about what it would be like to be home, and the very first night——"

Austin heaved himself over and sat up in bed, staring down at her in the dark. "This is something you started your own self. I didn't mention Nora."

"What difference does it make who mentioned her? She's still here," Martha said, and felt the bed give as he lay back once more. "I can't reach you the way I used to be able to," Martha said, after a while. "I guess it's just that I don't know you any more. You've changed, but I've changed, too. You know Nora better than you know me. You've talked more to her. I don't mean this unkindly, Austin, but I think we ought to see things as they are, instead of trying to make a false life together, for the sake of the children. It's something I realized in the hospital—that you have only one life and if you spend all your time and energy trying to force something that, in the very nature of things, is impossible and hopeless, you might as well not have lived at all. People ought to follow their deeper instincts and be what they are meant to be, even if it causes unhappiness. They can't be themselves and still go on pretending that everything is all right when it isn't. By being honest with each other, we can at least——" She stopped, informed by his breathing that he was asleep.

How could he do that to her? How could he not care, when she was speaking to him for the first time, opening her heart in a way that she had not done all the years of their married life? She had been through the most terrible experience, and the minute it was over, he had no more interest in it or in what she had been through. All that mattered to him was his own peace and comfort.

In a cold rigid fury she lay beside him, trying not to hear the deep regular breathing of the man who had beaten her down with his persistence and his unbending will, and now no longer cared enough about her even to stay awake five minutes. She was weak and exhausted and caught by the children she had borne him, but he was fine. He was still young and didn't care whether she lived or died, so long as he got his sleep.

She moved slowly and carefully, out from under the cover, being careful even in her anger not to waken him. . . . Not that she was afraid of him any longer, but she had to be alone, to think, to decide what she would do when she got her strength back. Because she wouldn't stay in the house with him a day longer than she had to. She would take the children and Rachel and find some place where they could live. It probably wouldn't be comfortable and beautiful like this house. They'd probably have to live in some little flat downtown, over a store, but in the summer-time she could rent a cottage at the Chautauqua grounds so that the children would have a place to play outdoors, and they would manage somehow. They would be independent, and free at last to make of their lives something decent and brave, and when the children got old enough to look after themselves, she could go to Chicago and find a job there. Rachel had managed, and what Rachel could do, she could.

How long Martha King sat in the rocking chair by the front window in the guest-room, with her robe drawn around her, planning, she had no idea. She looked out at the street and saw the street lamp as the life she had been meant to lead and the circle of light cast by it as the place she must get to. Drunk with certainty, with finality, with decision, when the grandfather's clock in the downstairs hall struck one, she went into the room where the baby's crib was. The nurse was lying on her back snoring and did not waken when Martha King picked up the baby and carried it into the guest-room where she sat holding it, the burden that had so little weight, that was no burden at all.

The baby did not waken, though it stirred occasionally and she felt the hands pushing for a second against her side. She examined the baby's face by the light of the street lamp: so small and helpless, so much in need of protection against the cruelty of the world. She would bring him up not to be nice, not to be polite, not to make the best of things, but in full knowledge of what life is, to make his own way, fight for what he wanted, and above all else to feel. To be angry when he was angry, and when he was happy, to bring the house down with his joy. All the things that Austin had failed to be. This child would have a chance. She would make it possible. It would be so.

She put the child back in the crib, and because it was cold, and she was not well and there was, after all, no place else to go, she got back into bed and lay there, with her eyes wide open, looking at the reflection of the street light on the ceiling.

Austin stirred, and put his arm across her, and she took hold of it, by the wrist, and removed it, but when she moved away from him, towards the outer edge of the bed, he followed again in his sleep, and curled around her in a way that made her want to shout at him, and beat his face with her fists. She pushed the arm away, roughly this time, but he still did not waken. The arm had a life of its own. All the rest of him, his body and his soul, were asleep. But the arm was awake, and came across her, and the hand settled on her heart, and she let it stay there for a moment, thinking how hard and heavy it was compared to the child she had been holding, how importunate, how demanding; how it was no part of her and never would be, insisting on a satisfaction, even in sleep, that she could not give. She started to push it away once more but her own arms were bound to the bed. Only her mind was awake, able to act, to hate. And then suddenly the delicate gold chain of awareness, no stronger than its weakest link, gave way. Circled by the body next to her, enclosed in warmth, held by the arm that knew (even though the man it belonged to did not), Martha King was asleep.